I0685312

JESSIE ARNOLD;

OR,

THE MURDER AT THE OLD WELL.

A ROMANCE.

BY THE AUTHOR OF "THE BLACK MANTLE," "LOVE AND MYSTERY; OR, MARRIED AND SINGLE," &c., &c.

———

LONDON:

PUBLISHED BY E. LLOYD, SALISBURY-SQUARE, FLEET-STREET.

———

MDCCCLII.

PREFACE

FROM the Patronage bestowed upon JESSIE ARNOLD by the Public, we have reason to believe our labour has not been in vain; and that we have succeeded in contributing to the leisure moments of some thousands, amusement and instruction. The example of JESSIE ARNOLD, the heroine of our romance, gentle readers, may be imitated by all who chose the good and noble course of rejecting every temptation to evil, and firmly adhering to every noble virtue. The example of the once happy father being dragged down into the abyss of despair from the paths of rectitude and comfort, by addicting himself to that monster curse, Gaming, may serve as a warning beacon to the sorely tried and tempted of the male portion of our readers.

London, 1853.

JESSIE ARNOLD:
OR,
THE MURDER AT THE OLD WELL.
A ROMANCE.

CHAPTER I.

THE GAMING-HOUSE.

St. James's-street was all life and gaiety. The hour was four in the afternoon, and the fashionable world had condescended to acknow-ledge that it was time to be up and stirring A September sun was shining sweetly upon the houses, giving even the artificial town something the appearance of natural beauty. Throngs of brilliant carriages, filled with gaily-dressed persons, filled the streets, the sides of which were lined with pedestrians hurrying onwards, as if the fate of nations depended upon their speed. Mingled, however, with this fast moving mass were aristocratic loungers, who thought it awfully grand to move at a snail's pace, and with an action as if every joint in their bodies ached. There were idlers, too, of another sort—those who were compelled so to be by dire necessity, and whose listless, sauntering gait arose from want of some object to stimulate them to exertion—persons many of whom would gladly have been the most active of the active, but they laboured under the misfortune of having no particular marketable talent which they could give to society in exchange for the means of existence.

The steps, too, of many handsome and spacious edifices had their occupants in the shape of idling exquisites, who preferred that slight elevation above the mob in which to study an attitude, or adopt one previously studied. These persons were discoursing with the lisping affected frivolity of their truly contemptible class, and saying nothings as glibly and with as great an air of satisfaction as if they were really of any importance.

And amid all this living, breathing, moving mass of humanity it was astonishing to see and note, which might be easily done, the utter selfishness that pervaded all classes. Each was intent upon its own particular objects and pursuits—each was utterly heedless what effect those objects and pursuits had upon others. Not a shadow even of that instinctive feeling of humanity which seems in some of the lower animals to bind an individual to its species could be found. The moan of distress jarred not upon the fine nervous sensibility of the fine lady, although a handkerchief impregnated with *eau de voilets*, instead of *marzanara*, would probably produce quite grievous consequences. The appeal of a starving fellow-creature had no effect upon the exquisite who would have fainted at the catastrophe of some common weed being mingled with the pure leaves of his havannah.

In large social communities, as they are facetiously called, there is no sociality at all. Every man wraps himself in the impregnable armour of selfishness. So was it strikingly manifest on the particular afternoon to which we wish to call the reader's attention. There were dukes and beggars, countesses and paupers, rags and gilding. In one hour some specimen of every kind of misery and of every kind of splendour and ostentation might have been encountered; yet all passed each other as if there had been no such thing as a community of feeling, as if mankind by its Maker was divided into different classes, formed of different materials, the rich and the titled, of course, being constructed of a sweet and tender texture differing widely from the poor and nameless.

In fact, people are very much in their hearts of opinion with the lady who declared her firm conviction that poor common people were as different from people of means and respectability as earthenware pipkins from fine China.

This lady desired the footman once to order the nursery-maid to bring the children to the dining-room, when, as a satire upon her exclusiveness, John roared out—

"Earthenware, bring down the best china."

But, to return from this digression, there was one house on the right hand side of St. James's-street, the inhabitants of which could have had but a small taste for the beautiful sunlight that was streaming through the mild and serene air, making the most dingy parts of the great city beautiful by casting over them the splendour of its beams, for the blinds were drawn down for the most part, and through them came glancing the light from lamps and chandeliers, struggling to show itself in the sweet sunshine, and losing sadly, most sadly by the comparison.

There would have been yet ample time for any indoor occupation requiring light without resorting to artificial means of illumination, and, to our thinking, that last hour of day when the sun seems taking a lingering and regretful leave of the world, is the most beautiful of the whole four-and-twenty, if we exclude the first hour of a summer's morning, when all nature is awakened by the first beams from the silvery east.

Still, however, as we have said, that house was lighted up within, and the Venetian blinds closed as much as possible in order to exclude the scene without with all its charms, and all its subjects of sad or happy contemplation. Many a passing glance was cast at its magnificent architecture, and some of those glances were sad and full of mournful meaning, while other faces assumed smiles, but not smiles of a mirthful character—no, they were rather those of triumph—some triumph of an unholy, unblessed character, which the heart has to deceive itself in before it can really think it one.

None lingered on the door-steps of that house but occasionally a haggard, pale, trembling man would leave it, and with staggering gait, and strange despairing gestures, hastily seek refuge from the popular gaze down some narrow turning—then again, sometimes one would come from the house flushed with the pride of some great success, and look about him with an air of easy confidence upon the throngs in the street, while his hand would be buried deeply in his pocket, clutching the treasure he had just wrested from some unhappy wretch in the *gaming-house*.

Yes, that house was a gaming-house—a den into which no kindly sympathy ever entered—the grave of love, honour, honesty, and every noble feeling of humanity.

Oh! it was well to shut out from those meretricious, gilded saloons the bright, beautiful, and glorious light of Heaven, for strangely would that sweet sunshine have jarred with the angry, revengeful, selfish feelings that were engendered in that place. Perchance it might have fallen upon the eyes of some wretch wavering on the brink of ruin, and, reminding him of other scenes and happier days, have wooed him from his headlong, horrible career, back again to virtue and to peace. Oh, yes, it was well in that place to shut out the light of Heaven.

If, however, on the occasion we speak of there was abundant selfishness, abundant heartless vanity in St. James's-street, there was likewise a something that redeemed the mass of humanity in some measure from the stigma of being totally bad. There was a heart beautiful in its fresh goodness and simplicity, as when it came from the hands of its Maker—one form upon which the sweet evening sun might well shine, borrowing new beauty from the graceful features it gilded. The form was that of a young girl, tall of her age, and yet scarce numbering sixteen summers—graceful as a young fawn—beautiful as the gorgeous imaginations of a poet, and yet sad—sad as if some heavy blow of fate had fallen upon her heart and dimmed its brightest energies; she slowly paced down that gorgeous street in the direction of the fatal mansion we have been describing.

When she neared it, she paused, and half turned as if seeking advice or direction from one near her. A boy stepped up to her. He was attired as a half-page, half-groom, and was in that intermediate state between boyhood and manhood, when it is difficult to say what sort of animal the creature will ultimately become.

"Yes, missus," he said, "that's the place—I watched the governor, missus. He is there as sure as eggs is eggs."

"You can wait for me, Charles."

"Yes, missus, Oh! wice, wice—wicious wice."

The young girl ascended the steps of the magnificent house, while the boy sat down on the lowest of them, and appeared in a very philosophical manner to be contemplating the throng of passengers that hurried by.

His reflections appeared to be rather of a melancholy order, for he shook his head a great many times, and asked himself in the most metaphysical tone imaginable,—

"What is life—what is death—what's masters and missuses, and what's servants—what's nothing?"

As these questions are very difficult to answer, we shall leave Charles to comment upon them at leisure, and follow the young girl, who

with saddened steps ascended to the open doors of that den of vice and horror.

A much more jealous watch than was apparent was maintained at the entrance to that mansion, for just about half-a-dozen paces within the hall were two green doors, carefully watched by a porter who sat by them, and allowed no one to pass who could not satisfy him either at once from appearance, or from representations, that he was not a dangerous customer, but one who *bona fide* came there to play.

The young girl attempted to open one of these doors, but she was immediately challenged by the Cerberus, who cried,—

"Hilloa! hilloa! what now? What do you want?"

"My father," was the reply, and she fixed her eyes upon his face with an expression of unutterable woe, such even as he quailed before.

"Your—your father," he added, after a moment's pause; "oh! we have nobody's fathers here. This is a place only for gentlemen—you can't pass in."

"I have come to see my father, Captain Arnold, and I must pass."

"But my duty is to stop you."

"My errand is higher—holier than your duty, and I come to save the father of five young children from destruction. In the sacred name of justice, of humanity, I demand admittance here."

"Captain Arnold—tall—pale—good looking?"

"Yes—yes. He is here?"

"He is. But I tell you what, miss, it's as much as my place is worth to let you pass. Neither can I send to the captain. If you want to see him, you must even wait till he comes out, and that won't be on this side of twelve o'clock, I'll warrant."

"For mercy's sake, let me pass. You know not what effect my thus seeking him may produce. My sudden appearance, and my urgent appeal to him, may draw him at once and for ever from the vortex into which he is plunging. Oh! for mercy's sake, let me pass!"

"I cannot."

"Nay, think again. If my exertions should be blessed with success, you will share in the blessing of that success, as having facilitated my endeavours. Again I beseech—implore you to let me pass."

"What's all this?" said a gentlemanly-looking man, in the undress of an officer of the guards, suddenly pushing open the green doors from the interior of the mansion. "What's all this about, eh?"

"The young lady, sir, wants to pass into the saloon," said the porter, in a tone of respectful deference.

"A young lady!—oh, my dear, absurd. You really must not think of such a thing, and

and yet—it would be a glorious bit of fun. I tell you what, Davies, you let her in—I'll hold you harmless; and, my dear, I dare say you will give me a kiss from those sweet panting lips for the accommodation."

"Sir!" said Jessie Arnold, for such was her name, "by your garb I mistook you for a gentleman."

"Mistook me?"

"Yes, sir. The son of a king were contemptible if he insulted a child who came to such a place as this on the errand of attempting to save a father from perdition."

"I beg your pardon," said the officer, in a low tone. "What I said was said heedlessly. Davies, on my responsibility, let this young lady go to the saloon."

The officer hastily descended the steps, with difficulty avoiding treading upon Charles, who very unceremoniously asked him if he knew where he was going, and walked rapidly away.

"Well, miss," said the porter, "I shall let you by. But you hit him rather hard."

"What mean you?"

"Why, don't you know him?"

"Indeed, I do not. How should I know him?"

"Whew! Why it's Fitzclarence, the king's eldest son; but go on. There will be a row, and no sort of mistake at all. Take the first turning to the right when you reach the head of the stairs, and whatever you do, miss, be so good as to come away again as soon as ever you can, because, you know—eh?—oh! she's gone—she's in a mighty hurry—what a row there will be."

*   *   *   *

A confused hum of voices came to Jessie's ears as she reached the landing-place of the gorgeously carved staircase, and that sound, if she had received no particular direction, would have amply sufficed to conduct to the saloon, where large fortunes were lost and won, and where more guilty exultation, and more terrible despair were witnessed in one week than in the surrounding ten miles of country, probably, in the whole twelvemonths.

Laughter, now and then an oath, the confused hum of conversation, and various noises contingent upon the games that were being played, reached Jessie most painfully. A deep sense of oppression came across her heart, and she was compelled to pause for some few moments before she could recover strength of mind and body sufficient to go through with her self-imposed task.

While she thus paused a door opened, and within the apartment it led to she could see a flood of light, and a number of persons dispersed about at different tables. The person who had afforded such a transient glimpse of the apartment into which she was so soon herself to venture, was a young man—indeed, he could

scarcely have numbered twenty summers; but Jessie thought she never should forget the terrible expression of his face;—handsome it certainly was, in features, but upon it there was such an expression of deep agonizing despair, that it was indeed terrible to look upon.

He held by the gilt balustrades at the head of the stairs for a few brief moments, while deep sobs came from his breast.

"My poor—poor mother!" he gasped.

That thought seemed to be too much for him, and in an instant he drew a pocket-pistol from his breast, and presented it at his head.

To rush forward and arrest his arm, was the work of a moment to Jessie. In the action her bonnet fell back upon her head, so that the whole of her exquisitely-chiselled countenance was visible, as well as such a mass of sunny auburn ringlets, that the despairing man looked for a moment as if he were in a dream, and quite bewitched by the wondrous beauty he so beheld in that most unlikely place.

"Hope," said Jessie; "all may not be lost. Hope—hope. I have come to save one; by Heaven's grace, I may save two."

The pistol dropped from his grasp, and a flood of tears came to his relief. He clasped his hands and appeared about to speak, but Jessie felt satisfied that the paroxysm of his despair had passed away, and hesitating not longer, she walked on and opened the door of the saloon.

What a blaze of real beauty and brilliancy of decoration burst upon her eyes, as she stood upon the threshold of that gorgeous room.

The lighting was brilliant, and yet had no dazzling effect on the eyes, for the interposition of ground glasses, tinted a pale gold colour, assorted well with the style of decoration of the apartment, and took off all appearance of glare. The most costly and exquisite draperies hung from the walls and windows, interspersed with looking-glasses, so arranged as to multiply every object in the room, as well as its own space indefinitely. The floor was covered with carpeting that made the heaviest tread perfectly noiseless, so that the numerous guests seemed moving through the air rather than walking, as they lounged from one part of the room to the other.

What pains had been taken to still the voice of conscience, honour, prudence, and common feeling, in that saloon. The senses were attacked by all that beauty and magnificence in order that remorse might, along with reflection, be stifled. Then, too, there were costly and rare wines, to be used by the visitors at discretion, so that a stimulant was always at hand to steep in oblivion the senses of the unlucky gamester.

For a moment or more no one seemed to notice the sudden appearance of Jessie Arnold, and then some players at a table near the door appeared all at once to be aware of the strange fact that a young and beautiful girl had found her way into that gilded den of iniquity.

With various exclamations they rose, and the attention of every one in the room was immediately attracted to where, pale as a marble statue, stood Jessie, eagerly scanning countenance after countenance, in search of the one so deeply, sadly interesting to her.

"Father, father," she said, as in a remote corner of the apartment she fancied she saw the object of her search.

With a cry of surprise, a gentlemanly man sprang towards her, heedless of who he hustled aside in his course.

"Jessie!" he exclaimed; "for God's sake! what—what—brought you here? The—the—children ——"

—"Are well, father," said Jessie; "but the father is sick of a mortal disease. Let me be the humble instrument of Heaven to save you."

She sunk on her knees at his feet, and while he looked upon the beaming and beautiful countenance of his child with remorse and self-accusation, she poured forth, in all the simple eloquence of nature, her earnest prayers to him to save himself, and all that was dear to him, by renouncing the gaming-table, its terrible allurements, and its, as surely as death, terrible end.

Even those men who were inured to vice in its every form, stood abashed and trembling before her. Not a word was whispered in that saloon while she spoke, such a magic power have innocence and virtue over even the worst and most degraded of the human species.

"Father," she said, "come away. Think of those who love you—of those who have no other mortal hope but in your love. Think, father, of my poor mother, and the smile of joy that lingered even in death upon her wan cheek, at the thought, expressed with her last breath, that she was leaving her dear children with a father who would be all to them that the tenderest parent can be. Even then, in our deep affliction, father, there was a ray of happiness about our hearth, because you blessed it with loving tenderness; we learned to think of our mother's loss with a chastened sorrow, because it was an affliction from Heaven—but now—now we weep and try to comfort each other through long, weary nights, and you come not to us. Your cheek is pale—anxiety and discomfort sit upon your brow—your hands are fevered—father—come—come—come to those who love you, and find true happiness in their gentle kisses, kind caresses, and murmured prayers. You hear me, and are moved. I can see you are. You turn away your head, father, to hide your emotions. If you have tears, believe them blessed, holy drops. Father —dear, dear father—forsake this place, now and for ever."

To describe the exquisite tenderness with which these words were uttered would be impossible. The tears that accompanied them—the appropriate and natural gestures—all combined to produce an effect, even upon the most iron nerves of the men present, which would scarcely have been exceeded had they suddenly heard the last trumpet summoning them to judgment.

Some slunk back out of sight, while others looked in the faces of their companions, to note what effect was produced in others by the words that nearly paralysed themselves.

But if the feelings of utter strangers were thus strongly acted upon by the innocence and natural eloquence of that young girl, how much greater may the effect be supposed to be upon the heart of him who possessed all the feelings of a father, thus to see his gentle and beautiful child reduced to the sad necessity of so pleading to him in the presence of strangers.

Captain Arnold was not destitute of the finer feelings of humanity. In fact, it is not unfrequently found that the most generous and noble sensibilities, and many of the very highest attributes of mind, are found associated with that insane love of play, which in its end must lead to degradation and despair.

We have no wish to exalt any vice; but there are some which certainly belong more particularly to better natures, and hence the terrible consequences of gambling, as it generally makes desolate a heart that else would be surrounded by domestic virtues and felicities.

Twice Captain Arnold tried to speak; but his voice failed him, and when he did articulate, all he could say was,—

"Jessie—Jessie!"

"Father," she added, "I am successful. You feel as I would wish you, as all who love you would wish you. Once again the light of joy will illumine your home, and we shall be so very, very happy.

A flood of tears came to her relief, and she wept hysterically upon her father's breast, for he had raised her from her suppliant posture, and supported her in his arms.

One man, then, did succeed in shaking of the spell in which the words of Jessie had bound the senses of all. That man was a *roue* of the first water—a nobleman—a notorious gambler—and as notoriously a bad principled individual as could be by any possibility picked out of his class.

"Why, Arnold," he said, "d—n me—whiz! Sink me if you haven't got to have your revenge yet."

"Peace, my lord," said Arnold, waving his hand. "Let not this innocent child's ears be polluted by your words. If you must speak, Marquis of Rollington, let it be as a gentleman, and not in your present strain."

"A gentleman, sir?"

"Ay, a gentleman. You need assume no threatening attitude. I do not intend to quarrel, nor to have what you call my revenge."

"Ha, ha!" cried Lord Rollington, with an affected laugh. "Arnold has been bitten by a mad girl, and is beginning to preach."

An angry flush came across the countenance of Captain Arnold, and he would probably have made a reply, which, according to the vicious code of honour among military men, would have provoked serious ulterior consequences, but his daughter still clung to his arm, saying—

"Father—father! behold one of the consequences of gambling in a forced association with such a man as that."

The Marquis of Rollington quailed beneath the glance that Jessie bent upon him, and her outstretched finger pointing in his face, seemed as if it carried some deadly influence to his very heart.

"An actress, by Jove," he said, making a great effort to rally. "The scene is well got up."

"Jessie, you have conquered," whispered Captain Arnold.

With a gush of joy she threw herself upon his neck. The tears with which she bedewed his cheek were those of joy—she forgot everything but that she was rescuing her poor father from the scene of dissipation into which he had too heedlessly allowed himself to be allured.

"Come away, come away," she sobbed. "Oh, father, you know not how happy those few simple words have made me—take a last adieu of this place."

He glanced round him upon the brilliant decorations of that magnificent saloon, and then raising his voice, he said—

"Gentlemen, farewell. The little scene that has been enacted here to-day will, from some of you, provoke contempt—but, remember, while the conduct of my child may adorn a tale, it will likewise point a moral, and in your remarks upon her, and the heroism which prompted her to rescue me from the toils that were clinging round me, it will be well, likewise, to remember that I am a soldier and a gentleman, jealous of my honour and ready to defend it. Come, Jessie, come."

"A thousand pounds to a hundred," cried the Marquis of Rollington, that "Captain Arnold is in this room again within ten days from now."

"Done!" said the dissolute Lord Rouse.

"Play, gentlemen, play."

In a few moments Jessie Arnold and her father were in St. James's street, which was still faintly illuminated by the setting sun.

CHAPTER II.

THE MURDER.

NEAR the little village of Mortlake stood a villa residence, which had fallen into such miserable decay, that although many adventurous people, who fancied themselves fond of the picturesque, came to look at it with a view of tenanting it, they had all gone away again without troubling the agent in whose hands it had been placed.

For a long time an announcement on a board at the end of the lane down which the house was situated, had stated that it could be viewed by "cards only," and an old woman had possession in order to let the cards in; but she went the way of all flesh in due course of time, and the house remained unlet. Then the board crumbled away, and fell down, after which the front door of the cottage residence itself hung by one hinge, and several of the shutters themselves adopted the same change of attitude, so that, cards or no cards, any one could walk in who liked, the only hindrance being the spiders' webs, which hung in thick festoons along the passage.

Neighbours, who were lax in principle, had from time to time stolen the choicest plants from the garden, and, as no one complained of the larceny, they by degrees came to the commoner sort, so that, at length, there was not a shrub worth a few pence left in the place.

One night then some one stole the copper, and the other neighbours, in great indignation, began upon the stoves, which rapidly disappeared. A dead set was then made upon the locks and the bells, and the window fastenings; then some one cut down a tree, and walked off with it, and some one else took off a few floor boards for fire wood. This was too bad, and a man, who lived nearest at hand, exclaimed loudly against the heartlessness of robbery, that very night going himself, and wrenching off their hinges four or five doors for his own use.

Things were at this pass, and there was every probability of the little villa disappearing by degrees from the face of the earth, when it suddenly acquired a most unenviable reputation, that kept it without visitors for some years.

It was a tempestuous evening in autumn upon which the occurrence happened, and it at once and for ever appeared to have put a stop to the depredations upon Merton Villa, which was the name of the neglected residence.

For some weeks a rumour had got abroad in the neighbourhood that strange noises had been heard to proceed from the villa after nightfall, and certain it is that an occasional flash of light had been observed from its windows, and when those who saw it had repaired in haste to the place, no one was to be found, nor any indications of the presence of any one. These occurrences excited disagreeable suspicions; but that was all, for, as yet, no one could say that those who evidently had made visits to Merton Villa where a whit worse than the kind neighbours who had made such active exertions for its demolition.

This quiescent state of things was not made to last, and the time was fast approaching when something very different from the speculation of fixture and timber stealers was about to be enacted within the walls of that deserted house. It would seem, too, that either a peculiar night was chosen on which to perpetrate a very awful deed, or that the elements themselves viewed with horror the dreadful crime they were compelled to witness.

It was towards nightfall that two men had walked into a public house near the village of Mortlake; after partaking of some spirits, they produced a large flask bottle, which they desired should be filled with brandy. They then, after some desultory conversation, walked away in the direction of Merton Villa, and nothing more was thought of them or their proceedings, until a circumstance occurred, which made the flask bottle a matter of curiosity, and circumstantial evidence against one of those men for a murder of the most diabolical description.

It appeared that an engagement had been entered into between a rustic pair to meet and arrange some lover's quarrel in the garden of Merton Villa, that being the most likely spot to be free from interruption until very late, indeed, for the fixture depredators seldom made their appearance until the small hours of the morning. The swain, however, by some accident, was late, and by nine o'clock the young girl, who expected to hear some fond excuses from her lover, for some real or fancied slight, stood alone in the garden at the back of Merton Villa.

The day had been gloomy, and as the clouds chased each other across the sky, the heavy watery-looking masses of vapour gave tokens that a storm was near at hand, and towards night the clouds visibly increased and loured, while the wind still howled and groaned through the hollow chimneys of the old halls and rushed through the tall trees in the avenue.

As daylight disappeared, the first signs of the coming storm were seen, and a drizzling shower fell with such constancy and steadiness as to threaten the traveller with the greatest inconvenience from the wet.

The weary labourer, with hasty step, sought the cabin where all he loved was contained, in the hope that he should escape the full effects of the shower; but in this he was mistaken, for the light rain which had hitherto fell now increased into a steady shower, from which there was no escape, and a thorough wetting awaited he who was exposed to its fury.

Still the wind howled as it passed through the trees and hedgerows, with a strange mixture of sounds, for the strength of the wind served to increase the sound as it rushed through the long tapering branches, which bent beneath the force of the current; but as that decreased, they resumed their natural position, then alternately rising and bending beneath the fury of the blast.

The heavy monotonous beat of the rain fell on the almost soddened earth in heavy drops, and against the closed casements of the house; a heavy mist now rose with the fall of the rain, and he who was well housed listened, as he watched the flickering flame of the fire, and felt its genial warmth, and thought upon the comfort he now enjoyed, and how very miserable it was abroad—for the wind whistled round the gable ends, and all odd corners and projections served but to increase its hollow moaning as it swept round the hut.

Such a night was barely fit for man or brute to be abroad in, and the careful farmer gave shelter to his cattle and flocks against such inclement weather.

The brooks were now full, and rushed onwards with a velocity, that the spectator who had seen them but a few hours before would scarcely credit, for they were then dry, and showed no sign of moisture; but when the ground got saturated, and the rain fell heavy and fast, they soon became full and overflowing, and they then rushed onward, filling the watercourses, and again dashing forward to the low grounds, eventually discharging themselves into some river; and the traveller, who but lately crossed the dry channel, on his return finds it filled by the rushing stream—the rivers rise, and the fords become swollen, and man and horses are stayed.

The night was pitch dark, not a star was to be seen, and the moon was not old enough to shed any light upon the earth; the clouds were heavily floating above, and but slowly passing onwards, but from them fell such torrents of rain that few had ever witnessed, accompanied, as it was, by the loud roar of the wind, which now blew a perfect hurricane.

Terrible must be the state of the poor and houseless, the absolutely homeless creatures, who have not the shelter that a dog has—who sleep in holes and under hedges, but on such a night as this these shelters were useless; they would be saturated before the night was two hours old; not a place could they find but what was saturated with water, and most places overflowed; nothing but the most abject misery and suffering could be the portion of these wretched creatures, to whom all the commonest comforts of civilized life were denied.

Still the loud howling of the wind blew,

accompanied by the heavy rushing sound of the rain, as it fell fast and thick ; now and then could be heard, when the blast was more than usually furious, the cracking and crashing of some giant of the forest—some limb of an aged tree had parted from its trunk.

It was on such a night, when dark and atrocious deeds might be expected to be done, that this young girl, whose name was Mary Sedgemore, stood trembling within the precincts of the deserted villa.

A clock was striking when she heard a door slam shut with great violence within the villa, and before she could make up her mind to fly from the spot, two men emerged from the building, one of whom carried a lantern, which, although shedding but a feeble light around, was yet sufficient to have detected her had she attempted to fly from the place. These men were conversing in low tones, but in the stillness that reigned around in that deserted garden Mary heard distinctly every word they uttered.

"Hark ye," said one. "I have not brought you here without a reason. In the progress of the plan we are pursuing—a plan which we know may bring us into great danger, it will be not only desirable to have a place of concealment for ourselves, but likewise for booty which may fall into our hands on account of the forgeries."

"True enough," replied the other; "but it does seem to me but a foolish thing to attempt hiding in an uninhabited house, because the slightest circumstance would betray the fact of some one being in it, and a search would result."

"Exactly; but you must know there is a hiding-place on these premises known only, I think, to me, and I found it out by accident, although, by cautious inquiries afterwards, I learned more about it. The first occupier of this villa was the owner of the land on which it stands. He had it built to suit his own tastes, and habits, and a fine thing he thought it when during the excavations, a spring of pure and beautiful water was discovered. He had a well sunk at great cost and labour—not an ordinary common shaft, but a well built reservoir, and, for the purpose of cooling wines and other matters, he had small chambers excavated in the form of arches at the sides of the shaft at various depths. These chambers I have not been in, but I am assured they exist, and my errand here to-night with you is thoroughly to explore them."

"Where is this well?"

"It is now covered over by some loose boards, above which again is placed earth and gravel, so that it would be next to impossible for any one not acquainted with the exact spot to find it."

"But wherefore was it so concealed?"

"Because the owner of the house, the man who took such pains to build the well, took a prejudice against it. He had not occupied his new abode three days when his only child was missed. The well was the last place searched, and there she was found."

"A prejudice, indeed!"

"Yes, as you say. After that he had the well covered up, and taking sick himself he died in a week. Now ask yourself, could a more admirable place be found for our purposes?"

"Scarcely, certainly. I am most curious to see this well, and still more curious to know how, without the usual apparatus, it is to be used."

"That I have. An iron bar, a pulley, and a hundred pounds weight—all of which I have secreted about these premises—will suffice for a descent, and enable either of us at any time to make a visit here, either to deposit the proceeds of the forgeries, or to take from our hoard. There is only this to be said, that in case of suspicion falling upon us, and our personal safety requiring a hiding-place, but one of us can take advantage of the old well, for it will require the other to replace the earth and gravel at the top."

"I understand."

They had been walking at a slow pace along one of the weed-encumbered garden paths as they spoke, and Mary might have escaped, for they had passed the tree behind which she had shrunk, but curiosity and an undefinable feeling of the necessity of staying to see and hear all that passed, chained her to the spot. She felt as if she had been brought there that night for the accomplishment of some design of Providence, and she remained without making the least effort to escape.

The man who had given an account of the well paused, and striking his heel into the gravel, he exclaimed—

"Here we are. Just wait for me a few moments, and I will get the articles I mentioned."

He handed the lantern to his companion, and then himself walked rapidly towards the house. He who was left behind then uttered some words which brought a pang of terror to the heart of the girl. He spoke in a low tone of frightful resolution, and in that solitude his voice sounded like the dark suggestions of an evil spirit.

"The well—the well," he muttered. "In the whole range of opportunity, could anything be more apt? He shall descend, but never rise again. I have all his secrets, and the one that most of all concerns me have I—namely, his determination to take my life, whenever I shall be no longer useful. Yes, the well is the thing, and it will keep a secret better even than the ocean. My knife — where is my knife? I——"

The sound of the returning footsteps of the other man now operated as a caution to his companion, and he said no more.

"All's safe," cried he who was so terribly menaced; "all's safe. Here are abundant materials for accomplishing a descent into the old well, and by rare good fortune, too, I have found a spade. True, it's broken, but it will remove the gravel more quickly than any other means we possess. Hold down the light."

He then commenced shovelling aside the gravel and earth, until he struck the spade against some woodwork, when, stooping, he lifted up two planks, and exposed the mouth of the well. He seemed quite to pride himself upon the simplicity of his apparatus for ascent and descent. It consisted of a round bar of iron, about the thickness of an ordinary coach axle, in the centre of which was an iron pulley. Then he had a long rope, to one end of which he tied a heavy weight. At the other extremity was a flat piece of wood, making a tolerably commodious seat. This rope was placed over the pulley, and the iron bar being laid over the orifice of the well, he steadied it by beating the ends firmly into the soil with a small hammer he produced.

"Now, you see," he cried, "we have everything complete. Either of us may descend and draw up again with perfect ease. The weight is a counterpoise, you perceive. Now, could anything be better?"

"Do you think it safe?"

"Safe?—perfectly. You shall see. I will lower the lantern to convince you there is no foul air, then you can go down yourself."

"Indeed I should rather not, except upon urgent necessity. I would rather be excused. By-the-bye, now, tell me truly, once and for all. Have you really told me everything which will ensure the success of the forgeries?"

"I have. I have given you the chemical secrets for taking out writing, as well as for making ink look of any age. All we have to do, and that will not be difficult, is to get genuine documents to practise upon. We shall produce no little confusion, for we can change the amounts of checks and notes at pleasure. There, you see, the lantern burns. There is no mephitic vapour in the old well."

"I see; and do you really believe the chambers you mention exist?"

"I do; but there is nothing like proof, so I mean to go down and see."

"Ay, that will be as well. I will keep good watch and ward above here, and when you come back, I will go down myself."

"What an emphasis you lay upon when," remarked the other, with a laugh, as he sat upon the board, and swung himself off the ledge of the well. "There, you see, by laying hold of the other rope how easy one may go. Good-bye—good-bye. Ha! ha! ha!"

"Good-bye."

Slowly the rope wound over the pulley, and deeper still went the man in that dark abyss, which his merciless companion determined should be his grave. Occasionally his voice came strangely from the bowels of the earth, as he shouted to him above the discovery of various little cavernous offshoots from the sides of the well.

"My knife—my knife!" muttered the projector of murder; "my knife to cut this rope, and so free myself for ever from as dangerous an accomplice as ever mortal man had. D—n! where is my knife?"

He searched his pocket in vain—the knife was not to be found; and as moment after moment passed away, he felt in a fearful agony that such an opportunity should escape him, for many and strong were the reasons that man had for the murder of his companion. Then the voice of the doomed one came again to his ears—

"All right," he said; "I'm coming up now."

The action of the rope was reversed, and it was evident he was pulling himself up slowly but surely.

With flashing eyes the other glanced round him for some weapon. He seized the spade, but immediately cast it from him again with a conviction of its inefficiency. Bitter and terrible oaths escaped his lips, and then suddenly he raised the hammer from the ground, and holding it in both his hands, he waited for the arrival of his fated comrade, with an expression of countenance perfectly diabolical; and yet time was when that same man, who contemplated so cold-blooded a murder upon one who had trusted him, would have melted to tears at a tale of distress, and been the first to stand up as the champion of innocence and humanity. The wild train of circumstances that had so altered his nature we shall know as our narrative proceeds.

The light from the lantern become more and more distinct, and now the dark mass that was emerging from the well came in sight. A slight terror passed through the frame of him who held the hammer in so threatening an attitude, and then he was still again as a marble statue.

"Well, you see," said he who was ascending, "it's safe enough."

He looked up as he spoke, for his head was very near the level of the well's brink, and in a moment a sense of his danger flashed across his mind. He seemed for the instant paralysed, and with a ferocious cry the other made a swinging blow at his head with the hammer. Instinctively he threw his head back, and the blow came upon his face, smashing one of his eyes from its socket, and falling with such a sickening smash as was horrible to hear. In an instant the blow was repeated—and then a shriek so wild and agonising, and so awfully loud, that it was heard far and near, burst from the frightfully injured man. The lantern dropped from his grasp.

"Down—d——n!—down!" cried the murderer.

He gave another swinging blow with the hammer. A cry of horror burst from his own lips. He had overreached himself, and missing his blow, fell heavily upon his victim. The rope flew over the pulley like lightning, and both went to the bottom of the well, locked in a dreadful embrace.

CHAPTER III.

THE HAPPY HOME.

The two pictures of human life we have presented to the reader, demand a third, and that third must be necessarily in the nature of a retrospect.

He who was dragged by the eloquence of his watchful and gentle child from the gaming-table in St. James's-street; and he who, with such diabolical feelings and such awful means, hurried a fellow-creature into eternity at the old well, were one and the same person.

We have but to present him to our readers in another aspect and we shall have the three great phases of his character. True, there is another, namely, the condemned felon; but that was short and rather a corollary upon the others, than a result of wild and wilful passion on his own part.

It shall be our task, now, ever holding before us the two pictures we have presented to the reader, to trace the causes—clear and hidden —the complex circumstances which induced one whose honour was once his most glorious possession—whose good name was untarnished as the sword he wore, to run a frightful career of iniquity, terminating it by a crime of so terrible a nature as murder.

We shall see, too, step by step, how from love, and joy, and peace, the gentle and beautiful Jessie Arnold came to be full of cares, deep anxieties, harrowing afflictions, and such bitter sorrows, as would have crushed a less enduring, Heavenly spirit to the dust. We shall see how she toiled and strove for those she loved, through good report and through evil report—murmuring never, yet ever self-sacrificing, until she regained the stars from whence, one would be apt to believe, she came, as some bright, pure, and beautiful exemplary spirit, to show the world the very model of a true, gentle, enduring, and trusting heart.

With pain shall we note, in the case of her father, how weakness became slowly greater weakness, until at length it blended with crimi-nality; and how, when once the rubicon was passed which separated crime from innocence, he recklessly rushed from small crimes to greater, until he became a monster he himself would at one time have shuddered at.

Years elapsed between the different states of Captain Arnold, for such great changes in human actions and human feelings are gradual— by degrees one feeling must trench upon another—vice begins first just a little to lose its deformity, and the mind becomes very philosophic concerning criminality, doubting if circumstances are not altogether to blame. Here some dereliction succeeds, and when once the first step is taken, the feelings lose all their abhorrence of iniquity, and vice becomes habitual.

Still there must be some one great undermining principle at work to produce such revulsions of feeling. Avarice is a prolific source of such changes—passion, of various kinds, another; but, most of all, the wild, desperate, delirious excitement of the gambler, may be instanced as leading more really good constituted minds astray, than any other cause, or than probably all other causes put together.

It was Captain Arnold's unhappy fate to fall a victim to that fiend, and, in so doing, as is invariably the case, he dragged many with him to destruction and misery.

*   *   *   *

It was fifteen years before the murder at the old well, and seven years before the scene which had occurred at the fashionable gambling-house, that in a sweet, sequestered spot in the Isle of Wight, where the beauties of earth, sea, and sky, were ever most strikingly developed, there resided Captain Arnold and his family, consisting of his wife, a fond, amiable woman, Jessie, the eldest girl, and three other children—a boy and two girls, the whole family as happy, intelligent, and lovely a family group, as any heart could picture.

Peace and love were the constant inhabitants of that happy and contented home. Captain Arnold had been in the navy, and when the war ceased, he had retired to find repose and enjoyment among those so dear to him. He was still a young man, and his career, although short in actual service, won for him golden opinions.

It was no small pleasure to him to have found so pleasant and peaceful a home, near that element whose grandeur he admired, and which he could not help loving, as that upon which he had earned the name of a brave man, by the performance of many gallant deeds.

His wife he loved dearly and fondly. His children were the idols of his heart. Many a visitor who had spent a long happy day with the Arnolds, left with a sigh and but a faint hope of ever in a domestic circle of his or her own realizing such joy.

No wish seemed ungratified, and none was ungratified, because that dear domestic circle looked for their purest, best pleasures in the society of each other. The naturally beautiful scenery of this spot, elevated all their minds, and Captain Arnold would often thank Heaven with a tear of joy sparkling in his eye as he saw his rosy-cheeked children frolicking on before him, as the little party were bent upon the exploration of some unknown pathway in the island or rocky wilderness.

There was for some years but one disagreeable sensation produced in the mind of Captain Arnold, and that was one which his reason told him he should disregard, but which his fancy nevertheless could not treat so cavalierly.

He, with his wife hanging upon his arm, and his children gambolling before him, was walking one evening in one of the sweet romantic cliffy hollows with which the favoured spot abounds, when they suddenly came upon an old woman, whose dress and general appearance bespoke her of foreign origin. She was sitting huddled up on an old grey stone, and like Macbeth's witches,

"Looked not like an inhabitant o' the earth."

Her attire bespoke extreme poverty, and although she did not beg of the party, Captain Arnold instinctively put his hand in his pocket, and taking from it a small silver coin he placed it in the lap of the woman.

Instead of being thankful for the gift as well as the delicacy with which it was given, she sprang to her feet, exclaiming—

"Do not cast alms to me. What I want I take. Yes, take. You and your fine wife may look surprised, but I scorn your alms. You and such as you support me, but I tell you I take it when I want it. There, go search for you coin, and give it to a humbler heart than mine."

"My good woman," said Captain Arnold, "in addition to your very loose notions of morality, you are making me but a very sorry return for an intended kindness."

"Curses on kindness," she exclaimed. "I've done with it long, long ago. There is no sympathy in common between me and human nature.

"She is mad," whispered Mrs. Arnold to her husband, "she is mad, come away—come away."

The woman heard the remark, and it seemed to inflame her passion quite to an ungovernable pitch—she glared round her like some wild animal seeking for prey. A violent torrent of invectives burst from her lips, and Captain Arnold, rather in pity than in anger, was passing on after his children, when she suddenly burst into a loud laugh, and then added in a voice, the very calmness of which was terrible from its striking contrast with her former demeanour,

"Beware! beware! Ha! ha! ha! You are happy, quite happy. Everything is smiling around you, and you believe yourself in such a haven of security as to be sheltered from every storm of fate, blow it from what quarter it may. Ha! ha! ha! make the most of the sunshine, for night is coming. Make the most of it. Your hours of joy, peace and content, are numbered."

"For heaven's sake come away," said Mrs. Arnold, "oh! come away."

The Arnolds left the spot immediately, but the words of the woman made a vivid and painful impression upon the mind of Captain Arnold.

The cottage, or cottage residence of Captain Arnold was beautifully and romantically situated. The house itself was a modern building—one of those houses which are prettily and handsomely built, and might be called a villa from its size and the extent of its grounds; much taste was displayed in its decoration, the spot chosen for its erection was, perhaps, the best that could have been chosen for many miles from the spot.

It was situated at the top of a beautiful little bay, some short distance from the water's edge, and completely protected from the bleak winds by the rising headlands which rose at either side of the little bay, and almost enclosed it.

Here, in the most disturbed state of the ocean, and the most squally weather, the water in this little basin was perfectly calm and free from disturbance, save a slight swell caused by the waves, which broke their force on the headlands at the entrance.

The grounds were laid out with considerable taste and care, the various seasons here were not without their peculiar beauties, for it had been the captain's care, that all that could enhance the beauty and adornment of his residence should be brought; flowers that bloomed in succession from the first of the year, till the last hardy plants, in protected situations, threw out blossoms, thus rendering the worst and dullest part of the year less sad and melancholy.

The windows of the principal apartments ranged the full height of the rooms, and opened out on to the lawns, which were well kept, smooth, and clean; the honeysuckle and the clematis circled their tendrils, and gave to the place a green and life-like retirement, while the sweet scents from the blossoms floated fragrantly on the balmy air.

The beauties of the garden were inexhaustible—flowers and fruits grew in abundance—but all of the choicest, and those things designed for use alone, were so arranged as to prove ornamental rather than a detraction from the neatness of the general view.

From the house many beautiful views were to be seen, the whole country was one wild scene of beauty, and turn which way you would, some new and singularly interesting landscape awaited you.

Then facing the house ran the ocean, and from the two little headlands a view of the sea might be obtained, that would amply compensate the little labour of walking up them. The morning's sunrise from the spot is a scene of beauty and splendour seldom witnessed, and once seen never forgotten.

In the little bay was moored the captain's sailing boat, in which, on fine days, and nearly calm weather, he would occasionally sail with his family a short way up and down the English Channel.

The day had been one of calm beauty, the sky was of that intense blue so seldom seen, but duly appreciated when seen; the heat of the day was much lessened by the gentle breeze that blew from the water, when Captain Arnold and his family left their delightful residence to witness the sunset from the headland at the end of the bay.

The spirit and gaiety of the throng was great, as they wended their way by the margin of the little bay towards the spot from which they could presently receive so much gratification from the view seaward.

They arrived on the headland as the sun was sinking; the beautiful hue of the waters, the gentle ripple, scarce disturbed by the slightest incident; neither rock nor bank raised a white curl on the waters as far as the eye could reach; all was serenity above and below, and save the evening breeze, which springs up at sundown, not a breath of air stirred sufficient to lift a leaf.

They stood silent and motionless, watching the declination of the sun, which now touched the edge of the waters, and in a very short time it had disappeared. There were no clouds to illumine with its departing rays, but the waters for a short space reflected them upwards, but it was but a few moments, then all was calm, silent, and subdued.

"My dear children," said the captain, after they had gazed some time in silence upon the magic scene, "to-morrow bids fair to be a fine day, and if there be not much wind, or appearance of it, you shall all sail out in the boat for a few hours."

Never was an announcement more welcome to them than this promise of their parent. They were passionately fond of sailing; their father was too careful to allow any one circumstance of danger to mar the joy of the scene—never, but in the calmest and most serene weather, did he ever trust his beloved family on the bosom of the deceitful deep.

They returned to the house full of delightful anticipations of the joys that to-morrow would produce.

CHAPTER IV.

THE CATASTROPHE.

THE morning was bright and beautiful. A soft air, just sufficient to fan with a delicious coolness the cheeks of the little party who were bent on an excursion of pleasure, was stirring. The water was as calm as some island lake, the surface of which remains for ever unruffled by those storms which heave up the bosom of the ocean, and spread death and desolation in their track.

Captain Arnold himself looked forward to a day of unmingled satisfaction, and as for his children, their delight knew no bounds when they rose, and peeping from the pretty latticed windows of their sleeping rooms, saw what a glorious promise of a beautiful day the sweet serene morning presented.

The dark words of the gipsy woman, if she were such, recurred not to the memory of Captain Arnold as he made preparations for the pleasant little marine voyage, which he thought would be a source of so much enjoyment.

Alas! who can foretell when pleasure may turn to pain—who shall say that our best grounded anticipations of good may not be the very circumstances which will inflict upon us the greatest possible evils!

The yacht in which the excursion was to be performed was one belonging to a friend of Captain Arnold, and in every respect as pretty a specimen of naval architecture as ever swam the waters. Even Mrs. Arnold, timid as she usually was of the sea, declared, when she saw the light graceful build, and tapering masts of the Zephyr, that she could have no reluctance to trust herself in so superb a vessel.

The morning was yet young when they started, and the bright sunshine was sweetly tempered by the awning that overshadowed the wide deck of the beautiful yacht.

There was certainly a peculiar colour towards the eastern horizon, which Captain Arnold noticed after they had been gone some few hours, and were nearly twenty miles from land, but it was with a transient seriousness that he noted it, and said to himself—

"I dare say to-morrow there will be some squally weather."

*   *   *   *

It was four o'clock in the afternoon, and the head of the yacht bore towards Cowes, when suddenly there appeared in the north-east the edge of a dense bank of clouds just peering above the long low line of the horizon. At the same moment a howling wind swept through the cordage of the vessel, stopping as suddenly as it had risen.

Captain Arnold no sooner perceived this

alteration in the aspect of the weather than he ordered the boatmen to put back, and endeavour to reach Cowes. This was immediately done, but their progress was slow, as the wind blew them from the spot they were making for, so they were compelled to take different tacks to enable them to near the land at all.

In the interim the wind rose, causing a greater ripple on the water, and the waves were crowned with a curl of white, which lasted but a moment. The sea-bird swept along the waters with a screaming sound, as if it rejoiced in the prospect of the disturbance in the elements that was so fearfully prognosticated.

The captain's family were much alarmed at these appearances, for well they knew that sudden and violent changes often happened in the Channel, which occasioned fatal accidents to those who were unprepared for the weather; but they did not attempt to seek shelter in the cabin, but remained on the deck with Captain Arnold himself, who did not see sufficient occasion to alarm them by sending them below.

The clouds quickly spread over the whole sky, coming up with great swiftness, a black mass of vapour obscuring the whole face of the scene: and that which had but a short time before been like a fairy scene, was now overcast with shadows and gloom.

The wind now rose and fell in loud gusts, and the sea heaved high its waves, which were now crested by a cap of white foam, which remained visible for a moment, and then was dashed into spray, mixing with the wind, and thus increasing the cold.

The little vessel was reduced to the smallest possible bit of canvas that she could sail under, and yet the wind drove it hither and thither, as if it were entirely at the mercy of the lightest breath of Heaven.

"You had better descend to the cabin," said Captain Arnold to his lady and children. "We shall have bad weather; the rain will fall presently, and you can be of no use; but probably in the evening——"

"Do you think there is any——"

"No, no," replied the captain, who really did not see much more than a heavy squall, and the prospect of being out at sea for a few hours longer than otherwise he would have been. But he had scarcely said this ere the wind rose, loudly roaring above the sound of the rushing waters, or the scream of the sea-mew; the rain fell in torrents, and a storm of fearful violence commenced.

The sea rose and fell in mighty waves, and the little vessel rolled and pitched so, that they often thought that she must go down on her beam ends; but as good fortune decided the matter, she always came up on the crest of the waves, riding like a cork on the billows.

They were now nearing the land, and the greatest anxiety prevailed in the minds of the captain's family to get to shore, for they feared to weather the storm out; and the captain himself believed that he could steer into the little bay near his own residence, without running much risk or danger, and hence he himself steered in the direction, but, long before he neared the wished-for spot, the gale increasing, they were driven close into the shore, where the yacht struck a bank with great force, but yet she rode off it and drifted with the current, as she was perfectly unmanageable; the rudder was unshipped, and the vessel striking repeatedly in a series of shocks, terror and despair seized the minds of the Arnold family, but at the captain's exertions they remained quiet, and he then ordered the boat to be lowered, and if possiblee they would risk an escape in that; but ths chief difficulty now lay in the boat, as it was scarcely possible it would live in such a sea a this.

To the great joy, however, of all on board, the boat was lowered, and floated lightly upon the raging waters, and hope revived in the breasts of the Arnolds as the only means they could think of for an escape was likely to become available.

Still the winds and waves raged in their utmost fury, and the heavy rain fell as fast as when it first began, and the little vessel continued to drift along, occasionally striking on the bank on which she had been driven.

The difficulty of getting into the boat was immense, and poor Captain Arnold, among so many affectionate calls upon his attention, knew not for a moment which first to apply himself to. He looked around upon his wife and children with an air of momentary distraction —but hesitation was not a part of his nature— and he said in a loud voice,—

"Hark all—I will remain here the last, but let the children be first placed in the boat, and youngest child the first of them."

A faint cheer of approval burst from the men —a cheer which was nearly drowned by the howling blast, that made it a matter of extreme difficulty to stand on the deck of the ill-fated vessel.

"You," cried Captain Arnold, addressing the man nearest to him, "you jump into the boat. I will watch my opportunity of throwing the children into your arms."

The order was promptly obeyed; and, watching an opportunity when the boat rose on the crest of a giant wave, the man sprung into it. The tremendous movement of the vessel, however, and the rapid rising and sinking of the boat, made the leap one of extreme hazard— true, he reached the boat, but in another moment such a dashing sea swept over it, that Captain Arnold believed it was swamped, and the only hope of a rescue for himself and family had gone. Such, however, proved not to be the case. The boat righted, although with a quantity of water in it, but the man had been swept away before he could secure a hold of the frail sides of the light vessel, and was nowhere to be seen.

Captain Arnold drew a long breath, and then cried in a loud voice, while his hair was wildly dashed about by the wind,—

"I ask no one to venture in that boat; I said I would be the last man on board this yacht, and if any one of you likes to leap to the boat I will keep my word, otherwise I must try it myself."

The men looked in each other's faces, and evidently shrunk from meeting the fate of their companion, and in another instant Captain Arnold, after whispering to his wife, cried,—"Cheer up, cheer up—all may be well—we are in the hands of Heaven—God bless you all!" sprung himself over the ship's side, and just succeeded in falling at full length in the boat as it sunk in the trough of a tremendous sea.

The position which he assumed in the boat was not only the most favourable for preserving its centre of gravity, but it was likewise one from which it was least likely he could be dislodged by a heavy sea. He lay on his back in the very centre of the boat, and grasped the sides firmly with his hands, so that he in fact dislodged much of the water that lay in it, and rose and fell as it was tossed on gigantic waves, or fell into the deep abyss between them, as if he had been part and parcel of the construction himself.

A cry of pleasure burst from the men on the yacht, and amid that cry Captain Arnold could hear the voice of his wife as she recognised the comparative safety of him who was so dear to her.

Now that he had once got fair possession of the boat, Captain Arnold considered the greatest difficulty was over. In fact, the chief danger now consisted in its being staved to pieces by striking against the sides of the yacht. Some of the crew immediately saw this, and, clinging to the disordered rigging, part of which was trailing over the sides, they lent most efficient assistance every time the boat drifted against the vessel, in preventing such a catastrophe.

Captain Arnold found that to maintain any higher position in the boat than a sitting one was quite impossible, and stretching up his arms he cried, in a voice that made itself plainly heard amid the din and tumult of the elements,—

"Throw me the children—throw me the children, as she rises on the crest."

One of the crew twisted his left arm around the rigging to resist the force of the wind, and the youngest child was handed to him. He was a powerful man, and taking a firm grasp of the child's clothes, he held it with his right hand, stretching over the vessel's side, ready to cast the little thing into its father's arms the first favourable opportunity that should present itself.

A crashing sound at this moment betrayed that the yacht had struck upon some other rock, and throughout all its loosened timbers were feeling the consequences of the concussion.

"She's going—she's going," cried the crew, and a rush was made to the side on which was the boat.

"Back, for your lives' sake, back," cried Captain Arnold. "One by one we may get quietly into the boat and be saved—make a rush of it and you swamp her."

"Easy, easy," cried the man who held the child. "The yacht will hold together for two or three such thumps as this. Now, sir." He cast the child fairly into Captain Arnold's arms as the boat was brought upon a wave nearly level with the side rails of the yacht.

"Thank God!" cried the anxious father, "one is saved."

The other two younger children were saved in the same way, and there remained but Jessie and her mother, the difficulty of rescuing whom was infinitely greater.

"Lie down—lie down," whispered Captain Arnold to the children; then in a loud voice he cried—"A coil of rope, here; cast me a coil of rope."

It was done; and in a few moments he had tied the children to the boat, which he felt was their only chance of rescue, so firmly that no sea could wash them out. Watching then his opportunity, just as for one half instant the boat was steady after it had reached the top of a wave, and before it plunged into the deep trough of the sea, he made a tremendous spring, and alighted in safety on the deck of the yacht.

"Now, my men," he cried, "I will keep my promise, and be the last on board this yacht. To you," addressing the sailor who had thrown him his children, "I commit this young girl. Watch your opportunity, men; be slow and steady, and you may all get into the boat. Be careful of the children, and God speed you."

The coolness with which Captain Arnold spoke had a wonderful effect in creating confidence among the men, and preventing the frightful confusion usually arising under such circumstances—a confusion which, in nine case out of ten, is the direct cause of the great loss of human life.

Practised in such matters, the sailors one by one got into the boat, including him who had the charge of Jessie, so that by the time the yacht had drifted on to another rock, against which it struck with awful violence, Captain Arnold and his wife were the only persons on board. The shock threw them both down; but the captain in a moment recovered his feet;

and as he did so, felt by a peculiar movement of the vessel, that it was slowly settling in the sea, and in a very few minutes must inevitably go down. With a strength lent to him by the urgency of the circumstances in which he was placed, he raised his wife in his arms, and waited for the boat to assume a favourable position for him to spring into it.

The roaring of the wind, at that moment, was truly terrific; the lashing of the broken cordage, and flapping of the torn sails, added to the noise; the whole combined, with the hoarse cries of the sailors, as one advised one thing, and one another, produced a scene t perfect terror.

The boat was still held to the yacht by a powerful cable, which had stood the most as- tounishing strains, and one of the crew sat with a knife in his hand ready to sever it, the moment Captain Arnold should have made good his foot- ing in the already over-crowded little vessel, to whose care so many lives were now committed in the midst of such a tempest.

For a moment the yacht became perfectly firm and steady. Captain Arnold knew too well what that meant—she was sinking. He roused up every energy for the spring he was about to take, for the boat was washing up towards him, on a heavy swell of sea. Nearer and nearer it came. Another moment and he would have been off the deck of the yacht, but before he could take the leap, a loud rushing noise took place below the deck and she lurched over like a dolphin, prow foremost. A shriek burst from the lips of Mrs. Arnold.

The man who was ready with his knife severed the cable, for he saw that, otherwise, the boat would be dragged to the bottom along with the doomed yacht.

A loud noise proclaimed the bursting up of the deck. There was one other wailing cry, and down went the yacht like a lump of lead, almost sucking the boat with it into the boiling vortex it created.

CHAPTER V.

THE FISHERMAN'S HUT.

THE next morning shone sweetly upon the varied beauties of sea and land with which the Isle of Wight abounds. A more calm, delicious day had never shone from out the clear blue sky, which was of that deep and beautiful hue so seldom seen in our variable climate.

No one could have believed that the quiet, lake-like sea, that gently rippled in upon the sandy beach, had, but a few short hours before, been lashed to fury, spreading death and desola- tion in its rage, engulfing in its far depths many a mute form which might otherwise have lived long to be the light and joy of many hearts. The sun shone with more than usual warmth. The wind, which had so lately blown a perfect hurricane, was subdued to the gentlest sighing zephyr, making most eloquent music wherever it went; and yet that wind was blow- ing from the same quarter with that which, some hours before, had snapped the stoutest cordage, torn sails to atoms, broken the masts of tall ships, and spread destruction in its course, that it seemed as if carrying on its bosom a legion of destroying fiends, who had been permitted, for a brief space, to wreak their wild fury upon man.

In a pretty, sequestered nook, near an inlet, where the gentle rippling sea was scarcely mur- muring, stood a fisherman's cottage. Like the humble wild floweret which escapes the storm that uproots the towering and majestic oak, the little structure had weathered the fury of the elements, affording a more secure shelter to the fisherman and his family, than the proudest palace could have done.

About the humble dwelling there was an air of quiet and mystery unusual to it. The children were hushed by their mother, and the fisherman and his wife spoke to each other in subdued accents.

The hut consisted but of two rooms, the inner one of which was a sleeping chamber, and it was towards this that the fisherman frequently directed his eye, as he held a whispered con- versation with his helpmate.

Now and then the woman would, with stealthy steps, creep into the inner room, and, after re- maining a short time, return and whisper to her husband that he was not much better and had not yet spoken.

"Heaven help him, for the sake of his poor children," said the fisherman, "as well as for himself; a better, kinder-hearted man don't breathe than Captain Arnold."

"You saw the yacht go down, John?" remarked his wife.

"I did. I was getting in shore as fast as I could myself, for a pretty few hours I had had, when I saw the last of the poor Zephry."

"It was, indeed, a frightful storm."

"Ay. Such a one as we haven't had on this bit of coast for many years—not since——"

"Hush, John, hush! I know what you are going to say."

"Well, well, I can bear now and then, Mary, to just say a word about our poor lost boy—it seems to relieve my heart—and often when I've been a long way out, and no one has been near to hear me but God, I have spoken his name, and it has come echoed back to me from some jutting cliff, as if—as if—"

The wife burst into tears as she clung to her husband's arm, saying, "There, there, John! enough, enough! you will make me unhappy for hours now."

The fisherman's reply was stopped, by the door of the inner room being suddenly opened, and a gentlemanly-looking man making his appearance from it.

"He's getting better, now," he remarked. "I think your watching will be sufficient, and I would not, on any account, recommend his removal to his own house yet."

"We'll take care of him, sir," said the fisherman; "we know Captain Arnold well. I little thought he, and all that belonged to him, were in the Zephyr yesterday."

A low moan from the inner apartment struck upon their ears, and the medical man, for such he was, accompanied by the fisherman, hurried into the room.

Captain Arnold was lying on the fisherman's humble couch. He was pale as death itself; his very lips were bloodless: and, although his eyes were open, they looked so sadly exhausted, as to be scarcely capable of turning a faint gaze upon the faces of his kind attendants. He made several ineffectual attempts to articulate before he could speak a word, and when he did it was in so low a tone that the fisherman had to bend his ear down to the mouth of the exhausted man to catch what he said.

"Are—are all saved?" he groaned.

"Hush!" said the surgeon, as the fisherman with a shake of the head, was about to reply; "hush! a relapse would be fatal."

"Speak—speak," groaned Captain Arnold.

"All your children," said the medical man, "are saved. They are at home, quite well."

"Thank God!"

A smile played over the father's face, and a transient gleam of colour came to his cheeks; but almost immediately it was gone again, and raising himself upon one arm, he said, in a tone of deep anxiety, trembling while he spoke.

"My wife—my wife!"

"Pray be tranquil, Mr. Arnold; in your present exhausted state you should endeavour to sleep if you can."

"Sleep—sleep! I ask you where—where is she?"

"Now really——"

"Peace, man—peace. You, John Anston, I know you, you will tell me the truth. Is she dead?"

The fisherman looked perplexed, and the medical man immediately said in a confident tone—

"All your family are safe, Captain Arnold. Now compose yourself, I beg of you."

"John Anston, tell me," he murmured, without removing his eyes from the fisherman's face; "as you hope for peace here and mercy hereafter, tell me truly—is my wife saved?"

A convulsive spasm came to the fisherman's throat, and he could but with difficulty say—

"The ocean swallowed my only child, Captain Arnold—the one darling hope, joy, and

pride, that God had given me, and yet you see me here, and I can say, His will be done."

"I understand—she—she——."

"Is lost."

Captain Arnold fell back on his pillow in a state of utter insensibility. He lay, to all appearance, as if quite dead; and the surgeon said in a reproachful tone—

"There now; there's no telling what mischief is done. What on earth made you tell such a thing to a man in such a state of physical exhaustion and prostration?"

"You may understand what you call physical things," said the fisherman, "but I'm an old man now, and I know something of human nature. If there's bad news for a man, let him have it with such kind words and consolations as one can think of, and then when he knows the worst he can bear up against it as a man should, and as such a man as Captain Arnold will."

"Ah, but don't you see, you have induced syncope, which may produce that same state of coma fuacer which I have had so much trouble to arouse him from."

"State of what?"

"Ah, you don't understand me, I perceive."

"I say, doctor, what do you think of missing stays in a trade wind, blowing like mad?"

"I really don't comprehend."

"Exactly; everybody to his trade, and on favour. There's the captain opening his eyes again; I knew he would."

Captain Arnold did open his eyes, and then he slowly raised his hand, beckoning the fisherman to come close to him. John Anston obeyed the signal; and when he was very near Captain Arnold whispered,—

"Tell me all—how—how was it? Tell me all?"

"I will. You recollect the storm?"

"Yes, yes—and the wreck—I recollect all till she went down—down. Yes, I recollect all till then."

"You remember the children being saved?"

"I do."

"Well, then, it seems the Zephyr was settling down when you and Mrs. Arnold stood upon its deck. As they who saw the whole affair tell me, you made a spring just as the vessel was going, and in course fell— you were sucked down with her."

"Yes—yes—go on."

"And the boat nearly shared the same fate After a few moments you rose to the surface but quite insensible. They pulled you on' board, but never saw Mrs. Arnold at all."

"They—they waited?"

"They did wait till all hope was past. The children were half dead with cold, hunger, and fright, when they got in here. You were brought to my hut, and this doctoring gentleman has brought you round again, though I thought you were a dead man—that's all, captain."

"All!" moaned Captain Arnold, and tears gushed from his eyes. "Oh, why was I saved? —why was I saved?"

"Why were you saved?"

"Yes—oh, why did not the same waves close for ever over me?"

"I'll tell you; and I'll tell you, too, why you ought to be ashamed of yourself for saying such a thing. The why was that you've got four children to look to. Be a man, captain. Storms will happen in the quietest seas, and a man is a poor sailor who would give up his vessel because even her mainmast had gone by the board."

"Really he ought to be kept quiet," said the medical man. "You are talking as loud as if you were out at sea."

"It will do him good," said John Anston. "It will do him a world of good, I tell you."

"Leave me," said Captain Arnold; "leave me now—leave me now." He turned his face to the pillow. They heard him weeping, and they left him for awhile to the sacredness of his sorrow.

CHAPTER VI.

THE FAMILY FRIEND.

On the morning of the day after the one which, owing to the extreme exhaustion of his frame, Captain Arnold was compelled to spend in the house of the honest fisherman, he was quietly and gently conveyed to his own once happy home—that home which he had fondly regarded as a haven of peace and love for life, where he could live securely, free from all but the usual casualties of existence, which no man of ordinary intellect even can otherwise than expect.

But now how utterly desolate did that pleasant well-kept spot appear. How the beauty had deserted the flowers. How the tall lime trees that shaded the house had lost, in his eyes, their graceful foliage—all, al seemed changed, as if a tempest of desolation had swept over that lovely and once enchanting spot.

Captain Arnold embraced his children, with tears in his eyes, and they wept freely, although their sorrow for the bitter loss they had experienced in the death of a fond mother was much tempered by their affection for their father, who, more than men usually do, had made himself familiar with the younger branches of his family, mingling with their sports and pastimes, and interesting himself largely in their growing hopes and wishes.

To Jessie, who was more of an age to comprehend him, although at that period she had not seen quite ten summers, he conversed seriously of his future plans and intentions.

"My dear Jessie," he said, "we have lost her whom we all loved so fondly, but most of all, have you and the younger ones lost the care of a kind mother. I cannot bear to part with any of you, so, my darling, we will all remain together, and by degrees, as you get older, you will be able to take a responsible position in my bereaved household."

The girl's voice was choked with sobs; she could only say,—

"Yes, father—yes;" and then she threw herself upon his breast in a paroxysm of weeping.

"Hush my darling," said Captain Arnold, although it was only by a great effort he kept his own tears from mingling with those of his child. "Hush, my darling Jessie. 'Tis true, your mother has been snatched away from us but we will try to bear up against our misfortunes with fortitude."

"And besides, father," whispered Jessie, "mamma is in Heaven."

"Yes, my child, yes."

Captain Arnold was forced to turn away his head to conceal his deep emotion.

"We shall see her again," sobbed Jessie; "I have told Willy and the others that we shall all see her again."

"Yes—yes—dear one, yes. We shall see her again, never more to part from her."

A sorrowful servant at this moment glided into the room, and in low accents said,—

"There is a gentleman below, sir, wishes to see you."

"I can see no one now," said Captain Arnold. "Say that—that a domestic calamity compels me—that is, I—I—have not spirits sufficient to see any one."

"Yes, sir."

The servant laid the visitor's card before her master, who, casting his eyes languidly upon it, read the name of Arlines.

"Arlines!" he cried; "my old friend Arlines; is it indeed he? Show him up directly; I long much for the companionship of one upon whose friendly sympathy I can fully rely in such a trying emergency as this."

Before this Mr. Arlines enters the room we may as well, considering that he will play no unimportant part in the drama of real life we have to lay before the reader, more formally introduce him.

Mr. Phillip Arlines was the son of a colonial judge, and upon the death of his father he had obtained a passage home in the vessel of which Captain Arnold was then lieutenant, and which happened at the juncture to be in the port.

It was on this homeward voyage that Philip Arlines had managed completely to win the friendship and esteem of Arnold. His manners and person were both agreeable, and he had one of those rare tongues with which Heaven occasionally gifts some of its worst creatures, that are almost sufficient to wheedle an angel out of Heaven. No wonder, then, that, thrown into his really fascinating society every day during a long voyage, Captain Arnold should think him the most agreeable and desirable acquaintance he had ever made.

Generous and unsuspicious as he was by nature, Captain Arnold had not had an opportunity of mixing sufficiently with society to become suspicious instead of confiding. He had been shut up in ships during that period of life when a man gets rid of that doctrine that all men should be assumed honest till you know they are rogues, and substitutes in its stead the much more practical and rational one of assuming all men rogues till you find them honest.

Hence, without a thought, he became quite on intimate terms with this Mr. Arlines, who, he little suspected, was an unprincipled man of the worst class. He had been such an affliction, in consequence of his dissolute conduct, to his father, that there was no doubt he, the father, had died partly of grief to see a son of his holding so disgraceful a career. But Captain Arnold knew nothing of all this, which had happened in the colony from which he brought Arlines ; and in England the dissolute young man was unknown.

The voyage occupied some months, during which Arlines contrived, in the most natural manner in the world, to win a good round sum from Arnold at cards ; but then he won it with such an air of regret, and seemed so really vexed at his own good fortune, that poor Arnold, far from suspecting the sharp hands he had fallen into, was more pleased than otherwise ; for he considered that the circumstance showed most strongly what an excellent heart his new friend had.

The intimacy grew stronger, and when Arnold's ship came to an English port he said,—

"Well, Arlines, I only hope that now we have arrived at the end of our voyage we have not arrived at the end of our friendship."

"My dear Arnold," replied Arlines, "if there is any one circumstance which I do believe was brought about specially by the goodness of Heaven, that circumstance consists in my meeting with you so soon after I had been compelled by the irrevocable fiat of death to bid adieu in this world to the best of fathers. You, my dear Arnold, by your admirable society and varied talents, have chased away the gloom from my heart which otherwise might long have oppressed it. Oh, what a treasure it is to possess a philosophic friend like yourself."

"Nay, Arlines, I am indebted to you," said the gratified Arnold, "for making a long wearisome voyage pleasant and attractive."

"Ah, there again," said Arlines with a sigh and a sad smile, " modest merit ever tries to hide its head."

"Pho, pho, Arlines, you know how gratified I am in your acquaintance. Tell me how and when we shall meet in London, whither I must post immediately."

Arlines named an hotel, which was not of the most respectable character, although Arnold was far from being aware of that fact, and they parted. Since then they had never met ; for when Arnold, upon his arrival in the metropolis, took the first opportunity of seeking his attractive acquaintance, he found a letter awaiting him to the following effect,—

"My dear Arnold—Judge of my surprise when I endeavoured to settle my deceased father's affairs in England, to find that I had been wrongly advised, and that, therefore, I must return again to New South Wales in order to take some legal steps with relation to his property in that colony.

"Before you receive this I shall have started ; for as time is really an object, I do not like to lose the first vessel bound for that part of the world. Upon my return I shall lose no time in searching you out.

"Wishing you all health and happiness in the bosom of your family, I am, my dear Arnold, yours ever truly,

"PHILLIP ARLINES."

Captain Arnold, for to that rank he was elevated immediately upon his return, felt the loss of the society of Arlines severely for a short time ; but all regrets were soon forgotten when he joined his family and became busied in looking out for some calm and quiet retreat, in which he could enjoy the society of those who were so dear to him. He left all actual service, and after some search had succeeded in settling himself in the delightful residence we have described to the reader—a residence which a long time was one of joy and peace ; but which, by the catastrophe which had occurred, became one full of gloomy thoughts, and sad, tearful, and tender recollections.

Of Arlines, Captain Arnold had heard nothing until now, suddenly, he dropped in upon him at the very moment of his great affliction, when the society of a friend, if he had been really a sincere well-meaning one, would have been of the greatest importance to Arnold.

With this brief introduction we will accompany Mr. Arlines into the apartment where Captain Arnold had held the gentle and affectionate conversation we have recorded with his beautiful child Jessie.

"Ah, my dear Arnold," cried Arlines, shaking him by the hand, with a tremendous amount of cordiality ; "I am delighted to see you. It seems to me a hundred years since we met—but—but—good God, how is this?—

you are looking ill—distressed. Gracious Heavens, what has happened?"

"Have you not heard, Arlines?"

"No—no—why—why—I am quite shocked at your appearance, my dear friend."

"Jessie, my darling," said Captain Arnold, "you can go now."

Jessie kissed her father's cheek, and then glided from the room, after which Captain Arnold briefly related to Arlines all that had occurred since they last met.

Grief and commiseration were never more admirably depicted in the countenance of a Garrick, than they were in the still handsome but dissolute-looking countenance of Phillip Arlines; nay, he had even tears at command, and shed them freely, so that Captain Arnold, even in the midst of his grief, blessed his happy stars that he had met with such a sympathizing friend.

"You see, Arlines," he added, "I am in a sad situation. You should have come here some time since, and then I could have given you a proper reception."

"My dear Arnold, do not speak of that. Lamenting, as I do, your very great calamity; feeling for you, as I do, from the very bottom of my heart, believe me, I am pleased, if I may use such an expression when I am so full of sympathy, that I have come to you in your distress, for the conversation, weak though it may be, of a well-meaning friend, may assist to wean your mind from a consideration of your heavy loss, and, in the course of time, you may learn to feel it less acutely."

"You are very kind, Arlines, but I cannot consent to take you from, most likely, a gay and happy circle, to produce a gloom upon your spirits, by——"

"Pho, pho," interrupted Arlines; "friendship is a sacred thing; I will remain with you as long as you like. Just you tell me when you wish to get rid of me, that's all. There may be many things, just now, which it would grieve you to do yourself, but which a friend can do for you. Tell me your plans and what you propose."

"I am really grateful to you," said Arnold. "In the first place I wish to leave this house; it no longer has any charms for me; all that was beautiful about it, has now faded away."

"Naturally. I can fully appreciate your feelings."

"I must remove to a distance, where the cares attendant upon bringing up my motherless little ones must occupy my mind."

"Exactly, exactly."

"I was thinking of living in or near London."

"You cannot do better. Take some residence near the leviathan city, and when you feel any unusual depression stealing over you, you can mix in a few of its gaieties, and shake it off. Besides, if you select some pretty spot in the suburbs of London, you may enjoy still many of the charms of the country, besides securing for your children a healthier and purer atmosphere than London itself could give you."

"Yes; I think that a good plan."

"A capital one. By-the-by, I am the very man to find a place for you. Excuse my question, Arnold, but between friends anything can be said—is your fortune considerable?"

"I have my pay and some property besides; I should say, I am worth, altogether, something near fifteen hundred per annum."

"Oh!"

"Yes; sometimes a little more, sometimes a little less, as the property differs in value."

"My dear Arnold, it is a handsome little income. You may be very happy yet; and depend upon me being, as long as I live, a friend to you and your family. A shade is over my spirits, at present, from sympathy with your afflictions, but when I can free myself from that, I hope, likewise, to rescue you from your state of depression, and that you may look back upon what has occurred with a calmer regret, and a trust in the wisdom of that Providence which never deserts a good man, even in the hour of his darkest tribulation."

CHAPTER VII.

THE CONSPIRACY.

IT was some evenings after the conversation we have recorded between Phillip Arlines and Captain Arnold, that the former was in London. He had received full power and instructions from Arnold to look for a house for him, and he had made up his mind that it would be a very strange thing indeed if, in addition to living upon him, he could not, in the course of time, so far abuse the confidence which the unsuspecting man had in him, as to ruin him entirely.

Phillip Arlines had got through all his patrimony, and was in that condition which forces a gentleman to live by his wits, as the saying is. He had been an inveterate gambler, and when he got fleeced of all his own means, he was graciously admitted into the fraternity of black legs which had been his ruin.

Arlines, however, must, by no means, be sympathised with as an innocent victim. He had played in the most dishonourable manner possible, and exerted all his ingenuity to win by trickery—that he lost, was only because the sharpers in London knew more than he did, and, consequently, got the better of him in the long run.

Still, during the process, they saw enough

of him to respect his talents, and to believe that he would make a very desirable confederate. When, therefore, he had no more money to lose, they made overtures to him, which he joyfully accepted, for there was not one lingering principle of honour or honesty in his heart to stand in the way of his commission of any iniquities, so long as the proceeds procured him the luxuries he so much admired.

The proposal to him was, that he should undertake a particular department of an iniquitous plan for fleecing people of their money at a fashionable gaming-house, which was, at that time, being newly built in St. James's-street, and which, by the neatness of its interior decorations, was exciting the curiosity of all the town. He was to act as the decoy to persons who otherwise would never think of gambling, to induce them to come to that house, where some of the parties were always to be ready to take advantage of the victim.

The fascinating appearance and gentlemanly manners of Phillip Arlines admirably calculated him for such a part in the nefarious plot. His name, likewise, was known; and he was, before his real character became known, much respected, and admitted to many respectable families, for his father's sake, who had been in life, as a man of honour and a gentleman everything that his son was not.

Phillip Arlines then was to be supplied with the means of going into good society, and if he brought but one or two victims in the course of twelve months into the hands of his rascally associates, the thing would pay very well.

As soon, then, as Arlines had made this arrangement, he cast a look about him to see who he could make its victims, and among a list of others, he took care to place Captain Arnold's name, accompanied by a note, in the form of a query, as to his property, concerning which Arlines, as yet, knew nothing, as he had not had, during their former intimacy, any particular stimulus to make the inquiry.

We are aware how, with assumed candour, he asked the interesting question of Captain Arnold, and got from him, at once, the amount of his income. Such a piece of news as that Captain Arnold had fifteen hundred pounds a year decided him, at once, to leave no art untried to make him a victim.

The property, he rightly argued, which could bring in anything like that amount yearly, must be of considerable marketable value, and it was that property, and not the current cash of the captain's, upon which Phillip Arlines fixed his eyes with a coveting and vicious gaze.

Rogue-like, then, and in direct opposition to the proverb of there being "honour among thieves," he began to think how he could bilk his companions, as well as victimise Captain Arnold; but in that he did not very clearly

see his way, only he treasured up the idea in his own mind, for future serious consideration, in case anything should turn up to give it a more practicable aspect.

On the evening we mention, Arlines was hurrying towards the once suburban village of Kensington, in order to hold a secret conference with the conspirators, one of whom, an attorney had a house there, in which all the minutiæ of the plans of operations were arranged from time to time.

The nefarious association consisted of six persons, viz., the attorney, whose name was Seldon; a certain noble lord, who was one of the hereditary legislators of his country, who, for the present, we will not name; Phillip Arlines; and three others, who acted subordinate parts, and whose connection with our narrative does not call for their separate and individual designations.

The hour was nine in the evening, and these worthies were assembled, according to a summons from Arlines, which stated he had something of importance to communicate.

They were tolerably punctual, and by a quarter after nine they were seated with as much solemnity as a privy council, in the drawing-room of Mr. Seldon, attorney at law, and as great a rogue as an attorney at law can possibly be, which we humbly opine is using very strong language indeed.

The noble lord, who affected to be extremely near-sighted, and to speak with a hesitating lisp, was placed in the chair, and the doors being secured, he said,—

"Ah—ah—well—Arlines—let's hear what's the tumult. Go on, my good fellow— who's the pigeon? Ah—order, gentlemen, if you please. If you don't kick up a row—ah—it's all one to me. Pass that Burgundy this way —ah."

Arlines rose and addressed the confederate scoundrels as follows:—

"Gentlemen, I have been quite indefatigable in pigeon fancying, and I think I have hit upon a fine bird, although not so valuable a one has as occasionally fallen into the hands of this honourable fraternity."

"No nonsense," said Seldon—"let's have the gist of the matter without any verbiage. I, as a lawyer, have seen so much of that in my time, that I'm sick of it."

"Very good," continued Arlines; "I have heard of Satan reproving sin, and was once told of a lawyer who offered to swear to something on his conscience."

"Ah—ah—ah!" simpered his lordship. "Push the Burgundy."

"Well, gentlemen, to proceed: what amount of real property ought to bring somewhere about fifteen hundred per annum? Come, Seldon, how much?"

"The property can't be worth much less than thirty thousand pounds," said the lawyer.

"Then the pigeon I have in view is a thirty thousand pounds one to all intents and purposes, for that's what he is worth."

"Good," said Seldon.

"Bravissimo!" cried his lordship.

"Who is he?" said another.

"A captain in the navy, by name, Arnold."

"Green?"

"No; Arnold."

"Now, curse you—you know what I meant. To be decidedly verdant."

"Decidedly. He is one of your open, candid characters—soft as water, and full as the Thames is of impurities of all sorts of sweet amiabilities."

"Good!"

"He has just lost his wife, and, consequently, is in great distress of mind."

"What?" screamed his lordship.

"What?" roared the attorney.

"What?" echoed the other conspirators; and the whole of them glanced at Arlines with unmitigated astonishment.

"I say he has just lost his wife."

"Well, but, ah—you said something about a consequence. Now, my good fellow, you must be mad. If I were to lose my lady, ah—I do think, out of thankfulness, ah—to Providence, that I should turn, ah—moral."

"Talk of a man's consequent distress, because he has lost his wife," said the lawyer. "Arlines—Arlines—we have met to transact important business, and not to be persecuted with any of your grave irony."

"Well, well, gentlemen, we can drop that portion of the subject," said Arlines.

"Ah!" added one of the conspirators, with a deep sigh, "I wish to God I could drop that portion of the subject. I've got a wife, gentlemen, who is a perfect horror. At one time, gentlemen, I thought her a fine woman, and married her—some persons or people, to be sure, warned me that she was a devil, but they were wrong, for she is a dozen devils rolled into one—she drinks like a fish—robs me on all opportunities—she——"

"Enough, enough," said Seldon; "to business—to business. What is the name of this captain?"

"I told you. His name is Arnold—he is coming up to London, and has placed himself entirely in my hands; in fact, I have become his factotum. Now, Seldon, your part of the business comes next."

"Exactly, and that is to make cautious inquiries, and thoroughly, and without doubt, ascertain the nature and value of his property, and whether all of it is in his own disposal or not. After that, my lord, comes your share of the business."

"Of course," said his lordship, "I must be introduced to him and help to inveigle him to play, affecting to lose myself, and bewail his losses."

"You have nothing more to say, Arlines?"

"Nothing, except that I want twenty pounds, for which I shall give the usual receipt among us, so that the sum can be deducted from my share of the proceeds of this adventure."

The money he required was, without any hesitation, handed to him, and in a short time the atrocious conference broke up, the noble lord repairing to his seat in the House of Lords, to support a measure for creating a bishop for the Island of Owhyhee, and the lawyer to his chambers, while the other vagabonds dispersed over the hells of the metropolis.

* * * *

It was one great cause of grief to Captain Arnold, that he had not even the melancholy satisfaction of consigning ceremoniously and affectionately the remains of his beloved partner to the earth. It grieved him much, making sad ravages upon his face and form, to reflect that she, whom he had pressed to his bosom as the wife of his affections, should be food for the creatures of the deep.

This was a reflection he never mentioned to any one, and was probably more intense and bitter on that account. He would awaken in the night with dreadful images of her mangled body floating before his eyes; and many and many a time he forgot, for a few moments, the young things who had no one to look to in the world but himself for succour and love, and wished himself with her who had possessed all his heart, at the bottom of the sea, sleeping as calmly as she was sleeping, and washed to and fro by the same billows.

Time only could assuage such feelings as these, and bring anything like relief to the mourner's heart. As yet his wounds were too fresh and green for him not to feel them severely.

Phillip Arlines he thought he could never be sufficiently thankful to, for he seemed indefatigable in his efforts, not only to amuse his mind, but to find some pleasant and suitable residence for him in London, or very near to it.

It was on the fifth day after Arlines had left the Isle of Wight that Captain Arnold received the following gratifying epistle from him:—

"MY DEAR ARNOLD,—House-hunting is rather more of a job than I thought it; but that has arisen, perhaps, because I have been more squeamish for you than I should have been for myself. I would not write before because I had found nothing to my liking, or, rather, nothing that I thought would be to your liking. Yesterday, however, I was more successful; indeed, I think I may say most successful.

"Some two miles from Hyde-park I have seen a pretty little box, which I think will suit

you. It is a villa residence, replete with con-
veniences, as the auctioneers say—the grounds
are not extensive, but quite sufficient to contain
a little of everything that it is necessary to
have.

"My own opinion is that it would just suit
you. The rent is a hundred and twenty-five
pounds per annum.

"Write to me by return of post, my dear
Arnold, giving me instructions what to do, and
some references in town who know you, for I
may be asked for such.

"Believe me, yours, very truly,
"PHILLIP ARLINES."

To this note Captain Arnold sent an immediate reply, giving Arlines full power to take
the villa on his account, and referring him to his
solicitors in London, not only for any reference
that might be requred, but for any money he,
Arlines, might want, on his, Captain Arnold's,
account.

This was just the sort of reply Arlines expected and wished, and out of the transactions
he could, he felt assured, have no difficulty in
pocketing some thirty or forty pounds for
himself.

In such a calculation, however, he met with
a little check, for when he waited upon Captain
Arnold's solicitors, although he was received
with abundance of civility the head of the firm,
who was a wary old practitioner, said—

"Mr. Arlines, we are very much obliged to
you for this visit, very much indeed, and the
letter you produce from our respected friend,
Captain Arnold, is very satisfactory—very.
We will take upon ourselves to act for him as
regards the house you mention, defraying all
necessary charges, without giving you any more
trouble, for your kindness already has been so
great, that if in a sheer business transaction we
did not relieve you, we should be very much to
blame indeed—very."

This was a damper, and the old attorney
seemed to mean that it should be so, for he
rubbed his lean shrivelled hands together, and
looked up at the ceiling, as much as to say,
"It's of no use your arguing the point—
I have made up my mind, and you get no
money out of me."

"But my good sir," said Arlines, "you
perceive that Captain Arnold expressly
authorises me to take money of you on his
account? You perceive that?"

"Oh! certainly—certainly—and we shall do
our duty towards our client and friend, Captain
Arnold."

"I want, then, a hundred pounds."

"Ahem—which will be paid upon the
production of vouchers, that such a sum has been
expended—ahem!"

"Then I am to expend it first out of my own
pocket?"

"Yes—ah—yes."

"But really this is very odd."

"Very—very."

"Then you will advance nothing?"

"Certainly not, without vouchers—ahem!
Business is business, you see, my dear sir—a
business man is one who minds his own business
and lets other people's business alone."

"Yes—but—"

"And goes about his business in a business-
like manner, and when he has any business to
do he—"

"Good morning, gentlemen," said Arlines,
with a bland smile, " you are perfectly right,
and I am quite wrong.—Good morning,
gentlemen. God bless you."

"Good morning, my dear sir. Heaven preserve you," said the old lawyer.

"D—n him!" muttered Arlines, when he
reached the street.

"That fellow's a rogue," remarked the old
lawyer, as he resumed the perusal of some
documents which the entrance of Arlines had
interrupted.

So Mr. Phillip Arlines, for once in his life,
reckoned without his host.

CHAPTER VIII.

THE REMOVAL, AND THE TEMPTATION.

MR. ARLINES was a politic man, and he
made up his mind that he would not, on any
account, quarrel with Captain Arnold's solicitors.
Oh, dear, no, not on any account, although he
was absolutely boiling with indignation at the
manner in which he had been treated by them.

He wrote to Captain Arnold, saying how
very kindly he had been received by them, and
ascribing it to some knowledge of his poor
deceased father—adding, too, how much he
admired them for agreeing with him, that there
was no necessity whatever for their advancing
any money.

Could hypocrisy go further than this?

In a postscript he gave his address in London,
and pressed the captain and his family to come
and be his guests, until he should be quite
ready for their reception.

After some demur about the trouble which
he was giving to the most disinterested and
best of friends, Captain Arnold, rather than
inflict an indelible wound upon the sensitive
heart of Mr. Arlines, accepted his invitation,
and made immediate preparations for a journey
to London with his children.

He had, since the catastrophe which had
ended so fatally, called several times upon the
fisherman, with a view of recompensing him
for the trouble he had had upon his account;
but John would accept of nothing, and Captain
Arnold, who was determined upon making some

substantial show of his gratitude, bought for him a new boat, which he ordered should be taken home the day after he and his family should have left the Isle of Wight, in all likelihood, at least as far as he, Captain Arnold was concerned, for ever.

Then there came the disagreeable task of severing himself from a spot he had loved so well—the packing, too, of the many articles he chose not to part with, because they were associated in his mind with scenes of affection and interest. These were mournful remembrances at the very least; but still he clung to them, and hours before it was necessary to think of actually leaving, everything was in a state of active readiness to bid adieu to the well know and once carefully-tended spot of earth.

The day was one of those calm, serene, and sunny days, in which no sound is heard, save the songs of the birds. No angry look of the heavens cast a shadow upon the earth—no breath breathed to disturb the fall of a leaf, or to bend the tall blades of grass—it was a day of calm beauty.

The sadness that oppressed the hearts that dwelt beneath the roof of Captain Arnold's dwelling, found no repose in nature, all without that abode of sorrow and regret seemed joy and gladness. The birds flew from bough to bough and tree to tree, and gave forth as merry a note as at any other season of gladness; but to those conscious of the melancholy event that had taken place, how great was the contrast, how the unhappy notes of gladness jarred their feelings and fell upon their ears like notes of dissonance.

The sun shone in the heavens with more than Italian splendour; but in the hearts of the inmates was more than Cimmerian darkness; joy and gladness without, sorrow and sadness within.

Captain Arnold and his family, ere they left the abode that had so long afforded them joy and sorrow, walked round it to take a farewell look, and bid a long adieu to all the well-known spots of beauty, to all those favourite resorts in which they had taken so much delight, in parting from which they experienced the severest pangs they could endure, save alone what they felt on the occasion of such a calamity as the one they had just had the sad misfortune of experiencing.

Their walk was a silent one—there was much that might have been said, yet the heart was too full of recent sorrow to say it. Their weeping eyes first met one object and then another, which had once been the peculiar care of the hand that was now cold in death, who was now they knew not where.

There was a small summer-house at one end of the garden; it was long ere they could approach this spot, for here the unfortunate Mrs. Arnold used often to spend a few hours in reading or instructing her children—here they often received the natural advice that was given out of pure love, and had for its object the welfare of the youthful throng that listened.

The tears that now fell were those of deep-seated grief, such as come from the heart of innocence; the beauty of the scene around was but dimly seen through the tears that stood in the eyes of those gentle hearts that accompanied the disconsolate father around the walks that he had so often perambulated in happier hours.

The little gate, and the path that led directly to the bay in which used to lie the cause of their recent misfortune, the yacht; and in that, too, they had passed many of their happiest hours. At this gate they paused with one consent, and looked long and fixedly at the little bay, now empty, the light and fairy-like Zephyr was no longer riding on its calm bosom, casting the only shadow on its pure pelucid waters it ever bore. Alas! they too well knew the cause of this absence; but though they noticed it, not one of them spoke of that which most strongly presented itself to their minds.

Captain Arnold opened the wicket-gate, and then walked out, followed by his children in silence. He walked quietly by the margin of the little bay, and then to the headland, which reared its form at the end.

They all strolled onwards, and ascended the acclivity, and once more a calm and beautiful prospect of the ocean presented itself to their view.

The sun was in its full meridian power—the sea-gull swept over the ocean's surface with a heavy, lazy sweep, and then settled upon its surface, floating over the gentle waves with the ease and lightness of a nautilus. Long and steadfastly did Captain Arnold gaze upon the scene as if wrapped in contemplation of its beauties, and when he turned from the spot, his eyes were filled with tears, and without a word he led the way to his own cottage, whither his daughters followed him in silence.

Another hour and they bade adieu to the beloved spot, never to see it more.

Travelling then, was not what it is now; on the contrary, speed, though an object to a certain extent, never was indulged in to that extent; but always left travellers in that happy frame of mind in which there was yet something more to be desired; this was fortunate for the individual who had all his desires fairly satiated, had nothing more to live for, and his existence might as well be terminated at once, seeing he had nothing more to hope for or to enjoy—he had done his utmost in this way, and no more joys were in store.

Captain Arnold and his youthful family came to London by the usual conveyance; he took that as the readiest, and which exposed them to no more real inconvenience than a private vehicle, and it was not until the following morning that they approached the suburbs of London.

Great excitement prevailed among the little group on their approach to this celebrated city, of which they had heard so much and expected so much, and of which they knew so little, that the captain's mind insensibly quitted the gloomy field of reflection and remembrance that recent events had so amply furnished him with, and his attention was compelled in favour of those dear beings who looked to him as their only protector, and answer the many childish inquiries they made of him.

This had a beneficial effect upon the whole group, for question and answer were provocative of question and answer without end; this conversation so entirely absorbed their whole faculties, that it soon caused sorrow to fade for awhile, and a smile of pleasure, though a languid one, played upon the countenance of the fond and affectionate father.

Here they were, however, in London—not in the heart of it, it is true—but the road was lined with that class of houses, which, near the outskirts of London, have a variety of imitation gardens in front, ornamented with a dwarf brick wall, surmounted with a flag stone and some spiked rails and a border of some kind of evergreen, which only boasts of that colour after a shower, or occasionally a stunted tree, whose fair proportions had been some time or other ruthlessly cut down, while a few branches, and often straggling subsidary branches, burst out of the degraded crown.

* * * * *

We will pass over some intervening space, which, although containing incidents of interest to the Arnolds, possesses nothing of sufficient importance to stay the even current of our narrative.

We will suppose them housed in their new home on the first day of their arrival there, and with grateful feelings surveying the various beauties of the situation, and the comforts, which, after all their mental distress, they could not but be cognisant of.

Captain Arnold felt a relief in the new features and scenes which surrounded him. Not that he much delighted in novelty for novelty sake, his mind was too constant in its affection, and remembrance was to him one of the dearest qualities he possessed to his own mind. He loved to recal all that was good and beautiful; he loved to see around him the same beautiful scene; the same earth, air, and sky; nay, the very waves had a claim upon his mind, for he loved all those countless charms that such a habitation as that which he had so lately occupied possessed; but, above all, he loved to see old faces around him. His own family had the closest ties to him, while his affections seemed not bounded by the narrow limits of his own family,

but extended to all those whom he was in the habit of meeting and having any communication with whatever.

The peasantry around the beautiful spot where he but so lately resided in the Isle of Wight lost a good, kind friend when Captain Arnold left that delightful spot.

But how great was the change that had taken place, how great the revulsion of feeling! She, whom he loved more dearly than his life, was gone—had been snatched from him by an accident—the more lamentable that it was on such an occasion.

The long familiar scenes became hateful; and the vast expanse of water that lay open to his view from the little woodland, became distasteful to him; for in the deceitful waves lay the body of his much loved wife, the partner of all his joys and sorrows, she whom he loved above all human affections.

His affections towards this spot were dried up; he could not bear to look upon it; the surrounding objects, so dear from old associations, were no longer pleasing, but brought with them that remembrance of an event that he would endeavour to banish from his mind, but which yet clung to him like his shadow.

Every walk he took, every turn, presented some object to him that recalled the deceased Mrs. Arnold to his mind, and involuntarily tears would start to his eyes, as he gazed upon some object of her care or admiration; some flower trained by her own hands; some plants she tended with more than ordinary care; some sweet view, or sylvan retreat that she had frequented: all these things brought her to his mind so forcibly and frequently that Captain Arnold felt the utter impossibility of remaining in a place that recalled so often and so vividly the dear object of his affections to his view.

It was from this motive he quitted the Isle of Wight, a place abounding in natural beauties, and took up his residence near London.

Since his arrival, (but a few hours,) his spirits appeared to recover somewhat of their former elasticity, and he busied himself in one little office and another to his children, who now only had claims of peculiar care upon him; for them, then, he would live and endeavour to protect them from the evils they might be exposed to in the commencement of their pilgrimage through life.

They looked over and admired the new residence. Many novelties arrested their attention, and called forth a flood of remarks and inquiries about things they saw for the first time; seeing them in new positions, and under different circumstances, caused a different emotion in their minds, and they were busy in conversation until it drew towards evening.

The sun gently declined towards the west, the clouds were slightly gilded by the setting sun, that threw a new and varied glory over the heavens. This was a novel and, to them, beautiful appearance; differing, as it did, in grandeur, and the sterner beauties of their own parts, this, to them, had a secret and sedative effect upon their minds.

They watched the sun as he traversed the remaining space ere he dipped behind the dark lines of trees that formed the horizon to their view. The gentle and subdued hour of twilight approached, when Jessie, who had been standing by her father, as they watched the sun's decline, said to him—

"Dear father, how different is the sunset here to what it used to be when it sunk in the waters of the ocean, ere we came here."

"Yes, my Jessie," replied Captain Arnold; "I wish all to be different, very different; I never can forget her who has been taken from us; but I could not endure the remembrance of her to be so painfully excited. We shall live here happy and long, I hope."

"I hope so, too," replied Jessie, with a sigh. "How very beautiful this place is, though its beauty is of a different kind to what we have been used to."

"It is," said Captain Arnold.

"And then the number of people, carriages, and the gaiety of dress, and so many things, may be said to distract one's attention."

Captain Arnold smiled as he listened to his daughter's remarks, and replied.—

"After a time, Jessie, the novelty of this will wear off, all this will be but common, and no longer excite your surprise, and yet changes will be frequent, until at length change itself shall cease to excite notions of wonder or surprise."

Thus, in pleasant conversation, they passed the evening. Not a thought or expression fell from the lips of any one of the party that disturbed the calm harmony, nor the current of pleasant thoughts, and Captain Arnold kissed his children and bade them good-night early on that evening, for the day had been a busy and fatiguing one to them all.

CHAPTER IX.

A DISTURBED REPOSE.—A DREAM.—THE EARLY MORN.

SLEEP, the kindly refresher of the mind and body, had fallen upon the household; even Captain Arnold had sunk to repose, and buried his cares in oblivion; not a sound was heard in the house, save the monotonous ticking of the old clock upon the staircase. It was that hour of sound repose in which a whole population lies buried in forgetfulness.

At such an hour as this a cry ran through the house of a heart-rending and fearful character, such as pained those who heard it, and caused them involuntarily to start up from their peaceful slumbers with barely the consciousness of their existence.

Captain Arnold jumped up from his bed alarmed at the cry, and scarcely had he attired himself in his dressing-gown, when another piercing shriek struck upon his ears; it was so loud, so long, and so shrill, that it was painful to listen to it; though those who heard it involuntarily paused in their employment, as if with the expectation of hearing it repeated.

Rushing from his room, Captain Arnold paused on the stairs to listen whence the sounds proceeded. A few moments convinced him they were from his daughter, for the sounds of sobs and sighs came audibly from her room.

By this time all who were in the house were now awake and about, for none could possibly remain asleep after such a cry.

The door was opened, and Jessie was found in a paroxysm of terror; and it was not until after much persuasion and kind remonstrance that she could be at all quieted; but even when she became aware that she was in the hands of friends she trembled excessively.

"Where is my father?" exclaimed Jessie—"where is he? is he safe?—oh, tell me he is safe."

"Safe, my darling Jessie," replied Mr. Arnold. "Here I am, I have been speaking to you. Don't you know me?—look at me, my child, and do not thus affright yourself—I am here."

"Thank Heaven!—thank Heaven!" repeated Jessie, "I feared—I feared——"

"Feared what, my Jessie?" inquired Mr. Arnold.

"Oh, it was but a dream—but oh, it was a terrible one. Thank Heaven you are safe."

"What was it, Jessie?—tell me dear," said Mr. Arnold, in soothing tones, endeavouring to engage her mind, and so draw her back to a full consciousness of her own and his security and safety.

"Oh, it was a terrible dream, father, a terrible dream, indeed; but I will tell you all about it——"

Jessie paused and shuddered, but after a minute or two she said,—

"I know not how it came to pass—I knew not how it was—but I thought I was alone in a garden, wild and neglected, and overgrown with weeds and long rank grass, scarcely a flower could be seen, but such has had become wild through neglect. The rose had turned to thorns, and the walks were undistinguisable from the beds, so over-run was the spot with wild and rank vegetation.

"I was alone. I walked in this garden, and mourned the neglect that had allowed everything to run to waste or to decay, when I was suddenly startled by the sound of men's voices in angry contention.

"I started at the sound, and turning, I saw two men struggling with each other. The words they uttered were few, but spoken in a subdued tone, and between their clenched teeth.

"During the struggle they gradually, but slowly, neared a desolate spot, about which lay a few broken boards and bricks; it was wild and over-run with weeds; not a single object that could attract the attention, save one, and oh, God! that was a well.

"There was no protecting cover to it; there were no means of saving any human being from falling into it. And at first when I looked at the spot I saw not the well; but as the two were struggling and drawing near it, I saw the old well.

"Nearer and nearer they came; my heart beat quick, and I stooped down with fear and the horrible expectation of seeing an event I shrunk from witnessing, without the power of uttering a sound, and my direst fears were every moment nearer being verified.

"Presently the two men stood on the brink; they endeavoured to free themselves, and the one to throw the other into the well. They doubled, and twisted, and every kind of action that under such circumstances could be performed, was done; and at length their exertions had reached a limit, and they stood locked in each other's embrace, motionless.

"A moment thus spent, and then the fierce struggle was renewed, with more desperate energy; they both bent over the old well, and then disappeared.

"A momentary stillness ensued, and then a sullen and heavy splash came from the depths of the old well. Oh, Heaven! they were swallowed up in its cold waters. I shook as with an ague, and impelled by an irresistible impulse, I crept nearer and nearer the well.

"A strange sound came from its depths. The water appeared to bubble and boil as if it were rising rapidly towards the top. I was near, but not near enough to see down the well. I had an ardent desire to do so, yet I feared to creep closer.

"Presently I could see the water rising and whirling round in giddy eddies, and the two bodies rose and were carried round in the whirl of the waters; the face of one I saw, but that one was unknown to me, and the other was—oh! Heaven preserve me!—that of you, my dear father.

"For a few moments, horror and surprise took possession of my soul, and I was incapable of motion. My nerve had deserted me, and my eyes were fixed upon that terrible spectacle, and I without the power of withdrawing them; but presently my faculties returned, and I screamed out for aid.

"The motion I made caused me to wake, and I suppose in my sleep, that I did cry out, and that is what alarmed you all."

"It was, my dear Jessie; it was that terrible cry that brought us all here; but let not that disturb you, we shall all soon sleep again."

"Not I," replied Jessie; "I dare not close my eyes again this night."

"What, let a dream scare you from your rest, love? forget it, and think it was but a dream."

"Ay, but such a dream—I shall never forget it the longest day I live. Oh! it was too terrible—too dreadful; ever to fly from my mind."

"Come, come, Jessie, is it not thus you usually speak and think; you know that it was but a dream, and I am here."

"I know it, father; and had you been away, I should have mourned you dead. I see you are here, and know that you are safe; but oh, should it be but some warning of a dreadful death that may await you—it is too terrible to think of."

"It is, my dear Jessie, and therefore we will forget it. You dreamt one thing, and another is the fact; can anything be more evident? When ought we to place faith in dreams? Certainly not when they are manifestly false. Can anything be shown you in a stronger light than this?—I think not."

"And yet, dear father, I cannot throw off the fear and terror I feel but now; indeed, the effect of them is, to leave me somewhat under their influence now; not that I doubted your existence, but I now feel the effects of my fears—I shall be better by the morning."

"I will not leave you, Jessie," replied Captain Arnold; "I will sit up with you. It will not be very long ere day will break."

"I do not wish to disturb you thus."

"Nay, I have made up my mind what to do, Jessie; I shall not go to sleep to-night again."

Most of the household retired to rest so soon as their curiosity was satisfied, and Captain Arnold fully dressed himself, and came down again for the purpose of spending the remainder of the night in his daughter's company, for he feared much that her mind might receive some terrible shock, were a recurrence of her dream to take place, especially that night.

He could but remark that it had made a great impression upon her already, and her pale features and the wandering expression of her eyes alarmed him.

Jessie had risen, and was ready to sit up till morning. They descended to a little parlour that looked out upon the garden. All was quiet and still; not a sound was to be heard, and the air was serene and mild; and Mr. Arnold took the opportunity of conversing with his daughter upon different subjects, so as to distract her attention, and hinder it from being exclusively taken up by the contemplation of her dream.

When they had been seated, and had been conversing for some time, the eastern sky presented the appearance of the approach of day; and ere another half-hour had passed over the gray tints had deepened and objects became visible.

The clouds now reflected the sun's earliest rays in faint tints that each moment were gradually deepening and becoming beautiful from their variety of form and colour.

It was then that Captain Arnold proposed to Jessie that she should accompany him into the garden to witness the beauties of the sunrise, and to note the appearance of the flowers as they opened their blossoms at the approach of the morning sun.

The dew was heavy on the trees and shrubs, and the flowers appeared with a new bloom upon them; the day each moment growing older, until the sun appeared fairly above the horizon, and the heavens were glorious with the beautiful tints reflected by the departing, and now fast fading, night clouds.

Jessie felt the full effect of the scene upon her, and the recollection of her dream was fast fading before this beautiful scene, and she expressed her conviction that it was only caused by the diversity of scenes—the recollection of the fatal catastrophe of the yacht, and the fatigue she had undergone; but now it had vanished, and she confidently believed she should forget it.

CHAPTER X.

THE MORNING VISITOR.—PLANS AND HOPES FOR THE FUTURE.—THE NOBLE LORD.— CAPTAIN ARNOLD NEARLY RESCUED.

THE Arnolds were likely to be happy in this new home, when the memory of her who had been so dear to them had somewhat faded, and they had borrowed from time a little philosophy, with which to console themselves for their grievous deprivation.

The morning following their arrival at their new home was a favourable one for inducing a love towards it. The sky was not cloudless, but the clouds that were in it added the charm of variety to its otherwise too glaring beauty. There was a soft gentle wind, too, from the south, which gave that waving beautiful motion to the foliage, which is at once graceful and life-like. They could not help being pleased with their new home. It was all they could have painted to themselves as desirable; and if the beauty of some particular tree or flower called up a fond regret that she, who had met death in the ocean, was not there to join in the general admiration, still it was a gentle regret, and one which hourly was becoming tinctured with greater resignation.

And then, too, when the sun was shining, and the birds were singing, how foolish did Jessie think herself for being terrified at her night vision, and how the dream which had disturbed her sank into utter insignificance before the beaming daylight.

How strange, she thought, that our dreams should be, in many cases, so very incongruous, and so utterly at variance with the remotest probability.

Captain Arnold joined her in the sentiment, and they were talking in more cheerfulness than they had done since their sad family bereavement, when, as we have stated, a ring at the garden-gate announced a visitor.

"That's Arlines," exclaimed Captain Arnold, "I have no doubt; I really shall never be able sufficiently to thank him for the trouble he has taken on our account."

Captain Arnold was right as to its being Phillip Arlines, although, as regarded his debt of gratitude to him, a very small sum, indeed, would have amply sufficed to discharge it. That was a discovery, however, which, sadly for him, the captain had not made, nor was he to make it, until too late to save himself from the awful consequences of an association with a man destitute of all honour, feeling, honesty, or virtue.

Arlines was announced in a few moments, and waving ceremony, Captain Arnold himself went out to meet him. Nothing could exceed the kindness of his reception, and nothing could exceed the consummate art with which Phillip Arlines replied to that reception. His manner of asking after the children was perfection— the perfection of deceit, if we may be allowed the term; and, finally, the free and easy way, with a dash of respect in it too, with which he called the captain merely Arnold, was quite irresistible.

"Arnold, my dear friend," he said, "tell me, now, is there anything connected with your new home in which I have erred? I know I may vainly hope to have imitated your own taste; but I have still striven, Arnold, to make the place have a kind of character about it."

"I cannot thank you sufficiently," replied the captain. "It is all we could possibly wish."

"Well, really, you don't know how pleased I am to hear you say so much. I believe the workmen that I placed on the premises, as soon as I had your permission to take them, thought me, decidedly, the most troublesome person they had ever met with in all their lives."

"And that was all on my account?"

"Oh, never mind that. I had something to do, and let it be what it may, I always consider that, if a thing is worth doing at all, it is worth doing well."

"By-the-bye, Arlines, now that I think of it, pardon me, but I am sure you must have made a great many disbursements for us, quite independent of what you have been so kind as to make yourself the medium of paying."

"Oh, pho—pho, Arnold! I gave you the bills, you know, and you gave me the money."

"Yes; but were there no little incidental expenses which did not appear in the regular bills?"

"Why," said Arlines, with a smile—and his smile was really good—" you know human nature thoroughly."

Captain Arnold looked rather gratified—and who would not, upon being informed, so sententiously, that he possessed such a remarkable fund of knowledge?

"You have seen the world," continued Arlines, "and studied mankind well; or rather I should say, you have one of those minds which at once and almost intuitively seize upon important truths, and then submitting them to the crucible——"

"Really, now, really."

"To the crucible of a vigorous genius, extract from them conclusions which would remain for ever hidden from less favoured mortals."

"Now, my dear Arlines, you allow your own generous and kindly feelings to run away with you."

"No—no."

"Yes, you do."

"Indeed, excuse me. I am very blunt—mean what I say, and, to my misfortune, it has lost me many a friend. Heigho! I have a most unhappy knack of saying just what I mean, without deduction or adornment."

"For which you are much to be commended."

"Well, it is, as human nature is constituted, a bar to advancement; and as for any little sums I may have expended for you, I really beg you won't mention them."

"But you must permit me——"

"No—no—now, really——"

"Really, I will pay them, so say no more about it, further than giving me an idea of the gross amount."

"The gross amount," thought Arlines; "it almost sounds like a pun; but he don't mean it. He is as green as grass in April. Why, I don't think in the whole I have spent twenty pounds for you."

"Are you sure?"

"Oh, quite—quite. Come, now, you are satisfied. Let it rest; and now shall I take the great liberty of saying, I have really not breakfasted?"

"Yes, certainly; but you shall breakfast, and if you don't wish to vex me very much——"

"I vex you? God forbid!"

"Very well, you will take these two ten-pound notes. Now, Arlines, I will have no refusal. You know a man is entitled to be

very positive, and sometimes very obstinate, in his own house."

"I am really mortified," said Arlines, as he pocketed the twenty pounds, with quite a regretful looking countenance.

"Nonsense—nonsense," said Captain Arnold. "Come now, to breakfast. Jessie—Jessie."

"I am here, father," said Jessie, stepping from a French window on the lawn.

"Jessie, look to Mr. Arlines for a few minutes, while I change my coat, dear."

"Yes, father."

"Make yourself at home, Arlines. I will be with you in a few minutes."

Jessie, as she emerged from the window of the breakfast-room on to the well-kept lawn, looked extremely beautiful. She was, as the reader is aware, just at an age when all the charms, all the innocence, all the childlike beauty of the girl is secretly mingling with the intellectual beauties of maturer life. No wonder that the licentious Phillip Arlines was struck with her at first sight, when he saw her at the Isle of Wight; but it appeared to him as if the sorrow she had gone through on account of her mother's death had elevated her years in understanding and feeling—certain it was, that she did not look so much the girl merely at the villa near Kensington, as she had done so short a time before at the beautiful marine cottage by Cowes.

"Will you come this way, Mr. Arlines?" said Jessie.

"Yes—yes, my dear," he replied. "You are looking very well. How do you like your new home?"

"I like it well, and think, in time, I shall like it better," replied Jessie, who, by this time, had re-entered the breakfast-room, followed by Phillip Arlines.

"By Heaven," thought the libertine, "she is a perfect Hebe. Upon this first interview will depend the terms upon which I shall remain with her. Dare I risk it?—yes, I will. She is an angel—quite an angel."

"Jessie," he said, "how blooming you look."

"Sir?" said Jessie, with a slightly-heightened colour.

"You are the handsomest girl in the neighbourhood, my dear. You will become quite the belle of the park."

As he spoke, he made a coolly audacious attempt to kiss her, but Jessie stepped back with such a look of disdain upon her countenance, that in a moment he saw he had made a false step, and calculated upon her being taken by surprise when such was not the case.

"Oh!" he said, "I did not mean to offend you."

"I am scarcely a judge of that," said Jessie, coldly.

"Excuse me. I—I——"

"Enough, sir. My father can determine better than I if I have a right to feel offence or not."

"Your father?"

"Yes, sir. My father, Captain Arnold."

Phillip Arlines was perfectly staggered. In is own mind he cursed himself for his precipitate folly, and at once saw the glaring error of judgment he had fallen into. He was for one instant at his very wit's ends, and knew not how to extricate himself from the dilemma into which he had so suddenly plunged. Time, however, was most precious. Captain Arnold would return in a few minutes. Something must be done, and that immediately too.

"Miss Arnold," he said, with an air of profound respect and contrition; "your complaint to your father will, of course, produce a quarrel—a quarrel between gentlemen produces a duel."

Jessie turned pale.

"I need not, I am sure, say that I intended no rudeness. It is for you to create endless disagreeables by a complaint to your father, or to let this matter rest as it is."

The door at this moment opened, and Captain Arnold made his appearance.

"Well, Jessie, my dear," he cried, "go and bustle about the breakfast—I am really hungry."

Jessie was glad of the opportunity of leaving the room, and Phillip Arlines drew a long breath of relief, as he said to himself,—

"I am safe—I am safe. A complaint from her to such a man as Arnold, would have knocked up the whole scheme of operations as regards him and my highly respectable associates. What an escape he might have had, and what an escape I have had. Who would have thought the little beauty would have been so very proud?"

An ample breakfast was placed upon the table, and soon Mr. Arlines was himself again, discoursing with his host in his inimitable, easy, confidential manner—a manner that imparted an importance to the wisest nothings—converting truisms into aphorisms, and completely hoodwinking the captain to the fact that his dear friend was only pumping him as to every minute particular connected with his property.

And Phillip Arlines was eminently successful in the process, for he ascertained amply sufficient as a groundwork of future operations, always assuming that Captain Arnold could be brought within the vortex of gambling.

More than ever, too, did Arlines now wish successfully to pursue the diabolical scheme that had been laid for the destruction of the trusting, unsuspecting man, at whose board he was sitting. He, in that interview, got up a new motive. The beauty of Jessie attracted him; her proud and haughty repulse of his attempted familiarity amazed him, while it added fuel to the flame of his passion; he respected her as well as admired her—to use the word love in such a case would be a profanation of the term.

"Proud as she is," he thought, "I will yet humble her—I must yet be very cautious. When her father is absolutely and irretrievably ruined, as he shall be, we will then see if this proud beauty will not come down from her lofty position."

Arlines then bethought him of one of the plans of operation which had been agreed upon—namely, the introduction by him of one of the conspirators for the purpose of aiding in urging on Captain Arnold to the gaming-table. Before he left, therefore, he took an opportunity of saying,—

"I have an intimate friend, the Marquis of Rollington. He is the soul of honour and good heartedness, and it would be a great delight to me if you and he were acquainted."

"My dear Arlines, bring him here."

"Shall we intrude?"

"Not intrude, certainly, but come when you like. Any friend of yours is welcome here."

"You are really very kind, Arnold; I will then, in this one case, avail myself of the kind permission, and to-morrow, if you have no objection, I will come over here with the marquis."

"Do so, I shall be much pleased,—but must you go now?"

Captain Arnold accompanied his dear friend with regret to the garden gate, parting with him with every manifestation of the greatest esteem and grateful feeling.

CHAPTER XI.

FELICITATIONS. — JESSIE'S DOUBTS. — THE MEETING OF THE CONFEDERATES. — THE CONTENTION.

"WELL, Jessie," said the captain, when he returned to the breakfast room, "in the midst of our grief, and with the memory of our great misfortune still green and fresh in our minds, is it not a great mercy of Heaven that we have so kind, so candid, and considerate a friend as this Mr. Phillip Arlines?"

"Those are noble qualities," replied Jessie, evasively.

"They are, indeed; and he possesses them. Mind, Jessie, should he come here when I am from home ever, treat him as my most valued friend, my dear."

"I will obey you, father; and yet——"

"Yet what, my darling?"

"I think, father, should Mr. Arlines, or any gentleman, call while you are from home, it would be better taste for them to go away than to call upon me to entertain them."

"Yes, ordinarily speaking; but Mr. Arlines

I wish to be the exception to such a general rule."

"I hope you always will be at home, father, when he comes."

"Why, Jessie, you speak doubtingly of him. You don't like Mr. Arlines, I see. Come, come, Jessie, do not give way to prejudice."

"I will not, father; and yet I do not like Mr. Phillip Arlines."

"And wherefore?"

"His manner is too—too—what shall I say? too uniformly soft and silky."

"Well, I own he certainly is the most unruffled person I ever knew; he has admirable self-command, but surely for that he is to be praised instead of condemned, you know. I believe him, in all respects, a man of honour, rare integrity, and of the most kindly feelings. Now, Jessie, come and take a stroll with me in our really pretty garden."

*   *   *   *

We will now leave Captain Arnold and Jessie to their own thoughts and conversation, while we follow the villain Arlines once again to the meeting of the association, which, for so heartless a purpose as the bringing ruin and distress upon others, had formed itself and was acting with an awful amount of success.

There was one thing which made Arlines more than usually anxious to meet his companions in iniquity, and that was, that he should make some definitive and understood arrangement, from which there should be no shrinking, that he was not to be in any shape or way interfered with in his personal pursuit of Jessie.

Her scorn of him had made him think her ten times better worth the winning than before, and he calculated upon the time when Captain Arnold's pecuniary distresses would effectually prevent him from throwing that protecting arm around his child, which he now would and could.

"If," thought Arlines, "through all the distresses which I fully expect will come upon him in consequence of the plans that are now in active operation, I can preserve a fair exterior as regards him, all will be well, and he will place a confidence in me, which will enable me to make such advances to Jessie as she may not have it in her power to resist."

With these thoughts in his mind he met the confederates, and having stated that he had procured an invitation for the Marquis of Rollington, he added—

"And now, before we proceed further, I have one thing to state, about which there must be no sort of ambiguity, and no possibility of a mistake."

"What's that?" was the general cry.

"I will tell you; Captain Arnold has a daughter. I admire her, and I will not be interfered with in that affair."

A shout of laughter was the reply, and it was only somewhat hushed by the attorney saying—

"I am sure, gentlemen, as far as we are concerned, Mr. Arlines is most welcome to anybody's daughter. However, there is one question we must ask Mr. Arlines, and that is, are his intentions matrimonial or not?"

"Decidedly not," said Arlines.

"Very well. Had they been of a matrimonial complexion, you see, it would have been to the interest of Mr. Arlines to let Captain Arnold know of the projected attack upon his pocket; but being quite the reverse, why, of course the conclusion is quite the reverse."

"Gentlemen," said Arlines, "however mortifying such a confession from me may appear, it is, nevertheless, a truth, which I am well aware of, that Miss Arnold does not look upon me with an eye of favour."

"Oh, indeed!"

"Yes; a matrimonial speculation in that quarter, I am quite convinced, would be quite hopeless. I have nothing to expect but from the ruin of the father, and—and——"

"His consequent inability to protect his child," added the attorney. "I think, gentlemen, that is a very proper sentiment, indeed, and amazingly satisfactory."

"Very," said the association.

"Then I am satisfied. All that I wished to guard against, was the fascinations of the noble marquis; but if he gives me his word of honour that he will subdue his exquisite charm of manner, I shall be intensely satisfied."

"'Pon my soul," said the marquis, "that's d—d good—ha, ha! You have my solemn gage I will not be fascinating. Ah!"

Having received this assurance, Phillip Arlines was, as he expressed it, intensely satisfied, not because he set any high value upon the fascination of the noble marquis, but he had a great opinion of his insolence and his effrontery—an opinion which induced in his mind a well-grounded belief, that had the subject not been settled by a previous understanding, he, the marquis, would have committed himself in some way to Jessie, which would have overturned the whole scheme, and placed Captain Arnold, at the end of a quarrel, quite free from the meshes that were being so artfully spread for his destruction.

*   *   *   *

The evening was just casting its gentle and soothing influence over the beautiful scenery which surrounded Captain Arnold's new abode, when Jessie, accompanied by the youngest child but one, went to walk in Kensington Gardens, of which she had heard so much, but within the precincts of which she had not as yet been.

Her father was busy writing letters, and it was upon his assurance that anybody might alone walk without fear of molestation in the royal garden, that she ventured.

The beauty of the walks, the majesty of the aged trees, and the general air of lofty grandeur about the whole place, were irresistibly attractive to Jessie, and she much congratulated herself upon being in the immediate vicinity of so attractive and delightful a place of promenade. At that time in the evening, too, there were but few persons in the gardens, a fact which tended much to enhance its beauties to Jessie, for she much disliked a crowd.

The child who was with her expressed his pleasure in unmeasured terms, and more than once escaped from her guiding hand to take a run all alone among the high grass and underwood that in some parts was to be found in great abundance.

So on they rambled till they got near to the Serpentine river, which, in consequence of some very heavy rains, had risen much higher than usual, and, consequently, looked a much more respectable piece of water than commonly.

Jessie was ignorant of the locality, and she kept a protecting hand upon her young charge as they neared the water. The child, however, observing some wild flowers floating near to the bank, suddenly rushed from her. It was but the action of a moment; in the next, the little fellow was struggling in the stream, and Jessie was awakening the solitude around her with her screams for assistance.

No one appeared to be at hand, and with a self-devotion that would in all probability have cost her her life, she was about herself to plunge into the water to the rescue of the child, when a loud, clear voice suddenly came upon her ears, shouting,—

"Hold, hold—he shall be saved! For the love of Heaven, spare yourself—he shall be saved!"

She listened a moment, and then from the opposite shore she saw some one make a tremendous spring; there was a heavy splash, and, what with the excitement of the scene and her extreme terror, Jessie dropped on the verdant bank, not precisely in a state of insensibility, but very nearly so.

Her first consciousness was, that some one was speaking to her in kind and encouraging tones, while she felt herself encumbered in some way that she could not rise—it was the child clinging to her, and hanging round her neck. The little fellow was uninjured, having been rescued with a promptitude that prevented insensibility from ensuing.

For a few moments Jessie could think of nothing else but her extreme joy at the child's deliverance; she was not able to arrange any of the circumstances in her confusion of mind at the time; she only knew he was saved, and she shed tears of joy at the deliverance of herself and her father from another calamity, only

to be equalled by the one which had already expelled them from their former once happy home.

"Pray do not be alarmed," said a manly voice, and yet it was sweetly modulated; "I am sure he is unhurt."

Jessie lifted her eyes to the speaker and saw before her a young man who, from the state he was in, plainly showed that to him she was indebted for the recovery of the child from the stream, in which he would too soon, but for such timely intervention, have found a grave.

"Sir," said Jessie, while the eloquent blood flew to her cheek, "sir, I—I have no words to thank you."

"I require no thanks," replied the stranger. "The happiness of being able, in consequence of an early acquired skill in swimming, to save a life is a dear reward indeed; moreover, I have given you pleasure——"

"Pleasure! oh, you have saved me from an amount of misery that would have embittered my existence."

The stranger seemed much struck with the language and sentiments that came from one evidently so very young as Jessie Arnold, and he replied,—

"Then am I repaid indeed. Might I advise that this little friend of mine should be taken home as quickly as possible and divested of his wet clothing?"

"And you too," remarked Jessie. "Pardon me, that I am so unmindful of what I owe to you. My joy at the deliverance of this child has taken my reason prisoner. Come to my father's house, and all the hospitality that he can render you shall be yours."

"I fear much to intrude myself upon a family who knew me not. 'Tis true I am far from home, and—and not exactly in a very pleasant or healthful condition with this wet clothing."

"Intrude!" exclaimed Jessie; "can that be a proper word on such an occasion as this?"

"For the sake of the little fellow I will hesitate no longer," said the stranger.

Jessie led the way, and the stranger followed her closely, holding by the hand the child, who certainly owed its life to his heroism and accidental presence at so opportune a moment.

The distance was not great, and as the little party walked quickly—for the stranger urged the necessity of keeping the boy in rather violent exercise, considering that his garments were so thoroughly saturated with water—they soon arrived at the garden gate of Captain Arnold's new house.

"Where is my father?" was Jessie's first exclamation. "Tell him I wish to see him immediately."

"Yes, miss; the captain is in his own room."

In a few minutes Captain Arnold made his appearance with no little surprise depicted on his countenance at the sight of a stranger with Jessie, but that surprise was soon turned into a feeling of the liveliest gratitude when Jessie said,—

"Father, this gentleman is our deliverer from a calamity only equal to what has already befallen us. He has saved Henry from death."

"Death!" echoed the captain. "Good Heaven, what has occurred?"

"A little accident, sir," said the stranger, "which I was so fortunate as to be near enough to prevent becoming more serious. Although I cannot but admire and respect the feelings with which your daughter pleases to regard the service I have been the happy instrument of rendering to you, yet believe me, sir, as I happen to be a good swimmer, and have no great horror of a ducking, I do not consider myself entitled to much thanks."

Captain Arnold turned very pale from the rush of feelings that came across his heart, and then with a faltering voice he said,—

"I see it all now. You have saved me, sir, from such a calamity as, superadded to one the recollection of which is still fresh, would have driven me distracted. Accept the heartfelt thanks of a father, sir—my warmest gratitude—my friendship."

"Your friendship, sir," replied the stranger, "I willingly and gladly accept, and beg that you will say no more."

Jessie, with tearful eyes, left the room with the child, and then Captain Arnold said,—

"Perhaps, after all, sir, you do not know who we are?"

"I fear," he replied, with a smile, "that in addition to borrowing a coat of you, I must introduce myself."

As he spoke he produced his card-case, and placed a card before the captain, on which was the name, "Alfred Pearson."

"Thank you," said Captain Arnold, and handing his card to the stranger, he added, "we are living here in a state of great seclusion in consequence of a death in our family, but I hope that you will honour us with repeated calls. Allow me now to conduct you to my dressing-room, where you can change your clothing for something more comfortable."

This process was soon accomplished; and in another half hour a very pleasant little party indeed, consisting of the captain, Jessie, and Mr. Alfred Pearson, sat down to tea in the drawing-room of the villa which had so providentially been saved from becoming a place of woe and deep distress.

As for the child, he was sleeping soundly, and to all appearance had suffered nothing from his temporary immersion in the Serpentine.

CHAPTER XII.

THE VISIT AND ITS CONSEQUENCES.—THE FIRST STEP IN A SAD CAREER.—THE CAPTAIN'S DOUBTS.—THE BLUE BOOK.

THE conversation became general and interesting, for the stranger who had so suddenly and strangely become acquainted with Captain Arnold and his family showed an amount of knowledge on almost every subject that was proposed to him, that, considering his age, was quite extraordinary.

While Jessie was present he said nothing directly of himself or his station in society, but when she had left, he turned to the captain, and in a mild, gentlemanly tone, remarked—

"Captain Arnold, your honourable profession which gives a prefix to your name, absolves you from any further explanation concerning yourself, but I am not so favourably situated."

"My dear sir," interrupted the captain, "you have placed yourself in a position, as regards me and my family, which no explanation of any kind could better."

"And yet, notwithstanding all your frank kindness, as I intend to value highly the privilege you have given me of occasionally calling here, allow me briefly to say, that I am the poor son of a poor gentleman; that I have been, until lately, residing with my mother at Bath, and that I am now in London to endeavour to establish my right to some small property which my father was unjustly defrauded of by the cupidity of a trustee or executor. Thus, Captain Arnold, you have my whole history in a few words. My father has been dead four years, and my mother is very ailing."

"Your frankness does you great credit," said the captain; "let us see you here as often as you feel disposed, and above all dine with us to-morrow: mind, too, if I can, in any possible way, be of assistance to you, command me."

The slightly heightened colour of Jessie that evening, as she bade the young stranger adieu, might have suggested to Captain Arnold something deserving of serious thought, but he did not see it, although Mr. Pearson did, and it gave him a thrill of pleasure, such as he had never before felt. He loved Jessie Arnold with one of those sudden passions which, although the produce of a moment, exercise, in so many cases, an influence over a long life, either for good or for evil, mostly for the former.

* * * *

Mr. Phillip Arlines would have been somewhat discomposed if he had been aware of what was taking place at the villa of Captain Arnold during his absence, and still more discomposed would he have been, could he have

had a thorough appreciation of the character of Alfred Pearson.

If Alfred Pearson were, indeed, destined to become an intimate friend of Captain Arnold's he was, assuredly, likewise destined to become a thorn in the side of Phillip Arlines, and a great obstacle to the prosecution of his plans. But such a knowledge he could not have, although, when he did see Pearson, he saw quite enough to give him uneasiness.

Captain Arnold was not the man exactly to be flattered, even by a visit from a marquis, but he did consider that a certain rank in society was a kind of guarantee for a certain amount of honourable feeling.

What police magistrate, from Lambeth-street to Bow-street, would think of sending a nobleman to the tread-mill for anything which he could possibly construe into a fineable offence?

The morning had not very far advanced; that is to say, twelve o'clock certainly had struck, but the fashionable morning was yet young, when Mr. Phillip Arlines arrived at the villa of Captain Arnold, with the Marquis of Rollington.

Of course, the reception was polite on the

part of the captain, and as for the noble lord he was all condescension and agreeability. Luncheon was offered and accepted, and the conversation flowed on in an easy and delightful channel.

Still there was something in the manner of Lord Rollington not exactly pleasing to Captain Arnold, and once or twice, in the course of conversation, he gave utterance to opinions and sentiments which did not exactly bear the impress of high and lofty morality.

The dinner-hour was yet far off, and Captain Arnold, after partaking with his guests of a handsome luncheon, proposed a stroll in the grounds attached to the villa, as the most pleasurable means of passing the time.

To this the Marquis of Rollington, notwithstanding all the nods and winks of Phillip Arlines, rather demurred, saying,

"Don't you think cards would waste an idle hour or two ?"

"I don't play," replied Captain Arnold.

"Certainly not," said Phillip Arlines ; "nor I. Come to the garden. No one ever got any good by gambling."

"Oh, now," said the disappointed marquis, "there you are decidedly wrong. Many a fortune, I grant you, has been lost at the gaming-table ; but, then, many a one has been likewise gained."

"Indeed !" said Arnold, incredulously.

"Yes: I never, at least, I very rarely, make assertions which I cannot justify. Now I happen to know, positively, of one case, where such a thing as a total retrieval of affairs took place. I was talking to a friend the other day, who was complaining that an evil destiny seemed ever to pursue him at the gaming-table, and I said to him,

" ' Your case is not a singular one, but there is only one course to pursue, and that is to persevere.' I knew a man once, not many years since, and he is now living in affluence, and I may say, splendour, who was reduced to the last stage of misfortune, but he rose above all. I will tell you the tale, as it will be one in point.

"He was a gentleman of good birth and estate, but fond of play ; for him there was no place equal to the gaming room ; the lights, the wine, the gay conversation, the glitter of the wealth that constantly changed hands, gilded the hours of life, and gave him that joy and excitation that can be found at no other place, nor under any other circumstances.

"A run of ill-luck set in against him for a long time, and he was not a man to be daunted.

" ' It cannot last long,' he would say ; ' it will be my turn soon ; I must have a change of fortune, for she is too fickle to stay long in the arms of my successful antagonists.'

"This was strictly true ; but he who has not the means or the courage to continue on in the same course is always ruined. And so it was with him ; for although a temporary turn of fortune took place in his favour, yet she again deserted him, and he was reduced to a state bordering on beggary.

"His estates were mortgaged, and he again continued to play, and was once more successful ; but he did not redeem his mortgages ; he said, ' No, I have the means, and I will either win an immense fortune, or I will lose all ; the last is improbable, as I have the means of continuing for a great length of time.'

"Things went on smoothly enough for a few years, and he supported a princely establishment with undiminished means. He had, notwithstanding, played deeply, and lost largely, but his gains had been great also, and hence he still continued a career of joy, happiness, and high station, such as few men in this world enjoy.

"The time drew near for the mortgage-money to be called in ; but he determined not to pay it until the moment it was due, as, till then, he could play with the money, and perhaps gain greatly with the sum in hand.

"This was unfortunate, for on the morning before the day the mortgage was to be paid, he was without the means of payment ; added to which, he had been served with a legal notice that payment would be enforced and the mortgage foreclosed.

"His state of mind was terrible, for he had an amiable lady and lovely daughter, for both of whom he had to provide. You may easily imagine what must that man's feelings have been : but he was a man of high courage and dauntless heart ; he saw what he believed must happen, perhaps with a blanched cheek, but a collected mind. His fate was sealed.

"He shut himself up the greater part of the day, and employed his time in arranging such of his affairs as he could, without the interference of money settlements, devised such of his property or effects as remained to him, and commended his wife and daughter to the care of some relation or friend who he knew would, for their sakes alone, extend a fostering and guardian hand to them.

"This being done, before the evening was well advanced he carefully loaded a beautiful brace of pistols, and placed them in his pocket, determining, that should the last venture he had it in his power to make fail him, he would, with Roman resolution, leave the world, in which he could no longer live as he had done, —determining rather to perish than bear the brunt of the tide of ills that fortune might have in store for him.

"He set out for the saloons, where the gaieties and pleasures of life awaited him, for the last time, as he believed. He was quite self-possessed, and returned the courtesies that were shown to him with his usual urbanity and respect towards those with whom he came in contact, engaged in conversations, both trivial and important, as they turned up by the circumstances of the moment, and no man could have said, judging from his appearance, 'That man has made up his mind to die by his own hand, before another sun shall rise.'

"But yet such was the fact; he had not only made such a mental resolve, but had arranged everything that could be arranged on so short a notice, and left directions for what could not be done then by himself.

"A little paler he might have looked, and a slightly compressed lip might have told a tale of determination of some kind, but that was scarcely visible.

"The play began; he did not at first play, but waited till the evening set in, and serious play commenced. The rooms were crowded by guests of the highest ranks and largest fortunes; many thousands were lost and won. At length, finding himself warmed with the scene before him, he took a seat at the table, and commenced his game with an adversary of whom he had won on former occasions.

"At first it seemed as if fortune frowned upon him, but yet his determination never wavered, and he played on and won, played again and won. He now breathed freely, and a lighter heart beat in his bosom; but yet he rose not while fortune smiled; who could desert her while she bestowed her favours? But he had an object in view; without a certain heavy sum, amounting to some thousands, he must lose his estate, and without that sum, or with anything short of it, he would not rise.

"Some hours had elapsed since he first sat down, and midnight was advancing. The hand of the dial was near the stroke of twelve. As the hour approached fortune deserted him, and as it was chimed by the silvery-toned bell, he was a beggar. Every iota he possessed had changed owners.

"For a few moments he appeared stunned; the place was in a whirl, and he could not distinguish anything that was going on near him. He arose mechanically from his seat, he could barely stand, the whole room went round, and he seized the back of his chair for support till the vertigo should subside.

"Two gentlemen were on the right; they were boisterous in their play, the wine had warmed their hearts, and they played for heavy sums, which they won or lost with the utmost nonchalance. His eyes rested upon them for a few moments, and he forgot his own wretched state in the excitement of the play. They both played with equal skill and tact, notwithstanding their exuberant spirits, and he looked on, not with the feelings of a man who is about to die, but as one deeply interested in the game.

"'Do you know those gentlemen?' inquired a well-known marquis, coming up, and looking for a few moments on the play.

"'No, I do not, though I believe I have seen them on one or two occasions before.'

"'The best player is to your right,' observed the marquis.

"'I think not,' was the reply; 'for he has lost the last two games, you may observe.'

"'The best player will occasionally lose; indeed, it must be so, for I have often lost myself.'

"'That is very true, but I think the individual to the left much the best, and also the coolest player, which goes far towards making him the best player.'

"'Are you willing to back your opinion?'

"'I should be so, but I have lost what cash I brought with me, and cannot do so in this instance.'

"'Oh,' replied the marquis; 'say nothing upon that score, you are too well known to be doubted; your I O U will be sufficient guarantee among men of honour.'

"He paused a moment, and turned the offer in his own mind; could he, with honour, accept the proposed bet, which, if he lost, he well knew he could not pay? The urgency of the case—it might be a turn of fortune—at all events it was a chance of life, and he did not feel inclined to throw it away. 'Should he lose,' he thought, 'he cannot complain; it was his own offer, and I shall have expiated all by my death.' The offer was repeated, and on the marquis saying,

"'An even ten thousand upon the game of the gentleman to my right,' he replied,

"'An even ten thousand let it be; I am agreed.'

"The bet was made, and the game carefully watched. It was with great anxiety that he traced every move that took place; no single motion of either player escaped his eye; they played very near each other, and it was not before the last moment that victory decided either ● the one or the other, as the individual betted upon by the marquis met with a reverse, and his antagonist became the victor.

"'It was well played,' remarked the marquis; 'but I thought my side would have won it. You are fortunate, sir; here are the notes.'

"As he said this he handed him the money. Need I say that the mortgage was paid off, and the man now lives in splendour, an example of courage and fortune?"

"But," said Captain Arnold, "after all, the fact of any one person receiving money by gambling, brings with it, to my mind, as a necessary consequence, the fact of some one or more being rendered miserable, perhaps even utterly destitute by its loss."

"Well, well," said the marquis; "let us

walk in the garden: if it must be so, we will be rural."

They had not proceeded far in the garden when the marquis suddenly called out—

"Look! look! here's a fight between two spiders ; two to one on that yellow one—two to one."

"Done," cried Arlines; "go me halves, captain ?"

"I don't mind," said Captain Arnold, with a laugh.

The yellow spider did beat the other, and then the marquis explained that his bet referred to pounds, so that Captain Arnold paid ten shillings, and Phillip Arlines ten shillings, which sums, insignificant as they were, the noble lord greedily pocketed.

This gave a sort of qualm to Captain Arnold, and for the first time a suspicion crossed his mind, that the Marquis of Rollington might not be what he assumed.

The captain, therefore, made an excuse to leave the room, to which they had returned, for a few moments, and consulted a Court Guide, wherein, sure enough, he found a full account of the Marquis of Rollington. He was, therefore, satisfied, and returned to the drawing-room with a conviction that a marquis might, after all, not be above all human feelings or human frailties.

It was about half an hour after this that Alfred Pearson arrived, and the surprise, as well as chagrin, of Phillip Arlines at finding any one else on intimate terms with the Arnolds but himself, was quite depicted on his countenance. As for Alfred, he fixed his eyes upon the face of Arlines, with a scrutinizing gaze, that was anything but pleasing to that gentleman, for he was well aware that he, Phillip Arlines, did not bear well to be looked at, and the gaze of the young man gave him a disagreeable suspicion that he must have seen him previously somewhere.

That such was the fact we shall discover as we proceed. Dinner rapidly succeeded Alfred's arrival, and, for a time, all were actively engaged at a well spread table.

CHAPTER XIII.

THE SECOND MEETING OF THE LOVERS.—THE WARNING TO CAPTAIN ARNOLD, AND ITS CONSEQUENCES.—THE CHALLENGE AND THE THREAT.

JESSIE did not appear at the dinner table, for she had taken a great dislike to Mr. Arlines, a dislike which, the reader is aware she had ample grounds for showing. Not even the presence of Alfred Pearson, and the charm of his conversation, could induce her willingly to sit down in the same room with Phillip

Arlines ; under the plea of a headache, she, therefore, escaped from the dessert-table, much to the chagrin of Pearson, who looked in vain for her who had now so great an interest in his eyes.

The conversation lost a great quantity of its hilarity somehow, after the arrival of Alfred. Perhaps the noble lord and his coajutor began to think the game was not so entirely in their own hands as they had flattered themselves, but certain it is, that they shrunk amazingly from making any allusion to gambling for some hours.

At length, however, his lordship summoned all his assurance to back him and said,

"Well, I vote for a quiet rubber at whist. Here are four of us, and no ladies, what do you say?"

"I really don't know if there are cards in the house," said Captain Arnold, laughingly.

"But you will send for them," added the marquis, "you were going to say."

"Oh, I'll go myself," said Arlines, "if you much wish it."

"No," remarked the captain; "I cannot think of that; I will have a hunt for a pack; there may be some."

"You will excuse me, gentlemen," said Alfred Pearson, rising; "but at the risk of falling somewhat in your opinion, and, perhaps, being thought even rude, I must decline playing."

"Pooh, pooh," said the marquis; "once in a way."

"I never play. The beautiful sunset, and rising moon, in the captain's gardens, will amuse me well for an hour or two."

So saying, he left the room which Captain Arnold had gone from some moments previously, and, with great pleasure, inhaled the pure air of the garden.

The sun, the bright harbinger of day, having run his diurnal round, was again approaching the glowing west, casting long shadows towards the east, an ominous warning to the truant schoolboy, who has stayed away from the presence of the village pedagogue, preferring to contemplate the beauties of nature to the study of syntax, that the time for his return to the paternal roof is fast coming. The long shadows of the trees, or the solitary oak standing in the midst of a large field, or of cattle on the pasturage, gives a variety of tint pleasing to the eye. The shadows deepen and lengthen each moment, casting a deep tint on the beautiful verdure of the meadow.

The gracefully waving corn, with its bright golden tinge, almost defies the power of night to deprive it of its hue or beauty, while the evening breeze brings up with it the fresh odours from the clover field. The fluttering flight of birds before they seek their places of concealment for the night, the call of the partridge to her young, this being her feeding time, all form objects of grateful and pleasing contemplation.

But turn we to the west, the glorious many-tinted west. The evening breeze has brought up some broadly expanding clouds, richly illumined by the god of day. The rainbow may be beautiful to look at; nay, it is beautiful, but it may not be compared to the broad shadows and glowing tints of the sunset.

Here, indeed, nature seems to have done her utmost, for

"All that is beautiful there is seen;"

and he must be a moodish soul who cannot find new beauties at every repetition of the glowing, changing, and ever variable scene.

Gradually and slowly sunk the sun, while over the broad expanse of blue ethereal sky floated many masses of vapour, whose beauty far surpassed the painter's art, and which reflected back the last glowing tints that shot upwards from the horizon; and here and there might be seen, dimly sparkling, a star, but so dim and so faint did it appear in the flood of twilight, that the observer would often look at the spot, believing his sight had been cheated.

Hill and dale were fast sinking into the shadows of night; true it was, that the trees which crowned the summit of the neighbouring hill were still gilded by the fleeting rays of lingering sun-light. The old hall's windows were still strangely beautiful, for they reflected the sun's rays in deep red tints, which might be seen afar off; but even that soon ceased to be, and now nothing but the grey twilight rested upon nature.

Still all was beautiful and serene; the heat of the day had been exchanged for the quiet hour and cool breeze which now lifted the dried leaves of the tallest trees, bringing with it a freshness and balminess grateful to all.

Delighted with the beauty of the evening, Alfred Pearson wandered alone in the garden; wrapped in deep thought and in pleasing melancholy musing, he spent more time than, in politeness to his entertainer, he was warranted in doing; but his absence of thought made him forget all save the scene around him, and the contemplation of the beautiful Jessie.

"She is as beautiful and as gentle as the Arabian vale laden with spices. Her father, too, a man of great sincerity and benevolence—candour is written on his brow.

"But what guests! The silly marquis, whose vanity is only equalled by his absurdity. Phillip Arlines, too, he is here; such a man, as I have strong reason to believe he is, ought not to be in such society; he cannot be a friend; if so, he is enough to taint the whole with a leprosy. I will make some inquiries respecting his standing in this circle, before I leave it. and if it be that he is not known, I will put

them on their guard against him; if not—if they do know his character, I——but—no—it cannot be that the father of my dear Jessie, for dear she is, can be connected, in any unworthy way, with Phillip Arlines."

While these thoughts passed through his mind, he walked up and down the garden, passing many of the beauties unnoticed; indeed his gaze was fixed upon the walk, and he saw not, until he had approached so closely that his garments touched some one, that Jessie Arnold stood before him.

"Miss Arnold," he exclaimed, in a hasty and apologetical tone, "pray excuse my absence; I have been longer a truant from the table than politeness allows, but I hope you will find an excuse in my admiration of the scene around me."

"Do not name it, Mr. Pearson," said Jessie; "absence from the wine-table can ever find a friend in me; but you did not appear to be so much taken up with admiration of the scene, as you were employed in contemplation."

"It is the scene that has produced such absence. I first admired it, and then a train of reflection followed, that caused me not to observe you. It is the same motive, I presume, that brings you to the quiet scenery of a garden by moonlight."

"Yes, the heat indoors was great, and I sought to refresh myself; besides, I am a great admirer of such scenes, for their own sakes."

"I am happy to hear it; such a taste expands the heart, and opens it to receive impressions from all that is great and good. To be a lover of nature is, to my mind, equivalent to candour and kindness."

"You compliment by inference, I perceive, sir," replied Jessie; "I am much obliged."

"Do you return my compliment, since you call it such, by throwing it overboard. I did not, however, confine my observation, in meaning, to this spot, but meant it as generally applicable; but I do think it is peculiarly applicable."

Jessie was silent for a few moments. She did not like to pursue the subject further, voluntarily, herself; but, at length, she said,

"I forgot, or, rather, I had not the power, to express my gratitude to you for rescuing my brother from such a dreadful death."

"Jessie—I beg pardon, Miss Arnold, I mean—permit me to hear no more of that; the act itself was its own reward, and such an introduction as that I have achieved, into your own and your father's society, would amply repay me, had I been really much injuried. Will you allow me to ask you a question respecting one of the guests I have met with at your father's table?"

"Certainly," said Jessie, somewhat surprised. "Do you know either of them?"

" I have reasons to think I know a little of one," replied Pearson.

" Which of them?"

" Mr. Arlines. Have you known him any length of time?"

—" My father has known him for some time; that is, he was on a voyage in the same ship, some years ago, and since that period I think he has scarcely seen him."

" Indeed. Well, I am very glad to hear it; but allow me to caution you against him; he is, to the best of my belief, a very indifferent sort of person."

" What can you mean, Mr. Pearson? I have never seen anything in Mr. Arlines' behaviour that made me suspect him of anything dishonourable, and I should be sorry to harbour such thoughts of him from mere suspicion."

" I believe him to be a man of a bad character—what is called a sharper, and an inveterate gambler, broken in fortune and in reputation."

" I should wish to inform my father of what you say; for should it be true, it concerns him as nearly as it can you."

" I can have no objection to your doing so, since what I have said I would have said to your father, Captain Arnold, had I the opportunity of seeing him alone."

" Then if you will remain here, sir, I will endeavour to bring him to you."

As Jessie said this she hastened towards the house where she had left him not long before. Her mind was much perplexed by the communication of Mr. Alfred Pearson, and half induced her to repent she had thus suddenly involved her in what might prove an important and exceedingly troublesome affair.

She soon, however, found means to detach her father from his two guests, Phillip Arlines and the Marquis of Rollington, and then earnestly begged that he would immediately accompany her to Mr. Alfred Pearson, who was in the garden, and who wished to make some communication to him.

Much surprised at this information, he hastened towards the spot, accompanied by Jessie, who could not patiently await the conclusion, but had an irresistible impulse to be present.

" My daughter informs me, Mr. Pearson, that you desire to speak to me; I shall ever be happy to hear what so esteemed a friend has to say."

" It is somewhat of an unpleasant nature, but it had better be done at once. Do you know this Phillip Arlines? and how long and in what circumstances?"

" It is a singular question: I have know him some time; but our meeting has been at but a very long interval; he is, I believe, a man of honour and attainments."

" His attainments are, I fear, in a line that do him but little credit," said Pearson.

" Pray explain yourself, sir. Have you any reason for believing him otherwise than I have described him, and only as I have known him?"

" I believe him to be a blackleg, a mere shifting gamester; one who has the manners and appearance of a gentleman, and trades upon them to deceive."

" This is very extraordinary and very serious. You can have no objection to say as much to his face, as I should wish the matter investigated."

" None, in the least," replied Pearson.

CHAPTER XIII.

THE ACCUSATION.—THE QUARREL.—THE ATTACK UPON ALFRED PEARSON.

On Alfred Pearson's answer, Captain Arnold immediately quitted the spot, much concerned at what had occurred, for he saw that it could but end in a quarrel. Yet what course could be pursued other than that which he was about to take? Of Phillip Arlines he had the best of opinions, and to Alfred Pearson he was under a deep obligation; but what motives could exist for the latter to malign the former? " But," he thought, " it is all a mistake, which can be cleared up by a little explanation; and, after all, it will be the best to have a complete and full investigation of the charge against Arlines at once; all bad impressions will then be most probably cleared up, and all will go on smoothly."

" Arlines," said Arnold, as he entered the room, " I wish for your presence in the garden; there is a little consultation going on which I think you will be desirous of joining."

" Certainly," said Arlines, rising; " perhaps, marquis, you will accompany me, if the affair be not strictly private."

" It concerns yourself," said Captain Arnold, " and you are, therefore, the best judge."

" Myself!" said Arlines, somewhat amazed.

" Yes; Mr. Alfred Pearson has some doubts about the nature of your pursuits, and I wish him to have them cleared up."

" Thank you," said Phillip Arlines, with a look of remarkable meaning, which he gave his companion. " I shall always be happy to meet any charge, and give a fair explanation. Marquis, may I beg the favour of your company? Your countenance may save me, for no enemy is so subtle as mere suspicion, and none so difficult of answer."

" I'll come with a goblet of wine," remarked the marquis, as he poured out a glassful, and holding it up to the light, he added,—" May the foul fiend, Suspicion, sink in despair, for I would not put out my arm to save him from instant annihilation."

At the termination of this speech he drank the contents of the glass, and rising, he followed Captain Arnold and Phillip Arlines out of the room, and the whole party soon after stood in each other's presence in the little garden.

Jessie watched them with observant eyes; she thought she could distinguish between the calm and gentleman like bearing of young Pearson, and the apparent indignation and haughty tone of Arlines, whose features at moments bore a sinister expression; but it might have been bias that gave her that impression.

There was a moment's pause when they met, and every one appeared embarrassed.

"This is a meeting of 'friends,' truly," said the Marquis of Rollington. "The employment of the bumper would give inspiration. Wine is certainly the cordial of the soul. Shall we adjourn?"

"Captain Arnold," said Phillip Arlines, with great self-possession, "I think you promised me some trifling amusement in the way of conversation."

"Yes," replied the captain; "I told you I wished you to hear a communication I have heard, and then I believe you will be able to convince Mr. Pearson that he is in error with respect to you."

"I know not, till I hear what I stand charged with," said Phillip Arlines, "Pray, sir," to Pearson, "what may be the nature of this that Captain Arnold alludes to, and which I am at a loss to name."

"Yes," replied Alfred Pearson, steadily, "it is this—you have been pointed out to me as a man of indifferent fortune, and a gamester."

"'Tis a lie, sir, whoever has informed you so," said Arlines, in the first burst of passion, but suddenly recovering himself, he added,

"I presume I speak to a gentleman, and one who will aid me in punishing any one who has so rascally traduced my character. Will you give me his name? I think I am entitled to demand that."

"I cannot do that."

"You make yourself responsible for the assertion," said Arlines, fiercely.

"Drown responsibility in a bumper," remarked the Marquis of Rollington, with a grave air.

"I have seen you myself more than once come out of a gaming-house in St. James's Street," said Alfred Pearson, "and should never have recollected your features had you not been pointed out as the character I describe."

"I think," said Captain Arnold, "that you must be mistaken; a mistake under such circumstances is so very likely and natural, that I cannot but believe, though actuated by the purest motives, you must be in error."

"No," replied Pearson. "I am not; had I any doubt, I would never have said what I have."

"Then, sir," replied Arlines, "you cannot refuse me your card."

"Drink deep of rosy wine," said the marquis; "drown all unkindness in a bumper. Come and try; if a bumper won't do, try a bottle, and if a bottle won't do, try more, and I'll warrant it will be effectual before morning."

"I have no acquaintance with you, sir," said Pearson, coolly, to Phillip Arlines.

"Then, sir," said Arlines, "since you will be neither answerable for the calumny you utter, nor give the name of your authority, I must send a friend to you in the morning, and make a last attempt to bring you to a sense of the position in which you now stand, and should that be unsuccessful, I shall brand you in society as a cowardly and characterless calumniator."

"Allow me to interpose," said Captain Arnold. "It is an unlucky affair. A low Mr. Pearson to communicate with his friend, from whom he has received so erroneous an impression, and then he may be able to rectify the error he has been led into."

"Certainly," said the Marquis of Rollington. "Captain Arnold's proposition is the most reasonable; and then, you know, we can return to the table, and drink deep—deep bumpers of nectar—wine, I mean, until we wash away all remembrance of the past."

"Mr. Arlines," said Alfred Pearson, addressing himself to that person, "if what you have said is, as I presume you mean it to be considered, a threat of a duel, allow me to save your friend some trouble. I will not accept an invitation at your hands until I am convinced that I can do so without descending to fight a man beneath me. I must be sure that your standing in society is such as to warrant the demand."

"I am precluded from following the bent of my own inclinations," said Arlines, with a sneer, and his eyes glared towards the spot where Jessie stood, somewhat alarmed at the quarrel; "and am thus prevented from doing that which the justice of the case requires, else your coat would not sit so easy on your shoulders as it does."

Alfred Pearson looked calmly at him, and never shrunk from the look of intense hatred with which Phillip Arlines regarded him; indeed, the latter shrunk from before the steady and dignified calmness of the former, and quitted the spot.

In a short time after, the Marquis of Rollington and Phillip Arlines quitted the house, after some conversation with Captain Arlines, in which both endeavoured to convince the other how sorry they were that such a useless quarrel should spring up in the house of the captain.

Soon after the captain returned to the garden, where Alfred and Jessie were walking and conversing together.

Captain Arnold conversed much upon the scene that had taken place between Pearson and Phillip Arlines, and gave it as his opinion that he must be mistaken in the character of the man, to which the other invariably expressed it as his firm conviction that Arlines was a mere adventurer and a blackleg.

The evening came on, and a cool breeze springing up, the whole party re-entered the house, and after passing some time there, Alfred Pearson rose to leave the house, which he did, after a kindly farewell from Captain Arnold, who again and again thanked him for the obligation he had laid him under, and desired to see him whenever he could find leisure to come.

A look from Jessie's eyes told him, more than words, how welcome he would be to her; and pleased with the thought that Jessie was not indifferent to his presence, he quitted the house with a light step and gladsome heart.

The moon was up, and shed her light upon the earth in liquid splendour; scarce an object that could not be discovered by the eye with ease, and yet this light threw broad and impervious shadows upon the land.

Large clumps of trees stood out in bold relief; but all beneath was as dark as the blackest midnight, so great was the shadow cast by the overhanging boughs.

Alfred Pearson pursued his walk, not wholly unmindful of the beauties that were scattered about him. He was a lover of nature, and admired her many phases, yet, on this occasion, he was so wrapped in his own thoughts, and those thoughts were employed on so important and pleasing an object, that he could bestow no more than a passing glance at objects that at other times he would have stood to admire.

As he neared one clump of tall trees, he threw a cursory view over it, and became again absorbed in pleasing reverie; but in passing he suddenly became aware that two men were present beneath the shade of the chestnuts, and ere he could turn to scrutinize them, he received so heavy blow across the head from a stick, that, had it not been for his hat, he must have been struck senseless.

A desperate attack was now commenced upon him, from which he defended himself with as much energy as an unarmed man could, for he had no weapon of any kind with him. He received several severe blows from the stick, when, making a sudden rush upon the man who used it, he contrived to

seize it, and retained a firm grasp of it, despite all the blows he received from the accomplice.

After a sharp struggle the stick broke, and Pearson retained a part of it, using it with such desperate energy that, notwithstanding the two men rushed on him with fury, he compelled them to retreat and seek their safety in flight, for assistance was near at hand, which they perceived.

Pearson made the best of his way towards Oxford-street, intending to get out of the park into the open streets, where he would be safe, as in the park he had no doubt a second attack would be meditated upon him. It was not long ere he came beneath the glare of lamp lights, and then the thought struck him to examine the stick he held in his hand.

"I could swear," he said, after minutely examining it, "that I saw this in the possession of Phillip Arlines this day at Captain Arnold's. Well, there can be no doubt but that he and his friend, the Marquis of Rollington, have committed this cowardly and dastardly attack. I'll save this till some fitting opportunity occurs of returning it to him."

So saying, he again pursued his way towards his lodging.

CHAPTER XIV.

THE ANONYMOUS LETTER TO CAPTAIN ARNOLD.—THE NOTE TO JESSIE, AND THE UNEXPECTED MEETING IN KENSINGTON GARDENS.—THE GAMING-HOUSE IN ST. JAMES'S-STREET.

THE morning following the events which we have just recorded broke upon the family at the cottage as they usually did, calm and serene to them, with no thought of the future to disturb their thoughts, though reminiscences of the past did occasionally do so; yet theirs were of a melancholy cast, something to regret, yet accompanied with a resignation that deprived the evil of its bitterness.

The breakfast had not long been cleared away, and the captain still sat reading the morning paper, and Jessie had left the apartment a short time, when a note was put into Captain Arnold's hands by the servant.

"Who can this be from?" mentally ejaculated the captain, as he turned it over from one side to the other; but he could gain no information from that, as the handwriting was a strange one to him, and the seal also. Then placing the paper down before

THE WRECK OF THE YACHT, AND DEATH OF MRS. ARNOLD.

him, he proceeded to open it, and read as follows :—

"SIR,—I was an eye-witness of the affair that occurred at the Serpentine, where a child fell into some weeds, and a person named Alfred Pearson lifted it out. I do not mean to underrate his act, which certainly caused him to soil some portion of his wearing apparel, more from contact with that of your child's than from any difficulty he incurred or danger he faced ; indeed, there was neither. As an adventurer it was his desire to get into your family, and endeavour to make his fortune. I am also informed that your daughter is to meet this Alfred Pearson this evening at six o'clock near the Bayswater-gate. Be present, and convince yourself of the truth of my assertion. Alfred Pearson is no more. and certainly not less, than an unprincipled adventurer, and one who will hesitate at nothing that will further his plans.

"AN ENEMY TO PROFLIGACY."

Captain Arnold pondered over this missive in silence and amazement for some minutes, perfectly at a loss how to act.

"I will ask Jessie herself," at length he mentally exclaimed. "It must be a fabrication altogether, without a particle of truth in it. I will show it to them both."

He paused a few moments, and remained in deep thought, and then said,—

"No; that would be precipitate. I will not do that. I will first endeavour to find if there be any truth in the assertions with which the letter is filled; else should this be true, I shall but put Pearson on his guard, without doing anything that can prevent the mischief that may happen to Jessie. Yes, I will go there, and watch for their coming, and then I shall forbid Mr. Pearson's presence at my table any more. Well, who could think there was so much iniquity in the world, that one should be compelled to be thus watchful and vigilant? This letter would never have been written without a motive. The ostensible one, a good one, of course. Believe it otherwise, and that it is written with the intention of injuring Pearson. Yet mere falsehood would carry its own refutation with it. That would never do. No, no. There must be some truth; but even that I'll not trust to chance. I'll be convinced of it, and for that purpose I'll be near the Bayswater-gate at six this evening. Should this be a falsity, I shall be happier than if I find it true, and I shall be convinced that it is a wicked libel. Surely Jessie cannot be so imprudent as to go, though he were bad enough to invite her."

Thus musing, the captain rose and left the house for his morning's walk, without mentioning, as he first intended, the contents of the letter to his daughter.

During that morning, Jessie was busy in her little garden, and on various matters in the house, in which she usually moved about, when a letter was placed in her hands.

The superscription was in an unknown hand, and the seal a plain one. She opened it and saw that the contents were as follows:—

"MISS ARNOLD,—My presumption in thus addressing you, directly, and without the knowledge of your father, must be excused on the ground, that I prefer a request to you, which, if granted, will result in benefit to him, for it will enable you to baffle the cunning of men who have now obtained his confidence, and who seek but his ruin.

"Meet me this evening at the Bayswater-gate, at six o'clock, when I will, at length, relate circumstances that you may use to save a parent from utter ruin and even disgrace. Believe me to be sincere in what I say, and judge for yourself. Much as I value your regard, I will risk it all, but you shall be convinced of the propriety of the step.

"Yours, sincerely,

"ALFRED PEARSON."

Jessie was at first shocked at the letter, and it fell from her hands, and she at first determined to seek her father, and show it to him, and doubtless would have done so, but he happened at that moment to be from home, and this resolution melted away in the maze of thought that ensued.

Jessie thought of the letter of Alfred Pearson, and could think of nothing else, but the more she thought of it, the less could she understand.

She could well see it was not a common assignation—not a mere affair of gallantry—indeed, it had not the remotest appearance of such, or even the air of a love epistle. She thought it breathed nothing but respect, and an ardent wish for the welfare of her father.

What could he mean? was it anything in connection with Phillip Arlines—what other connections had her father that she knew of? One question she asked herself, over and over again, in the vain hope of anticipating the nature of the communication she expected to receive.

At length, however, being unable to answer all her queries, she determined that evening to attend the place of appointment, and learn that which she had endeavoured to find out from mere conjecture.

Having thus made up her mind, she now looked forward to the time of meeting, with evident anxiety.

*   *   *   *   *

Captain Arnold, that evening, felt anxious and angry—not with his daughter, but at the uncertainty of the event that had yet to happen. He knew not how or when the appointment had been made between Jessie and Alfred Pearson; but he presumed it must have been on the evening of the day in which the quarrel took place between Pearson and Arlines. He little thought she had received a letter—a letter, too, that had been concocted by the same hand that wrote the anonymous letter that he had received himself—that they were but the victims of a villain.

He quitted the house early that evening, so that he should have ample time to be at the appointed spot, long ere either of them were there, so that he could watch and speculate upon their arrival.

He took his station within sight of the gate, keeping himself carefully concealed from observation, and there remained some time in expectation of the approach of some of them.

He waited there a considerable time—many people came and went, leaving many others to supply their places; and, notwithstanding, there appeared as many more, the mass appearing never to diminish; but among them he saw not Alfred Pearson nor his own daughter, and the clocks had chimed six some minutes, and yet he saw not those he sought.

He began to breathe freely, and feel he had

detected the malice that must have actuated the writer of the letter against Pearson, but he had scarcely done so when he beheld Jessie walk up to the gate.

If Captain Arnold could feel angry, he would then have been extremely so, for he began to be certain that she would not come; but she was alone, and he determined to prevent her meeting Pearson, by at once remonstrating with her upon the folly of the course she was pursuing; leaving his place of concealment, therefore, he at once walked up to her, and gently took her arm.

She started at such an act of familiarity, but her confusion was scarcely abated by the presence of her father, who said—

"Does your conscience smite you, Jessie?— what brought you to this spot?"

Jessie made no reply, but taking the letter she had received from her reticule, she handed it to her father, who read it attentively, and then said,—

"You have committed a great mistake, Jessie, in not consulting with me ere you attempted to carry on a communication with Mr. Pearson."

"Dear father," said Jessie, "I hoped that by coming here, I might have been the means of hearing something that would have served——"

"You could not, child. I have no connections such as this would imply—but you must cease to have any kind of correspondence with Mr. Pearson. I fear that he is, at the best, but an unworthy man; and I am sure you cannot be aware of the impropriety of your conduct, or you would never have been here to meet him."

Jessie was about to reply, when some one came up, and took Captain Arnold's arm; it was Philip Arlines.

"Well," he said, "who would have thought of meeting with Captain Arnold and his daughter at this place?"

"It was rather a singular motive, I must say," said the captain. "My daughter——"

"Father," interrupted Jessie, "I beg this matter may sink into oblivion."

"No," said the captain; "Mr. Arlines is so old a friend, I cannot refrain from telling him the whole of the story."

He then related all that had happened, and concluded by saying—

"I have now no doubt but that his calumnies of you were mere inventions."

"I know it," said Arlines; "he wished to get me from the house, as, having seen me in society in which he would not be received, he feared I should find out his purpose and foil him; but I will make a few careful inquiries about him, and you shall know the result."

"If Mr. Pearson is to be arraigned and accused," said Jessie, turning to Arlines, "he shall be treated fairly, for I will inform him of it; it shall be for him to make a few inquiries respecting you, Mr. Arlines, and see if you are as pure as he is."

"Jessie," said Captain Arnold, "I do not wish to be angry with you; you had better precede us, and go home."

Jessie did as she was desired, not without, however, a tear starting to her eye, and she sorrowed to think she left her father in company with Arlines.

The captain accompanied Arlines to an hotel, where they had some wine, after which he became much excited; the wine had been drugged sufficiently to make him consent to any proposal his companion might make, and he agreed that he should show him some of the lions of the metropolis. This was no sooner said, than, turning out of St. James's Street, they entered a house, where, after certain signals from Arlines, they were admitted, and at once entered a saloon filled with visitors, and illumined by the most dazzling light, that for a moment confused his sight.

CHAPTER XV.

THE FIRST APPEARANCE AT THE GAMING-HOUSE.—THE WINNER.—THE ALTERCATION IN ST. JAMES'S STREET.

BEWILDERED by the glare of light in the saloon to which he was so suddenly introduced, and half stupefied from the effects of the powerful potion which had been administered to him by his unscrupulous friend, Phillip Arlines, poor Captain Arnold was in anything but a frame of mind which would enable him to exercise caution or discrimination.

"This—is quite—quite magnificent," he said.

"Ay, truly," replied Arlines. "The rooms are not full at present, but, during the four-and-twenty hours, you would see here most of the great public characters of the day. The place is highly respectable. In fact, quite select."

"Oh! of course, of course,"

The captain's eyes were beginning to get a little accustomed to the glare of the chandeliers, reflected in endless variations by superb mirrors, and he could take more particular, although not very accurate, notice of the really princely saloon to which he had so suddenly, and, on his part, so unexpectedly been introduced by his disinterested friend.

The room seemed of vast dimensions, but that effect was chiefly produced by the skilful arrangement of looking-glasses; superb carpeting, which completely destroyed all noise from the movement of feet, covered the floors;

while the massive draperies that adorned the windows prevented any of the rude sounds from the street penetrating that abode of luxury and feverish excitement.

Oh, if man would take half the pains upon virtue he takes upon vice, and add them to the intrinsic beauty of rectitude, how different a world might this be! But we universally find vice and immorality arrayed in the most charming colours. Surely, they mistake human nature sadly, who talk of the stern simplicity of virtue being attractive—it is not so to the mass of minds, who, with a limited power of ratiocination, reason superficially, and are attracted rather by the glitter of sin than the cold colouring of morality.

To them anything not virtuous and good appears everything which is bright and beautiful; to them, of course, the gaudy trappings of the theatre offer a brilliant contrast to the cold severity of the whitewashed conventicle; and certain are we that the affectation, for we can call it no otherwise, which induces your mightly virtuous people to deny all ornament and beauty, has done more, or as much as any other powerful cause, to thin their ranks.

Miss Edgeworth says, pithily, "whoever makes truth and goodness disagreeable, commits high treason against virtue;" and the saying should be written in letters of gold, for it contains an admirable philosophy.

Why is it that all the most abundant resources of art are to be found principally in mansions devoted to purposes of gaming, or worse object? Why is it that greatly virtuous people will not condescend to allure folks to virtue by the same means that they are so frequently allured to vice? Make the paths of justice, morality, and religion, which might be easily done, as flowery and beautiful as those of wrong, vice, and infidelity, and we shall find fewer strayers from the right road.

But to return from this digression. Captain Arnold sat down on a sofa, and gazed around him for some time in surprise, which shortly gave way to a feeling of pleasure, as he marked the intense harmony and beauty of the scene by which he was surrounded.

True, he did not see the agitated countenances of the players—he did not see the keen smile of avarice on the part of a winner—nor did he, situated as he was, mark the pale cheek and wild glance of indescribable agony that sat upon the countenances of those to whom fortune had not been propitious.

He was not sufficiently near the gaming-table to notice such particular facts, nor was he, perhaps, in a sufficiently cool state of mind to become so observant had he been closer. All to him was beauty, magnificence, and admirable taste.

Phillip Arlines saw the effect which the scene was having upon his imagination. He marked with exultation, first, the look of amazement, and then the look of pleasure, with which his victim gazed around him, upon the truly magical scene, and he augured well from the effect which was produced upon Captain Arnold's imagination for the success of the diabolical scheme which was concocted for his destruction.

"He soon forgets his daughter," thought Arlines. "Truly success is greater that I thought it would be. This is glorious."

In about ten minutes he spoke to the captain, saying, in a low tone,—

"Well, Arnold, what do you think of this place?"

"It is a place of enchantment. I never saw anything so princely in all my life. Surely, where there is such pure and admirable taste, there must be——"

"Excited feelings," added Arlines. "You are quite right. Play goes on here, but you perceive it is robbed of all its grossness. It is merely for amusement, and we never see a frown upon any face—ahem!"

"Indeed."

"Yes. Now that I have introduced you once, you can come again; and whenever time hangs heavy on your hands, and you want solace from some brooding care, come here, and look upon the superb statuary—the magnificent decorations, and inestimable paintings, with which the house abounds."

"I will—I will. A more delightful recreation could not be conceived. There is a very atmosphere of richness and beauty about it."

"There is; but I must warn you of one thing. You know human nature is sometimes not quite what it should be; and in the holiest sanctuary there will occasionally creep noxious things. Now, in spite of the precautions to keep the place quite respectable, I am afraid there are two or three persons who come here for play professedly, and are not very particular, you understand me, how they win, so that they do win."

"Exactly—exactly."

"Well, then, be cautious. Take my advice, and never play at all, unless I am with you."

"You are very kind."

"Oh, don't mention that. I know pretty well who is safe and who is not in these saloons; and I strongly advise you, in order to prevent anything wrong, to be cautious."

"My better plan," said the captain, "will be only to come occasionally with you."

"Why, yes, it would. I did not like to propose that, as it seemed a kind of restraint upon you; but, unquestionably, it would be the safer and better plan."

"Then I shall adopt it; and I can only add that I am very much your debtor for introducing me here. Gambling I detest;

out, as you say, in this magnificent place, where the very best company congregate, it is not—not exactly—you see——"

"Exactly. That is just what I mean. You take a very proper view of the case. By-the-bye, at the first visit it is always expected that you should risk a guinea or two, just as a matter of initiation."

"Oh, certainly. A guinea or two risked can do no harm to any one. That is very different from gambling."

"Oh, quite another thing. Come along."

Phillip Arlines took the arm of the captain, and led him to one of the tables, whispering to him as he went towards it,—

"Do as your hear and see me do. These are men of honour at this table."

There were but three persons seated at the small table, to which Arlines led the captain, and they were conversing while they played at cards in the most affable manner in the world.

"Ah," said one, as Arlines approached, "here is our friend Arlines. How do you do?"

"Quite well, I thank you. This is a friend of mine; I have been desiring him never to play even here with any one he has not been introduced to by me."

"And quite right too. We are forced, even here, sir, to keep ourselves a little select."

"What are you playing at?" said Arlines.

"Vingt-un. Will you bet?"

"I don't mind."

He took his purse from his pocket, and laid five-pounds on a pack of cards.

"Allow me, gentlemen, to do theme," said Captain Arnold, "if you please."

"Certainly—certainly."

He laid a five-pound note on the same packet that Arlines had selected, and in a few moments they both won.

"Ah, you are fortunate," said the loser, with the utmost blandness of tone and manner. "Will you try again?"

They did try again, and lost—but then they tried again and won. We need not follow them through varieties of good and bad fortune, but suffice it to state that of course Captain Arnold was in the long run permitted to win by the scoundrels, who were thus urging him on to a course fraught with ruin and despair, and that by one o'clock in the morning he found himself a gainer to the amount of about sixty pounds.

It was Arlines, who, looking at his watch, suddenly said,—

"Bless me, I had no idea it was so late. One o'clock; how the time flies when we are pleasantly occupied."

"One o'clock," cried Captain Arnold, springing to his feet, and suddenly recollecting what consternation he might be producing among the little ones at home, by his long and most unusual absence. He thought of Jessie,

and his heart smote him at the supposition that she would think he was staying out to punish her for her indiscretion in making private appointments with Alfred Pearson.

"Indeed it is one," remarked another of the gamesters. "Well, I thought we were on the other side of midnight."

"I fear, gentlemen," remarked Captain Arnold, "that as a winner I have no right in honour to rise from the table till you please to do so likewise."

"Oh, no—no—no," cried the whole three. "We have no such absurd notions here. You come and go as you like, sir, winner or loser."

"Exactly," said Arlines. "I was going to tell you that no one is expected to remain here one moment longer than his conscience or inclination may dictate."

"That is very liberal," said the captain, rising. "I do now wish to return home, and I can only say, gentlemen, that I shall be very happy to meet you again."

"With pleasure, sir, we shall see you," was the reply.

A few moments more, and Captain Arnold, with his dear friend, Phillip Arlines. stood in the cool early morning air in St. James's-street.

"Upon my word," said Arnold, "I don't half like walking off in this way with sixty pounds."

"My dear fellow," replied Arlines, with a laugh, "think nothing of it. I have seen as many thousands walked off with quite as coolly."

"Have you indeed?"

"Yes, and I don't see why you should not have a little occasional amusement in coming here."

"Why, certainly I have every temptation."

"You are certain, by playing only with these, of receiving honourable treatment, and you cannot come to much harm, you see."

"Harm? it appears to me that I am coming to some good. Here am I a winner of more than I ever lost or won in all my life at any game of chance or skill."

"So much the better; and now, captain, will you allow me to plead for Jessie; she is young, innocent, and easily imposed upon. Take no further notice of this little affair of Pearson's; just forbid him your house, and have done with him."

"But really—I—I don't know what to think about it. His heroic conduct in saving my child——"

"What, do you really think the child was in any danger?"

"I cannot say, but to doubt on a subject of gratitude is so very painful, and I am always tempted to err on the right side. I will see him once more, and speak to him freely on the subject of that note to Jessie."

"I am here, Captain Arnold," cried Alfred Pearson, suddenly walking up to the astonished pair. "I am here, sir. I have done myself the honour this evening of calling at your house, and finding you from home, and in company with this man, a suspicion crossed my mind that he had allured you to the house I have had the pain of seeing you even now emerge from."

There was an earnest and manly sincerity about the tone of the young man that forcibly struck Captain Arnold, and he was for some moments silent and confused. Arlines seized the opportunity of the moment, and at once gave a bias to Captain Arnold's thoughts, by saying,—

"How do you like a spy upon your private actions? Verily this new acquaintance gives himself a strange license."

The word spy appeared to rouse some anger in the captain's mind, and he turned menacingly to Alfred Pearson, saying,—

"Sir, while I am fully inclined to admit the claim you have upon my consideration, on account of all the service you have rendered to me, I cannot think that gives you any kind of right to become a spy upon my actions."

"Captain Arnold," said Alfred Pearson, with emotion, "I can easily perceive that the man you now have with you has acquired a dominion over your unsuspicious nature, which I may in vain try to shake, but a time will come when the words I now address to you will wake some suspicion upon your mind, reverting to your memory with a painful consciousness of their truth. You are being led on by that man to ruin."

"Ruin!" echoed Captain Arnold.

"Ay, worse than ruin."

"How dare you," cried Arlines, "thus malign me? Slanderer, I don't know what hinders me chastising you on the spot for your insolence!"

"But I do," remarked Pearson, coolly. "Cowardice hinders you. You dare not lift a finger against me."

Arlines trembled with passion, but still he hung back, and in the fullest manner verified the charge of cowardice brought against him by the other.

"Conscious guilt," added Alfred Pearson, "would unnerve you, even if you were sufficiently stung by my words to induce you to strike me."

Captain Arnold looked from one to the other in amazement, and very much wondered at Arlines's powers of endurance.

"The assassin," continued Pearson, "the man who would attack, aided by others, an unarmed man, may well shrink from an encounter on terms of equality."

Arlines turned ghastly pale.

"What is the meaning of this?" said Captain Arnold. "What do you allude to when you use the word assassin, Mr. Pearson?"

"I allude to an attack which was made upon me last night, when I left your house, by this Phillip Arlines, aided by others; an attack which nearly cost me my life, although I did succeed in beating off the cowardly assailants."

"Indeed! Can this be true?"

"No!" cried Arlines, in a half screaming voice. "It's false as hell! Quite false— quite!"

"I have proof."

"False—false! I defy your proof, I defy it!"

"Very well," said Alfred; "the law shall settle that question. Captain Arnold, do you know this piece of walking-stick?"

"That—why—why, Arlines, you had such a one. It is very like yours."

"I wrested it from the hands of one of the ruffians," added Pearson. "It is a damning proof of who were my assailants. You shall have an opportunity of defying the proof, Phillip Arlines; and once more, Captain Arnold, I warn you that this man is making an attempt to drag you down an abyss from whence there is no return. He is a gambler— I may add, a swindler. Beware of him, and never gamble with him, or any one to whom he may introduce you."

"Talk as you please," said Arlines. "You are yourself smarting under a sense of exposure. You thought to establish yourself as a welcome visitor in Captain Arnold's house; and now that you find yourself signally foiled, you are throwing charges about at random, to make what mischief you can."

"I cannot decide in this case," said Captain Arnold. "You must, however, be mistaken, Mr. Pearson. Mr. Arlines is, I assure you, quite incapable of acting as you describe."

"Your own unsuspicious heart would acquit him," replied Pearson; "but the outrage is too great for me to pass unnoticed. I believe my murder was aimed at. There are men who care not, if a life stands in the way of their objects, to destroy it. Phillip Arlines is one of them."

"Come away, captain," said Arlines. "He is mad or drunk."

Alfred Pearson turned and beckoned to a man, who was standing some dozen paces from where the brief and angry conversation had taken place. The man immediately advanced, and then Pearson, pointing to Arlines, said, in a calm voice,—

"That is your prisoner."

"Prisoner!" cried Arlines, stepping back a pace. "Why—why—you don't know what you are saying."

"Is your name Phillip Arlines?" said the stranger.

"Yes—but—but——"

"You are my prisoner, then. I have a warrant against you."

"This is serious," said Captain Arnold. "How did this occur?"

"I applied and obtained a warrant for his apprehension, on a charge of making a murderous assault upon me," replied Pearson. "The magistrate thought the broken stick I produced good evidence, since it has this man's initials upon it; and I can swear to it as being his."

"Why—why," remarked the captain—"I really don't know what's to be done. This is awkward. You deny the charge, Arlines, you say? Really, Mr. Pearson, you must be labouring under some very extraordinary error."

"No, Captain Arnold, I am not. The circumstances all combine to fix the guilt of the cowardly attack upon this man. Officer, do your duty."

"You must come along with me," said the officer, taking a strong hold of the arm of Arlines.

"One word," said Arlines. "Captain Arnold, I am quite innocent of this charge. I lost my stick, or it was stolen from me, before I got home last night. How it came into the possession of this young man I cannot say. Perhaps, to-morrow, at the police-office, I may make him change places with me. Will you do me the favour of attending?"

"Where?"

"At Marylebone," said the officer, "Come along, sir."

Captain Arnold shook hands with Phillip Arlines, who was then led away by the officer.

"Now, sir," said Alfred Pearson, "can you doubt?"

"Mr. Pearson, the whole affair is so extraordinary, that you must give me leave to suspend my judgment till to-morrow; and as I cannot possibly tell just now who is wrong or who is right, I would rather hear nothing more about it. Good night, sir."

"Good night, sir," said Alfred Pearson proudly; and without another word, he left the captain, and walked hastily away.

The captain stood for some moments in a state of bewilderment. So many strange occurrences had been compressed within the last six or eight hours that he could hardly believe them all possible; and then to terminate with the arrest of his dear and devoted friend, Phillip Arlines, in so unceremonious a way, and upon such a charge, was the crowning curiosity of all.

"Well," he said, drawing a long breath, "when will this night's adventures cease? There have been truly some most extraordinary circumstances. I have won sixty pounds most unexpectedly—Phillip Arlines arrested—Alfred Pearson accused of all sorts of iniquity; and yet carrying himself so very like an innocent man. I don't know what to think."

At this moment two o'clock was given forth by some neighbouring church clock, and Captain Arnold at once awoke to the necessity of getting home as quickly as possible. He walked with a very rapid pace; and there being few obstructions in the streets, he in a short time found himself in the neighbourhood of his own house.

A light burned in the window of a lower room, and after climbing the gate, for he would not ring, lest he should disturb the younger children, he made towards it, and looked in.

Jessie was there, sitting at a table. Her head was resting on her hands, and she appeared to be sleeping. Some books lay upon the table, as if she had endeavoured to beguile time of some of its tediousness by reading. The long, untrimmed snuff of the candle proclaimed her inattention to it; and it was with a pang of self-reproach that he recollected how long he had left her to endure the reproaches he had cast upon her for what, after all, was but a venial fault, if, under the peculiar circumstances, it could be called a fault at all.

"That letter of Pearson's," he thought, "was certainly a strong inducement to her to meet him; and here have I left her for many hours, thinking me very unkind. Curses on the gaming-house, and all its magnificence! What are they, compared with one smile from my darling Jessie?"

He found the outer door yielded readily to his touch, and he crept softly into the apartment where poor Jessie had kept a long and lonely watch.

She was sleeping, but weeping even in her sleep. It was some moments before Captain Arnold could command himself sufficiently to awaken her, and before he did so, he heard her once, in a gentle tone of affectionate reproach, pronounce the word,—

"Father!"

The captain took two turns round the room then before he could quite overcome the choking feeling that arose in his throat. He then gently touched her arm.

"Jessie—Jessie," he said; "my Jessie."

She looked up on the instant, and, with a burst of passionate weeping, she flung herself into her father's arms.

"Hush! hush! my darling," he said; "wherefore this emotion?"

"Oh! father! father! it was cruel to leave us so very long. Did I deserve so great a punishment?"

"You much mistake, Jessie. I did not remain away from home to punish you."

"Thank Heaven—thank Heaven! Oh! what a weary time it has been—so many hours. Had I but known, I could have been content; but I was tortured with suppositions that you had met with some accident."

"No—no. I was with a friend merely, and the time stole on quite unawares. I really had no notion it was so late, or rather early, till one o'clock."

"I am repaid for all by seeing you safe and well; I am very happy now, father, and you are not so angry with me as you were."

"Not angry at all, my dear, now; I was vexed, of course, at your going to meet any one clandestinely."

"But the contents of the letter, father, were such as to make me think some danger threatened you; and as you know I have not a favourable opinion of Phillip Arlines, I suspected him of concocting some mischief."

"You have a prejudice against Mr. Arlines?"

"Possibly, father."

"And another in favour of Mr. Pearson?"

"I hope that is not a prejudice."

"Well, well, now go to bed, Jessie. We will talk more of this in the morning."

"Mr. Pearson has been here, and declares the note sent to me, in his name, to be a forgery."

"Indeed!"

"Yes; I suspect, and so does he, that it emanated from Phillip Arlines, who attacked him last night, and would have murdered him, if possible."

"Jessie, you have heard but one side of the question. You speak too confidently of things which you may be wrongfully informed of."

"And yet can I for a moment doubt——"

Jessie paused, for she thought that if she proceeded much further, she should be compelled to tell her father of the little scene which had taken place between herself and Arlines in the breakfast-parlour, and of the threats by which he had succeeded in inducing her hitherto to preserve silence on the subject.

"Good night," she added, "good night, father. I am, indeed, very weary. Good night!"

"Good night, my dear; God bless you."

Captain Arnold was far from being satisfied with himself when he came to reflect upon the proceedings of the evening in the solitude of his own chamber. He had inflicted much uneasiness upon Jessie for the gratification of a pleasure which he had always denied, and really despised.

He wondered what could have induced him to go to the gaming-house at all, and then he wondered still more that he should have been persuaded so easily to play, and he felt much vexed at winning the sixty pounds. Dim suspicions of Arlines would now and then float across his imagination, but they were very dim, indeed, and finally Captain Arnold fell fast asleep, and dreamed again of the splendid saloon in St. James's street, which had so taken his fancy and beguiled so many hours of their absolute tediousness. He thought he was there again, winning immense sums of money, which he saw in prospect would lift him and his children to a height in society he had never before thought of aspiring to. Fatal—fatal visions!

CHAPTER XVI.

THE MORNING.—THE POLICE OFFICE.—THE CHARGE, AND THE REFUTATION.—THE THREAT.

CAPTAIN ARNOLD felt himself in the morning feverish and impatient. The wine which he had partaken of with Phillip Arlines left more effect behind it than any undrugged liquor could have done, and the deceived captain fancied when he rose that he could have almost drunk the Thames dry, to alleviate the scorching thirst that consumed him.

After a long draught of spring water, he felt somewhat revived, and with a deep-drawn breath, he said—

"Well, this comes of excitement and late hours, I suppose. Confound that saloon and all its pictures, and all its statues. It seems to me that I have paid a heavy price in health and peace for the temporary enjoyment of them."

A walk of about half an hour's duration in the beautiful grounds of his villa did much to restore him to his wonted equanimity of mind and health of body, and he returned to breakfast with renewed vigour and a clearer conception of the overnight's proceedings than he had had.

"What am I to think," he muttered to himself, as he neared the breakfast-parlour. "I have every reason to think well of Phillip Arlines, and every wish to think well of Alfred Pearson; yet one of them must be unworthy of my friendship and esteem—which, is the question. How can I decide? As for the mere fact of Alfred Pearson being alive to the beauty of Jessie, and feeling and affection for her, however I might interpose to prevent an imprudent marriage, I cannot blame him utterly. I ran away with my wife in spite of

" 'Fathers, and mothers, and cousins and all.' "

By this time he reached some stone steps which led up to the window of the breakfast-room, in which he saw Jessie, certainly a little paler than usual, in consequence of her deprivation of rest the preceding evening, but otherwise calm, and, to all appearance, tranquil and composed.

PEARSON'S ADMIRATION OF THE INSENSIBLE JESSIE AFTER RESCUING THE CHILD.

The first meeting was a little awkward on the captain's part, for he could not tell himself he was altogether conscience free in the matter; on the contrary, a feeling of self-reproach came over his mind that his beautiful child should owe the deprivation of any of the roses that were accustomed to bloom upon her cheeks to him.

"Well, Jessie," he said, when the morning meal was nearly over, "I have some news to tell you."

"News, father?"

"Yes. Mr. Pearson appears to be quite in earnest in charging Arline with making an attack upon him near Hyde Park, and has given him, Arlines, into custody upon the charge."

"He told me so much," said Jessie, softly.

"And he told you he suspected Arlines? The circumstance of the stick may be explained away."

"How, father? I saw Mr. Arlines leave here with the stick."

"Why, he says he lost it."

Jessie shook her head as she remarked gently,

"I have heard and read of very strange circumstances and coincidences, but it is very odd that Phillip Arlines should quarrel with Alfred Pearson, and then that Arlines should lose his walking stick, and then that it should be found by some one, who then should make a brutal attack upon Mr. Pearson, and then——"

"There—there," cried Captain Arnold, "that will do. You should have been a boy, and I would have made you a barrister. You certainly would have argued well on the probabilities of this case; but I must go now, and all I can say is, that I will impartially and honourably investigate the matter."

"Then, dear father, I am quite content."

Captain Arnold imprinted a kiss upon his daughter's cheek, and then hurried off to the police-court, where Phillip Arlines was to be brought up on the serious charge Alfred Pearson had brought against him, and which, with the evidence of the stick, seemed likely enough to be substantiated.

The whole of the circumstances seemed to point to Arlines as the guilty party. There was his quarrel with Pearson, and his threat to be revenged on him. Then there was the fact of Arlines leaving Captain Arnold's house just soon enough before Pearson quitted it to lay in wait for him, and perpetrate the outrage, while last, though not least, came the fragment of the walking stick, which Phillip Arlines would find the greatest difficulty in denying to be his, should he be so ill-advised as to attempt such a task.

His conviction on the charge appeared certain, and the officer who had arrested him said as much to Pearson.

"He will either be fined five pounds," he said, "or the case will be sent to the sessions. But the magistrate cannot let him off on such strong circumstantial evidence."

Such was the state of affairs when the police-office opened that morning. Mr. Arlines was brought up from his not over-comfortable lodging in the station house, and Alfred Pearson was ready to detail again the facts he had already deposed to when he procured the warrant for the immediate apprehension of his dishonourable antagonist.

A row between persons of any respectability in society always produces in a police-office a degree of excitement edifying to behold, and the night charges are discussed in as summary a manner as a tiresome overture, when a drama of no ordinary interest is expected to succeed it.

Captain Arnold arrived in good time, but he had no opportunity of speaking to Arlines, although he had with Pearson. The latter, however, would not have addressed the captain, had he not first been spoken to, considering the unceremonious manner in which he had been treated the evening before; but when Captain Arnold said,—" Mr. Pearson, I come here biassed neither way, but prepared to hear and acknowledge the truth," the young man answered,—

"I thank you, sir. My earnest wish and prayer is that the truth shall be made apparent. Let Mr. Arlines clear himself, and my voice shall be raised in favour of his acquittal."

A bustle then in court announced the end of the night charges, and in another moment Phillip Arlines appeared at the bar.

There was a confident look upon the face of Arlines as he appeared in the police-court, which seemed to say, "I am quite innocent, and can confound you all by proving it;" while Pearson, on the contrary, looked pale and harrassed, as if what he was doing was more for duty's sake than because he consulted his own inclination.

Report had very much exaggerated the quarrel which had ensued between Arlines and Pearson, as well as the attack which had been made upon the latter; so that upon the whole it was rather a disappointment and a mortification to the good folks who had squeezed themselves into the police-office not to find him, Pearson, some frightful complication of surgical bandages.

"Call Mr. Pearson," said the magistrate.

Then ensued the usual little bustle, during which everybody turned round at least once, and then looked at Pearson when he made his appearance as if he had been some rare and curious specimen of humanity.

He was duly sworn, and then the magistrate added,—

"Now, sir, will you detail your complaint against the prisoner?"

Alfred Pearson spoke in a firm clear voice, that had no sort of shrinking in it, and carried in its cadences an irresistible air of truthfulness and simplicity.

"I had been dining," he said, "at Captain Arnold's villa, near Kensington, when owing to my recognising the prisoner, Phillip Arlines, as a man who had been pointed out to me as a professed gambler and a sharper, I took upon myself, he being likewise at Captain Arnold's house, to tell the captain the character of his guest. This produced some words between me and Captain Arnold, during which the prisoner uttered various threats, which at the time I disregarded, but which are of importance in this charge. In consequence of the altercation, a disagreeable feeling appeared to have sprung up, and Arlines left along with his friend. I remained but a very short time behind him, and on my route to town I was savagely attacked, and am confident, from the violence of the attack, that my murder was intended. I fought off my assailants, and in the struggle secured this piece of a walking stick, which I can swear to as belonging to Phillip Arlines, the prisoner."

"How many persons attacked you?" asked the magistrate.

" Two."

" And you could not recognise them?"

" I could not; the place was dark."

" Then you cannot positively swear to the prisoner at the bar?"

" I cannot."

" Well, Mr. Pearson, have you any witness?"

" I call upon Captain Arnold, who I perceive in court, to depose to his knowledge of the stick."

" Captain Arnold," cried the clerk, and the captain, stepping forward, replied,—

" I am here."

He was immediately sworn, and then said,—

" To the best of my belief, this is a portion of a walking stick I have frequently seen in the possession of Mr. Arlines."

" Further," said the magistrate, " I presume, you know nothing of this transaction?"

" Nothing further than confirming Mr. Pearson's account of what passed at my house."

" Well, Mr. Arlines," added the magistrate, " what have you to say to this most serious charge?"

" Simply that I am innocent."

" Ah, but, you see, the circumstances are very suspicious. If you persist, however, in a denial of the charge, I shall send the case before another tribunal instead of summarily adjudicating upon the case myself."

" I do persist in my denial, and I have some witnesses in support of that denial. There is a list of my witnesses."

He handed a paper to the magistrate, who read,—

" The most honourable the Marquis of Rollington, the honourable Lord Rouse, Sir Mathew Elmleye, Baronet.—God bless me! do you mean to say you have these witnesses?"

" I have; and request the Marquis of Rollington be called."

" I am here," said the marquis, stepping forward.

The magistrate immediately rose, and an immense bustle ensued, which ended in the marquis being accommodated with a seat on the bench, and being the observed of all observers; while Pearson stood by, wondering what piece of artful villany was now about to be enacted.

" Will your lordship," said the magistrate, " upon your lordship's word of honour, please to state what you know of this affair?"

" Silence!" screamed the usher; and the noble lord, in a voice of great dignity, commenced—

" What Mr. Pearson has stated as regards what happened at Captain Arnold's villa is substantially correct."

" Yes, my lord," said the magistrate. " Oh, correct."

" Upon my honour."

The magistrate bowed so low that he almost put his nose into the official inkstand that was before him.

His lordship continued—

" Mr. Arlines and I left the villa of Captain Arnold together, and if two people attacked Mr. Pearson, I must have been one of them."

A smile of incredulity curled the lips of the magistrate, and he shook his head as much as to say, " No, no; who could for one moment suspect a lord of anything wrong?"

" Upon my honour, as a peer of this realm," added the noble marquis, " Mr. Arlines complained to me a short time after we had left the villa of Captain Arnold of having lost his stick."

" Cut his stick, yer means," said a voice from among the crowd.

The magistrate sprang to his feet in a state of the most horrible virtuous indignation.

" Who said that?" he cried. " Officer, who said that? Who dared to interrupt his lordship? Bring him before me, and I'll commit him for three months as an incorrigible rogue and vagabond! Who was it? Gracious Heaven! is justice and a lord to be interrupted in this most disgraceful way?"

Of course the officers showed their efficiency, and pushed everybody about dreadfully, but somehow or another they couldn't find the culprit; and although a vague idea of convicting everybody as rogues and vagabonds, and so making sure of the criminal, came over the mind of the magistrate, he gave it up, and sat down quite pale with rage and defeated indignation.

" My lord," he said, " I deeply regret—'

" Oh, don't mention it—don't mention it," said the marquis. " I was about to say, that Mr. Arlines had lost his walking-stick, upon my honour, and that after that he walked home with me to my house, where he supped with me, and Lord Rouse, and others, remaining there all night."

" And he assaulted no one?"

" Upon my honour, no one."

" Then," said the magistrate, " there is an end of the case. I discharge the prisoner. Where is the prosecutor? He must be a hardened, a very hardened individual, to bring forward such a charge as he has against any friend of our lordship."

" I am here," said Alfred Pearson, stepping forward; " and, before this case is thus summarily decided, I claim to be heard, and I will be heard."

" You—you will?"

" I will; and you dare not deny me the right, sir. Is this man now sitting by your side to be——"

" Pho, pho, clear the court, clear the court. The case is disposed of. I won't be bullied.

Clear the court, I say. Turn him out directly."

The officers made prodigious efforts, and Alfred Pearson found himself in a few moments in the street.

CHAPTER XVII.

THE LOVERS' FAREWELL.—JESSIE'S EN-TREATIES.—THE CAPTAIN'S UNEXPECTED LOSS.—THE QUARREL.

THE evening succeeding the day upon which the affair at the police-office terminated was calm and beautiful; the sun was sinking in the west, bidding his diurnal farewell to earth in all the glorious majesty of the many-tinted clouds.

Jessie, with a heart sad at the recollection of recent circumstances, walked up and down the garden, solitary and melancholy. The affairs that in her father's mind had taken so decided a turn to the disadvantage of Alfred Pearson, found in her mind no argument against his truth and sincerity, nor did his want of evidence against Arlines exculpate the latter from the charge in her mind, though it had in that of the magistrate's and her father's.

Alfred Pearson, she felt convinced, would not have made the statement he had if he had not been sure of it; the loss of the stick averred to by the marquis she considered very suspicious, and in her own mind fully believed in his guilt.

She saw not the setting sun surrounded by all the glories of an eastern sky; the many hues of the clouds now attracted not her warmest admiration, and lifted up her thoughts far above worldly things and creatures; the glowing west no longer exposed its fleeting grandeur to her gaze, for she looked not on it, and her eyes were cast upon the ground, and she pursued her slow pacings up and down the path regardless of all around her.

Her thoughts were many, and as varied as the hues of the changeful west, and, like them, concentrated on one point, and that point was Alfred Pearson.

She was near the end of a walk where a low wall was built, and on which many climbing plants grew, and was much alarmed by a sudden noise. She looked around her, but had scarce time to do so when the figure of a man was seen vaulting over the wall.

Jessie uttered a faint scream, and was about to seek safety in flight, when he approached her, saying, in a respectful tone—

"Do not be alarmed, Miss Arnold, 'tis I; do you not recollect me?"

She stopped and instantly recognised the form of Alfred Pearson.

"Mr. Pearson," she said, "I had no idea

of seeing you thus; your presence is so sudden."

"It is," replied Pearson, sadly. "I have no other means of seeing you and bidding you farewell."

"Farewell!"

"Yes, I have been forbidden the house by Captain Arnold, and have, therefore, no right to be even here; but I could not leave you, Miss Arnold, without seeing you and bidding you farewell, and at the same time having a few words of conversation with you ere we part."

"Part? Surely you cannot mean to take what my father says as being so serious?"

"I regret that I have no alternative, else I had not done so, I assure you. That man, Phillip Arlines, has got his ear so completely, that I could not be acceptable in the same house with him."

"I regret that much; Arlines, I am convinced means no good; his objects all tend to self. Indeed, I have so great an abhorrence of the man, that I could not believe anything he said."

"I would that your father could see his character as clearly as you do; but that I fear will not be until he has suffered from his too great and close an intimacy with him. I am more convinced than ever that he is a shameless adventurer, and a profligate gamester, and, in my opinion, that marquis is no more than an accomplice."

"Then you think he is no marquis at all?" said Jessie.

"I do not say that, for there are men in all grades and ranks of life who, having ruined themselves by companionship with such men, and are brought to that pass that they no longer look upon such actions as degrading, hesitate not to seek the means of retaining their old pleasures and habits, as those which were the cause of their downfall."

"Can such men really exist," sighed Jessie, "who, knowing the evil that others have inflicted upon them, seek to do the like evil to others?"

"Yes, Jessie, there are; and it is from such men your father has the most to fear. But I came not here to speak of them. You are aware of their intentions, and will not do me the injustice, I am sure, to think I seek aught save the good and kindly thoughts of those I have been received by. Say that in some moment of leisure you will think of Alfred Pearson, when he shall no longer be present with you—tell me this, and I shall be in some measure compensated for the injury I have received; I shall then know I have one friend in this house."

"You have," said Jessie. "I can never forget the debt of gratitude I owe to you; neither can my father, who, I am sure, ere long will be convinced of your truth, and the baseness of these men."

"I live in hopes," replied Pearson, "that such may some day happen; but, till that time arrives, I must forego the happiness of visiting this house."

"It may not be long," said Jessie, with a sigh. "I am sure that iniquity cannot prevail against truth."

"It often does," said Alfred Pearson, "and I am not casuist enough to pretend to explain the reason; but while I know that you, Miss Arnold, will think of the absent Alfred Pearson, I shall have a balm that will go far to ease the wound that has been inflicted. Accident will again throw us into each other's society, and renew those meetings, which I had hoped would never end save in mutual and closer ties."

As Alfred said this, he gently pressed the hand of Jessie, whose heart throbbed audibly, and she trembled, scarce knowing what to say, or how to bring the interview to an end, for she felt it was like to grow to a great length, and more might be said than was, perhaps, under all circumstances, prudent.

Alfred had watched her countenance with anxiety, and his features wore something like a ray of hope as he witnessed her emotion, when a sudden and furious ring at the garden gate startled them both.

"It is my father," said Jessie.

"And Arlines," replied Alfred. "I hear them talking very loudly."

"What will you do? Do not see them. Avoid them if possible," said Jessie, "else I fear the consequences may be still worse than what has already happened. It is evident they are not fit to talk with by the loudness of their tones."

"Here is a hedge," said Pearson, "which will conceal me until they have passed, when I can quit the place."

"Do so," said Jessie.

Ere he stepped into the clump of trees he took Jessie's hand and quietly pressed it to his lips, and in another moment he was out of sight.

Jessie was so flurried by what had passed, that she stood irresolute what course to pursue; but a second more violent application to the bell startled her, and awakened her to the necessity of disappearing, which she did, and entered the house by a side door.

"Pooh! never mind," said Arlines to the captain; "the loss is trifling. Recollect, you were a winner yesterday."

"But I have lost all I have won, and a thousand pounds besides."

"Well, that is true; but Dame Fortune never sits on any man's shoulders long, and will do as much for you another day."

"I may meet with the same ill luck, Arlines, and then where shall I be?"

"Do not think of it; it is absurd and impossible. Fortune never yet ran against any man for so long a time."

"I have heard of instances——"

"Yes, you have heard of men who dared venture until they were nearly ruined, and then they fell short of risking the last stake which would have restored them all they had lost, and much more besides."

"I hope it may be so; it was a magnificent place, I must admit."

"Yes," said Arlines; "such a place you will scarcely find in Europe. All that is beautiful and fashionable is there, and the most renowned characters of the day, even crowned heads, or, rather, blood royal."

"Indeed, the company we met with, though strangers, were singularly well bred, and concealed the chagrin naturally felt upon a loss."

"Yes," said Arlines; "that is the perfection that a man of the world and a gentleman aims at in society—never to lose his temper and self-possession under the most trying circumstances; and I am sure you must admit that if was done to perfection."

"I do—I do," said Arnold; "nothing better. I believe, Arlines, that my features did not betray me when I rose up a loser?"

"Considering it was your first loss I should say no; but your seat at the Isle of Wight has prevented you from mixing much with that society for which you appear so eminently qualified to shine in."

"You think that a stranger could tell by my features that I was a loser, then?"

"Not exactly; but there was not that exclusive command of features that can only be obtained but by practice; but, to tell you the truth, dear Arnold, I never expected you would have endured it half so well."

"Indeed; but perhaps a thousand pounds is of more consequence to me than to them."

"Often, but not always. A duke may be poor, you know; his expense is proportionate to his income."

"Exactly; but let us go in."

They were about to quit the garden, when Alfred Pearson, who had overheard every word of their conversation, stepped from behind the bushes that concealed him, and advanced full in front of them.

They were both so astonished at the sudden appearance of Pearson, that they stopped in silence, and he then said,—

"Captain Arnold, my advice may be deemed impertinent, but let me implore you to consider the course that man is likely to lead you. I know him, and a deeper dyed villain never lived. Put up with your present loss, heavy as it is; but you will have an easy escape from such a scene of profligacy, ruin, and disgrace, that will embitter your days, and make those unhappy whom you would wish to render happiest. You have lost a thousand pounds; let it be the price of security for what you have, and let this be your last appearance in a gaming house."

"D——n!" cried Arlines, whose rage knew no bounds. "I will teach you to talk to gentlemen thus."

He made a desperate rush at Pearson, who stepped back from the fury of so sudden an onset; and then by a well-aimed blow, struck him down, and he rolled on to a flower bed, crushing and destroying everything in his progress.

Alfred Pearson then passed out of the gate at which Captain Arnold and Arlines had just entered.

CHAPTER XVIII.

CAPTAIN ARNOLD'S SITUATION.— THE LETTER TO ALFRED PEARSON.—THE SUDDEN ARREST OF ARLINES.—THE BOND.

THE words of Alfred Pearson did make some impression upon Captain Arnold's mind. Indeed, there was a tone of fervid truthfulness about them that could not fail of producing a strong feeling with regard to the candour and sincerity of the young man.

Had the captain's mind not been in the state of excitement it was, the warnings and the advice, both admirable as they were, must have had more than a momentary effect; but in the condition he was, and exposed to the baneful influence of the associate who was with him, the effect was but transient, instead of being lasting and efficacious.

Alfred Pearson was gone before the discomfited Phillip Arlines could gather himself up from the flower bed into which he had fallen from the straightforward knock-down blow which he had received.

When he did rise his face presented such a picture of diabolical rage as perhaps scarcely ever before had sat upon a human countenance. He was perfectly furious, and, with a courage given him by passion, he would have pursued Alfred Pearson with frantic eagerness, had not Captain Arnold restrained him, saying,—

"Let him go—let him go. Have of him the satisfaction which one gentleman cannot refuse another; but do not condescend to a brawl."

"D——n!" roared Arlines, "I will have his life. Let me pursue him. Revenge I will have!"

"Nay, consider where you are," urged the captain. "Be more calm and composed. Think of my situation, and the counsel I expect from you."

Arline's rage was not decreasing but his prudence was increasing; and, although the same deadly hatred swelled in his heart against Alfred Pearson, he was not sorry to be held back from following him, and running the danger of another personal encounter with him.

It was not the nature of Phillip Arlines to be prompt in quarrel, or to resent any injury by a personal encounter, which would put his courage to the test. No; he was one of those malignant spirits who like to brood over what they consider their injuries, and think slowly of the means of avenging them.

He, therefore, suffered himself to be led into the villa by the captain, who flattered himself that he had succeeded in calming the rage that had really burnt itself out, and only remained smouldering and awaiting some more fitting opportunity to show itself.

"Now, my dear Arlines," reasoned the captain, "be patient, and we will think of some course to adopt as regards this headstrong young man, who has completely forfeited all regard I may have had for him."

"The scoundrel!" muttered Arlines. "I tell you my opinion of him, Captain Arnold; he is some needy adventurer, who has an eye to your daughter."

"My own suspicions run that way. But my mind is so—distracted, I was going to say, but annoyed is the better term—at the loss I have experienced in the gaming-house, that I forgot while he was here to mention it."

"My advice to you is certainly that you forbid him your house."

"That I shall assuredly do if I find, upon questioning Jessie, that he has endeavoured to make any impression upon her affections. Whatever may have been my opinions concerning him, they are now much changed, in consequence of his violent hostility to you."

"And, besides, if he affected any interest in your daughter's heart, it is to you he should have applied for permission to prosecute his suit, instead of watching you from home and then clandestinely holding meetings with your daughter."

"Do you think he has watched me from home?"

"There can be no doubt about it whatever, Captain Arnold. And there is one part of Pearson's conduct which I think deserving of the very severest reprehension—that is his presuming upon the gratitude of a young and artless girl as he has done by calling here in your absence upon so very short an acquaintance."

"That is, certainly, most ungenerous. I shall, in the strongest terms, inform him of my opinion."

"You have his address?"

"Yes; his card lies on the drawing-room table now."

"T en my advice to you is at once to write to him forbidding his future visits altogether, and declining his acquaintance. If he then should venture here, your own sense of honour can dicta'e to you what to do."

"A good plan. I will write at once; and then, that business being despatched, we can talk over this loss of mine, which really at the present time is troublesome."

Captain Arnold then wrote the following letter to Pearson, and then read it to Arlines, who approved of it very much :—

"Sir,—There are circumstances which quench even the liveliest feelings of gratitude. Your conduct in saving my child from the possible consequences of an accident, I consider such as to entitle you to my warmest esteem; but I need not enter into particulars further than saying that, for subsequent conduct not of an honourable or candid nature, I beg to decline the honour of your future acquaintance, and particularly reque-t that I may never hear of your calling at my house.

"I am, Sir, yours, &c.,
"AUGUSTUS ARNOLD."

This letter Phillip Arlines put in his pocket, promising that no time should be lost in posting it, and then he said,—

"Now, Arnold, that this little uncomfortable affair is so far settled, we will return to a consideration of your loss, which really should not for a moment distress you."

"Not distress me?"

"No; I will tell you why. You are sure to win it back again: you have but to persevere, and keep on increasing your stakes, when ultimately you must be a winner."

"Indeed!"

"Yes; that is the *rationale* of gaming. You have lost a thousand pounds: well, what then?"

"Why, then, I am a thousand pounds the poorer."

"For the present; but the way to place that all right is to go on playing. Don't you see, you cannot be always so unlucky."

"But I may."

"Impossible—impossible. Come again to-night, and redeem some of your loss; I feel assured you will. Trust to me, and play systematically, and you must come off a winner, and have all the amusement for nothing."

"The amusement is quite of the terrific order," remarked the captain, with a shudder. "A battle has not one half the excitement about it."

"Powerful minds," remarked Arlines, "require power'ul excitements, or else they prey on themselves, and wear out the body altogether. Besides, in going to this house, where for once you have been unlucky, you are sure of being in the very best society, and of receiving the most honourable treatment."

"My fortune is not very large."

"Oh, pho! pho!"

"And a few such losses as this would much embarrass me,"

"A few such losses? Why, you must not calculate upon them. Suppose, now, you go to-night and have a cast for two thousand."

"Two thousand!"

"Yes and lose."

"The deuce!"

"Well, then, you are three thousand minus."

"Of course."

"Then you stake four thousand."

"Tremendous!"

"Not at all: you lose or win. If the former, you stake eight thousand; if the latter, you win one thousand at once, and can then leave off if you like and play for small sums. Don't you see you *must* win."

"Well, I—I really do see."

"You cannot help it. By such a plan you cannot fail of becoming a winner. You perceive you invariably win, if you continue playing long enough, your original stake, whatever may be that amount."

"Certainly. Then if I persevere I win a thousand pounds without a doubt."

"Exactly so."

"But it strikes me as just possible that one's antagonist might not feel inclined to go on with such a system. It would be rather awkward, after doubling one's stakes for some time, and losing, to be left in the lurch."

"Ah, but at the house to which I have introduced you you will find none but men o. honour."

"There is something in that."

"That is everything. Come to-night. Make up your mind."

"I will venture."

There was at this moment a loud ring at the gate bell, and a servant came into the room to say that Mr. Arlines was wanted by two gentlemen.

"Two gentlemen!" exclaimed Arlines. "Who can they be, and how came they to know I was here?"

"Never mind that," cried the captain. "If they are friends of yours that is sufficient. Ask them in; they will be welcome here."

"But, really, the intrusion——"

"Is none at all."

At this moment the door was rather unceremoniously opened, and two men entered the room. The foremost one advanced to Phillip Arlines, and, laying a hand upon his arm, said—

"You are my prisoner, sir."

"Prisoner!" cried Captain Arnold, with unfeigned surprise.

"P isoner!" echoed Phillip Arlines, with feigned astonishment, for he had been on the tenter-hooks of impatience for some time past for the appearance of these very men.

"Yes," added the man; "I arrest you at the suit of Scratch, Darem, and Co., for the thousand pounds you were security for."

"What! has my old friend, Anderton, failed to pay?"

"He has. He lies dangerously ill, and cannot attend to business; so you see, Mr. Arlines, you are arrested, unless you can get some one else of undoubted respectability as well as yourself to put his name at the back of the bond."

"I am lost—lost!"

"Good God! what is all this?" said Captain Arnold. "Explain it to me, Mr. Arlines."

"The story is short. I have a friend—a dear friend—on whom I can rely. He wanted a thousand pounds, and knew he could be able to pay it by a certain day; and so he can, but you hear he lies on a bed of sickness. I became his security, and behold the consequence."

"Ah," remarked the officer, "I will say it's too bad, because Mr. Anderton can and will pay as soon as he get's well. But, you see, sir, the attorneys care for nothing nor nobody so long as they get costs."

"And I must go to prison," said Arlines, with a deep sigh. "Farewell, Captain Arnold, farewell!"

"Nay, nay," cried the captain; "cannot this be arranged?"

"Why, yes," said the officer, "if any gentleman will put his name on the back of the bond."

"Arlines, Arlines, why did you not apply to me?"

"To you! I could not bring my mind to do so. I knew your generosity would have prompted you to assist me immediately, and I likewise knew how safe it was, and yet I could not bear to ask you to incur even the shadow of a responsibility."

"You are too scrupulous. Officer, release your prisoner, and I will place my name to the bond."

"Will you, sir? Then all I can say is you're a real out-and-out gentleman. Here's the bond, sir; I happen to have it in my pocket-book, for Scratch and Darem said to me, 'If,' says they, 'Mr. Arlines, when you nabs him, can get some friend as is respectable at once to put his name to the bond, let him go; and so they gives it to me, you see, sir."

"This is a promissory note for a thousand pounds," said Captain Arnold, reading it.

"Yes, yes," said Arlines. "Do not sign it on my account, although it is a mere form."

"Pho, pho, I will."

The captain signed his name, during which some telegraphic signs passed between the parties, which had he seen would have effectu-

ally opened his eyes to the fact of a perfect understanding subsisting between Mr. Arlines and the officers.

CHAPTER XIX.

THE THIRD NIGHT OF GAMBLING.—THE CAPTAIN'S DESPAIR.—THE PROPOSAL OF PHILLIP ARLINES.

ONE hour after sunset the streets of London begin to present that peculiar and brilliant appearance that is caused by the magic display of lamps and lights in the many shop windows.

It was the hour of appointment made by the captain to meet Phillip Arlines, and once again to tempt his fate at the gaming-table. It was a melancholy thing to witness the course of events with one who had passed so blameless a life in the bosom of such a family—to see him now the dupe of an artful, designing villain.

Captain Arnold felt an uneasiness at heart that he could not divest himself of, and his loss much annoyed him, for he could not hide from his own knowledge that he could but ill afford to spend such a sum in such a manner; and his walk was embarrassed, and his manner irresolute, as he made his way towards the spot where the vice of gaming flourished.

He was perceived by Arlines, who immediately saw the state of his mind, and rightly guessing the cause, he stepped up to him, and said, in a friendly way—

"You don't look well, Arnold. I hope nothing has happened to disturb your digestion or equanimity? That fellow is not worth thinking about, much less causing yourself any uneasiness."

"Who?"

"Pearson."

"I was not thinking of him," replied Arnold. "I am well enough, thank you; how are you?"

"Oh, as I ever am; it is but little that ails me, you know. I am one of those that wear well at all times, and under all circumstances. A glass of wine will restore you to your wonted spirits."

Thus walking and talking they arrived at the house where Arnold had lost his money. The doors were immediately thrown open by the attendant, who knew at a glance that Arnold was no stranger, and that probably he was a victim to the demon that presides at these pandemoniums.

In they went, and the dazzling light once more fell upon Arnold's bewildered gaze. The lights, the company, the gaiety of all that surrounded him, the luscious and delicate wines,—all tended to raise his spirits, and infuse a species of gaiety in him that, false and fleeting as it was, served so far as to render him only anxious to enjoy the moment, and gave him a desire to mingle in the scene that was being enacted.

"You notice that gentleman who is playing at the table yonder?" said Arlines to Arnold, as they stood aloof and watched the play of the others; he with the medal."

THE MEETING IN THE GARDEN BETWEEN JESSIE AND ALFRED PEARSON.

"Yes," said Arnold.

"He won it some years ago from an old man, after he had won all he possessed besides."

The old man rushed from the house precipitately, and was followed by the conqueror.

"'My medal—my medal,' said the old man;

and no other answer could he obtain from him for some time, until he at length said,—

"'The medal was given me upon my promise that I would never part with it; and I have now lost it irrecoverably.'

"The old man's grief was so great, and so

severe, that he returned the medal to him, as he cared nothing for it, looking upon it as a mere stake, and of no great value.

"A few days afterwards he was requested to call at a handsome villa, which he did, though he was ignorant by whom he had been invited: and when he got there was shown into a splendid house, handsomely furnished, and then into an apartment, where he met with the same individual with whom he had played, and who introduced him to his daughter—a beautiful creature.

"Well," said Arlines, "to cut the matter short, he fell in love with her, and they were both married soon after, he received a handsome fortune with his wife, for the old man possessed a large property; but he was little known at this house, and, not being trusted, he was compelled to abstain either from play or risk his medal, which he for a time lost, and its restoration was so grateful to him that he never ceased heaping favours and wealth upon his son in-law.

"It is not many months since he died and left him heir to great possessions, and strictly enjoined him to wear the medal that had been the original cause of their close connexion and relationship. This, as you may very well imagine, he has no objection to, but continually wears it and the old black ribbon just as it was bequeathed to him."

"He has lost heavily," remarked Arnold to his companion, who had been endeavouring to amuse the captain's mind by the above relation.

"Yes, he does so occasionally, but then he plays constantly and never in the end loses. Sometimes he loses largely, but then, you see, he always plays, and perseverance in the end puts money in his pocket."

"But the risk must be great," said Arnold.

"No, not at all. But will you join the game? The table is vacated."

Captain Arnold again found himself in the height of the game. His spirits rose, but yet he trembled, and he knew not that he was closely watched by his friend Arlines, who never lost sight of him.

He played with varying success, sometimes a winner and sometimes a loser. His mind was at moments a prey to the pangs of despair, when he contemplated his loss; and then again his feelings would rise from the depths of wretchedness to a rush of joy at some sudden turn of fortune, and he would then contemplate the wealth he believed himself acquiring, and the good to which he would apply it. Then came the revulsion of feeling, the knowledge that he was losing; and then he became seriously and painfully absorbed in the progress of the game before him.

It was his last stake, his last sum; and it was with a painful and trembling interest that Captain Arnold watched the course of the game

he was playing, the result of which would be of the greatest importance to him; and he saw with much anxiety that the game was running against him.

It was but a few moments more and he sat there with the knowledge that he had lost a very heavy sum—three thousand pounds had changed owners.

This was disastrous; but Arlines whispered encouragement into his ear, and the stake was doubled. Six thousand pounds was now staked upon the merest chance in the world. What a sum to be dependant upon the colour or name of a card!

The card was turned and the sum changed owners.

The antagonist of Captain Arnold now rose, and coolly placing what he had won in his pocket, he was about to quit the table, when Captain Arnold said,—

"Do you not play any more?"

"No," he replied, "I don't feel inclined. I have an engagement to keep, and I cannot stay here any longer, I shall wish you, therefore, a good evening."

Captain Arnold was much annoyed that his antagonist should thus quit him, at a moment when he had just enriched himself at his expense, and now refused him his revenge. He rose also.

"You cannot mean," he said, "that—that you leave now, when you are so large a winner?"

"Hush! hush!" whispered Arlines. "You know I explained to you it was a rule of the house that any one might leave off playing when he chose."

"Explain be d——d!" cried Captain Arnold.

"For Heaven's sake, Arnold, be calm."

"Calm——"

"Sir," said the captain's antagonist, "I am sorry I am compelled to leave now, but I will meet you another night, and resume our game at the point precisely where now I am obliged to leave it off. I have the honour, gentlemen, to wish you a very good evening."

Arnold sank into a chair, and said no more. He then leant his head upon his hand for some moments, after which he suddenly cried,— "Wine!—wine!" in a tone that startled every one in the rooms, and made him for an instant the general contemplation.

The players, however, in these saloons were too accustomed to such sudden outbreaks of temper on the part of those who lost largely to take any further notice of the captain's sudden ebullition of feeling, and in another instant everything was going on in its ordinary channel.

The wine was immediately brought to Captain Arnold in obedience to his vociferous demand for it, for in such places the proprietors find it largely to their interests to provide an unlimited supply of stimulants to their guests.

He quaffed off four or five large glasses in as many minutes, and then rising he said to Phillip Arlines, who was watching his proceedings with no small degree of interest,—

" Well, it cannot be helped ; I shall meet him again. How much have I lost ?"

" Oh, not much—not much. Don't you recollect ?"

" Not exactly. I don't feel quite clear about anything just now, do you know."

" No, indeed."

" No. If I didn't know the contrary, I should almost imagine I had been drinking."

" Oh, dear, quite the reverse. No one could accuse you of being in the slightest degree intoxicated."

" I should like to hear anybody do so. I ain't a quarrelsome man, but I defy all the world."

" Very proper—very proper, indeed. Do you think of going home now, captain ?"

" Why, yes, I think I shall. To-morrow evening I will meet that vagabond again who has won my money, and have my revenge out of him. I recollect the system—always double."

" Hush ! hush ! For Heaven's sake do not expose to every one who may be within hearing how we play."

" Ay, ay, mum's the word—caution. What's o'clock ?"

" Late, or rather early. I am going a part of your way, and we can walk together. I have something rather particular to say to you, and I can say it as we go along."

" Very good. Won't you take a glass of wine ?"

" None for me."

" Then I will. Wine, here, wine."

Captain Arnold tossed off some more wine; and then, leaning heavily upon the arm of the man who was tempting him to destruction, he left the gaming-house.

CHAPTER XX.

THE PROPOSAL.—MR. PHILLIP ARLINES' EX-TRAORDINARY CLEVERNESS.—THE CON-FEDERATES.

No sooner had Captain Arnold quitted the gaming-house than the fresh air of the streets tended to restore him somewhat to himself, instead of, as is usually the case with most people, increasing the state of intoxication in which he was.

He and Phillip Arlines walked and talked for some time, until the latter thought this a favourable moment to open upon a project he had in his mind, and which he had long thought of.

" Well, you have been a looser to-night,

Arnold," said Arlines ; " but you may yet be a gainer by the affair,"

" I can't say I clearly see how it is to be done," replied Arnold.

" A steady perseverance will do all that I have predicted. Another game, and you might have turned the whole of your cash into your own pockets again."

" But he would play no more, and there is a certain stop to all plans of gain ; for how can you win when a man won't play ?"

" That appears unanserable, but it is not so ; on the contrary, you might have played with any one else and done the same. But you need not fear ; we shall see him again, and then you can have your chance of winning your cash back."

" I know not what to say," said Arnold, carelessly ; " I may or I may not, I cannot say just yet. Circumstances alter cases considerably, you know—I may not feel inclined."

" That, of course depends so entirely upon yourself,' replied Arlines, " that I may say you have the means of meeting completely in your hands."

" True ; but the sum I have lost is a heavy one to be so disposed of, and all for the mere gratification of a moment."

" You look at it in a wrong light, Arnold," said Arlines. " It is not so ; you do not play so much for the mere gratification of playing ; were it so, none would play. It is because there is a changing of notes, and because there is so much of uncertainty in the result. There is a sum staked against a sum, and it is to win this you strive. There is something like ex-citation in the thought ; your whole heart and soul is engaged, and it is for this reason you play, and not for that you mentioned."

" Well, you may be right, Arlines," replied Arnold, " I won't deny it."

" I could," rejoined Arlines, " say much ; and there is one thing I wish to say, and yet scarce know how to say it."

" Indeed !"

" Yes, it is this. I could put you in possession of a plan to recover all you have lost, and to net a considerable sum by the transaction."

" Could you ?"

" I could, I assure you."

" And how could it be done ? If you know you will name it."

" There's the difficulty," said Arlines."

" The difficulty ?" repeated Captain Arnold. " I cannot for my life see it."

" It is this : there are certain conditions to be complied with first. So important an affair cannot be the mere subject of a communication which can have but little or no object ; on the contrary, the secret I posess would be worth a most ample fortune instead of aught less."

" Then those who have a fortune could only buy it. I know that at that price only that one thing could be purchased ; but let me know, though only for the sake of knowing, the price you set upon this wonderful secret."

"I will tell you," replied Arlines, gravely. "It is this. Make your daughter, Jessie, my wife, and I undertake to put you in possession of a secret that will enable you to make a large sum of money."

"My daughter's the price ?"

"It is so," replied Arlines, "and were it not that the price is great, and the value commensurate, I would not ask it."

"It is a matter that requires more consideration than I at the present moment can give to it."

"Well, well," replied Arlines; "it is a matter to be thought of. Consider it well, and think it over in your own mind, and then determine."

"I will," said Arnold, as he laid his hand on the bell at his own gate, for they had walked thus far talking to each other.

"Then I will bid you farewell," said Phillip Arlines, as he shook the captain by the hand.

"Good night, Arlines !" replied the captain, returning the pressure of Arlines' hand.

The two now parted, Captain Arnold to his own meditations, and Phillip Arlines to his, which were of a totally different character.

"The plot thickens," he thought; "but why should I play other people's game ? Why should I be content to take a share when I can grasp the whole ? It shall be so.

"It would, independently of any other motive, be a good thought to turn the tables on Rollington. If I could outwit these men who deem themselves impregnable, that they are assailable on no point, and who never yet omitted to take advantage of the first chance that was offered them.

"Yes, yes, it must be so; the marquis would, indeed, do the like if he had the opportunity.

"If I can I will marry the daughter of Arnold, this Jessie ; there will be some trouble, I dare say, but her scruples will be easily overcome by parental authority; and when I am once her husband it will be to my interest to protect the captain from Rollington and his confederates.

"Indeed, it will be to my interest to render them perfectly innoxious, and this can only be done by depriving them of their means to do so. This I can easily do by setting them on the captain, and causing them to lose all, or nearly so, for the purpose of drawing him, in which of course they fail by his knowledge of what they have in view.

"This would, indeed, be a capital idea—an excellent idea ; and it shall not be my fault if I do no carry this into operation. But Arnold must win ; he is becoming anxious and

uneasy at his losses. It will not do to frighten him, else all his lost."

Full of these thoughts, and well pleased with the plan he had formed of tricking his companions in iniquity, he walked quickly, and presently came in collision with some one, and, on turning round, saw his fellow associate, Rollington.

"Ah, Rollington," he said, "where so fast ? You are in haste to-night."

"Not in the least, for I am at you service," replied his companion.

"Then come this way; I am going townwards. I should die of ennui if I had to live out in these dull quarters."

"No doubt. A man could only drink himself into a melancholy madness, and then, by way of a change, send one to St. Luke's."

"Ah, well, you have time enough for that yet."

"You have been home with Arnold, have you not ?" said Rollington.

"Yes, I have."

"Well in what sort of a humour did you leave him ? He drank very freely."

"He did, but got better afterwards ; the air operated to his advantage ; but he was in a fitful mood. Do you know I strongly suspect that if he keeps losing we shall lose the game altogether."

"You don't say so ?"

"I do. He seems to chafe over his loss very much. I think it will be advisable to let the line of luck take a change."

"He may play no more then," replied Rollington, apprehensively.

"I have no doubt of that; he will be more inclined to play boldly, thinking he will have an equal chance. Now, however, he thinks he has a run of ill luck which he cannot overcome, and which it is merely ruin to try."

"Well, well, we must see what can be done in the affair; it would be a pity to spoil all."

CHAPTER XXI.

MR. JOHN SMITH AND THE I O U.—A DIM RECOLLECTION OF LAST NIGHT'S OCCURRENCES.

THE morning following the last events just recorded was bright and fair, but this sadly contrasted with the state of body and mind in which Captain Arnold found himself.

A dim but very indistinct recollection of what took place on the preceding evening recurred to his mind. He knew where he had been, and that it was in the company of Arlines, and some others, and had played.

Further than this all was vague and uncertain; he fancied he had lost, but could not say whether he had or had not.

His state of uncertainty was greatly aided and increased by a dreadful headache; his temples throbbed violently, and he turned in his bed, but it was an effort that he could scarce be induced to repeat.

The captain's reflections were but little consolatory, for he blamed himself for the part he must have enacted during the previous evening. His regret was increased when he found his recollection was so uncertain and indistinct that he could not tell what he lost, if lose he did, which somehow or other he believed he did.

This was particularly a source of annoyance, and he accused himself of acting with the most egregious folly, an unpardonable want of common discretion; and he made so much of a resolve as a man under his disagreeable condition could do, that he would not go near such places of amusement again.

Many incoherent and undigested thoughts passed through his mind as he lay a victim to the after effects of previous intoxication, which were anything but such as to render reflection either easy or pleasant; and the captain felt but ill pleased with himself and the world in general.

Soon after a servant knocked at the door of his room, saying,—.

"Please, sir, there's a gentleman below who wants to see you."

"To see me! What's his business?"

"I don't know," replied the attendant; "all he said was I was to tell you he wished to see you."

"Then go and learn who he is."

While the girl was gone, Captain Arnold rose and dressed himself; and when she returned she said that the gentleman's name was Smith, and he wished to see Captain Arnold particularly.

"Smith—Smith?" replied Captain Arnold. "I have no knowledge of such a person, nor can I conceive how he can call upon me, or what for."

His thoughts, however, tended but little to help him out of difficulty. He soon dressed himself, and descended the stairs, and entering the apartment he perceived Mr. Smith, a very common kind of personage, who rose, however, to receive him.

"Good morning, sir, said Mr. Smith.

"Good morning," replied the captain. "To what am I indebted for this visit?"

"Ah, I see you do not recollect me, Captain Arnold. That, however, is of no consequence; but allow me to say, sir, that I recollect you."

"Possibly; but as I do not know you, you will be good enough to afford me the explanation I require."

"Certainly, 'tis but reasonable: my name is John Smith. You recollect, I daresay, where you were in St. James's-street last evening, in company with your friend, Mr. Arlines."

"Yes," said Captain Arnold, "I do;" and at the same time Captain Arnold felt exceedingly nervous from some cause that he could not well explain, even to himself.

"Well, sir, I had the honour of playing with you, and accepted your memorandum for the amount of your losses."

"My losses!" repeated Arnold, somewhat surprised. "What, I lost then? Well, I suppose I did."

"You did, indeed."

"And what was the amount of my losings?" inquired the captain, dubiously.

"Only a trifle—a mere trifle I assure you, Captain Arnold," said Mr. John Smith, in a very off-hand, easy manner, handing at the same time an I O U that the captain had given him.

"Why, I suppose I could not have lost much," said Arnold; but his eyes dilated considerably when he perceived the sum.

"It is quite right, as you perceive," remarked Mr. John Smith.

"I am not quite sure of that," remarked the captain, still holding out the I O U before his eyes; "I could never have lost this sum. It is monstrous, and impossible."

"Not only possible, but true," remarked Mr. John Smith; "and I will submit to an appeal to any one who was present, although such a course has never yet been pursued with regard to debts of honour."

Mr. John Smith laid great stress upon the last three words; but it had not the intended effect upon the captain, who was too much absorbed in the contemplation of his loss to notice the insinuation.

"It must be some mistake—I could not have forgotten such a sum so completely as I have this," he remarked, rather to himself than to his visitor, though perfectly audible.

"You had taken a little wine, Captain Arnold, and perhaps more since, and hence your forgetfulness of the circumstance."

The captain paused; he had been drinking wine he knew; but yet such a loss, he thought, would have sobered him.

"The hand writing is yours, is it not, Captain Arnold?" said Mr. John Smith, losing patience.

"Yes, I believe so; I am not sure."

"This is very extraordinary, I must say; however, your admission is enough. Lost or not, you have given your signature for six thousand pounds, and you would scarce do that, did you not owe it."

Just at this juncture Mr. Phillip Arlines was announced, and the captain desired he might be admitted.

"Captain Arnold," said Arlines, "I am happy to see you up; I feared I should disturb.

Ah! you have your opponent of last night with you; perhaps I am *de trop*."

"Not at all, I assure you," replied Captain Arnold, shaking hands; "you are the very individual I wished most to see above all others. Perhaps you can help to solve what to me appears to be a mystery."

"I'll do my best," replied Arlines, laughing.

"Well, look at that I O U, and tell me what you think of it."

Arlines took the paper and read it through very attentively, and then returned it to Arnold saying, unconcernedly,—

"It is all right, I believe; and, besides, Mr Smith is too respectable a man to have anything to do with aught dishonourable."

"I lost this sum then you think?"

"Yes, you did; I saw you write the I O U myself," replied Arlines; "and you promised to pay it this morning."

"Did I?" said Arnold, much surprised. "I have not the smallest remembrance of it."

"It is as you have been informed," said Mr. John Smith; "and I hope I have not to learn that I did wrong in accepting your signature."

"You had better pay at once," remarked Arlines; "you are sure to have your revenge."

"I have not so much at my banker's," said Arnold, after a moment's pause; "but I can sell out."

"That will do," said Mr. Smith. "If you will give me written instructions to your broker to sell out stock, that will answer as well as a cheque."

Upon this Captain Arnold wrote the required letter of instruction, and handed it over to Mr. John Smith, who instantly returned the I O U, and, with a bow, took his departure.

This was a great blow to Captain Arnold, who considered the loss of so much money as a great piece of folly on his own part; and, at the solicitation of Arlines, he left the house to enjoy the cool morning air in the garden.

"By the way, Arnold," said Arlines, "do you recollect a proposition that I made to you last night before we parted?"

"I have some remembrance of something being said, though I cannot say what it was; perhaps you can inform me."

"It was this," said Arlines, "that if I were your son-in-law I could then put you in possession of means not only to recover all you have lost, but a considerable sum besides; indeed, you might make a handsome fortune."

"But then Jessie——"

"Must be mine."

"That could not well be, for I would never coerce her to marry. It must be some one of her own free choice, for I hold the influence, even of a parent, ought rather to be used as a corrective than an inductive in cases of this kind; but she is yet by far too young to think of marriage I hope for years."

"But that does not prevent me from becoming her suitor. Let me be received as an acknowledged suitor, and all others discouraged, and leave me to make my way to her heart myself."

"I can't tamper with my child's affections," replied Arnold. I must leave that affair to be settled at some future time, but not now or without her consent; but tell me what was the plan, you cannot mean to make that a condition."

"Oh, no, no; the plan I had was the same as what I told you of before, and that is to persevere, and win you must."

"Yes; but my next stakes will be twelve thousand pounds, and that will go nigh to make a beggar of me. To play at that fearful rate would, indeed, be reckless; but I have not the capital—I must cease to play."

CHAPTER XXI.

THE words of Captain Arnold made some impression upon Phillip Arlines; and as he quitted the captain's house he thought that they had acted somewhat too indiscreetly in thus early winning so heavy a sum from so careful and considerate a man as Captain Arnold. He ought to have won before, and become thoroughly initiated in the game, so much so as to feel that there was a much greater fluctuation in luck than the gamesters usually permit.

It was with the view of impressing his companion in iniquity with this view of the case he made his way to a tavern in the neighbourhood of Piccadilly, where he expected to see Viscount Rollington and his companions.

He reached the spot, and was not disappointed in finding them already assembled, and he greeted them.

"Why, how now, Arlines," said the viscount, facetiously. "I have not seen you look so moody and melancholy for I don't know how long. Surely you are unwell, or unmindful of the glorious success we have had."

"It is the cause of all this that makes me melancholy," replied Arlines.

"Well, tell us the truth, then, for we are too impatient to hear riddles."

"It is this, then," said Arlines; "you have won heavily of Arnold."

"Yes, and have the money, or its security, by this time."

"Yes, you have; but it was not paid without some reluctance, and unless the tide of luck changes you'll lose your bird."

This intimation produced a considerable effect upon the features of all present, and Viscount Rollington, after a pause, inquired,—

"What would you advise. Arlines? You are our director in this affair."

"I would strongly advise you to let him win."

"Win," said one. "It's a hard case to part with cool cash at any rate."

"It may be," said Arlines; "and yet, if it be not done, I predict that the next time he sits down to play will be the last, if I can induce him to do so much."

"It requires much consideration," said Rollington. "But, Arlines, do you really think that if he were to win he would be induced to play again? He is not anxious to come the old soldier, is he?"

"Ah, that ought to be thought of," said a gentleman in green spectacles.

"As for the latter part of your inquiry, Rollington," said Arlines, "it must answer itself; for the captain cannot play the old soldier, since he can suspect nothing."

"Certainly, I see."

"Well, then, as to his playing again, I am sure he would, for he does not really dislike play—on the contrary, he has rather a taste for it, but is afraid to indulge in it for fear of the consequences. He has seen none of the vicissitudes, none of the chances; it has been all loss to him and no gain, and hence it is that he is fast losing even the pleasure he first felt."

"Well," said Rollington, "I think we ought to forego a little immediate triumph to ensure us a good round sum, such as you say Arnold is worth."

"Yes, he is ours, I know, if we act with discretion; and an ample fortune will be divided amongst us, which we are as sure to lose by over precipitancy."

"Well, then, it shall be so; and the next time we meet him," said Viscount Rollington, "we will allow him his revenge. Shall that be the resolve?"

"Yes, yes," replied those present; "let him win."

While this scene was being enacted among the confederates, with Arlines and Rollington as their chiefs, to lure to destruction their unfortunate victim, Captain Arnold himself was in a state of mind not easily described.

Fully alive to the impropriety of the course he was pursuing, and the utter ruin and degradation of character that would be the certain consequences of his present course of conduct, he was yet unable to form any stern resolve by which he might throw off the malignant genius that hovered over him like a black and threatening cloud.

A prey to remorse and the most melancholy reflections, he re-entered the house after Phillip Arlines's departure, and shut himself up in his own room, anxious to escape from the observation even of his own daughter, whom, indeed, he wished not to face.

He became painfully aware that his recent transactions could be neither more nor less than of a gambling nature, and that, too, accompanied by excess in the use of wine. These reflections became very painful to him, and he walked about his apartment with a disordered step and aching heart, for he was really much distressed in mind at what had occurred.

Thus he continued for some time, alternately blaming his own folly, and then contemplating the precipice upon which he stood. Of Phillip Arlines, Arnold often thought, and many doubts crossed his mind, and the words of Alfred Pearson more than once occurred to his recollection; but Arlines had such a hold upon his imagination, that the captain could scarce be said to be able to free himself from the influence he possessed over him.

A low knock at his room door now aroused him. He wished to know who was there, for he almost feared to meet the gaze of Jessie, and something told Arnold that it was his daughter who thus demanded admission. While he was debating in his own mind, or rather while he was thus standing irresolute, the knocking was repeated in a louder key, and Captain Arnold at once opened the door quietly, and looked into the passage, where he saw Jessie standing with a saddened countenance.

"What, Jessie," said Arnold, "did you knock?"

"Yes," she replied, "I did; I feared you had not heard me."

"What do you want?"

"I want to speak to you if you can spare me but a few minutes, father."

"Come in, my dear child," said the captain, affectionately taking her hand, for he saw that she was very sad and melancholy, "and tell me what it is that you want."

"I come, father, to beg that you will go no more away from me during the evening; it makes me very unhappy, and I don't think you yourself appear the happier for it."

"Hush! hush! Jessie, you should not talk thus; I was but in the company of Mr. Arlines and Viscount Rollington."

"Ay, father," replied Jessie, sadly; "but it is they whom I so much dread. There are no others that we are acquainted with, or even have known, whose habits are the same."

"You speak, I fear, Jessie, from prejudice against Mr. Arlines. He is an old friend, and one to whom we are under some obligation to treat with consideration and respect."

"While he deserves it, father, certainly; but tell me, has he done so recently?"

"And why not, Jessie?"

"Need I say ask your own heart, father? How have you returned home lately—heated, and filled with disappointment, unwell next day, and then more appointments with this man."

"I have appointments, it is true, with Mr. Arlines. Jessie, and I have been out with him and others; but do you not watch your father's conduct a little too closely that you note an occasion when he has taken a glass or two of wine more than usual? Is this decent, Jessie?"

"Father, father," said Jessie, "your own heart does not dictate such an answer to me. Your sadness and unhappiness does not arise from that cause, but, I think, from the loss of money to Arlines and some of his confederates."

"I have lost a little; but money, you know, Jessie, is not happiness."

"No, father, I well know that happiness and money are not identical; and yet the loss you have sustained has made you very unhappy, therefore the connection is very intimate indeed. One is very much dependant upon the other, and you would never like to hold your way in society by means upon which these men exist and make an appearance."

"I have your welfare, Jessie, and that of my other children too much at heart ever to do anything that could in any remote degree affect them or you. Believe me, Jessie, you are inexperienced, and much and needlessly alarmed."

"I hope so, indeed; but, father, will you make me happy, and say you will not go out any more with Mr. Arlines?"

"My dear Jessie, I cannot consent to bind myself—it would be needless and very absurd. Your uneasiness is groundless: I love you all too much to hurt you; but you are unnecessarily harsh upon Arlines."

CHAPTER XXII.

THE TURN OF FORTUNE.—THE LAST STAKE. ARNOLD'S INSENSIBILITY.

THAT evening—the same as that of the day on which Jessie Arnold had made an appeal to her father in the hope that she would be able to extract a promise from him that should have for its object his absence from the company of Phillip Arlines; but she failed, signally failed, and was put off by her father with the assurance that he loved her and his children too well to wrong them—that evening the captain was again in the St. James's-street hell, and with him, of course, Arlines, Rollington, and others, known and unknown to him.

The scene presented the usual gaiety and splendour, the usual and many temptations; but Captain Arnold talked much with Rollington and Arlines, and did not at first play. Indeed, he amused himself for some time by looking on, and appeared not much inclined to play; but, ere long, he found himself seated, and engaged with an opponent.

Fortune at first frowned, and then the captain became a winner of a stake, and all his money was again his own, besides the amount of his stake. If ever Captain Arnold felt a sudden revulsion of feeling from sorrow to joy it was when he knew that he was better off than when he first began.

Arlines observed the effect this temporary turn of fortune gave him, and instantly guessed the state of his mind, and he came forward to speak to him.

"Well," said Arlines, "did I not tell you you must win? I knew fortune could not entirely desert you—on, the contrary, she would be sure to right you."

"Yes, I have at last won; but my stake was all I have gained, and that, you know, is not much; but yet, little as I have, I would not like to risk it again."

"Risk it again!"

"Yes, I think it is now just the moment to rise and leave off."

"Leave off!" exclaimed Arlines, in astonishment. "You surely would not think of it."

"I have seriously thought of it," replied the captain; "I intend to do so too. Would you yourself not seriously advise me to do so?"

"Certainly not. Never turn your back upon Fortune, is a maxim which I would advise you to adhere to."

The captain hesitated, and appeared to think in his own mind that this was the most favourable moment that could happen for him to leave off; another might not occur, and then he should be lost. All came with fearful force to his mind, and lastly the appeal of Jessie was not without its effect, and the captain had just in his own mind resolved to play no more, when Arlines said,—

"Do you not hear your opponent crying for his revenge? Give it him if you play no more; it is a rule you cannot well break through—a courtesy which each individual expects, and which cannot well be refused."

"I claim my revenge, Captain Arnold," exclaimed the last player. "I never played so badly. I was unduly beaten; I ought to have been a winner."

"Indeed!" exclaimed Arnold. "We can't all be winners, you know."

"I am aware of that, sir; and I have reason of late to know it."

The captain, however, took some wine that Arlines handed to him, and drank several glasses off, and after some more conversation he sat down to resume the play, when an accident occurred that alarmed the whole of the assembled company.

A sudden and tremendous crash took place, followed by total darkness, that caused all present to believe that the world was suddenly about to cease to exist. The great chandelier had fallen, and covered the principal table with

ARNOLD FINDS JESSY ASLEEP, ON HIS RETURN HOME

fragments. Many gentlemen found themselves covered with minute particles of glass.

Phillip Arlines never quitted Arnold, but kept him engaged in conversation until all the effects of the accident were swept off, and then he said,—

"Will you resume your game with your opponent, whom I have not seen these few minutes ?"

"He has no doubt left," replied Arnold. "I ought to have done so too, for I really believe the fall was a warning to me not to stay any longer."

"Pooh! pooh!" said Arlines. "Here,

Rollington," to that gentleman, "did you ever hear of going home ?"

"Impossible !" replied Rollington; "I cannot believe it; besides, there's the gentleman who is patiently seated watching the moment you are ready to resume play with him."

"No, no," said Arnold; "I shall play no more this night, I assure you."

"Well, well, do as you please," said Arlines; "but you will not leave us till we go ? Have some wine, I have had none myself."

So saying, he ordered wine.

Captain Arnold drank heartily of wine while he was in this heated atmosphere; and being artfully kept engaged in conversation by first one and then another, his spirits became elevated, and he was soon in a state to hear their offers for playing again.

It was not long before he felt himself again seized with the desire of acquiring large sums by these means, and Arlines said,—

"That man who has just risen has won a heavy sum; his fortune, I believe, is made. Why, don't you do the like?"

"I have tried, you know, and how very unlucky I have been."

"I think the reverse; you are a winner, and yet you call yourself unlucky. Well, it is unusual to consider winning a misfortune."

"True; but it was at the twelfth hour, you know," said Arnold.

"What matters that? you had it in time, and cannot complain. At all events, fortune acted kindly, and you not only recovered what you had lost, but more also."

"I did."

"Well, then, you cannot complain of what you have received at her hands. Do as you please, but your career has opened well for you; if you neglect it you will be no gainer, though fortune smile on you ever so kindly. But I shall reap no benefit, therefore follow your own inclination."

"Well, Captain Arnold," said the individual with whom he had been playing, "do you intend to grant me my revenge? You are a winner by me, and I presume, as a gentleman, you will grant me what I require."

This appeal was made when Captain Arnold was surrounded by friends and many strangers, and all eyes were upon him as his opponent spoke, and placed him in a position only to accede; for what motive could he allege for a refusal? Certainly none that would be considered as current there; and, beside, he could not refuse, primed as he had been with wine and conversation by Arlines and Viscount Rollington.

Captain Arnold, therefore, intimated his compliance with the request that had been made him, and once more sat down to the table, where he was soon immersed in the vortex of all the anxieties and pleasures that so completely fill the soul of the gamester.

Phillip Arlines stood a little apart, with his eyes fixed on Arnold. With a look of intense interest, he watched every movement; every stray expression fell upon his ears with distinctness; all else was a blank, and Arlines saw but Captain Arnold and his adversary, who was engaged at play with him.

Rollington, too, watched the play with much earnestness and even anxiety. Many others also stopped in their play, for the play had become high, and heavy stakes were lost by Arnold, who played on recklessly, despite the losses he had sustained and the heavy sums he was staking.

The whole place, splendidly illuminated as it was, shone upon anxious and interested faces. Not a muscle moved, nor a breath was heard above the rest,—all was quiet and still save the two players, and their words were short and few.

The stakes were won—Arnold had again lost; but he doubled his stakes. If this were lost also it would be his last stake, for it would make him a beggar.

The lips of the captain were dry and hard, and bloodless, and his features showed the extreme anxiety, the fearful state of mind up to which he had been brought; his temples throbbed quickly and he breathed short.

His companion was the reverse; he, too, was anxious, but there was an air of calm and quiet about him that contrasted strongly with Arnold. A compressed smile was on his lips, which he subdued for the sake of decency rather than aught else; he was cool, confident, and cunning.

The play was over—Captain Arnold lost; he rose, staggered, and exclaimed,—

"Lost! lost! all lost!" and fell back in the chair in a state of insensibility.

Restoratives were immediately sent for, and a coach at the same time, which, when it arrived, he was placed in, still insensible, by Rollington and Arlines, and then orders were given to drive him homewards.

CHAPTER XXIII.

INTERVIEW BETWEEN PHILLIP ARLINES AND JESSIE ARNOLD.—THE PROPOSAL AND REJECTION.

THE next morning was one of much sadness to Jessie Arnold, who knew from the late hour that had arrived, and her father yet kept his room, that he had been in the company of Arlines, and had probably lost some money. This was a sad and melancholy reflection to one so young and so innocent.

The incidents of her early life were few; joy and contentment had hitherto been her lot, and sorrow and misfortune were strangers. But then her mother lived; but now, deprived by a lamentable accident of maternal aid and guidance and thrown upon the resources of her own mind for guidance and conduct, she appeared, young and beautiful as she was, to be suddenly animated by superior intelligence and rectitude.

What a change from her former life was this! Sorrow and sadness sat upon her brow; her sorrow was not for herself, but for her father, whom she believed to be the dupe of a designing and artful villain. In her judgment of Phillip Arlines she might have been influenced by the statement of Alfred Pearson; but all the latter had said was daily becoming more and more evident; and she, therefore, implicitly credited all he had said, and firmly believed in her own mind that Arlines was a much worse character than was even represented to her.

Her regret was very great when she discovered the influence this man had upon her father and his unwillingness to believe any assertion that agreed not with his notions of honour and of Arlines, for he deemed them identical. And yet Jessie thought that recently her father could not avoid judging from what he must have witnessed in Arlines' company, but that he studiously avoided the subject.

While these and like thoughts passed through her mind, a knock at the street door announced a visitor.

"That man Arlines, I dare say," sighed Jessie, "to see my father, and obtain from him a promise and an appointment, or probably induce him to confirm one alleged to be given over night. I am sure Arlines would not be particular as to what he asserted."

At this moment a servant entered the room, saying—

"Mr. Arlines, miss."

"My father is not yet stirring, tell Mr. Arlines, and that I do not think he can be seen for some time."

"I said so, Miss Jessie; but Mr. Arlines wishes to speak to you."

"To me!" said Jessie, surprised.

"Yes, Miss Arnold," said Phillip Arlines, pushing past the girl, and entering the apartment.

The servant retired, and Jessie, much embarrassed at this assurance, for some seconds scarce knew how to act; but at length she said, rising, and looking at him very earnestly—

"And what, Mr. Arlines, can you have to say to me?"

"Much, Miss Arnold," said Arlines, with an air of gallantry that to Jessie appeared most disgusting and annoying.

"Let me hear it, sir, as shortly as possible, for I have but little time to spare; and yet I think you had better reserve it for my father's ears than mine."

"Not so; for what I have to say concerns yourself most nearly."

"Indeed!"

"Yes; listen to me, Miss Arnold. It cannot but be evident to you that I have long felt those feelings towards you which can only be engendered by the pure and beautiful like yourself."

"Sir!" said Jessie, looking gravely, but not discomfited at this address.

"Yes, Jessie—allow me to call you by that name; it is a name I adore."

"Come, sir, this is trash. I cannot sit with patience and listen to it."

"Nay, say not so; young maidens are impatient, I know; but such a point is a tender one, and I am anxious not to overstep the bounds of prudence. But you will, I am sure, grant me that indulgence the circumstances claim, and show me that courtesy usual on such an occasion."

"I cannot show you the courtesy I do not feel; and, certainly, neither you nor your address deserve any."

"Say not so, charming Jessie; I have your welfare at heart. My love for you—and I love you most tenderly—has long since caused me to seek an opportunity of declaring my passion for you; but I have hitherto been unable to effect my object. Deign, then, dear girl, to look upon my suit with favour, and to return my affection with your own love."

Mr. Arlines at this juncture approached Jessie in a familiar manner, and attempted to take her hand; but she repulsed him, saying, while indignation glowed in her face,—

"Keep your seat, Mr. Arlines, I did not expect to be thus insulted, and yet I ought to have done so."

"Insulted?"

"Yes, sir. I repeat, insulted. I have allowed you to finish your proposal, because I would not make any mistake about the nature of it; but be assured I can now thoroughly appreciate your character."

"I am happy at least in being understood," said Arlines, with unblushing effrontery, again attempting to seize her hand. "I feared you would misconstrue me."

"No, no, you need not have feared that, and, although others thought I did, yet I have never mistaken you. This insult I shall inform my father of, and you may depend upon it that it forms a sufficient reason to induce him to close the doors against one who ought never to have been allowed to enter them."

"Close these doors against me—complain to your father, Jessie? Surely you are dreaming: it can never be done."

"Not be done?" exclaimed Jessie, much annoyed and alarmed at the tone and manner of Arlines, which carried a conviction to her heart that, but for her distrust of the man, she could have sunk to her seat.

"No, not be done, Jessie. Your father is in my power. All he possesses is under my control. Say what you will to him, and urge him to break faith with me, and I can ruin him, and consign him, any day I please, to a prison. Be advised, and keep your own counsel."

Jessie could hear no more, but, with a look of indignation, she walked to the door. Before leaving the room, she turned and said,—

"I could not have believed that I stood in the presence of so bad a man. It is unfitting

I should continue longer in such society. If what you say be true, how true also must that be that we have been told concerning you."

Arlines was much vexed at the manner in which Jessie had treated him, and her last words were bitter even to him, inured to vice, profligacy, and crime as he was; but the most innocent have often the greatest power to inflict a severe wound.

Captain Arnold rose soon after, and by the time he entered the room where Phillip Arlines was yet seated the latter had recovered his equanimity, which had been somewhat disturbed by Jessie. He had had time to make up his mind as to the course to be pursued.

Arnold's appearance was greatly altered indeed; the effects of wine were visible, drugged as it was, yet the effects of mental anxiety and distress were plainly visible over and above the effects of mere intemperance. Arnold at first avoided the eyes of Arlines, but at length said,—

"Last night has decided my fate; I'm a ruined, a lost man. Why, oh, why did I yield to your invitations and solicitations to go to such a place of ruin? Had it not been for you, Arlines, I should yet have been a happy man, and now ruin and distress surround me."

"This is useless lamenting, Arnold," replied Arlines. "Your loss, great no doubt, ought not thus to affect you."

"I am mad, Arlines. I dare not look my children in their faces when I think of the ruin and distress I have brought to their door—ay, they'll even be turned from the house that shelters them."

"You need not apprehend such harsh measures as that; all may not yet be so bad as you anticipate. Think and recover the tone of your mind, and you will see that even yet much may be done to save yourself."

"Save myself—how—when? When did you ever hear of the soft heartedness of a gambler? The debt is due and will be rigidly demanded."

"There are yet means by which much of your property may be regained. I doubt not but by exerting my influence to the utmost, I may so far be able to aid you by delaying the time when the demand is to be made."

"Do, do, and I will thank you. And yet why should I thus delay payment? It must come, and all will be lost."

"But your children, Arnold, will require a home for a time. Stay here, therefore, and I will exert for your benefit all the influence of myself and friends.

"Arlines, I must trust to your friendship then to save me as much misery as you can."

"I will, I will; do not despair yet. A time may come when you will regain your property."

"It can never come—it can never come," said Captain Arnold, vehemently.

"But it can and will, if you will be guided by my advice."

"Your advice, Arlines? What do you advise me to do now? Something that will still sink me deeper in the slough of despair."

"You are hardly yourself now, Arnold, and I will say more another time; but this much I will say, that you may make money fast, but it will most probably offend the niceties of honour and over-delicate feelings; but believe me, you must discard these feelings under the pressure of circumstances."

"I will discard them all, Arlines, if you will but teach me how to gain the means of providing for my family—my children. I am yours body and soul. The despair I have at my heart maddens my soul."

"Then we shall soon understand each other, and I will not fail in exerting my influence in your behalf," replied Arlines; and as he did so, a smile of triumph crossed his features, as he looked upon the bowed form of Captain Arnold.

CHAPTER XXIV.

THE MEETING OF THE CONFEDERATES.—THE MODE IN WHICH ARLINES SEVERS THE CONNECTION.—ARLINES' UNLUCKY ENCOUNTER WITH ALFRED PEARSON.

THE tavern we have before alluded to in the neighbourhood of Piccadilly, where the confederates met on a previous occasion, was on this day a scene of some confusion and contention among the same individuals who had, on a previous occasion met there.

There were among them faces that betrayed anger and alarm, some that viewed everybody with distrust; something had been done that did not exactly agree with their notions of right and wrong, but they were of a peculiar character and confined to themselves.

There was much bustle, and many were talking at once, and, as may be imagined, there was but little understood, and that generally only by the individual who uttered it; so that though much was attempted, little or nothing was done.

Viscount Rollington was there, and essayed to speak, so as to make himself heard, several times, above those who were constantly attempting to do the same thing; until at length he succeeded in saying—

"At least we will hear what he has to say to us before we finally pass judgment. I have had none of the money or the security, and until I have I shall be rather disposed to look with suspicion upon Mr. Arlines' conduct."

"Suspicion? I look upon it as a dead certainty that we are all pumped as dry as sand bags," said a fat man, with an immensity of whisker.

"If he has played the traitor, or intends so doing, I for one will never leave him, but expose him thoroughly."

"Ay," replied Rollington, "and so will I; but I can't bring myself to the belief that he really and coolly intends to cut us out, as it were, of our fair and just booty."

"If Arlines has all the securities about him, or in his possession," said a sallow-faced man, with black moustache and imperial, "I tell you what you may depend upon then."

"What—what?" exclaimed several.

"Why, that he'll keep it all. He's too crafty to be induced by any consideration to part with it. He has enough to indemnify him against all our ill opinions, or even our vengeance; besides, he cares but little for that."

"Be that as it may," said Rollington, "we must do something to mark our sense of such a man's misconduct, and shut him out from our society for the future."

The hubbub and confusion suddenly ceased, and silence reigned around as the door opened, and every eye was turned towards it, when Phillip Arlines was seen to enter the room, calm and triumphant.

"Arlines," said Viscount Rollington, speaking, after a moment's silence, "we wished to see you most particularly."

"I am happy I am here," said Arlines, coolly.

"We were talking of you, and wishing to ask of you a few words of explanation."

"Which I shall be most happy to give you," replied Arlines, "as I always am; but what is the subject of explanation?"

"It relates to the play of Captain Arnold," said Rollington.

"Ay, I understand."

"And we want to know who has the winnings, and who won them?"

"They are in my possession, though won by another—at least the securities are."

"Then short reckonings make long friends; make now the distribution you have promised so long."

"No, hardly; I have toiled so long that it is time I looked after myself."

"But our agreement; we agreed to share all among ourselves. Surely you would not act so greedily as to throw them overboard."

"Quite; for you well know that every man for himself, and Providence for us all."

"Providence, indeed! I think I see Providence staying us here."

"Ah, so do I; it would be a queer sort of a job, such as Providence never contemplates."

"Come, come," said Rollington, "you cannot, Arlines, mean to act with so much rascality."

"Indeed I do. I find that I have to think and act for you all, and that I had to do work for too many; and I began to think that I could do it all by myself."

"I will take care and expose your conduct; you shall no longer mix with the crew you have been in the habit of doing. Your vile conduct shall be a by-word, and you shall be feared and detested—a man who kept not faith with his own friends."

"Ay, ay, that's all very well, Rollington," said Arlines; "but it strikes me the more you stir in this affair the worse you yourself will appear. Don't it strike you that your name, sounded as a conspirator for such a purpose, will but slightly aid the already inodorous name of Rollington? I think that such knowledge on the part of the world would be an effectual bar to any further intercourse in society. This to you, Rollington, must be apparent, though not to your companions; but it affects them in the same way, for the conspiracy, while it was quiet and secret, once blown, attaches a blighting reputation to all concerned, and they become, for a time, at least, innoxious, and lose the means of carrying on the war against mankind, by which they lived."

This was too true and too evident to all, and silence ensued, during which Phillip Arlines formally took his leave of his former friends by a mock and grave pantomime which he performed, and then quitted the room, unmolested by any one, so much were they staggered and astonished.

Phillip Arlines having thus severed the connection between himself and the men who had been hitherto of service to him, quitted the house, much elated with the result that had just happened; but he had scarcely passed three paces from the step of the door, when he met Alfred Pearson face to face. Arlines motioned him to stay, and advanced towards him, saying,—

"Mr. Pearson, I believe?"

"Yes," was the short reply.

"Then I beg to congratulate you upon the progress you have made in the affections of Captain Arnold's pretty daughter."

"Is it your intention to provoke a quarrel? and have you forgot the result of a former meeting?" said Alfred Pearson.

"No, no," replied Arlines; "my object is but to inform you that I have the entree to the house, and visit Jessie when I choose. Do you intend to try your luck there, eh?"

"I shall try my luck, as you call it, upon kicking you for this insolence." And, so saying, before Arlines could be aware of his intention, or make an effort to save himself, Alfred Pearson seized him by the collar, and with a strong but sudden effort, he turned him quite round, and bestowing several hearty kicks upon him, gave such an impetus to his person that he forced him into the tavern he had just quitted in a very undignified posture and haste.

Alfred Pearson for a moment or two awaited

the egress of Phillip Arlines, but not seeing him he did not consider he was bound to await his coming longer than he pleased, so at once walked in the direction he was going before the encounter took place, without meeting with any interruption whatever.

The road he took was in the direction of Captain Arnold's villa, but as he neared it he slackened his pace, and as if he had suddenly made up his mind as to what course he would pursue, he turned on one side and entered an hotel, where he called for pen and paper.

While this was being brought he walked about in a hurried manner, as if impatient of delay.

"Yes, I will write—I will write. I have obtained such information that may much advantage Jessie or Arnold to know it. It may save him from destruction. True, she will look upon the letter with suspicion, having been duped by that scoundrel; but I will make the attempt."

The articles he required being brought, he wrote the following brief note:—

"DEAR JESSIE,

"Pardon this intrusion; but it is dictated by necessity, which I can fully explain to you if you will meet me in Kensington-gardens to-morrow evening, as I have something to inform you of relating to Phillip Arlines, and a number of others, who have conspired together to ruin your father. As you value your own and his welfare consent to meet me.

"Ever yours,
"ALFRED PEARSON."

This note was sealed and directed, and then Pearson began to think of the most eligible means of delivering it. He was well known himself to the captain and his servants, and if he went he should by his presence, probably, increase the captain's displeasure, and he sought not to incur indignity even at the hands of Arnold himself; but then, he argued, that his delivering the letter by some means to the servant if an opportunity occurred, would assure Jessie of its authenticity.

He was now in the immediate vicinity of the villa, and had paused to consider the best means of getting speech of some of the servants, when some one touched his arm, saying,—

"I begs pardon, Mr. Pearson, but doesn't you wish to see Miss Jessie, that is, Miss Arnold? I am sure she's been very melancholy since you were here last. I never seed nobody so sad since our cook lost her sweetheart, who died, as the doctor said, in a state of gallops."

"S ate of what?" said Pearson, in amazement.

"Gallops."

"I never heard of such a disorder."

"Nor I, sir; but I suppose it's some old illness under a new name. But Miss Jessie, sir?"

"Ay," replied Pearson, giving the man a piece of silver, who was one of Arnold's servants, "I wish you would give her this letter, unobserved, as early as possible."

"Ay, that I will. I can make a good go-between, I warrant. I never misses nothing, and makes no mistakes; and if you want to see me at any time, if you go to the 'Goat and Compasses' you are sure to find me when I am not at work. That's my playground, sir; it's a good and dry skittle ground."

At the end of this piece of information the Mercury made the best of his way to his master's, carefully concealing the letter in his hat.

CHAPTER XXV.

THE LETTER TO JESSIE.—THE APPOINTMENT.—THE CONVERSATION IN KENSINGTON GARDENS.

THE letter which Alfred Pearson had confided to the care of the singular specimen of humanity that had the fortune to be man-servant to Captain Arnold, was not long in reaching its destination, for there were plenty of opportunities of delivering it, as Jessie was much alone, Captain Arnold's reflections being of such a nature as to make him eschew the company of his children, whose happiness he had sacrificed to such pleasures.

"Miss Jessie," said John, peering into the apartment where she was seated, melancholy and unhappy in her own thoughts.

"Well, John, what do you want?" she inquired.

"Are you all alone, miss? and are you sure nobody's looking?"

"Bless me, what's the matter with you, John? You surely are beside yourself this morning. What do you mean?"

"Why, miss, there has been somebody beside myself, and I mean that I don't want nobody to see this here bit of billy doo as I have here for you. 'Twas guved me by Master Pearson."

"By whom?" said Jessie, as the name of Pearson reached her ears.

"By Master Pearson; he bid me give it to you, miss, when alone. I hope I knows the way to give it alone, and leave it with somebody."

So saying, John advanced and laid the letter on the work table, at which she was seated, and then made a precipitate retreat, leaving Jessie and the letter by themselves.

It was several minutes ere Jessie had the courage to take the letter, for at first some scruples came to her mind; but there was the letter, and they were at last overcome.

"From Alfred Pearson," she said, with a

sigh; "what can he desire to say to me? I would that he had remained our visitor, and that bad man, Arlines turned from the house; there is more between him and my father, I fear, than he will admit."

While these thoughts passed through her mind she took up the letter, and perused the contents with a painful interest, which was not lessened by the information the letter contained.

Indeed, it was some minutes ere she could recover from the surprise and consternation into which it threw her. It evidently affected her deeply, for agony was depicted on her beautiful countenance, and bitter tears fell fast down her pale cheeks.

"Oh, my father! my father!" she at length sobbed, "to think that it should be perceptible to all save yourself. What new misfortunes await you, Heaven only knows! I would I could induce you to compel the absence of Phillip Arlines from this place. Surely there must be some motive for his insolent conduct to me. He never would have ventured upon it, but upon the knowledge that he held his place in this house upon surer grounds than that of mere friendship, which his baseness would be sufficient to sever had it been bound in adamantine bonds."

She paused, and her grief absorbed all her faculties, until exhausted by it, she leaned her head upon her hand, and was soon in deep thought.

"How shall I act? Shall I break through my father's commands not to see or hold any communication with Alfred Pearson?" were her first thoughts. "My father certainly objects to it; but then the circumstances of the case are urgent, and such, I think, as would warrant a daughter in disobeying the commands of a parent. The object, too," said Jessie, "is such that would justify my doing so. His happiness and fortune are certainly in danger; and shall I not attempt to rescue him from unseen traitors? Yes, I will see him, and hear what Alfred Pearson has to say. I would that my father had listened to his counsel rather than to that indisidious man, whose whole and great object is to lead him to destruction. Alas! alas! much may already be accomplished, and hence the insolence I have suffered. It may be one of many insults I have yet to suffer—one of the many wrongs I may have to endure; but no, my father would never suffer that, if ruin did fall heavily upon us. No—no, we are and may be poor, but not slaves."

*   *   *   *

The next day was exceedingly cold and boisterous; the sharp wind seemed to make its way with biting severity and keenness and to make its way to the body, despite clothing, and even doors and walls; and as the evening set in a desultory hail storm fell, at times leaving off, and then again coming down with greater severity than before.

The whole face of nature appeared cheerless and gloomy; not a single ray of gladness or comfort could be found out of doors, and in the neighbourhood of Kensington the prospect was cheerless and dull in the extreme. The very lamps looked duller and more useless than heretofore, and the evening set in dark and inclement.

Yet, notwithstanding the hail, the wind, and the darkness, Jessie had resolved to keep the appointment; and when the hour approached she wrapped herself up carefully in a warm cloak, and left the house quietly without attracting the attention of any one.

During her walk thither a doubt of the propriety of the step she was taking crossed her mind, but soon vanished before the clear light of reason, and the firm conviction she felt that it was purely for her father's welfare that she thus exposed herself to censure.

"My motives are good, and the object I have in view is such that ought to animate the heart of every daughter, and urge her to use every exertion to stay the course of such events as I fear too strongly are in course of action."

With a sad and troubled heart Jessie Arnold threaded her way to Kensington-gardens, despite all the opposition the angry elements offered. She but drew her cloak the closer around her at each angry blast, and stepped more firmly forward than before, and in a short time she stood within the bounds of Kensington-gardens.

The wind howled through the trees, and the hail fell fast and struck with great force upon the hands and face of Jessie, who endeavoured to screen herself from the effects of the storm by getting beneath the tall trees that there abound.

Here she had been but a short time when the figure of a man appeared slowly approaching the spot where she stood. Oh! how her heart beat with expectation, for she believed it was Pearson. She had not seen him since the night they parted in the garden, when the captain and Arlines entered together, and on that night Arnold had incurred his first loss.

It was not long ere Alfred Pearson saw the form of Jessie, for he it was that was approaching; and, flying towards her, he extended his hands to her, saying,—

"Jessie, dear Jessie, I hardly dared expect you, especially such a night as this; indeed I felt I did wrong in writing to you to bring you thither on such a night."

"Say nothing of that, Pearson," said Jessie, mildly; "the inducement to come was the strongest you could offer me. My father's welfare I have too deeply at heart to neglect doing anything I can to save him from destruction."

"And only you, Jessie, can; I fear advice from any one else would be useless, and be received in the light of impertinent meddling; and yet I have yours and your father's interest at heart so strongly that I have incurred this reproach in order, if possible, to be of use to you."

"Thanks, Mr. Pearson, you have my best thanks; but tell me, what is it that you have to say that will be of my avail?"

"It is this: I have made many inquiries respecting this Phillip Arlines, and I have found out that he is, indeed, one of the greatest scoundrels that are let loose upon society."

"Indeed, are you sure of that? It will be but useless to tempt my father's anger, if I fail in convincing him of that; for anything short would, to him, smack so strongly of ill will, that he would be harder than ever to be convinced."

"I am aware of all that, Jessie; and have you thought how to avoid it? I have made inquiries as have fully confirmed me in all my previous opinions of that man; and these inquiries can be verified with proof. Every assertion I make I can prove, and prove, too, to his satisfaction."

"But how can my father become acquainted with the proofs you possess?—how make him aware of Arlines' baseness?"

"That is the only difficulty," replied Alfred Pearson; "and one which I canno get over save by your assistance."

"And that can be had," replied Jessie. "I will do all I can to save my father from the ruin I am sure that man's character is certain to bring upon him."

"'Tis true, dear Jesse, 'tis true; but the task you have is difficult, I know, and perhaps unpleasant; but then it must be done, and the only way in which he can become acquainted with the true character of Phillip Arlines is by your telling him frankly all I have said, and endeavour to obtain his permission for me to produce the proof I speak of. I can bring those who can give positive and undeniable testimony as to his character and pursuits, both of which are bad to a degree."

"I will do it—I will do anything," said Jessie, "that will free my father from the thrall of that man Arlines."

"Thanks, dear Jessie; it will in some measure tend to remove the apparent doubt cast upon me, as well as serve himself by your doing so; but let me hope that I have not thus suffered in your estimation."

"No—no," replied Jessie; "I never doubted you from the first. Oh, that my father had not been so infatuated by Arlines!"

"Thanks, dear Jessie, for your good opinion of me. May I hope that it will ripen to a better feeling than that which you even now profess? This is scarce a time and place for me to express those feelings of affection by which my heart is bound to you; but my opportunities are so few, I hope I may be forgiven, and even that what I have said is not without an echo, though a distant one, in your own heart."

Jessie was silent: she knew not how to speak; her heart was too full for words; and she attempted not to withdraw the hand that Pearson held and pressed to his lips.

Time flew on, and Jessie left Kensington-gardens in company with Pearson, who saw her safe to her father's door.

CHAPTER XXVI.

PHILLIP ARLINES' RESOLVE.—THE ROOKERY, AND AN INTRODUCTION TO AN OLD FRIEND.

THE evening of the same day in which Phillip Arlines quitted the company and dissolved the partnership between himself and his old associates, and in which he met with the unceremonious treatment from Alfred Pearson, was spent in a tavern where he was not known; and there he sat drinking and turning over in his own mind the various chances that presented themselves of seizing Captain Arnold's whole property.

Many doubts and difficulties presented themselves, which one after another were dissolved as they arose in his mind by his own resolutions and the many counter propositions that presented themselves in succession, until at length he became convinced that the only two great obstacles in the way lay in the persons of Jessie Arnold and Alfred Pearson.

Arnold's fortune alone was not sufficient to gratify his passions, but Jessie must be his also; and he hoped to effect that by increasing the power he possessed over Arnold himself, and forcing him into crime after crime; and as for Pearson he knew not what to do.

To allow Alfred Pearson to be about town watching his steps, and keeping an espionage upon all his acts, would be utter ruin, and all that remained would be, by some means or other, to dispose of him; but how to do that was the difficulty. Put Alfred Pearson out of the way, and the thing might be done; Jessie herself might become assailable, but not while he whom she loved stood by her.

These thoughts passed and repassed through

ARLINES APPREHENDED FOR THE UNPAID BOND.

his mind, and yet he could come to no conclusion; he could not determine what to do, because he could in no way see his course clearly.

"He must be removed," he thought; "but how to remove him is a question to be solved—a great difficulty it is. To put him out of the way is easy enough, but how to escape detection is beyond my comprehension. To attack him at some moment when he is not prepared would be the thing; and yet should he contrive to recover from a first onset, the chance I should run would be too hazardous to make he attempt. No, no, I cannot do it."

"But no matter, Jessie must be mine; she will be mine when I have the power of placing her father in gaol. Yes, she will be mine then —she will save her father and submit with a good grace; but then Pearson must be disposed of ere this can be done."

Let him, however, turn his thoughts into any channel, propose any object to be done, and the end of his mental efforts would be the fact glaring him in the face that Alfred Pearson would thwart all, and, as a necessary consequence, he must be got rid of as quickly as such a purpose could be effected.

There he sat in moody meditation, with his brows bent, as if some stern and bloody thoughts were passing in his imagination. There he sat for a long time as if he were a statue, instead of a human being living and breathing.

At length he suddenly started from his reverie, and his countenance was lit up with a ray of fire as he said,—

"Yes, I have it, I have it; I know the man who will do this job for me—ay, and keep his own counsel to boot. My old friend George Gosset shall be the man: I pray Heaven he may have escaped the gallows or transportation, both of which he has likely enough undergone ere now. But I will seek him in the Rookery, his place of abode when not under the patronage of high people and the government."

So saying, he arose and left the tavern, and then made his way towards St. Giles's for the purpose of finding out a man with whom he had been intimate years since when they were both engaged in low and petty crimes.

This man, George Gosset, he knew, was one who never hesitated to commit any crime, and who had more than once been imprisoned for a length of time; but having lost sight of him for a long period, and knowing Gosset's partiality for aliases, he had some misgivings about his having suffered either capital or secondary punishment under one of them.

To this man's abode then he was making—not to his abode, for that was scarce known to any one—but to the immediate neighbourhood of it, with which Arlines was as well acquainted as Gosset himself, having, years gone by, sought refuge there from power.

Besides, he knew many of the houses, their pass-words and their cognomens, and George Gosset's was Cross-eyed George from the fact of his being cross-eyed or squinting.

It was somewhat late before Phillip Arlines reached the Rookery.

To give the reader a description of this place would be but to disgust him with a picture of the lowest depths to which humanity could descend— a picture of squalid misery and wretchedness, of crime and debauchery, not to be equalled, perhaps, in any city in Europe, Paris alone excepted. Old and young, male and female, were often mingled together without any discrimination whatever.

It was to such a place as this that Phillip Arlines now wended his way. The spot was to him full of old recollections; and many things sprang to his mind that he had long since forgotten or ceased to think of.

At length he came to a low public-house, but with extensive and rambling premises. Long red curtains were drawn across the windows that looked into the street, and the door, when opened, produced a queer grating sound, and immediately attracted the attention of those at hand or behind the bar.

At a signal from Arlines he was shown into a small room, the door of which opened behind a projection, and crossing which he was led into another room, where several men were seated carousing before a fire, but perfectly silent in their mirth and conversation, which was scarce above a whisper, and which could not be heard in the next room.

Another signal was made by Arlines, and a stout, good-natured, but lynx-eyed man, stepped forward, with an apron round him, which at once proclaimed him to be the landlord, who looked at him inquiringly.

"I don't recollect you," said the landlord, as he gazed upon Arlines' features.

"It is unnecessary you should," replied Arlines; "recollections are not pleasant at any time."

"Well, what would you have of me?" inquired the landlord.

"I want to know if George Gosset, known as Cross-eyed Goorge, is alive."

"He is," said the landlord.

"In the country or on his travels?"

"He has been home for some time, but he is not in the best case."

"No matter, I wish to see him. Can you tell me where I can find him?"

"Who are you?" said the landlord. "You know the signal, 'tis true, but I can't tell you where to find Gosset; I might be able to do so myself with some trouble, but I must know who you are."

"It is some years since I was here," replied Arlines, "and it is some years since I saw Gosset; he knows me well enough. I have something for him to do; but I decline making myself known—you can understand why."

"Exactly; but I now think I recollect your face. I will bring Gosset to you."

"No, no, I would sooner see him where he may be, if he be alone; I want no one else to stand between him and me."

"Very good, sir, then follow me," said the landlord. "George is alone in his own room; he had a bit of a spree last night and has scarce got the better of it."

Arlines followed the landlord through a variety of rambling passages intersected by stairs here and there to such a degree that it formed a puzzle to any one who had not resided among them for years which to take.

At length they came to a back room, very high indeed in the house, when his guide opened the door and said,—

"Here's a gentleman wants to see you, Gosset; he has given the signals all correct, and I suppose it's all right."

The room into which Arlines had been shown was one of small dimensions, but that was of little consequence, seeing the whole of the furniture consisted of a single table and two chairs; a bed lay up in one corner on the floor, and Gosset himself lay on it. There was a fire in the grate, and a dim, dubious kind of light given out by a candle of exceedingly small dimensions.

On hearing the landlord's words Gosset started up, and stared upon Arlines with a ferocious expression of countenance, as though he expected he would have done him some mischief, but Arlines coolly crossed the room, and took one of the chairs, and seated himself before the fire.

"That's cool," said Gosset, "to walk into a man's place, and sit down before his fire without saying as much as with yer lerve, or by yer leave. Come, come, that won't do with me, not while my name's George Gos——"

He stopped short, however, in telling his name, for it was a thing that he did not wish known to more than possible.

"George Gosset, you intended to say," said Arlines. "I came on purpose to see you, and have had some trouble to find you out. Come forward, man, and let's see you. Don't you recollect me—it is some years since we met?"

Gosset arose and seated himself opposite to Arlines. He was a big, muscular, and sturdy man, of a peculiarly disagreeable appearance, which was increased by his squint, red, bristly hair, and coarse beard. Strength he certainly did possess, and his appearance certainly did Arlines credit for believing that such a man would be ripe for any crime you might offer to pay him to perpetrate.

CHAPTER XXVII.

INTERVIEW BETWEEN ARLINES AND GEORGE GOSSET.—THE PLOT.—ARLINES' MEDITATIONS.

Gosset looked long and fixedly at Arlines, and after he had done so for some minutes he said,—

"I recollect you well enough now; though I did not at the first moment call to mind where I had seen you. Arlines, Phillip Arlines, is your name."

"It is. I scarcely thought you could have recognised me so easily, and yet I have deceived many who once knew me well enough. Well, how has the world used you, Gosset?"

"Oh, badly enough, badly enough," growled Gosset; "it was once different from what it is now, as you know. I have been out of the country, and, besides that, I have been laid up in limbo."

"You have been unlucky then; you used to be a handy clever fellow, and never got bowled out. How was it?"

"Oh, I don't know; I was out of luck, and that is all I know about it. The jobs were

bad—the times bad—and I was known to be so easily comeatable, which makes great odds against a man."

"So it does, so it does, George. Are you about anything now, or keeping snug?"

"Rather the latter, but for no one reason more than another. You are in good case, I see; your old luck still holds by you, I suppose? What a lucky dog you are, to be sure. The old times have gone by, else we used to do a thing or two, and then there was plenty of the usable to be had; but now I can't ask a friend to drink."

"Nor need you," replied Arlines, throwing down a sovereign. "Have what you like up, George, and then we can talk over our old affairs, and perhaps new ones, at leisure."

Gosset seized hold of the sovereign, and immediately left the room, but shortly after brought with him a variety of things, chiefly for drinking, but some of a more solid nature.

"I have eaten nothing since last night," said Gosset, as he placed the things down on the table. "I was out on a spree, and feel precious queer: I shall have a good appetite presently when I have had a little of the liquid."

"Drink, George," said Arlines, "and never mind me, I can sit and watch you; I have had enough to eat."

"Well, go on then," said Gosset, "and I will do the same; I can hear you just as well as if I were not eating. If you have anything to do, I should like it, for we have nothing stirring here; indeed, it's nearly starvation for us all."

"That is the reason I came to you to propose a job, which, though dangerous and dark, will be a profitable one to you."

"Eh? anything, no matter what, will do for me. George Gosset ain't particular as to what—cutting a weasand—nothing, if it is safe."

"Then you have just hit it, George. The fact is this: there's a fellow that stands between me and five hundred pounds. Now, if he were dead, I am sure to have that sum. I am, as you may suppose, rather anxious to get him out of the way by some means or other."

"Why haven't you done it yourself then, eh?" inquired Gosset.

"He knows me too well, and I should most likely be accused of his murder; therefore, it will be necessary for me to be somewhere where I can be seen and sworn to as being absent from the spot where he might be quieted."

"Oh, I see; you are still cunning, Phillip, as usual—an alibi's your plan. But it's a risky job, and I ought to be well paid if I undertake it."

"Half of what I get you shall have. Five hundred pounds is the sum. I will give you two hundred and fifty pounds if you can quietly do the job."

"I'll try my hand; but you must let me know the particulars—at all events the when, and where, and perhaps the how."

"That must depend upon circumstances. You are, however, as strong as ever you were, I suppose, and can stand a bit of a struggle?"

"I should think I could; but I don't like that work, there's such a squalling going on that's much above concert pitch, and everybody hears it. I don't like a job of that sort."

"Neither need you; all you have to do is to deal him one blow with a bludgeon, knife, or anything else that will quiet him and prevent any disturbance. You can then walk quietly away, and nobody knows anything about it; but in case he should seize you,—he is strong and active, though neither so tall nor bulky—"

"Never fear for me. What parts does he usually beat about on? That must be found out; and I must also see him before I should like to do anything for fear of hitting the wrong man, and so spoil the whole affair."

"That you shall know in good time. I believe he is often about Kensington, which will be a good spot to meet with him some night when no one else is by. There is his address; you can be about his neighbourhood, and soon ascertain who goes in and out, and their name. I must leave the rest of this business with you, for I must not be seen in it nor with you, in case there should be any disturbance."

"That will do," said Gosset; "I will go and make an acquaintance by sight with Mr. Pearson, and then make sure of my man; but, Arlines, you know, we must be true to each other."

"Of course," replied Arlines; "what could we gain by treachery? We might aggravate the state of another should any misfortune happen, but you may depend upon it we cannot gain anything."

"Exactly; but as I have the worst part of the job, and that part, too, upon which the heaviest penalty is incurred, it behoves me to have something upon which I can rely."

"What would you have, George? I am reasonable and open to any fair proposition; but do not think I shall spare more than half —that's the bargain; and, besides, I don't think more would be fair at all."

"I don't ask yer for more," replied Cross-eyed George, with a desperate attempt to look knowing over the froth of a pot of ale. "All I want, you see, is to make sure of that portion, because if anything should happen to you I could make no claim upon your relations, you know."

As George Gosset said this, he winked, and a grim smile passed over his countenance, and he placed the pot on the table, but half emptied.

"Well, George, for the life of me I cannot tell what you mean. If you desire the money down I must tell you I can only get it at all by this young fellow's death, and, therefore, I cannot give it to you."

"I don't desire it, Arlines; I haven't asked you to do so. Give me a bill, or agreement, or some writing of the sort, to the amount of my share, so that I can claim it, and all will be well."

"That I will do whenever you like."

"Exactly. Well, you can get it done when you like, for it must be some days at least before I can do the job; but I must keep clear of all other business."

"Yes; if you should get tied up 'twill spoil the whole plot."

"Exactly; but I must live also, and I can't go waiting about upon nothing, you know, and must, therefore, draw upon you for a few more of these golden pictures."

"Well, here are two more," said Arlines, "and I will give you more in a few days; meanwhile make yourself well acquainted with the neighbourhood of the place, and the man I have named."

"Never fear; I will not fail," said Gosset. "You and I, Arlines, have done business together before this time, you know."

"Ay," replied Arlines, "I have had some odd adventures since I saw you last, and some sharp escapes."

"You are safe so far, and I believe it must be the devil himself if any one ever gets the better of you. You were ever recognised as a cunning, daring fellow, ready to engage in any undertaking, however serious."

"Yes," said Arlines, "I think I have done some things pretty well; but I must now quit you. You understand exactly what I want?"

"I do; and will take care to do all of it by myself."

"Exactly; I shall depend upon you, and you only. Good-night."

Arlines now arose, and his companion assisted him to descend the stairs, which, as has been noticed, were very intricate and difficult of navigation, especially in the dark.

It was not long ere Arlines was in the street, and he immediately made the best of his way from the neighbourhood, in which he did not wish to be recognised.

Once clear of the Rookery, and Arlines slackened his pace, and his thoughts then reverted to the scene he had just enacted with his old associate in crime.

"What is the next step?" he said. "How to bring Arnold to such a sense of his condition that I can mould him to my purpose; and then Jessie—the beautiful, but scornful Jessie—she shall be mine, and sue for my protection. I must set Smith on them, and then come in as the kind friend, who exerts himself for the welfare of the family. I ought to earn thanks for that, at all events."

As Phillip Arlines muttered these words, a smile crossed his countenance, but of such a sneering, sickly character, that would have made any one who saw it shudder.

Dark thoughts passed across his mind, and his heart was the abode of deep and dreadful deeds yet to be done. It was a spot wherein were forged those acts that afterwards caused much misery and wretchedness to others.

Phillip Arlines was not the man to hesitate at aught that was to be done without detection. On the contrary, he was as bold and skilful as he was cunning and careful; and such a man was formed, we might say, looking at the means to the end, on purpose to commit great mischiefs with impunity.

The night was now well set in, and Arlines made his way towards his own lodging, intending to visit Arnold in the morning, and make some proposition to him after being of use to put off Smith for him, and save him for a time.

CHAPTER XXVIII.

CAPTAIN ARNOLD'S DESPAIR.—THE VISIT OF MR. SMITH, AND THE ASSISTANCE OF ARLINES.

THE morning following the events just recorded was gloomy and cold. No kindly ray of sun was felt nor seen glowing through some crevice among the black clouds that floated above; an ungenial easterly wind too sprang up, and caused the doors to be closed to keep as much of the disagreeables of the weather out as possible.

That morning Captain Arnold lay in his bed to an unusual hour. There he lay, a prey to the most agonising reflections, and to the most bitter repentance; but what could repentance do?—nothing.

It is common to repent; repentance is not intended as an atonement, but a punishment: it is as much an effect of a previous cause as pain and death should follow swallowing a poison.

Arnold was now a ruined man—he felt and knew it. All his property he had thrown away in exchange for pleasure and morbid excitement.

For the pleasure of the gaming-table he had exchanged all he possessed, and after that he parted with the wealth and the inheritance of his children. They looked to him for a future provision; but they could scarce be said to possess the means of present support.

Every particle of what he possessed was gone; not a shilling had he to spare, and how soon he might be compelled to quit the villa he

knew not; but he shrunk from every knock, or the sound of the bell, fearful lest its summons should be merely the forerunner of the announcement to him of the presence of some unwelcome visitor.

Thus he lay a prey to every fear and emotion that can render life wretched, fearful of rising, and feeling unable to do so, lest he should see the melancholy and sad faces of those whom he had made beggars, and were even yet dependant upon him for their daily support.

How to obtain the means of employment he knew not; he was scarce able to compete with the rapidity of action and the endurance of daily fatigue that is required of those who have to earn their bread by the sweat of their brow.

Suicide more than once came to his mind; but from this he shrunk; and, besides, he dared not quit his children and leave them at the mercy of a world too ready to take advantage of any opportunity there might be of robbing the orphan, or those without aid or friendless.

He had lain tortured in this manner for some hours perfectly awake, but unwilling to be noticed by any one, when a loud knock at the street-door, as well as a ring, proclaimed that some one approached who would scarcely be denied.

Arnold for a moment shrank beneath the clothes, as if to hide himself, but soon abandoned the idea, or rather the momentary impulse that had seized him.

The next moment a knock came at his own door, and after some parley it was ascertained that Mr. Smith wished to see him. It was some moments ere he could make up his mind what to do, whether he should refuse to see him or not; but then he asked himself—

" What will it avail me to refuse? perhaps exasperate this man, and compel an immediate relinquishment of even the villa itself, the least important part, but the most immediately in use; and I had better see him, and know at once what it is I have to suffer."

In accordance with this resolution he desired that Mr. Smith should be shown into the room where he was then, as he determined to remain where he was.

Mr. Smith entered the apartment with a quiet manner, much after the same fashion that a sleek and well-bred tom-cat would enter the apartment, save that his boots creaked in the most approved style.

" Your servant, Captain Arnold," said Mr. Smith, with a gentle inclination of the head; " I fear I am rather an early visitor. You look but poorly this morning; I hope I have not disturbed your repose?"

" No," replied Arnold. " Be so good, Mr. Smith, as to let me know what happened in St. James's-street, for I am much in the dark, and I fear I had more wine than was prudent."

Mr. Smith smiled dubiously, and advancing towards Arnold, said—

"You bore it exceedingly well then, Captain Arnold, for neither I nor any one else saw anything of the sort. You appeared very well indeed."

"I lost much I am afraid. I presume your visit is connected with what I lost upon the last occasion I was there?"

"It is so," replied Mr. Smith; "we have all of us now and then our changes in luck. Fortune declares for us one day, and against us on another, and unless we hold her with a tight rein, we are likely to lose all we might otherwise recover from her."

Arnold took this speech as alluding to his own position, and an intimation that Mr. Smith would scarcely deem it safe to give credit in an affair of this kind. It was with a deep sigh, therefore, that Arnold said—

"Will you be kind enough to inform me what it is that I am in your debt?"

"Certainly, certainly," replied Mr. Smith, who immediately began to feel in his pockets, and procured a pocket-book, in which were placed many documents; and after a short search among them, he produced one which he handed to Captain Arnold, saying as he did so—

"There is the memorandum; it is in your hand, and, therefore, questionless."

Arnold looked at the document with a gaze that would have caused an emotion of pity in all save such men as Mr. Smith, who quietly crossed his legs and coolly looked on. He saw not, nor cared not, for the agonized expression that sat on the features of him who was now before him. He looked, but yet he could not withdraw his eyes from the terrible document.

There he saw clear enough characters that in so many words declared him a beggar—ay, his very children were beggers too, and in another hour they might have neither home to go to nor food to satisfy the cravings of hunger.

A deep groan burst from his breast as he, with a trembling hand, returned the document to Mr. Smith, who replaced it in his pocket-book, and the pocket-book duly replaced in his coat pocket.

"And is that the truth?" at length exclaimed Arnold, in a low voice, but so hollow that had they heard who often heard him, they would have thought something was the matter. "Is that the sum, and did I lose to that amount?"

Mr. Smith placed his hand upon his heart (had he one?) and said, in a subdued tone, but with a smilin gcountenance,—

"Upon my honour, as a gentleman, Captain Arnold, you lost that sum, and that is the voucher you gave me, written by yourself before several persons of distinction."

Arnold's countenance, though he expected this result, betrayed the agony of his mind, and several minutes elapsed ere he could speak, and he said—

"This is a heavy sum; I must beg you will hold this voucher a few days for me, when I shall be better prepared to settle."

"A-hem!" said Mr. Smith. "You see, Captain Arnold, debts of honour are usually ready money transactions; and the sooner these things are settled the better."

"But surely you do not doubt my word; you cannot expect I should produce all this at a moment's notice? I must dispose of some property,—nay, the whole, before I can liquidate this sum."

"Of course I did suppose what was entered into would be performed at once; any other course is not recognised among gentlemen."

At that moment a knocking was heard at the door, which greatly relieved Captain Arnold, for he thought it could be no other than Phillip Arlines; and his arrival he considered opportune, as it would give him the benefit of his advice and countenance in his present emergency, and perhaps assist him to put off Mr. Smith for a few days longer.

Captain Arnold was not mistaken in his supposition about the arrival being that of Arlines, for in a few moments more he entered the captain's bedroom unannounced; and, pretending not to see Mr. Smith, he said, advancing to the captain—

"Captain Arnold, I hope my sudden intrusion will be excused; but last night's misfortune, or rather piece of ill luck, I thought might have disarranged your plans, and I desired to see you to offer my services as far as they can be of use."

"Thank you, Arlines, thank you; you could not have come at a better time. There is—a—Mr. Smith—you see there, behind you."

"Eh? Ah! Mr. Smith. I beg your pardon, but I did not observe you behind the door."

"Don't name it, Mr. Arlines. I am happy to see you so well and active."

"Yes, yes, very well. But, Arnold, I fear by your countenance that the worst has happened. Cheer up, Fortune is never long on one side, and she'll favour you by-and-by."

"But in the meantime, Arlines, I must starve."

"Pooh! pooh! nothing of the sort. I have not lived thus long in society not to know better than that. You will retrieve all, depend upon it you will. Nay, do not shake your head because you are troubled with melancholy. Dispose of this man—Mr. Smith, I mean—and then I will converse with you."

"That's what I wish to do; but I cannot, for he will not accede to my wishes, and I have no power to do anything else."

"What do you propose to him, then?" inquired Arlines.

"That he should wait a few days to enable me to dispose of all I have to satisfy the debt I owe him."

"And he will not accede?"

"I believe not."

"If I am answerable, you will not shrink from relieving me from the responsibility at the appointed time, will you?"

"Certainly not; I will do whatever you can induce him to agree to, for I am helpless."

"Mr. Smith," said Arlines, "Captain Arnold is a man of honour; and I will pledge myself that he will fulfil his engagements if you withhold your claim for a week or ten days."

Mr. Smith rose, and, bowing, said—

"The word of Mr. Arlines, added to Captain Arnold's word and voucher, is quite a sufficient guarantee for any engagement; and to show that I am willing to oblige you, I will take no further proceedings till after the expiration of that time."

CHAPTER XXIX.

THE MEETING.—SIR RUMPION MEADOW-BANKS.—THE ROBBERY.

CAPTAIN ARNOLD, when left alone with Phillip Arlines by the disappearance of Mr. Smith, who quitted the place upon the assurance of Arlines that he would be answerable, knew not how to address himself to the latter. He it was that had brought him to ruin, and yet he had just used his influence to stop the evil for a time.

"I am ruined," Arnold at length said, in a distressed tone, to Arlines.

"I hope not," replied Arlines; "at all events, we must see what can be done. Something may yet be done to retrieve what is lost."

"I have not the means; I have nothing left—it's useless to hope."

"Not so; meet me to night as usual; and though you may not play, yet you may be of use in some way or other. I have not any time to say more now, but will when I see you."

Arlines quitted Arnold immediately, as he desired not to hear the reproaches or the regrets of a man whom he had ruined, and whom he designed to become his tool in many deeds he yet contemplated should be done.

Arnold passed a day of misery. He quitted his home early in the day, and soon after Arlines left him, for he could not meet the faces of his children, whom he had so grievously injured. He wandered about the whole day, and resting awhile in taverns until night should come on, and the time arrive when he should meet with Arlines according to his promise.

The day, which had promised to be fine, was now nearly closed. The sun had not descended below the west for an hour, ere the wind, which had hitherto been lulled, now came on again with increased violence, and heavy clouds rode across the sky, passing the moon's face, and hiding for a space the clear silvery light she shed upon the earth.

The wind was fresh and laden with moisture, which, with the heavy gathering clouds, proclaimed a tempestuous night. Nor was it long before such a prediction became verified, for the rain fell, though lightly at first, heavily, and bore the appearance of being very likely to continue.

The streets were quickly deserted by all those who were abroad for pleasure and amusement, while those who were compelled to endure it hurried to and fro with the greatest rapidity they were able, endeavouring by their haste to shorten the period of their exposure to the inclemency of the weather.

The streets looked dreary and deserted; a few vehicles now only remained in the streets, though but a short period before the thoroughfares were crowded with carriages that were hastening towards their destinations. But now the contrast was great; the few that remained were only those for public convenience, and heavily laden carts and waggons, which dragged their slow length along, while the patient steeds bore the pitiless pelting of the rain, and slowly plodded on their way.

The howling of the wind as it rushed over the house-tops and through the streets was loud and constant, while the rain, which fell in showers, was carried drifting forwards, beating furiously against all that opposed its progress, and woe to the unfortunate wight who was compelled to face the weather.

The nearly empty streets were dark and quiet, but the occasional foot-fall of some compelled wanderer was to be heard, and the dull heavy beating of the rain as it fell against the door or shutter of some elevated house which stood more than ordinarily exposed.

The early part of the evening the moon had shed its kind influence upon the earth, though it was occasionally obscured by the passing clouds; but now it was totally hidden, for the heavy surcharged clouds covered the whole hemisphere as far as the eye could reach.

The rain in the meanwhile descended in heavy torrents, and the wind blew with violence, causing such a scene of desolation and dreary misery as can nowhere be seen save during a wet night in London.

Long before the storm was as its worst Captain Arnold was housed, but it was in the well-known hell where his ruin had been completed, and here it was that Arlines had appointed to meet him, and he came.

Arlines played but slightly on that night, but he lost, and then left off to watch othe players, which he did narrowly, though not obtrusively.

Among those who played recklessly and won largely was Bumpion Meadowbank, a knight of some little notoriety and fashion of the times, whose requisites for distinction were his extreme affectation and his recklessness in matters of fortune.

Sir Bumpion Meadowbank had been out more than one summer, and yet he stood his ground; he played, and yet often won, and on this occasion largely.

Phillip Arlines watched him closely, and appeared to be much interested in his actions, and at length he said to Arnold—

"Watch that Sir Bumpion, Arnold; for I cannot do so any more without exciting suspicion."

"Very well," replied Arnold; "but what do you intend to do with him; you don't appear to know him?"

"I do not, and so much the better. He has an abundance of cash and we have none."

"Well, what of that? It will not help us if he have more than enough."

"Indeed it will not if he be allowed to keep it; but we shall be all the better if a transfer is made of cash from his pocket to ours."

"Yes; but I confess I can't see how that is to be effected," replied Arnold.

"Well, never mind now; a short time will explain the mystery. I shall require your assistance, Arnold, in an affair that will need a little nerve and exertion."

"I will do anything to oblige you," said Arnold, quite unsuspicious of what the object of Arlines was.

Time wore on, and yet Sir Bumpion Meadowbank still sat at the table, and, to a certain extent, a winner. He played heedlessly enough, but much of this was affectation, and he was never known to hesitate about perjury when he owed or lost at the table.

At length, however, it grew late, and the knight rose, recollecting he had an appointment to meet some one,

"Come this way," said Arlines to Arnold, as he drew him towards the door.

They quitted the gaming-house, and Captain Arnold followed Phillip Arlines, who conducted him under a doorway, where they had a full view of the door of the gaming-house, and could see who came out.

"Now," said Arlines, "if he calls a coach we are done; but I think he won't wait for that, as there are none about here now."

"What do you intend to do?" inquired Arnold, much puzzled at what was passing.

"Why, we must have the money yonder fool has with him. We must have it; aid me to quiet him, and we shall be free to use his money. We must watch him till he comes to some quiet street, where we can easily set upon and manage him."

Arnold was about to reply, when Arlines drew him back, and said—

"Hush! hush! not a word. See, there he is—that's well; if he go up that turning we are safe to secure our prize."

Motioning Arnold to follow him, they gradually neared the object of their attack. Arlines placed his hat on the wrong way, so that the back and fore-part come over each ear, producing a strange effect, and certainly enough to disguise a gentleman in appearance. He recommended Arnold to do the same, which, from mere force of example, he did.

Phillip Arlines had plied Captain Arnold pretty freely with wine, and had him, to use his own expression, quite ripe for anything. This was true, not, however, from that cause; but Arnold was so abased in his own eyes, that he had neither spirit nor energy enough to have declined anything Arlines might have urged him to do as necessary.

"If he make any resistance," said Arlines, "you must strike him hard, just so as to render him insensible, and then we can possess ourselves of his cash, and be away before a word can be uttered."

They now came up with him, and Arlines made a blow at Sir Bumpion Meadowbank's head, which, missing its object, came heavily down on his shoulder.

Instinctively turning, he faced Arlines, and made a rush at him, with the intention of seizing him and calling out for aid; but Captain Arnold, thinking this the proper moment for his interference, threw out his foot, and aiming a blow with his clenched hand, he caused him to fall heavily to the ground, where he fell upon a curbstone, stunned and senseless.

"Be quick," exclaimed Arlines, "and search his pockets; we have no time to lose."

This was done by Arnold, who stooped down and did what he was desired from mere impulse, without thinking or exercising the least reflection or will.

Arlines did the like, but the search was soon over, and scarce a minute had elapsed from the first blow to the walking away of Arnold and Arlines.

The latter, after he had inquired of Arnold what he had obtained, said that he had but little, and the two amounts were put together and shared alike, though it might have been suspicious that so small a sum was found upon the person of the unfortunate man, and yet he was seen to have won much more.

Before the victim of Arlines' avarice could regain his feet and give an alarm, both he and Arnold were some distance off, and beyond hearing. Crossing Piccadilly, they both went up Regent-street, and amused themselves in the Quadrant, and after a while returning to Pic-

THE OFFICIOUS VALET DELIVERS PEARSON'S LETTER TO JESSIE.

cadilly, Arnold quitted Arlines, and proceeded towards his home.

Home! alas! such it was to him, and yet he dared scarcely show himself there. His thoughts were of the most painful description. His loss of fortune was a heavy blow to him, more for his children's sake than his own; yet the loss of honour, which until this event had never been sullied, afflicted him still more.

It was done so suddenly, and by mere impulse of the moment. He was brought so abject as not to have it in his power to refuse or withhold any assistance or co-operation.

It was with melancholy and sorrow most acute that he arrived at his own residence and rang for admission, and retired straight to his own apartment, not desiring even a chance of entering into conversation with Jessie, whose kindness and sorrow he felt like daggers to him. He shut himself up in his room, there to think over events that had happened, and were likely to happen.

CHAPTER XXX.

THE PROPOSAL AND THE BILL OF SALE.— CAPTAIN ARNOLD'S HOME.

SLEEP Captain Arnold could not; a short and uneasy slumber would for a short time wrap his senses in oblivion; but he awoke from it with a troubled frame of mind and feverish body. It appeared as if he had been dreaming, and could not recollect his dream, which had been so indistinct that he had forgotten it.

Thus he spent the night with a thousand vague and indistinct shadows, that exercised their gloomy influence over him, floating in his mind, and yet so ill-defined were they, that he could not signify which it was that tormented him most.

He was awake early, but fell at length into a troubled slumber, during which Phillip Arlines came to see him, and to converse with him upon several matters that were of importance to them both, but especially so to Arnold.

Arnold, scarcely conscious of what he was, or where he was, was some time before he could address even a word to Arlines when he entered the room, from a recollection of what had occurred the night before in Piccadilly.

"Arnold," said Arlines, as they shook hands, "I am the bearer of unpleasant intelligence; but I thought I had better be the bearer than leave you to be surprised and annoyed by and by."

"What can be the matter?" inquired Arnold, looking up in trouble and amazement. "I hope nothing of last night has been found out?"

"Nothing at all, and nothing more unlikely to happen, I assure you. By-the-by, that was well managed, and done cleverly. Such another or two would be the means of giving you a chance of retrieving your past misfortunes."

Captain Arnold shook his head mournfully, and then said with a sigh—

"I fear, Arlines, that I shall never encompass that object. I would that I could, not for my sake alone, but for those whom I ought never to have injured."

"Nay, you were fully entitled to do what you chose with what was your own, and they have no title to give you any uneasiness. But leave these considerations alone, and turn to brighter thoughts, and let hope be your guide."

Again Arnold shook his head, and said,—

"Well, well. I can't help what is passed. Misfortune and dishonour have both overtaken me, and punishment will follow. But what is that you came to tell me?"

'Merely this—Mr. Smith has called upon me, and urges an immediate settlement, and says it is so unusual a thing to give what he calls credit that I had some difficulty in quieting him for a time, upon the promise, however, that I would obtain from you some definite promise and arangement for its settlement."

Captain Arnold did not reply for several seconds: he felt that he was indeed poor and helpless; the very bed under him was another's, and both he and his children were liable to be turned out at a moment's notice. At length he said in a low tone,—

"What can I do? He has all, and I remain here but from sufferance; what more would he have, or I to give?"

"This much; give him a bill of sale of the whole, and that instrument he can instantly raise money upon, and thus he need not disturb you in your home for some time at least."

"That I cannot object to," replied Arnold, who never thought or dreamed of offering any opposition to making the whole of his fortune over to the man he believed had won it fairly of him, and who was fully entitled to come and take immediate possession of the house, and all it contained, without any opposition.

"Then if you do that you will relieve me of my responsibility, and at the same time it will induce him not to be hasty in dispossessing you; indeed he will not have the same motive to do so."

"What motive, more or less, could he have?" inquired Arnold.

"Merely that of obtaining quiet legal possession, for the longer that was delayed, the more trouble it would give him; but I told him there was no fear that you would act otherwise than rightly by him, and he said, no, he did not think you would, especially as he had my guarantee. So he had his eye fixed upon my security."

"He need not be under any apprehension on that account; I will give it him whenever he will get it prepared."

"Then this evening we will meet him and do all that is necessary, and then this matter will be ended; after which we must contrive something else that will relieve you of some of your most pressing difficulties."

"Be it as you say," replied Arnold. "I will meet you; but as for aught else, do not let it be of the same complexion as the last. I would sooner suffer any extreme."

"But recollect, Captain Arnold, there are others, who, being dependant upon you, will at all events cause you to be not quite so scrupulous as, if you yourself were the only consideration, you would or might be. But no more of this; I shall see you this evening."

"Yes, certainly, I will be sure to meet you at the appointed time."

Phillip Arlines then quitted Captain Arnold, and left the house, and congratulated himself upon the success with which his scheme had been conducted so far, and that it was probable enough that all would go on as he had designed it should.

That evening would at least set the question of property at rest. Captain Arnold would, indeed, be a beggar, and as such the more pliable and easy to be brought to his purposes. He thought, too, that when the father was steeped in crime and misery, and that only he, Phillip Arlines, stood between him and utter destruction, that the daughter would abate something of her pride and hatred.

"To save her father," he argued, "Jessie will consent to my proposal. She shall be mine, as I chose to take her. When I can command the fate of the father—when I can say, you die this death or that—that it is in my power to consign you, not only to poverty and punishment, but to disgrace also, then the proud Jessie Arnold will sue for mercy.

"The signing of that bond converts a questionable deed into a legal act; and though he could not recover the money according to law, yet with this bill of sale all can be done, and in a very short time from this Arnold must quit this villa for a place of much more humble appearance and pretension."

The day passed heavily with Arnold, who knew not what to do with himself. He now lost that relish for the love of home he once so strongly felt—and why? It was no longer a home to him: it was a spot full of the most poignant reflections.

A reproach was evident in every well-known article of furniture—each face that he saw he felt carried a well merited reproof to his heart. The comforts and joys of home were to him for ever fled.

The ruined gamester, whether he be the victim of his own folly or another man's cunning and fraud, has no title to think of home. Now, indeed, he has none, he could sell—barter, nay risk, not only home and all it contained, but life and honour,—ay, all that could be staked, it matters not what—still the stake must be paid when the ruthless creditor chooses.

Captain Arnold had done all this—at least he had done so much as leads to the rest, so much as leads certainly to what follows as that one event precedes another. Gaming is a sure introduction to misfortune, and few know how to escape her clutches. Captain Arnold had done this much: he had ruined himself, and made his innocent family beggars. He had connected them with crime in the person of himself, and it is always a question as to where such things shall end.

These thoughts tortured the mind of Arnold, and he again quitted home early in the day to seek in excitement and the change of place that riddance of reflection which so often pursues those who are for the first time immersed in the toils of crime and folly.

This being Captain Arnold's situation, no wonder it is then that he sought to drown all remembrance of his errors by hurrying forward into all kinds of scenes that tended to excite his imagination, and cause him to think of something that would keep his attention from his own affairs.

When the evening drew on he made towards the spot where he was to meet with Phillip Arlines and his confederate, Mr. Smith.

He was a little before his time, but he had not long to wait before they came; and then the three adjourned to the house of a solicitor, who drew up the document, and had it engrossed ere they arrived at his office.

"You are aware, Captain Arnold, of the nature of this document?" inquired the solicitor.

"Yes, I am," was the reply.

"Then I believe we may proceed to execute it," the man of law remarked.

The fact was that Arlines and Smith had a notion that if they had the deed drawn up by a respectable man it would add an appearance that must stamp it as a genuine transaction— nay, the very thing that would materially assist them should any question ever be raised.

The deed was duly read over by the solicitor, and then he handed it to Arnold to sign. This he did with a tremulous hand and an aching heart.

This done, the solicitor received his costs, and the whole party quitted the house and stood in consultation for a few moments, and then it was agreed that they should separate, as Arlines had some business to transact, and would meet Arnold an hour or two later.

Captain Arnold was no sooner alone than he ejaculated in an under tone, but one which evinced his feeling—

"I am now a beggar; I and my children are without a home and scarce the means of procuring a single meal. All—all is gone! We are beggars—we are beggars!"

So saying, he hurried forward, he scarce knew in what direction, with the hope that he should escape the inflictions consequent to his station and circumstances.

CHAPTER XXXI.

THE ESPIAL.—THE LETTER TO PEARSON.—
THE ATTEMPTED MURDER.

THE villain, George Gosset, employed by Phillip Arlines to take the life of Alfred Pearson, had well laid his snares, and taken every precaution he could think of that would ensure the destruction of his victim.

This man was ruthless and bloodthirsty, and had no compunction at shedding human blood provided his own neck was not endangered thereby; and this he believed to be a case in which he ran no danger of detection.

He had carefully watched the house in which Pearson resided, and in the course of time become well acquainted with the appearance of everybody who came out or went in without himself exciting any suspicion, or even being noticed or seen by any one in the house.

Opposite to Pearson's residence there was a low public-house, one that was situated at the corner of a mews, and commanding a view of the door, out of which all proceeded who entered or left the house. The roof of the parlour was low, and but very few went there during the day; the custom of the place was chiefly at night or in the evening.

Here Gosset used to sit at the window pretending to read the newspaper, but in reality watching the door of Pearson's house with a lynx eye, and none went in or came out but he carefully noted them; and it was difficult to detect which way Cross-eyed George was really looking; few people could tell; it appeared to be a perpetual secret, which he never divulged to any one.

He was well disguised by a suit of clothes that were very unlike anything he ever wore, and which he would scarce ever wear again.

Here he sat day after day until he had fairly become acquainted with the person of, as he believed, Alfred Pearson; but, to make sure of that, he called to the boy who scoured and cleaned the pots, and waited in the tap, saying—

"Who is that gentleman who has just passed? I have often seen him."

"Oh, that's Mr. Alfred Pearson, sir; he's a nice gentleman, a werry nice gentleman."

"He lives about here, I should say, then?" inquired Gosset.

"Yes, he does, and if you looks you'll find him go into that house opposite, and then come to the front winders."

Gosset did watch, and was now sure of his victim, and the next thing was to entice him to some lonely spot, where the deed could be attempted without any danger from interruption.

This was a consideration of the first importance, because if time and place were favourable, Gosset swore to himself with a deep oath that he should no longer be a living man, for he feared no one man; and, to do the monster credit, he did not. Few men were better adapted for the commission of such crimes both mentally and physically.

Thoroughly inured to crime, and capable of great physical energy and strength, little doubt remained on the mind of Arlines but that the wish of success of his diabolical scheme of the murder would be carried out fully and successfully.

Gosset now sought Arlines, and explained to him what he had done: he had ascertained the identity of Alfred Pearson.

"Well," exclaimed Arlines, "and is this all you are going to do? You know the man, and yet he lives."

"Yes, yes, Arlines, I know that very well. We shan't be able to kill him in the open street; now that's nearly the only place he walks through. Can't you invent some plan by which you can draw him from home to some particular spot, where I should be in waiting for him, and give him a reception he little expected?"

"Yes, I have a thought," said Arlines, suddenly recollecting himself. "I will obtain a letter in the handwriting of some one whom he knows, and send it by post, desiring him to meet her under the wall by eight or nine o'clock at night."

"Ay, ay, that will do," replied Gosset— "that will do; but make it nine if you can, because it gives one a better chance."

"I will do so," replied Arlines; "but be sure you do it effectually—no half measures. Hit hard in the first place, and your work is accomplished; but if you give him half a chance he will turn upon you, and he can use his limbs I promise you."

"What, you have found that out, have you, Master Phillip? Well, well, never look so glum, man, over it; but you know that you were meant for roguery and I for a fight. What's the odds if you did get beaten when you attempted my line? Why, I should fail if I attempted yours."

Swallowing this compliment with the best grace he could, Arlines gave his companion some further instructions, and then they both parted, Arlines to concoct the letter, and Gosset to seek some congenial public-house where he could pass the time until the evening set in, where he would seek the appointed spot, and lay in concealment until the unsuspecting victim of Arlines' treachery should be at the appointed spot.

In the meanwhile Arlines wrote a short note in the handwriting of Jessie, begging that he, Alfred Pearson, would meet her that evening under the wall of Kensington Gardens, when she would inform him of something that had happened, and begging his advice and assistance.

This letter was posted so that it should reach him but a short time before the moment for the appointment was due, so that Pearson would have no time to reflect upon what course to pursue; and he must either go or reject it, which latter was very unlikely.

The letter reached Pearson, who happened to be at home—indeed, he had been detained on account of some trifling indisposition. When he opened and read it he at once determined upon meeting Jessie.

He could not doubt the genuineness of the letter, for, from the little he had seen of Jessie's writing, this was much like jit. He looked upon it as a mark of her esteem and confidence, and would not have missed attending upon any consideration.

True it was that he considered the place and hour somewhat at variance with Jessie's timid character; but then he thought that the most fearful girl would make a heroine in such a cause as that in which Jessie was engaged—namely, the rescuing her father from ruin.

"Some heavy misfortune has overtaken them, I fear," he thought, after reading the note for the twentieth time; "that villain, Arlines, has succeeded in bringing him to the brink of ruin, I dare say. Pity it is that such a man should have been gifted with such a tongue: it is merely used but to betray."

Again he mused in silence for some minutes, and then he exclaimed—

"Nine o'clock—why it's eight now; I shall not have much time. It is more than probable that she will be there before the appointed hour. I will set out at once, and get there as soon as I can."

This thought no sooner crossed his mind than he grew impatient, and was soon after on his way to Kensington Gardens.

The evening was cold and chilly; a raw dampness pervaded the air, and there being no moon, the heavens were as dark as could be imagined. There being many heavy clouds, the stars were not visible, and save where there were lamps, there was nought that could be seen but at a very short distance indeed.

Alfred wrapped his cloak around him tightly, and at the same moment increased his speed towards the spot where he expected to meet with Jessie, for if she were waiting there for him he felt that she must have but a dull and wretched watch.

The distance between the spot appointed and that which he had left was soon traversed, and Pearson approached the spot that was named to him in the note.

"She is not here at all events. Well, I am glad she is not, for I should have been very sorry if she had been waiting in this dull and miserable place for me."

He paced up and down in silence, awaiting with impatience the coming of Jessie Arnold. There was another there, also, who awaited but his coming close enough to him to deal him a deadly blow with a heavily loaded stick; and this was George Gosset, who watched his victim's motions with all the malignancy such a nature was capable of feeling against anything human.

At length, finding he came no nearer, he stole from his place of concealment, and noiselessly approached Pearson, for it was so dark that it was almost impossible to see aught in such a place surrounded by trees as it was.

Raising his stick and holding it a moment or two in the air, he brought it down with all his strength, but in descending it caught an overhanging bough that deprived it of all its velocity and weight, but yet it came sharply upon Pearson's head, who reeled beneath the blow.

Gosset saw he had been baulked in his blow, else Pearson would in all probability have been deprived of sense, perhaps life. As it was, he was nearly stunned, but he quickly recovered, and endeavoured to escape by flight, for he saw not who had struck the blow.

"Help! help!" he cried, loudly, at the same time making what speed he was able.

Gosset muttered an oath, and renewed the attack by giving him another desperate blow that crushed his hat in, and brought him down on his knees almost insensible; yet still from instinct he called out "Help, help!" in a loud and clear voice; and while doing so he was, for the third time, stricken; but the blow scarcely took any effect, when he arose, and made a desperate attack upon Gosset, whom he seized, and by some means threw him down. They fought for some time, until at length Gosset struck him down with the heavy bludgeon he carried.

He stood a moment, and then again raised the murderous weapon to extinguish the last spark of life, if any was left, when the park-keepers appeared, having heard the cry for help. Gosset saw them, and retreating beneath the trees, made off unseen. They lifted Pearson up, and carried him to the nearest lodge in a state of insensibility.

CHAPTER XXXII.

AFTER THE ATTEMPTED MURDER.—THE DEPOSITION.—CAPTAIN ARNOLD'S DESPAIR. —THE TAUNT OF THE BETRAYER.

So severe and savage had been the assault upon Alfred Pearson, that it was at first believed by those who raised him from the ground and conveyed him to the Park lodge that he was really dead. Indeed, he showed no sign of animation whatever, and a great deal of consternation arose upon the subject. Of course, the nearest medical man was instantly sent for, and even he when he came had some difficulty to assure himself that the vital spark had actually not fled, but still lingered in the insensible form of the seriously wounded young man.

"This is a very serious case indeed," he said; "and unless the injuries are much less than I suppose them to be, or there is a renovating power in this young man's constitution such as we rarely meet with, he cannot live till the morning. It is necessary that a magistrate should take instant cognisance of the circumstances. I daresay I can restore him to consciousness, but I should prefer doing so when some proper authority is here to receive any statement he may wish to make as regards the persons who have inflicted these wounds upon him."

This advice was too sound and rational to be neglected, and one of the Park keepers was immediately dispatched to procure the assistance of the police.

Meanwhile poor Pearson remained in a state of total oblivion of all around; and it was not until the surgeon began to think the keeper would soon return, and likewise that the danger of his patient might be increased by allowing him to remain so long insensible, that he proceeded to take active measures to restore him to consciousness.

By the assistance of those about him, he succeeded in about ten minutes in eliciting some signs of animation from the wounded man. Pearson unclosed his eyes, and uttered a deep groan of anguish.

"He is recovering," remarked the surgeon. "After all there is no knowing what may be the result of this case. It often happens in practice the most apparently dangerous flesh wounds have not affected any vital part, and the patient gets well with great rapidity."

"Jessie—Jessie," groaned Pearson, and he swung his arms wildly about him as if in a perfect delirium.

The surgeon shook his head.

"I fear," he said, "we shall get no account of the transaction from him."

"Jessie—Jessie—my Jessie," again said Pearson; and the men present were shocked at the tone of deep anguish with which the name was uttered.

At this moment a tap was heard at the outer door of the lodge, and upon its being opened three gentlemen made their appearance, accompanied by the officer who had been sent to communicate with the police. Two of those gentlemen were magistrates, and the third was a gentleman connected with the rangership of the park, who had been accidentally with one of the magistrates when the information of the outrage was brought to him. They expressed the utmost sympathy with the condition of the young man, and the magistrate in whose particular district the occurrence had happened, said—

"A deposition as to the circumstances of this attempt at murder, for such it must have been, will be very important if now coming from the wounded party. Do you think he is able to make any statement?"

"It is difficult to say," replied the surgeon. "We can try. He seems delirious."

"No—no," said Pearson, in a faint voice. "I am better now, and can tell all—all."

"That will do," said the surgeon. "He is perfectly sane."

The magistrate stepped forward to question Pearson, and at the same moment a footstep was heard passing the lodge.

"See who that is," he said. "We should have all the evidence we can respecting the construction to be put upon the statement this wounded man may make. If he who is passing be a respectable person, pray ask him in to hear the deposition."

One of the keepers hurried out, and accosting the stranger who was passing, he said—

"Sir, a gentleman has been murdered, we fear, in the park. He is not dead, and is about to make some statement of who attacked him, which it is necessary as many persons should be witnesses to as possible. Will you step in and hear it?"

"Certainly," was the reply; and the passing passenger at once followed the keeper into the lodge. There was nothing in the expression of the stranger's face but surprise and sympathy as he entered the small room; but when he, after leaving the magistrates and the surgeon, advanced sufficiently near to have a view of the person wounded, he started back, and in a voice of astonishment and emotion exclaimed—

"Gracious God, Mr. Pearson!"

The sound of his name spoken so loudly, and with so much emotion, caused the wounded man to turn his eyes upon the speaker, and he immediately said—

"Captain Arnold! Is it possible?"

It was, indeed, Captain Arnold himself, who had been taking his way slowly homeward on that eventful evening, full of sad and gloomy thoughts, when he had his progress arrested by the request of the park keeper.

"Yes," he said, "I am Captain Arnold. By what dreadful mischance do I see you in such a condition?"

"You know this wounded gentleman?" interposed the magistrate.

"I do; his name is Pearson. I need not say how much I am grieved to see him in such a condition. Mr. Pearson, when we last parted it was not as friends, but now all sorts of disagreements are forgotten. What can I do for you?"

Pearson turned his eyes upon the captain's face, and said sadly—

"If, indeed, I am dying, I would fain see Jessie before my soul wings its way to eternity."

"You shall—you shall," said Arnold, deeply affected "But let me hope your case is not so bad."

" I am sadly hurt."

" Gentlemen," said Captain Arnold, turning to the magistrates, " this gentleman has laid me, by saving the life of one of my children, under the deepest obligation. We have, however, had a little disagreement, in which, I fear, I have been to blame. He desires to see my daughter. Will you permit me to gratify him and please myself by allowing me to fetch her? God forbid that I should place myself in the way of this interview at such a time as this."

" Certainly," said the magistrate. " Go at once, sir. We will take what evidence Mr. Pearson has to offer in your absence. Go at once, sir."

" I presume," said the other magistrate, " and in so doing I do not wish to give offence to any one, that you, Mr. Pearson, acquit entirely Captain Arnold of any part in this affair ?"

" Entirely and completely," said Alfred Pearson.

Captain Arnold turned upon the magistrate as if he were about to make some angry remark; but his better judgment came to his aid, and he passed out of the lodge without uttering a word.

His intention was really to find Jessie, and bring her as speedily as possible to the park lodge, where he verily believed Alfred Pearson was dying. He walked very hastily; but he had not proceeded a couple of hundred yards when he heard the voice of Phillip Arlines calling to him from the other side of the park wall, over which, at that part, it was easy to see any one.

To meet Arlines at such a time was agony to Captain Arnold, and he resolved to avoid him. Increasing his pace, he gave no heed to his repeated calls, and the last he saw of him was in clambering over the park wall to pursue him.

Determined, then, more than ever upon avoiding him—for he knew that an objection would be raised to Jessie's visit to the dying Pearson, and, alas! he, Captain Arnold, was by far too much in the power of his arch tempter even to resist his mandates—escape from him, then, seemed his only plan, and he fled with great haste he knew not where.

It was not sufficiently dark for him to elude pursuit by plunging into any door-way or behind any tree, so he had no resource but to actual speed. He dashed down a lane which presented itself to him, after he had gone a couple of miles at least, still hotly pursued by Arlines; and, finding a gate open in a wall, he rushed through it, closed it behind him, and found himself in the grounds of an apparently extensive mansion. He no longer heard the pursuing footsteps of Arlines, and he glanced around with no small curiosity on the place of refuge he had thus found.

It was a lone and deserted spot, and a desolate one, too; for here, at one time, the young, the gay, the beautiful, and the good passed hours and days, nay, years of happiness, alloyed to some, but unalloyed to others; and this spot, which was now shunned by the simple peasant, was once the abode of those whose spirits were long since freed from all earthly trammels, and none would willingly have passed through what had at one time been the ornamental grounds surrounding the mansion after sunset, to have insured himself a life of ease and plenty for ever after.

The old mansion was fast falling to decay; but it was a scene that the lover of the picturesque might contemplate with feelings of pleasure, tinged, perhaps, with melancholy, that so venerable a pile should be fast falling to decay, and giving a sure indication that it would not, without help, sustain itself in its present gloomy grandeur, if the hand of man did not interpose to stay the ravages of time.

It was composed of deep-red brick, but now this colour was in many places perfectly obliterated by time and the weather, for many a raging storm had exhausted its beating fury upon this noble structure, almost blackening its very walls. The long rows of tall, straight windows were relieved at either end by circular corners, rising in the manner and shape of towers, whose tops were turreted, and in and out of which the aged ivy crept, while its glossy leaves reflected back the sun's last rays towards the ground, for the mansion had been constructed on a hill towards the west, and the lawn ran in an inclined plane from the building, while the hill rose gently behind it.

The rays of the setting sun glowed upon the windows, which reflected back the fleeting rays with a blaze of red light peculiar to such moments, and which could be seen for many miles round by the simple peasantry, who, not knowing the cause, would whisper to each other that some fell spirit was holding its orgies, and that the old house was in a blaze of light, and the windows were always illuminated on the western side of the mansion.

Indeed it stood so high and lofty that, save a few giant trees behind, it was the last object that the sun shone upon, while the valley below lay in dim twilight; and it was this, to them unaccountable, appearance of light that much of the fear they were inspired with owed its origin.

The building had at one time been surrounded by a strong wall and ditch, while it was approached by a long and well preserved avenue, the entrance to which was through a large pair of folding gates, and a lodge; but the gates had long since fallen to pieces, and offered no bar to the curious who desired to visit the spot.

The shrubs that once adorned the grounds had now run up, and presented an impenetrable mass of tangled and dark foliage, and rank weeds choked up the paths; the jay and the daw built their nests upon the tree tops, while the owl and the bat appropriated many dark nooks and crannies in the thick ivy and mouldering walls and chimneys of the building.

Behind it lay what had once been servants' offices, stabling, and other necessary outbuildings to such a mansion; but these, too, were in a state of decay—indeed, much worse, for they had not the solid strength of the walls of the main building itself. The windows in most cases were either partially or wholly broken, presenting a truly pitiable aspect.

The rooms were numerous, and many of them extremely capacious, and when well appointed and well lighted must have had an imposing effect, for they would vie with many saloons. Such a house, with a generous owner, in the season of festivity, would have been a scene worth engraving on the tablets of the memory, and handing down to posterity. Now, however, all that remained was the ruins; grand and even beautiful as they were, there was yet something that cast a shade of melancholy over the mind of the observer as the association of ideas called up images of the past but to be contrasted with that which was.

Judging that Arlines must have passed on, Captain Arnold, thinking he had delayed long enough to make himself perfectly safe, thought of emerging from that place which was so singularly deserted by its owners, or those who had been left in charge of it.

So rapid had been his flight from the neighbourhood of Hyde Park, that he had not the least idea of how much ground he had gone over, or of where he really was. There was such a stillness and loneliness around him, too, that he became quite infected by it, and full of strange superstitious thoughts and fancies.

After a time he made a struggle to free himself from such imaginative terrors, and resolved to walk on until he should meet some one who would be able and willing to direct him his proper way.

"Alas, poor Pearson," he said, with a sigh; "he has fallen a victim to Arlines. I cannot doubt it; and I, too, am so deeply and inextricably entangled in the meshes of his dark and terrible policy, that I struggle in vain to escape from him. Where will be the end of all this misery and degradation into which I am plunged?"

The unhappy man shuddered as the real state of the case came up before him in a terrific shape—a shape which had become each day lately more and more familiar to his imagination. The word, suicide, kept continually recurring to him, and that he told himself would be his end in this world.

He groaned aloud as he repeated the words, "Suicide—suicide." Oh, there was a time when the very thought of such a consummation would have appeared to Captain Arnold the very acme of moral cowardice; but then his soul was free from crime, his honour unpolluted, and he could stand unflinchingly before the world a man of courage, a man of honour, who might in the strong armour of his known integrity defy the fates to inflict more than a passing pang upon his heart.

Now, how changed was all this! Fallen—fallen—fallen from his high estate. Lost—degraded utterly, where was he to turn for support against the misfortunes of life?—where was he to find the moral courage to face the crowding evils he saw too surely in the dim future? Suicide! Yes, suicide was the horrible resource. To assume the arbitration of his own mortal career, and, uncalled-for by his God, to stand in the awful presence of the Majesty of Heaven, with his own blood upon his hands, to answer the dreadful question of, "Man, what dost thou here unbidden?"

These were feelings that ran riot through his brain; and had he at that time, on that evening, possessed the means of at once and easily hurling himself into eternity, it is likely he would have done so, in the excess of agony that beset him at that still hour in that lonely spot.

All hope of reaching home, and then the park lodge, in time to fulfil the promise he had made to Alfred Pearson, was now gone, and Captain Arnold had a firm persuasion that by then the young man was surely dead.

"I am a curse," he said, "to all who know me. The shadow of my own evil destiny seems cast upon all who have any sort of connection with me. Oh, if any one would raise a hand against my life, sparing me the sin of self-murder, I would plead for their forgiveness at the throne of Heaven for the welcome deed."

In this state of terrible excitement of mind he walked about a mile before he met any one, and then he heard a solitary footstep approaching. The sound recalled him back to earth again, and summoning as firm a voice as he could, he said,—

"Can you direct me towards London?"

"Yes," was the reply. "The nearest way is through the churchyard."

"What churchyard?"

"Barnes. There it lies. You are close to the wicket gate. It is always open. Then you follow the new path. You cannot miss it. You will reach Hammersmith first."

"Thank you—thank you!"

Captain Arnold pushed open a small wicket gate which was close at hand, and not without a feeling of awe creeping over him, he entered the precincts of the dead. He walked slowly

THE ATTEMPTED MURDER OF PEARSON BY GEORGE GOSSET.

and quietly, for he felt that that was hallowed ground, and would not, by a rude footstep, disturb the solemn devotional stillness that there existed.

"Oh, would," he moaned, "that I were as these are, sleeping the calm sleep that knows no waking, in peace and in hope."

A slight wind rustled through the trees—the broad shadow cast by the church and the grave-stones gave a striking and singular appearance—every piece of moulding threw a long shadow down the front of the church, while the tower and steeple caused a long belt

of shade to be thrown right across the church-yard.

Here, indeed, was the quietude of the grave —extreme solitariness seemed to inhabit the churchyard, and he who walked among the old graves would scarce be able to resist the impression that such a scene was calculated to convey. Contemplation here might be pursued unbroken among the last homes of the dead.

The old yews threw a deep shade in one corner of the chuchyard, on a gloomy spot, which even the lover of the sad and solitary would approach with a feeling of deeper awe than even those spots where the mouldering remains of humanity lay; for then there seemed something like life, were it only that which had been.

The old church was an object of mystery, interest, and even wonder. On one side the moon's rays fell, fully illuminating the whole edifice, while the opposite side was thrown into complete shade, the windows reflected back the moonlight, and presented a strange and beautiful appearance.

The dews of night had fallen heavily, and the grass was wet, while the white vapour hung low in the hollow places, floating about here and there as if it sought to hide itself in the holes of the earth.

The iron tongue of the church clock chimed out the hour of midnight, and its vibrations were heard distinctly upon the night air; this was the moment for reflection, when the inhabitants of this hemisphere lay wrapped in deep slumber, save the few that conscience or despair robbed of their sleep.

Scarce a living creature moved, the bat had slunk to the shade of the trees, and all were at rest save the solitary owl, forced by the sharp sting of hunger to leave his abode in search of food; but he moved as if he feared to disturb the wrapt repose of the night, and swept noiselessly through the air.

Wondering where he was, Captain Arnold passed on, and it was not for some hours, and after repeated inquiries, that he found his way to his own house.

Upon the very threshold stood Phillip Arlines.

CHAPTER XXXIII.

THE PRESSURE OF WANT.—THE TEMPORARY REFUGE.—THE CONSENT TO MORE CRIME.—A DAUGHTER'S LOVE.

IT was some moments before either party spoke; Phillip Arlines preserved a strict silence, and Captain Arnold was unable, from surprise and vexation, to utter a word; and had he been capable of expressing himself, he would have found a difficulty in doing so; for he could neither give shape nor form to his feelings, they were so mixed and various: but all he could with any certainty and distinctness have expressed was, that he neither expected nor desired to see Phillip Arlines.

At length the lattter, seeing the captain's confusion, said—

"This is a fortunate meeting, Captain Arnold; I had scarcely expected it."

"Why, it is late," said the captain, "and I should have been home before, but for an unpleasant rencontre."

"Indeed?"

"Yes—but I did not expect to see you here," said Captain Arnold.

"Perhaps not," replied Arlines.

"You said," continued Captain Arnold, "that you desired to see me; have you anything fresh to tell me?"

"No," replied Arlines, "but to ask you what was going on at the park lodge this evening when I saw you come out?"

"You saw me?" said Captain Arnold. "I was called in to see a wounded man, and hear his last deposition; for he was supposed to be dying, or so near it, as to make it necessary to obtain what information they could in this manner."

"Who was the unfortunate man?" inquired Arlines, with a sneer.

"Who he was, or is, I am convinced, by your asking the question," replied Arnold, "in the manner you do, that you well know, and could as correctly name him as I can."

Phillip Arlines laughed, as he heard the captain pronounce these words, in a careless manner, and said unconcernedly—

"I should judge, then, it must be young Pearson from your manner. Well, never mind, it is one enemy the less; but what do you purpose doing now you are home?"

"I have promised him, as a dying request, that I will allow him to see Jessie before he is quite gone."

"Do not do it," said Arlines.

"Do not do it!" exclaimed Arnold; "why not? Surely there can be no harm in that."

"It is not worth while doing it, for it can confer no benefit upon either; and as for Jessie, it will but strain her feelings to the utmost to see a man dying and flying from life as fast as the hours fly; it will but make her ill, and perhaps do her serious mischief."

"I think the same thing may occur if she did not go to him. Besides, I have promised to him my word, and should not like to break my word with him under such circumstances."

"He is dying, and therefore it is of but little consequence what he thinks; he will never be able to tell you you broke your word; and what else fear you?"

"I fear nothing," replied Arnold, "upon that score; though I should feel but ill satisfied with myself if I consented to break my word with a dying man; for if sincerity be used towards any one, it ought to be pursued towards those who are in such a sad condition."

Arlines sneered as the captain uttered these words, and an expression of more than diabolical meaning came across his features, and he said—

"Captain Arnold, I cannot but think this was unnecessary; if you throw aside all such considerations as your daughter's health, the hour, the inutility of such a measure, and the harrowing nature of the interview, yet still it must be an unnecessary measure."

"I do not see how you can make it so," replied Arnold.

"Why, if he recovers, such a measure must be of the worst consequences, as it will tend to cement an acquaintance that it is desirable should be utterly broken off; and if he do not recover, he will need no extra emotion to urge him on his journey, which he is sure to travel; therefore it is needless; and by this time, he is either better or worse; if better, he will recover, and if worse, I doubt if you will get there before the breath leaves his body. Consider well, Captain Arnold, it can do no good, and stay away."

"I will, at least," said Arnold, "show that I have the inclination to keep my word with him. I will go, and so shall Jessie. I would it had never happened; he saved a child of mine, and it shall not be said I refused to put myself or my child out of the way to gratify his dying wish; I will go and take Jessie with me."

As he said these words, Captain Arnold pressed forward with the intention of going in, but Arlines stood before him, and gently pressed his arm with his hand.

"A moment or two more, Captain Arnold," said Arlines, softly, and with a peculiar expression of countenance, that caused Captain Arnold to step back, and gaze on him with astonishment.

"What would you say?" demanded Arnold, with dismay, for he feared what was to follow, though he knew not what it was.

"That this interview must not take place: I forbid it."

"You forbid it?"

"Yes; you force me to be explicit. I have endeavoured to persuade you, but it is hopeless, and now I must command, for I do not wish it to take place; therefore, do not let Jessie go to this man, who may be, for all you know, dead by this time."

Arnold felt sick at heart, and yet he determined to make one more effort for personal freedom, and said—

"Mr. Arlines, I am master of my own actions and my children's; I shall, therefore, go."

"Indeed, you must not! You dare not go, when I say you shall not. Dare to disobey my injunctions, and you shall then really and truly find the power I have over you; for you are at my entire mercy in every way you can imagine. Beware, therefore, how you make me your enemy; for, without my friendship, you would scarce live, and, if my enmity were raised, you would be crushed indeed, and your children at the mercy of the world."

"But, Arlines," argued Arnold, in a subdued tone, "this matter cannot, by any possibility, be one that will interfere with any plan of yours; therefore, then, allow me to fulfil my promise."

"It does interfere, and, therefore, I prohibit it," replied Arlines, decisively, "and once more, Captain Arnold, permit me to say that you must do nothing that I object to. I have my own plans, both for myself and you, by which you may be as much benefited as myself; but I have the conducting of them; and, therefore, only know what is, or is not, inimical to them, and, of course, act accordingly."

As Arlines uttered these words, he turned from the door, and quitted the spot.

It was some moments before Captain Arnold recovered from the shock that the conduct of Philip Arlines had given him; he was stupified and utterly incapable of understanding clearly where he was, and what he was about to do. Indeed, he found himself in his own house, seated on a sofa, with his daughter Jessie kneeling at his feet, sobbing with extreme grief, without being well able to account to himself how he came there.

Jessie's grief was the first thing that he became sensible of, and after a moment or two's hesitation, he said—

"Jessie, my dear Jessie, do not grieve so; it will break your father's heart. I have had enough of trouble and disagreeables of late; but we will bury that in oblivion. Come to my arms, Jessie, and tell me that you will not grieve that we are not as we once were."

"Oh, my dear father," said Jessie throwing herself into her father's arms, in an agony of grief, "it grieves me to the heart to hear you talk thus; but you are unable to comprehend what I say, and the sad tale I have been telling. Surely this man, this Arlines——"

"Name him not—name him not!" said the captain, with a deprecatory action; "we will think of ourselves, dearest, and in doing so we shall alone find true happiness."

"I know it, I know it, dear father," replied Jessie; "but you do not attend to what I have been telling you; and yet it is a terrible thing."

"What is it, my child?" said the captain, who began to collect his senses, and to fear some new evil had happened during his absence.

"My little sister Rosa," said Jessie, "she is——"

"Dead!" exclaimed Captain Arnold, starting back, for he saw by Jessie's countenance and grief the worst that could happen had now overtaken them.

"Yes, she is dead—alas! my poor sister!" exclaimed Jessie.

A fresh burst of grief now came over her, and she sunk on her father's shoulder.

Captain Arnold's feelings were painfully

excited. All the grief that he so keenly felt at the loss of his beloved wife, but which of late had been stifled by the peculiar nature of his circumstances, and the extreme anxiety they had produced upon his mind, now burst out fresh upon him, and he was scarcely able to offer the slightest consolation to his daughter; indeed the little he did was done in a manner more calculated to arouse her grief; so sorrow striken was he that he became an object of pity from his utter prostration.

This extreme grief could not last long; the chamber of death subdued and calmed those violent outbreaks of grief that had previously threatened to destroy his mind, and induced a more quiet and gentler flow of sorrow.

It was while in this state of mind, that Jessie then proceeded to inform him of their all but state of destitution; they required everything, and yet they had nothing; and, more, they were beset by persons coming there constantly for money.

"What are we to do?" said Jessie; "we are in debt everywhere, and can obtain no more credit: indeed, those who have given us credit are clamorous, and threaten the worst to obtain payment of what is due to them."

Captain Arnold was struck with the true picture of the state of his affairs, and struck his forehead with his hand, and, after a few moments' pause, he said—

"Jessie, I will obtain some of the necessary means to stay the clamours of creditors, and to purchase all that is needful; at least, in the morning, I will go out and strain every nerve I have to do so, and doubt not but I shall be successful. In the meantime, my dear child, be calm, and grieve not too much; we have had a terrible loss. My poor little child I grieve is gone; but she has gone, I hope, to join her mother in bliss. Say no more. say no more, Jessie: I cannot bear it; grief and sorrow have made me what I am, and anything from you, or were I to lose you, Jessie, my heart would break, my mind would be one scene of chaos, and reason would never revisit her throne."

Seeing her father's agitated state of mind, Jessie endeavoured to instil some hope of the future into his mind, and begged him for their sakes to be firm and resolved, and all yet might be well.

She then left him; and the captain sat for nearly two hours without changing his posture, and then he threw himself upon his bed, and fell into an uneasy slumber.

———

CHAPTER XXXIV.

THE UNSUCCESSFUL SEARCH FOR AR-LINES.—CAPTAIN ARNOLD'S REFLEC-TIONS.—THEIR REMOVAL.

THE next morning Captain Arnold rose earlier than usual, and after visiting Jessie, he visited the remains of his once promising child, and with a tear in his eye, kissed the cold lips that had often expressed love and affection for him, but which now had ceased to move, and then, half maddened, he quitted the house.

*   *   *   *

Captain Arnold had promised Jessie to do his utmost to relieve their wants, and had that morning quitted his house for the purpose of so doing; his intention was to see Arlines, and obtain from him, at any price, the necessary means to enable him to prevent any very unpleasant occurrence.

His only resource, indeed, was Philip Arlines; all other hopes were flown, and he could do nothing without his aid; he was, indeed, dependant—utterly dependant upon that bad man.

He sought him at all the usual places where he had ever seen him, or heard him spoken of. He walked over the most frequented spots, with the hope that he might meet with him accidentally, but yet without success. Hour after hour fled, and yet he was unsuccessful; he could not find him.

Night drew on, and yet he was unsuccessful. His heart was now heavy, and he feared he should be unable to keep his promise to Jessie, and another day would pass, and no aid could he afford them.

"But night approaches," he thought upon reflection, "and I am more likely to meet him then, and I shall have a better chance of obtaining all that I wish for them."

Buoyed up with the hope that all would yet be well, so far as his limited wishes then led the way, he proceeded to St. James's-street, and to other parts, where Arlines, and such as Arlines, congregate and prey upon the vitals of society.

Arnold now entered many of these dens, and with an anxious countenance sought to find out Arlines from among the many individuals who crowded around the tables; but no! he could not recognize the hated, though sought after, form of Phillip Arlines.

It was with an aching heart that Captain Arnold quitted these places one after the other, and yet he could not find him whom he sought. That night, at a late hour, Captain Arnold sought his home and his bed.

Jessie, however, was sitting up to see him, and with a sweet look she watched the expression of his countenance; and when she saw the look of pain and despair that sat there, she read his want of success, and forbore to ask him a single question, but bade him good night, and then quitted the room.

But little sleep visited Arnold's eyes that night, and in the morning he arose but little refreshed, and his heart sunk more and more within him, when he saw the pale, sorrowful countenance of his children.

He endeavoured to speak a few words of comfort to them; but it was in sad and sorrowful accents, and conveyed but little hope, especially to Jessie.

Again he quitted his home in search of Arlines, and was again unsuccessful. For five days had he searched after him in vain, and when he reached his home on the fifth day, suffering under all the horrors of disappointment, and of fear for the welfare of his children, he found a strange, uncouth-looking man was seated in his hall.

A second glance, and he knew that the worst had happened.

They had an execution put in the house; there was no use struggling against it; for now that one had begun to press them thus, all would follow, fearing to be too late to secure their own share of the spoil.

He sat down with his hands before his face, and gave vent to his grief in bitter tears.

He left home on the following morning, and again made a fruitless search after Arlines; but he returned home earlier than usual, and desired Jessie to come to his room. He was very pale and agitated. He could not brook the idea of remaining in the house until he was turned out of it under legal process.

"Jessie," he said, when she came into the apartment, "Jessie, my darling, we must quit this house, it is no longer a home for us,—and seek some obscure spot, where we can obtain shelter until something happens to enable me once more to appear as I have been. But never mind your father's misfortunes, my girl; do assist at a moment of need. Your sorrowful face I can scarce bear to look at. Collect such things as belong to yourself and sisters, and, when it is dark, we will all quit the place in company."

"Yes, dear father," replied Jessie, throwing herself in his arms, "I will not be many moments; and I hope we may be happy in a place of less pretension than this."

So saying, Jessie quitted the apartment, and as she did so, Captain Arnold uttered with a sigh—

"Poor Jessie—a place of less pretension; yes, indeed, with very much less pretension. May Heaven protect her better than I can! she little thinks what she has to go through."

Captain Arnold was wrapped in sad reflection—reflection embittered by the knowledge that his fall was to be attributed to his own folly and criminality; he had been the dupe of an artful and designing villain, one who was as unscrupulous as he was heartless, daring, and fertile in schemes of villany—and withal a consummate master of the powers of persuasion; a man, who, if he could not wile away the prey from the jaws of the ravenous wolf, could at least gain the unsuspecting confidence of the most cautious and selfish.

"Oh! that I had taken the repeated warnings of those who knew better than I did the nature of this bad man; who has doubtless all the crimes that can be committed against human society hanging heavily on his soul; but he cares not for crimes—sorrow and repentance he knows not; but the day may come yet, when he shall suffer bitter pangs for those he has caused me."

At this juncture Jessie entered the room with the two children, both of tender ages; at first he saw them not, and then started.

"We are all ready, father," said Jessie, "and will go whither you direct us."

There was something so sweet and so resigned in Jessie's looks and voice that touched Captain Arnold's very soul; he arose, and without speaking kissed them, and went to the door as if he were about to go out, but shrunk from doing so.

Jessie saw his hesitation, and immediately stepped up to him, and said—

"Father, we wait for you to take us to our new home; it is now dark, and if we have far to go, these" (pointing to the other two) "are young, and it will grow late before we get there."

Arnold said nothing, but opened the door wide enough to let them out, and then followed them.

The children each carried with them a small bundle, that contained as much wearing apparel as could on such a short notice be collected together, and with these they contrived to pass from the house without being interrogated by the officer as to their contents.

Arnold saw this, and he said to Jessie—

"Walk with me, Jessie—do you take the hand of one and I of the other; they will walk much better then, and we can converse as we go on, for we have some distance to go."

"Where is it, father?" inquired Jessie.

"I don't know, my child," replied Arnold.

"Don't know, father!" exclaimed Jessie, in some surprise. "What will become of them?"

"I mean, Jessie, I have yet to hire a lodging, and it may be difficult. I have been sorely disappointed in my attempts to procure assistance, but it cannot be long before I obtain what I want. Do not be sad, Jessie; you are now my only comfort, my only joy; when I see you sad I am more than wretched."

"Say nothing about it, my dear father, I will do my utmost to be cheerful, though when

I see you I can scarce refrain from open grief, you do not now look as you used to, you are pale and comparatively thin. Were we once in a lodging, however mean and poor, I would then be happy; if you were clear of our greatest enemy, then, indeed all would be sunshine and joy; our hearts would bound with gladness, and though our food were but a dry crust of bread and a glass of water, we should feel contented and happy."

Captain Arnold felt the words of Jessie were a deserved reproach, and sighed; but he knew that he was the mere tool of Arlines, and that without him he must perish, and with him he would be engulfed in iniquity.

*   *   *   *

It was several hours after this ere they found a lodging, one that would suit them or which they would suit, for it happened, as on most occasions, that few were to be found, and Arnold's purse being of so little value that he dared not venture upon any place that was but of the meanest and most abject kind.

After a long search they obtained one, a single room and a large closet, which by the landlady was termed a room also, up an innumerable quantity of stairs; this he was compelled to pay for in advance, for the old woman would have as soon thought of letting them have the place for nothing as to let them in without money in advance.

Two miserable beds were placed in them, one in the room and the other in the closet, for which they had paid a small, but, considering the place and its accommodations, a large rent, and a heavy sum considering the state of their finances.

"This," said Captain Arnold, looking round him for some seconds, "this will be your future home for some time to come, at least until I am fortunate enough to obtain the means of which I have been robbed. Yes, Jessie—it is so, but I cannot now help it, nor can I even complain or free myself."

"Only try, my dear father—only try—I will work for you day and night. Have nothing more to do with Phillip Arlines, and I will strive with a smiling countenance; but it will not come to that; surely some kind friend will——"

"Say no more, Jessie," replied Arnold, "we must endure this for a time—you are all fatigued and have had no food for some hours, and I will go and procure such as is to be had in the neighbourhood."

CHAPTER XXXV.

JESSIE'S REFLECTIONS.—THE NEW ABODE.—
DESPAIR AND ATTEMPTED SUICIDE.

DURING Arnold's absence, Jessie looked over the apartment, and sighed as she thought of the great difference there was between their present and past situation; what a change from all the comforts, and even elegancies of life, to the mean abjectness of a low lodging in a crowded neighbourhood, such as that in which they were now placed, and in which noises and disturbances of all kinds were rife.

Then there were the two children, brought up to expect and receive every attention and kindness; they, poor things, understood not the meaning of all this, though they saw and wondered at it.

Jessie herself shrunk from contact with all she saw; but dared not do so during her father's presence; it would have increased his unhappiness, had she done so, and she would not do that, if she could avoid it; but now that he was absent, she sat down, and a violent outbreak of grief immediately ensued.

The two children gazed at her in awe and astonishment, and for some moments knew not what to make of it; but then by degrees they came up to her, and entwined their little arms round her, and begged she would not cry. This, for some time, increased her tears, and then she embraced them tenderly.

After some time her grief abated, and she thought more calmly; the prospect was a bad one, and their situation, she thought, must be at its worst, and a change in her father's circumstances must take place some time or another, and at no period like the present, for it was most needed.

The place was low, mean, and unwholesome; she had never seen the like before, nor could she, indeed, have thought such places in existence; but then, it might become dearer to her, if happiness dwelt there; and should her father shake off the monster, Arlines, whom she believed to be at the bottom of all her father's misfortune, she would indeed be happy.

Here they might live in obscurity, unknown; —and if they lived not sumptuously, they could at least, she hoped, be able to obtain such necessaries of life as would allow them to live n moderate comfort.

Alas! she little understood how difficult it might become to obtain the means of existence even, in poverty and indigence; she little knew that they had come to a point, beyond which they could scarce travel; and the few shillings that remained in Captain Arnold's purse were his last, and how to obtain a fresh supply he knew not.

Jessie had never been brought up with any

notion of the means by which existence was supported; how, indeed, the world managed to live. Money had always been abundant, and her father had never expressed any apprehension on the score of obtaining any, as men of business are wont to do; she was, therefore, utterly ignorant of all that concerned the business of life.

Indeed, Arnold himself was much in the same state of ignorance, and was almost as helpless as a child, for he had no resources.

* * * * *

The night passed over, and the following morning dawned upon their sadness.

The sun rose in a mass of vapour, that was but dimly and obscurely illuminated with the dull heavy red that often betokens an unpleasant day, and the wind, which had blown freshly all night, with occasional showers, now increased in strength as the day broke.

The inhabitants of the town, as they awoke, heard the fearful howling of the wind, as it rushed across the city, and, as it met with any impediment to its course, it howled and shrieked, as if in very anger; while the occasional heavy plashing showers of rain beat heavily against the windows, causing those who were compelled to leave their houses to shudder at the prospect that lay before them—a dull and cheerless day.

As the day advanced the shop-keepers began one by one to open their shops; and to look out on the unhappy prospect that lay before them. "A bad commencement," they would mutter, "and no hope of amendment."

Many were the speculations of the early riser, who first perambulated the streets—as to the effect of falling tiles, broken chimney-pots, cowls, and stray flower-pots, which lay here and there scattered about in all directions; and many a one would have no small fear of the same thing occurring when he was about to pass by some unlucky house, the roof of which might in some one part be insecure, and shower its slates upon his devoted head.

The rain again descended in torrents, and the wind still continued to howl and rush onwards with unabated strength: the streets were, even at an early hour, nearly deserted by those who could find any excuse for sheltering themselves; and even now, when the time was come for passengers to pass to and fro on their route to their several occupations, the streets were not half as full as they were on fine days, and those who were about hurried on with hasty steps to shorten the time of their probation in such weather.

The violence of the wind and rain was unexampled, and when any unfortunate being came to an open place, or some unlucky corner, he would be met with an eddying wind that would overwhelm him with rain water.

The streets were washed clean by the quantity and violence of the rain, which now continued without any intermission whatever; the water-spouts were full, and in many places overflowing, to the great inconvenience of those who unwillingly came near them.

Few things stirred in the streets, save those which public convenience or private profit compelled, and no passengers but those whose occupations compelled them to be abroad.

Many speculations might arise in the mind of a stranger as to the various causes that induced so many people to be out and exposed to such weather; the amount of necessity, it would be imagined, must be very great; and so it is, but it is not of that kind of necessity from which we shrink with feelings of fear and sorrow.

It is not distress, but distress might ensue, were it abandoned; it is merely a business necessity. All who are engaged in any kind of trade or profession in London know the value of time, and cannot afford to lose it because it happens to come in an inclement season; people are inured to such weather.

They had need be inured to such a night as this, for it was terribly wet, cold, and dark; not one mitigating circumstance could be found to balance the gloomy qualities of the night.

Hour after hour passed, and Captain Arnold, who had been out since morning, returned not. He had quitted his home early; indeed, before Jessie was awake. She had lain the greater part of the previous night awake, thinking of their present condition, and towards morning she fell into a troubled slumber, during which Arnold quitted the place in search of Arlines, to obtain from him some assistance.

At length he came home, wet and weary; dispirited he was, and more so than he had yet appeared.

"Father," said Jessie, "I am glad you have returned. I feared something had happened to you; but now you are returned again, we shall be happier."

Captain Arnold smiled a sickly smile, and moved his lips to reply, but no sound issued from them; he had not strength to reply.

Day after day did Arnold pursue his wanderings in the vain hope of finding the arch villain, Phillip Arlines; but he was unsuccessful, and each evening a deeper gloom spread itself upon the unfortunate man's features, and he sat dejected and silent; he spoke not, nor moved.

Jessie all this while became daily more and more alarmed; she knew not what to do, or what to expect, or whom to consult. She had no soul to ask advice under such circumstances. She had no friend.

The name of Alfred Pearson crossed her imagination, and a flush crossed her pale face; she could not apply to him—no, no; she might starve, but not apply to him. He could afford it, no doubt, and that, too, with more gratification than could be expressed. His advice and assistance were, no doubt, always at her command; he would have died to have saved her—yet she shrunk from approaching him under such circumstances.

Little did she think that he was at that moment lying almost helpless from the effect of wounds; she could not know it.

In the meantime, their condition became worse and worse, and Captain Arnold could see no hopes of extrication from his present misery, and his mind became seriously affected; he dwelt impatiently upon the desperate character of his fortunes, and at length determined to commit suicide.

"I shall at least escape from this scene of misery and misfortune; and as for my children, they can do no worse, and I can do no nothing for them; all I could do I would, but that, alas! is now nothing, and to live and see them endure all the agonies of gradual starvation, I cannot and will not."

His thoughts then ran upon the best means of procuring the necessary drug, poison being the method which he deemed best in his own mind, and he, therefore, determined upon procuring enough of some deadly drug to effect his purpose.

It employed his thoughts some hours, during which time he imagined a variety of schemes, but rejected them all one after another, until he hit upon one that he thought would be effectual.

He determined to go about from chemist to chemist, and obtain small quantities of laudanum; and when he had a sufficient dose, he would return home and swallow it.

In pursuance of his plan, he arose early the next morning: it was a comfortless day, cold, dreary, and wet; no signs of any alterations for the better—far from it; it was heavy and dark, in unison with the frame of mind of the unfortunate Arnold, who sneaked about from shop to shop, purchasing small quantities of the deadly drug.

When he had obtained what he considered enough, he returned to his miserable abode, and determined to spend his last hours among his children.

He entered the apartment, and, with the few small coins that remained, purchased a last and scanty meal, which he gave into Jessie's hands, and desired her and her sisters to partake of it.

Jessie looked at her father, and thought she perceived a strange alteration in his manner; but attributed it to some fresh cause of grief and vexation he had probably endured during the day; and she made no remarks upon it, but did as she was desired.

Captain Arnold seated himself, but he would not partake of the meal; but contented himself with saying he had taken refreshment out, and did not require it.

His eyes were filled with tears, as he saw the two youngest devour their meal with avidity, so unlike what he had ever witnessed before, that it became quite painful to him, and yet he could not withdraw his eyes from off them.

Jessie, indeed, ate but little; her hunger was moderated by the appearance of her father, who more and more alarmed her, by the strangeness of his looks, and the earnestness of his gaze upon the children and herself.

The meal ended, Captain Arnold expressed a wish that they should all retire; but first he embraced them all, fervently kissed them, and then bade them all a lingering and affectionate adieu.

To Jessie he was unusually affectionate, and shed tears abundantly over, blessed, and bade her take care of the younger members of his family living.

"It must be done now," said Arnold, when they were gone, and the door closed. "It must be done now, or not at all; 'tis hard to quit so much true affection, but I can't see what must follow—starvation and misery; they will be cared for when I am away, and, while I remain here, I am a clog to them, and a hindrance."

So saying, he lifted the phial to his mouth, but scarce had the liquid touched his lips, when it was dashed to the ground, and its contents spilled.

CHAPTER XXXVI.

THE LAST APPEAL.—THE PROMISE.—THE TEMPTER AGAIN.

CAPTAIN ARNOLD started when he felt the bottle was dashed out of his hand, and saw the contents were entirely lost. He arose, and turned towards the person who had thus deprived him of the means of destroying himself, and then beheld the pale and terror-stricken form of his daughter Jessie, who had watched her father from the door.

Jessie had noticed the strange behaviour of her father, and had determined not to ask for any explanation, but to quietly wait and watch the result; and it was while she thus stood in readiness that she saw her father put the phial to his lips, and she rushed forward and saved him by its destruction.

For some moments there was a dead silence between the father and daughter. Poor Jessie was too much terrified to speak; and, as for Captain Arnold, what could he say to his innocent and beautiful child, who had saved him from an act of cowardice and a crime at once? He felt a flush of shame come to his face, and spread itself over his brow, as he thought of the

THE DEATH OF CAPTAIN ARNOLD'S YOUNGEST DAUGHTER.

great sinfulness he had meditated. What could he say to her whom he had so little affection for, that he had attempted leaving her in her early youth, unprotected and a prey to every ill fortune which a harsh, unfeeling world never fails to inflict upon the destitute and humble?

He felt as if he had been fighting some battle, and, because he had become doubtful of success, he had endeavoured to fly from the scene of contest, leaving those he had sworn to protect at the mercy of some merciless and implacable enemy.

He trembled, and yet he dared not look on his innocent child. Tears came to his eyes, and yet he dared not speak to her.

At length poor Jessie herself, with a gush of emotion that was terrible to her, found voice to utter that one word, which, to a parent's ears, is so full of sacred meaning.

"Father, father!" she sobbed, and threw herself into his arms, whether he would or not.

Captain Arnold was sufficiently subdued before; but now he gave way completely to his newly awakened feelings, and he wept like a child.

It was some minutes before he could speak,

and then in heart-breaking accents he said,—
" Jessie, my child — my innocent Jessie !
Can you still love him who has made you suffer
so much ? Are not your feelings towards me
chilled and blunted ? Oh, Jessie ! after all
that has passed, can you—dare you—do you
love me still ?"

" As ever—as ever !" sobbed Jessie.

Captain Arnold was powerfully moved, and
he shook like one at the point of death, while
he turned of an ashy paleness, and a faint sensation came over him of an alarming character,
accompanied by a dreadful state of debility.

Jessie felt his arms relax their hold of her,
and, looking in his face, she became alarmed at
its dreadful paleness.

" Father—father !" she said, in the frantic
tones of grief—" father, dear father, speak to
me ! Oh, speak !"

" I—I am better now, my child," he
said—" much better. The mind is too powerful in its emotions for my bodily strength. I
am not the man I once was. A draught of
water, dearest, will recover me. Some
water !"

Jessie quickly procured him some ; and, as
he cooled his fevered lips and throat, he felt
much relieved.

" Jessie," he said, " this is all very terrible.
Who would ever have imagined such a scene as
this ?"

" Forget it, father—oh, forget it !"

" I cannot—I cannot !"

" Then remember it only as an hour when
your mind awakened to better and holier
thoughts. Change from time forthwith,
father, and seek for happiness where alone it
can be found."

" Where, Jessie—where ? In the grave
do you mean?—in the grave ?"

" Father—father ! do not speak thus. You
know not what you say."

" Yes, Jessie, yes—too well—alas! too
well."

" No, father. From this moment you may
date a new life, which may bring you happiness, if not so perfect as that you once
possessed, yet sufficient to enable you, in
peace and calmness, to await the end of all
trouble."

" It is too late," said Captain Arnold, with
a deep sigh—" it is too late, I say."

" That it never is," she replied. " Too
late, father, to make peace with Heaven. Ah !
no. Suppose I had erred, and some one had
said it was too late for you to forgive me ?
No, father ; do not delude yourself with the
shallow argument that, having erred, it is too
late to mend, and, consequently, you must go
on erring. It is not too late. One week—
one day—ay, father, one hour, will prove 'tis
not too late. The very determination to
shake off evil associates—the resolve once made

to lead a new and a better life, will bring
with it a new solace, which will prove to you,
as with a voice from Heaven, that 'tis not too
late."

Captain Arnold looked in the face of his
beautiful child, like one newly awakened from
a dream.

" God of Heaven !" he cried, " is it possible
that I have possessed such a treasure, and not
known its value ?"

" You will reflect, dear father, upon my
words—you will consent to be happier—I see
it in your looks. You will, for your own sake,
and for my sake, be an altered man. Nay, you
are altered now—you are not what you were
one short hour since—you are happier, far
happier, even now, because you think of doing
better."

" Jessie," he gasped, " if I had but a
hope."

" You have. Hope never dies but with the
heart which should cherish it. You have hope ;
it is now fluttering in your breast. Dear—
dear father, you will change, and by some
noble, because some honest means, earn the
subsistence you have been robbed of."

" Are you my daughter," he gasped, " or
some ministering, pitying angel, sent by
Heaven to save me from myself ?"

" Your own—own child," she cried. " Look
at me, father : I am your own Jessie."

She sunk on her knees at his feet, and
looked imploringly in his face. There was a
holy fascination in her look which made her,
indeed, more resemble a being of Heaven than
of earth ; and Captain Arnold, as he looked
upon her, was strangely moved.

" My child," he said, " this is, perhaps,
all providential."

" It is," she said.

" And it may be (for out of evil springeth
good) that the awful purpose of my soul, which
was thwarted by you, may be the means of—of
—bringing me like a wanderer—back again—
to—to joy—to peace."

His voice was broken, and he wept freely
on the breast of his beautiful child, who
welcomed these tears, accompanied as they
were by hopeful words, as the harbingers of
better thoughts and a happier future.

Now she strove to bring to him something
like cheerfulness, by speaking cheerfully herself, and painting the possible, rather than the
probable, future, in far more glowing colours,
perchance, than the most favourable view of it
would warrant.

" Father," she said, " you must recollect
how many thousands are as poor, as utterly
destitute as we are, and without a tithe of your
abilities and your resources, if you wish to
place them in a productive channel : no doubt
you will find many real old friends, who would
gladly know where you are, and, knowing

that, will, with pride and pleasure, assist to place you in some line of life, which may put us far above many of the necessities of actual want."

" Think you so, Jessie ?"

" I do. I am certain."

" There are, indeed, many who know me. God bless you, my child ; go on—go on, your words fall like balm upon my heart."

" Then, father, the past, except such, perhaps, as has been full of the heart's contentment, will fade away, appearing more like a troubled dream than a frightful reality."

" Yes, yes, my child ; yes."

" We shall be happy once again ; we will find some humble, cheerful home, where we shall be very happy, shutting our hearts against all evil thoughts, father. You will ever find in me a child loving you fondly, waiting upon your lightest word, and tending you with that tenderness that love alone can show."

"My Jessie—my darling !"

" Dear father, you are happier now. Tell me that you are ?"

" I am, I am !"

" And never again will you see or speak to him who has been your ruin ?"

" Hush, hush ! You mean——"

" The villain, Arlines !"

Captain Arnold trembled, as he said, in a low tone,—

" Oh, would that he were dead !—would that he were dead, and that I was quite sure of never again looking on his awful face. Would he were dead."

" To you, father, he may be dead. You will promise me never again to seek him—never again to hold communication with him. You will promise me that !"

" Yes, yes," said Captain Arnold. " You speak truly. Once free from him, and I may find peace for the short time I linger here in a world which has to me been lately a scene of horror, horror, horror, Jessie !"

" And yet you will live, father, to be happy in it. To-morrow we shall both look upon the morning with far different eyes to what we have for a long weary time beheld it, for we shall recollect how much better we understand each other, and how happy we have resolved to be ; for people may, in a great measure, be happy or miserable, according as they make up their minds."

" Oh, Jessie ! Jessie ! where learnt you such words as these ?"

" I have been thrown much upon my own sad thoughts, father, and I am thankful that from them I have extracted a good, instead of a bad philosophy."

" Oh, Jessie, you do not utter the reproach, but I can discover it in your words. I have left you too much without friend, without counsellor, without one kindly word."

" Nay, do not speak so, father, because all that is past now. Let us look at the future, for that is our own. The past we cannot command."

" Yes," said Captain Arnold, abstractedly, as if communing with his own thoughts rather than addressing Jessie. " Yes, much may surely be done. There must still live some who recollect me in my brighter, happier days, and who will yet held out a helping hand to a fallen comrade."

" Many ; very many," said Jessie.

" Yes ; very many. I am not old. I have strength left, and any employment, so it be honourable, is preferable to the awful life I have been leading."

" Much, much."

" The villain Arlines has been my destruction ; but an honest man may, from the ashes of his fortunes, like another phœnix, rise again defying evil."

" He may, father ; he may !"

" You have conquered, Jessie. A glorious victory. Henceforward I am a new man, and more worthy of being your father."

The door of the miserable apartment at this moment was softly opened ; both father and daughter heard the sound, and instinctively turned their eyes in that direction, and, with both surprise and indignation, they beheld, standing on the threshold, no other than Phillip Arlines.

Jessie advanced a step, and in a commanding tone, she said,—

" Villain ! pollute not this humble abode by your presence. Away, and with you the horror —the pity of those you have, by your own wickedness, made unhappy."

" Bravo !" said Arlines, clapping his hands together. " Bravo ! very well done, indeed ! bravo ! How are you, Arnold ?"

" Phillip Arlines, begone," cried Captain Arnold. " Trouble me not ; begone !"

" Humph !" said Arlines. " That's unfriendly now—very unfriendly ; but I don't mean to go, nevertheless."

" You shall go !" cried Jessie.

" Shall I ?" cried the villain, as he strode into the room. " Indeed, young lady ! Look at your father. He dare not use such bold words. Look at him. Ha, ha, ha ! Jessie Arnold, you should learn meekness and humbleness."

Captain Arnold groaned, and appeared totally unnerved, and unable to move from the chair on which he was sitting.

———

CHAPTER XXXVII.

THE SUCCESSFUL PIECE OF DUPLICITY.—
CAPTAIN ARNOLD'S LAST CHANCE OF RE-
DEMPTION.—THE TEMPTATION.

PHILLIP ARLINES looked round the room
with a smile of malignancy and triumph, as if
he traced in every sign of poverty and want—
and there were many; they might be traced in
every article present, and by the absence of
others—the work of his own plotting and con-
triving; he could say to himself, " I have done
all this—here behold my power, and my success."

Yes, Phillip Arlines triumphed; he was as
bold as he was bad, and as malignant as he was
insensible to human suffering and human want;
what cared he what they suffered—what crime
they committed, so that the lion's share
was his ? Crime after crime would he drive
men to with a goad of iron, and yet not allow
them even the wretched reward of crime—the
wages of iniquity.

At length he fixed his eyes upon the unhappy
Arnold, who appeared unable to shake of the
influence or power this man had over him; and
though he spoke to Arnold, yet he fixed his
eyes on Jessie, and, while a demoniac smile lit
up his features, he said,—

" Come, come, Arnold, I wish to have a
word or two with you. We will both walk
a short distance."

Phillip Arlines arose and walked to the door,
leaving Arnold to follow him.

The unhappy Arnold rose to his feet, and
moved towards the door, without any definite
notion of what he was about to do.

" Father! father! dear father!" exclaimed
Jessie, endeavouring to throw herself in his
way, and hanging on his neck, " go not, I implore you, with that bad man: he will but lead
you to destruction; he will but point the way:
he will not follow, but reap the produce of
other men's crimes, and while they perish,
miserably perish, he will revel in safety and
luxury."

" Arnold," said Phillip Arlines.

" I am coming," replied Captain Arnold;
then turning to Jessie, he said, " I will be
back shortly—fear nothing for me."

He then disengaged himself from Jessie, and
rushed down the crazy stairs after Arlines,
leaving Jessie standing the picture of grief and
terror; she staggered back into the miserable
apartment, and sunk insensible upon the floor.

Arnold and Arlines walked some few paces
in silence, Arnold scarce knowing what he was
about, while Arlines enjoyed his triumph and
the other's confusion, determined to wait till
the other should speak.

" Arlines," said Arnold, after a brief space,
" you have found me out in my poverty and

want, and which, had I never seen you, had I
but listened to the voice of others, would never
have been my lot. I have nothing more to lose
—what, therefore, can you want with me ? you
can gain nothing, and yet if you did not think
so you would never have sought me under such
circumstances."

" This is partially true and partially false,"
replied Arlines; " but it matters not; I want
you, you know, and that between us must of
itself be a sufficient cause for action; and, moreover, what I require of you must be performed."

" Arlines, we had some ties of friendship,
which, if they no longer exist, yet let me
implore you, by the remembrance of them, to
quit me, and let me either perish by myself in
my poverty, or exist upon the produce of the
scantiest paid labour man can perform."

" Ha! ha! ha!" laughed Phillip Arlines;
" you are growing romantic, and have suddenly
forgotten the necessity of the present moment,
like children who fancy the life of a labourer in
a cottage presents nothing but industry and
enjoyment instead of short food, racking pains;
and dishonesty fills up the measure that honesty
could not fill."

" No, no, you mistake me; I never dreamed
of such a thing. I am for no cottage or poverty,
however varnished over, save when it is contrasted with a continued series of crime—crime
which must lead eventually to the worst of consequences—an ignominious end."

" The end of life is of little consequence,
Arnold," replied Arlines, with a laugh; " 'tis
but the present moment, and not the probable
duration of our lives, that we must look to. I
care but little for hanging, or dying in bed,
provided I know that the former would come
no earlier than the latter."

" For God's sake leave me, and let me
struggle on in my misery and poverty; if ever
mercy or pity stirred your heart, hear me, and
grant this request; 'tis the last you shall be
troubled with," said Arnold.

" I am glad to hear it, but, nevertheless, I
shall not grant it: 'tis not my intention; I
have resolved not, and I am not to be beaten
from my matured resolves."

" As you hope for mercy hereafter, let me
quit this dreadful line of life; as you expect
that your dying moments——"

" I don't expect anything in my dying
moments but death, Arnold; I suppose your
saint-like and sanctimonious daughter has
taught you all this cant and folly ?"

Arlines had scarcely uttered these words
when he was seized by Arnold by the throat,
who shook him violently for several minutes,
saying, with the violence of a mad-man,—

" Dare to say aught against the pure
innocence of one whom your vile and debased
nature cannot comprehend, and I will commit
one crime which shall at least have one good

and redeeming phase in it, and that is in ridding society of such a concocter of villany as you are."

Arlines spoke not a word; his face and lips were white with fear and rage; and, when Arnold had released him, he forbore to speak for some moments, fearing to trust himself with speech; but he gave such a deadly and dreadful scowl upon Arnold, as to make the latter shrink from him in horror and disgust.

When Arlines could trust his voice to speak, he said to Arnold,

"Well, Arnold, what do you think I can now do for you? ought I not to consign you to a prison, and leave your children to starvation, and probably worse? for human nature cannot always struggle with want, and resist the pleasure of the tempter."

Arnold was silent; he could now easily see the precipice he stood upon. Arlines could bring heavy punishment upon him, and deprive him of the only pleasure he could now know; and that was the society of his children.

"I ask you again, Arnold, what can you expect of me, save that I should punish you for your madness, consign you to a felon's cell, and leave your children to the mercy of the world?"

"All I ask is, that you will leave me! you have had that of me that ought to cancel this," replied Arnold.

"I have not, and I shall neither forget nor forgive; service alone may efface the indignity I have suffered. You must render yourself useful to me, and then I will give you the means of existence; do so I bid, and you may be able to maintain yourself and children in the same style that you have been used to."

"Ay, but at what price, Arlines! Think of that, Arlines, think of that."

"That is precisely what I do not think of," replied Arlines, "because there is no need; on the contrary, all I think of is the clearest, best, and least dangerous plan of raising that by which we live and enjoy life;— gold."

Arnold spoke not in reply, he saw that he was at his mercy, and to struggle longer was but to struggle with fate; however, he determined to listen to what his companion had to propose.

"You see," said Arnold, "what it is to be struggling for life in poverty and absolute want! the crushing of the hopes of your children— the bringing of them up in painful penury— with all the cramped notions and meanness of appearance and behaviour; these are consequences sure to follow any lengthened struggle of this nature. Then do you not think it is but reasonable that you should endeavour to maintain your position in the best way you can? at all events, they will benefit by it."

"What does all this mean?" said Arnold; "tell me at once what new scheme of villany you have to propose, and what it is you require me to do?"

"I will," replied Arlines; "but first understand me—you must be useful to me, and the first moment I even suspect that you are tampering with my wishes, the next will see you inside the walls of a prison, from which you will never emerge; and your children will sink in dishonour and poverty."

Arnold shrunk before the fierce and demoniac gaze of Arlines, as he uttered these words, and he felt fully the power this bad and unscrupulous man had over him, which he was well assured he would exact if he deemed he had sufficient provocation.

"I never deceived you," replied Arnold; "my faith with you has always been kept: can you say the same?"

"It does not signify; my answer to your questions are immaterial, but yours are to mine as I must direct accordingly; but we know each other now, and I hope there will be no more occasion to revert to this kind of conversation any more, nor shall I unless you compel me to do so. I have," he continued "another scheme in my head: it is no game of chance, it is a bold and politic stroke, which, if well done, is certainly successful, and incurs no danger, while it will give us an ample return."

"What is it you have determined upon doing?" inquired Arnold.

"It is this—there is an individual who has but recently died abroad, and who possessed large sums in the funds: now they will be unclaimed, and go into the hands of the commissioners for the reduction of the national debt; my object, therefore, will be to get the money out."

"But how can you do that?" inquired Arnold.

"By your personating the dead man, and signing the necessary documents authorising the sale; and thus we obtain the proceeds."

"It will surely be detected; the government will be too active and well acquainted with all that occurs to render it possible."

"The government is composed of as great a mob of soft-headed, conceited fools as ever broke bread, who deem themselves infallible; and are, therefore, secure, perfectly secure, from all such attempts—but a day will come when some unfortunate discovery, some accidental circumstance, or some bungling attempts will open their eyes, and exhibit to the world their inefficiency, and not only them, but all others similarly engaged."

"Who is the individual I am to personate?" inquired Arnold.

"Merely a Mr. Warren, who died at Spa, in Germany; he has nobody to look after his estates, or himself; no one is acquainted with the amount of property he possesses."

"When," said Arnold, "is this to be done?"

"The sooner the better," replied Arlines; "I think to-morrow will do best; the sooner we have the money the better; it is probable that a few hours only may be the utmost we shall have to suffer."

"I am scarely in a condition to appear to personate a wealthy man," remarked Arnold, as he looked upon his now worn and seedy garments. "I am not fit at all as regards my personal apparel."

"That need be no hindrance. Here are fifteen pounds! take them, and satisfy your wants; meet me to-morrow, at eleven, near the Mansion House, and all shall be arranged; and recollect it will put a thousand pounds in your pocket."

So saying, Phillip Arlines, satisfied with the impression he had made on the naturally good and honourable, but weak, mind of Captain Arnold, quitted the spot.

CHAPTER XXXVII.

ARLINES' PROPOSITION.—ARNOLD'S WEAKNESS.—A FLUSH OF FORTUNE.

CAPTAIN ARNOLD was easily moved; his mind had not that character and cast that gives a tone to the man and renders him usually an unyielding animal; on the contrary, the last words had the most permanent effect; and so it was on this occasion that Arlines had made his wonted impression upon Arnold's mind; and also the present aid which he had given him was of the utmost value to him, standing on the brink of starvation as he was.

It was not long ere Arnold purchased such necessaries as were needed, and returned to his own miserable apartment, which appeared more mean and miserable since he received this temporary aid from Arlines. Jessie looked at her father as he entered the room; her eyes were bedewed with tears, but Arnold dared not meet her gaze. She was virtuous and beautiful, and guilt was no fitting companion for her.

Yet he felt that he was doing his best towards his children, though the world would condemn the means by which it was done.

Jessie, however, could not converse with her father upon such an unpleasant topic as that which most occupied his thoughts.

Having satisfied their hunger, and seen them cared for for the night, Arnold sought the readiest means he could to render his toilet complete, and fitting for the new character he had to sustain on the morrow; the risk he saw of detection was great, as many would be present, and some might know him, or the man whom he was to personate.

These thoughts troubled him; but yet sleep drowned all these cares, and he forgot them all.

*   *   *   *   *

The next morning Captain Arnold rose, and attired himself for the street; he breakfasted with Jessie and his children. He took an affectionate farewell of them, and gave Jessie money to obtain such necessaries as she would require during the day. Jessie looked with a beseeching countenance upon her father, as he quitted the apartment, and Arnold hastily left the house, fearing another scene similar to that that had occurred on the previous day.

Arnold now walked towards the city, to meet Arlines, by appointment.

He arrived at the Mansion House a few minutes before the appointed hour, and he walked up and down the pavement, in front of that building; but he had scarce done so, when Arlines came up to him, and said,

"Follow me, Arnold, and I will explain all that is to be done."

Arnold did follow him, and they both entered a tavern situated somewhere at the back of the Mansion House, where they seated themselves in a private room, and ordered refreshments.

"You understand perfectly what you are to do?" said Arlines. "You are to personate a gentleman by the name of Warren, who has really died abroad, and of whom they know nothing."

"But who is to know that I am Warren?" said Arnold; "nobody can identify me by that name, and then they will refuse to grant the transfer."

"If they do not I will eat my hat; and, I hold, it is not good for the digestion. I am your witness, and I know you as Warren; and this will carry you over any difficulty of that kind. Come on now, I will introduce you to the broker, and all will be well."

"Do you think that this affair will be ended and completed to day?"

"I do. I have been in communication about it, and I believe all is ready, merely waiting for your appearance; and if so, you will have a thousand pounds in your pocket before you walk away."

"What is the amount of the property you are about to obtain?" inquired Arnold.

"Five thousand pounds," replied Arlines,—"come with me now, and it will soon be over."

Arnold followed Arlines out of the house, and they at once proceeded to the house of an eminent broker in Change Alley, and then they all proceeded to the Bank of England, and in a very few minutes all was done, and a successful piece of villany had been perpetrated without detection.

"Don't you think you ran more chance of detection from employing another?" inquired Arnold.

"We ran the less, for, the more respectable the broker, the less the risk; as all that he did would, to a certain extent, partake of his respectability,—and serve to blind the Bank people."

They returned once more to the same tavern, where Phillip Arlines took out a mass of bank notes; from among which he gave Arnold some amounting to a thousand pounds.

"There," he added, "that will float you for some time to come; and it is strange to me, if we cannot obtain a fresh supply long ere that is gone. I shall see you again before very many days have elapsed."

As Arlines uttered these words, he bade Arnold good day, and quitted the tavern. So great was Arnold's amazement at all that had occurred, that he was scarcely able to say anything, but went hither and thither so long as he found himself in the company of Arlines; but once abandoned to himself, he was some minutes ere he could well make up his mind what course to pursue, and then he found himself at his own door; instinct it would appear alone had brought him there; and he determined to ascend the many stairs to the miserable place, and at once take his children from their present state of misery.

He entered the room. Jessie was alone— she had been weeping; and she was pale and agitated; the former he was used to; he could not, however, bear to see her in this state, and, going up to her, he kissed her, and said—

"Jessie! Jessie! do not rend my heart thus; I am unhappy enough; but you make me more so than aught else can. We shall not always be thus low, but prosperity will again dawn upon us, and we shall live in happiness and luxury."

"I care not for that, father—I would never desire to be better off than I am now, provided our future life was not to be crossed by that vile man."

"There is much that cannot be explained to you, Jessie; you do not know the world and its ways—say no more about it, and gladden your father's eyes with a smile."

"A smile father?" said Jessie, looking mournfully in his face.

"Yes, a smile; why, not, my dear and beautiful Jessie? Why may a father not expect a smile from his daughter?"

"Can the features smile, while the heart is sad and sorrowful?"

"But it must be so no more, my child," said Arnold, throwing down the notes and gold he had received of Arlines on the table, where they lay in a glittering and tempting heap; "there is gold, and that will drive away sadness."

"But it brings dishonour, father; could any blot like that ever have attached to your name before your acquaintance with this man?"

"Jessie, I never knew the sharp sting of want and hunger; we have known it—and, if I can prevent it, it shall never occur again."

"At what a price, father—at what a price! I would sooner eat bread and drink water only, than I would touch any of that gold."

"Do not drive me to distraction, Jessie— remember there are others—your two little sisters as well as yourself—they cannot put up with the sharp pangs of hunger, if we can."

At this moment, a sharp rap came at the door. Jessie arose and answered it. No sooner was the door opened, than the landlady, a coarse, fat woman, bounced into the room, and said in a masculine voice,

"Now, Muster Arnold, or what's your name, I want's my rent; I can't trust you no longer, for I don't know you and you does no work; so some fine day yer will be a-bolting, I suppose, especially if yer dosen't get nabbed for something or t'other."

"How much do I owe you," said Arnold to the woman.

"How much? there's a pretty go! Now I tells yer what it is, yer only poking fun at me, and I'll not bear insults: not know the rent of yer own room, and can't double that!—well, I'm blessed! but that's the way with you stuck-up people; yer don't know what you owe and what you don't; and, what's more, yer don't know when to pay, so I comes up myself; for, if my husband gets it, he'll be sure to lose it somewhere or another."

"There," said Arnold, throwing down a sovereign, "take what I owe you out of that, and I leave your apartments to-night."

"To-night, sir? Dear me," exclaimed the woman, who no sooner saw there was ample means of payment, than she began to be civil and loquacious. "You can't be going to-night, it's so very cold, and the dear young creature, your daughter, will certainly be ill after it."

"We leave this evening; have the goodness to hand me the change."

This was decisive; and the woman then took for three weeks, which she declared was regular, as she had received no warning. The change was handed over, and the woman quitted the room.

"Jessie," said Captain Arnold, "we had nigh been turned into the streets; and your poor sisters would have had to walk until we should have found any one charitable enough to take us in; and you know, Jessie, whatever our destitution might have been, we should have been near perishing."

"Father! father! you used not to reason thus," exclaimed Jessie. "It pains me to hear you. I will go where you go; and may Heaven grant us its merciful regard!"

She arose, and immediately set about attiring the two younger girls for the walk, and, in a little while, she informed her father, with tears in her eyes, that she was ready to follow him as soon as he pleased.

Captain Arnold arose, and taking his daughter's arm, they quitted then miserable lodging, and went in search of one more suitable to their present prospects and means. It was a matter of exultation to Arnold, but yet he could not express all he thought and felt to his daughter. She knew not all that had happened, and he could not make the necessity of his position sufficiently distinct to her; so he walked on in silence, followed by the two youngest children

CHAPTER XXXVIII.

DIFFERENCE IN THE REFLECTIONS OF ARNOLD AND JESSIE.—THE NEW APARTMENTS.—SATISFACTION AND SADNESS.

CAPTAIN ARNOLD, with his daughter, walked for some distance, and then he called a coach, as that part of the town he desired to reside in lay at some distance, and with his children he entered the vehicle, and desired to be driven to Regent-street.

Jessie sat in silence; her grief was too great for utterance; the force of circumstances was hurrying her father forward in a course that she believed must eventually end in destruction. Their present prosperity, she thought, must be but temporary—it could not continue without her father continuing in the society, and acting under the advice, of such a man as Philip Arlines, whose honour and honesty were far beyond question—merely words of no import, save in the ear of the stranger, and then it was but an ignis-fatuus that led to destruction.

What course could her father have recourse to she knew not to keep him in the state he evidently desired to live in. The neighbourhood that he was going to was one that would require more means than she believed him capable of procuring with honour; and without it what was life?

Where was it all to end? She was incapable of answering the query, or rather she subdued the probable answer that rose upon her mind. It was such a one as a daughter might indeed shrink from contemplating, since it convinced her of his extreme danger and probable disgrace in the eyes of the world, and his suffering the penalty of adopting, at the artful suggestion of Phillip Arlines, courses that must, some time or other, be exposed, and render him amenable to the laws of society.

While these sad and disturbing thoughts passed through the mind of Jessie, her father's mind was in a state of tumult scarcely to be described.

His release from the immediate and unpleasant consequences of extreme poverty greatly elated him, as also the possession of a sum of money beyond his expectations, that at least put poverty so far in the shade that he could not contemplate her save as something distant and remote, too much so to disturb the equanimity of his mind.

Then again he would enjoy the style of living he had been used to, and his daughter Jessie would not be compelled to be the inhabitant of the miserable place where they had come from; she would now, he thought, be more happy, and his children also.

Now and then a heated flush crossed his brow as he thought of the mode by which he had acquired the means to do all this; and he now and then asked himself if he could honestly congratulate himself upon the change he was then making. Had he not debased himself still lower even in his own estimation, and that he was no longer the man of honour he once called himself with justice?

No—he was not; and each day, each new act, each new thought, tended to deprive him of the pious consciousness that once was the barrier between his honour and debasement.

His connection with Phillip Arlines he could not bear to think of; he considered it now at an end. He did not want his assistance, and could do without him; he would, therefore, have no more to do with him, and time would erase the deeds, that necessity compelled him to enact, from his memory—the past would be forgotten in the happiness and integrity of the future.

Thus had Captain Arnold glossed over in his own mind the events that had passed, and coloured highly those which he presumed would come.

They had now arrived in Regent-street, and the coachman inquired where they would go next. Captain Arnold told him to drive slowly down Conduit-street, Bond-street, and he would tell him when to stop.

The vehicle then slowly drove down, and Arnold eagerly watched each window as they passed, and at length noticed one in which there was a bill placed, notifying, to those whom it might concern, that there apartments might be had furnished.

Arnold desired the man to draw up and knock at the door, which he did, and then he entered the house to examine them, being fully certain that he should have them at any price. He was introduced to the landlady—a tall coarse woman, with a large turban, from the summit of which waved a large feather.

"Pray, madam," said the captain, "can I view the apartments you have to let?"

"Oh, yes," said the landlady, with a loud lofty voice, "you can. You want them, I suppose, eh?"

"Either them or some other, as they may be suitable or not," replied the captain, somewhat angered at the insolent tone and bearing of the big woman.

"Will you walk this way then, sir?" she asked, laying great stress upon the sir.

ARLINES CONDUCTED BY THE LANDLORD TO GOSSET'S HIDING-PLACE.

There were but three rooms, two bed-rooms and a sitting-room, which last was the front drawing-room. They were certainly handsome apartments, and well furnished; the carpets and rugs were of the best quality, as was, indeed, the whole of [the furniture, which was both fashionable and costly.

"Do you see anything that you would desire to be altered or amended?" inquired the land-lady, with a consciousness that nothing more could well be desired than the accommodations her apartments afforded.

"Nothing that I can at this moment see,' replied the captain. "What may you ask as rent?"

"Three guineas a-week," replied the woman, decisively.

"Three guineas!—'tis a heavy charge; but I presume that includes all?"

"All that is usual," replied the woman, evasively. "Have you any family, sir?"

"There are but myself, and three children," replied the captain.

"Three children—three children!" replied the landlady, in astonishment.

"Yes, you were a child yourself at one time,

madam, however long ago that may be," said the captain, with some asperity.

"But then I didn't let lodgings," replied the landlady; "eh, dear no, and I can't take in children, especially three, they destroy furniture, and create a disturbance."

"Young children may do so," replied the captain, "but mine have long since passed the age at which such mischief as that you apprehend is committed."

"Then how old are they?" inquired the woman, puzzled at what was said to her.

"Just ask the young lady in the coach to step up here," said the captain, "as I wish her to look at the apartments."

This was done, and Jessie entered the apartment in which her father and the big female were conversing.

"This," said Arnold, "is my eldest daughter; the others are younger, but long since passed the age of infancy."

"Ah," said the big female, "this young lady is quite different from what I thought, by the way in which you spoke of them."

"Then we may agree about terms, then, I suppose?" said Arnold,

"Yes, sir; what reference will you please to give?"

"None," replied Arnold, decidedly; "I never trouble my friends about such matters; and most of them are out of town as I came in; but I will pay in advance, and I dare say that will be equal to it."

"Quite," replied the big female, as she gathered up three sovereigns and three shillings, talking at the same time, and placed them with the utmost indifference into her capacious pouch that dangled at her side.

"I will send up the servant, who is at your desires, immediately."

She then bowed with a lodging-house keeper's gentility and assurance, and quitted the apartment.

"Any boxes?" inquired the servant, as she entered the drawing-room.

"None till to-morrow, when they will be here from the hotel," said the captain, whose colour came to his face when he recollected that Jessie was there to hear the lie he had so readily invented.

"Is there anything you would like now, sir?—a fire?"

"Yes; and let me have some refreshments as speedily as you can. Jessie, my dear, see that all things are as they should be, here is money," and he threw down several gold pieces. "I will go and bring the children up."

So saying, he quitted the apartment, and went to the coachman, whom he paid, and when returned with the children.

The air of warmth, comfort, and even of luxury, that pervaded the apartments was such that it conveyed the most pleasing emotions

and satisfaction to the mind of Captain Arnold, who leaned back in his softly-stuffed chair, and surveyed the place with delight.

Jessie alone, amidst this display, felt a sadness at heart, that caused her to feel a relief when the usual hour of rest came round, and she retired to the solitude of her own chamber.

CHAPTER XXXIX.

CAPTAIN ARNOLD'S PROMISE TO JESSIE.— INTERVIEW WITH ARLINES.—THE TEMPTATION.

THE next morning after the installation of Arnold into his new lodgings, was one of cheerful and sunny appearance. Captain Arnold was himself much elated; indeed, the intoxication of success and good fortune had taken complete possession of him, and he appeared not to be the same man he was a few days before.

Arnold had but little conversation with Jessie since he had come there; but he knew her feelings were different to his own; and his silence was a proof that he could not but admit that hers were, at least, more founded in reason than his own—they were more correct than his own, and this silence springing from such a cause became the more difficult to break as each moment passed by.

The situation of Jessie was nearly the same, with regard to her father, though it sprang from a different cause. She was unwilling to disturb the even course of his thoughts, nor add a pang to those moments which appeared to pass so happily with him, though her own heart was full to bursting.

Sadness and sorrow sat there, for she still thought she heard the threat of Arlines ringing in her ears, and her father's fate was a doom from which he could not escape, while he continued the companion and dupe of that man; and she was sure such a crafty man could not act otherwise than as a tempter, and then seize the plunder his helpless victim had been led to grasp.

"Father," she at length exclaimed, after a long silence, "father, have you thought of any plan by which we may all be maintained in this style without having recourse to that vile, bad man who has been the cause of all our misfortunes?"

Arnold was startled at the sound of her voice; there was so much sweetness in its tones that it struck a chord in his own bosom, and all the father was in his heart in an instant. It was some moments ere he could reply, and then he said,—

"I have not yet done so, Jessie; it will take some days, and much thought, before I can well determine, and then it may be a work of time before I can obtain what I want."

"And in the meantime, father——" here Jessie paused.

"I shall not want, Jessie; I have the means, and will not place you in any disagreeable situation such as you have already suffered. You, and your sister and brother, will remain here for many months, without any alteration in your present state and comforts."

"'Tis not of that I would speak," said Jessie, "but of that man who is the cause of our recent calamities. I hope, father, that I shall never be compelled to stay with him in the same house."

"No, Jessie, I shall have no more connection with him," said Arnold,

"That is one of the best things I have heard you say, father, for some time; but I fear that he is a man of vile and vindictive feelings; that he will follow you from place to place, and, either by threats or cajolements, induce you to join with him again."

"No, no, never, Jessie, never. I would defy him—I would not succumb to him. I have no need of him; we are now free of each other—he is no intimate of mine."

"I am glad of it," replied Jessie—"very glad of the assurance; but what will be the end of this expensive place; can we do all that?"

"Yes, Jessie, we can, and pay for it, too; and before my purse is low, we shall have it re-filled by legitimate means."

"Thank God, then, that is the case," said Jessie, fervently; "but, father, are people paid so well who have to work for their living, as to be able to afford such a place as this to live in? or, if they are, is this the best and cheapest mode of procuring such luxury as this by which we are surrounded?"

Arnold paused for a moment, and hesitated. He had never viewed the matter in this light before; but at length he said,—

"Yes, Jessie, my appearance and home may much influence my future prospects, and if it should turn out eventually that I cannot afford it, we can easily withdraw from it, and live in a more humble one; we shall, moreover, have time to seek for and choose a more compatible home."

Jessie sighed, for she thought she saw the clinging of her father to former habits and tastes. She could not blame him, had she felt herself entitled to do so; her heart chid her for being too rigid in her notions of right and wrong with her father.

"At all events, I have made up my mind that I will have nothing more to do with Phillip Arlines."

As he uttered these words, the drawing-room door opened, and Arlines himself darkened the entrance. His features bore on them a sneering expression, as if partly in triumph, and partly in conscious serenity. He turned and gazed upon Jessie, as much as to say, "You shall see how he will keep his promise, when it suits me he shall break it."

Captain Arnold spoke not; he was much astonished, and too bewildered by this sudden appearance, to have the power of concentrating his thoughts upon any one course. Jessie feared her father's wavering disposition, and with the view of recalling him to himself, she turned to Phillip Arlines, and said, with an air of dignity and composure,—

"This, sir, is a private apartment, and one in which your presence is both unannounced and unwelcome; and it will better become you to quit it, than stay here, were your presence is a positive intrusion."

Arlines bit his lip, but the sneer left not his countenance, as he said,—

"My visit, Miss Arnold, was not intended expressly for you; therefore, nowithstanding your intimation, founded upon your natural enough mistake, I will remain till I have had a few words with my friend Captain Arnold."

"And those need be but very few, Phillip Arlines," said the captain, rising; "there is the door—your road lies that way—we are henceforth strangers to each other."

"We are not strangers to each other, Captain Arnold," said Arlines; "I repeat it, we are not strangers."

"We have not been," said the captain, "and the greater my misfortune— but we are strangers for the future."

"I tell you again, Arnold," said Arlines, bending on him a keen glance, that made Arnold shrink, "I tell you again, and again, we are not strangers, past, present, or to come; and mark my words well, for I know what I say, and you do not."

"Arlines," said Arnold, "I have but received ruin and misery at your hands, and expect no more for the future; therefore, I have come to the determination of never associating myself with you. Attempt not to disturb my resolution; for I have resolved it shall be done."

"Then, hear me, Arnold: 'tis not you, who have associated yourself with me; but I, who have aided you; you came to me, you sought after me, and inquired after me at every place I frequented for days; you sought me and my assistance; you and your children would have starved, had I not assisted you, and saved you from a workhouse."

"'Tis in vain to argue about the matter," said Arnold; "I have said it, and am resolved to abide by what I have said."

"Are you mad, Arnold?" said Arlines, glancing at him with a furious gesture.

"Never more sane in my life," replied Arnold coolly, "and a proof of it is, that I am not moved."

"And are you sane enough to understand me,

Captain Arnold? why I could make you an inmate of a gaol by one word!"

"If your threat be good for anything, it would serve me as well as yourself," replied Arnold ; "and where I go in that case, there Phillip Arlines goes to."

"We shall see that," cried Arlines, stamping with rage.

"We shall indeed ; and now hear me, Arlines," said Captain Arnold, growing warm, " hear me. I will not be your tool, or your companion. Leave me to myself and my own fate ; I despise your threats, and defy your utmost malice and power. Do what you can, say what you know, and more, but be assured I will sacrifice even life itself to punish you ; and now, for the last time, quit this apartment, quit this house !"

Arlines was silent for a few moments ; rage and malice gleamed from his eyes, that gazed on Arnold and Jessie with the expression of the rattle-snake disappointed of its prey by some unlooked-for means, and he said, in a low, hissing voice,

"Listen to my last words, Arnoll. I leave you now—ay, and that, too, to your own course—go on, you shall have rope enough from me ; but, at length, you must come to me, and then be assured the time will be at hand when my foot will fall upon your neck. I could crush you now ; but these new-blown hopes shall blossom awhile ere they wither ; it will be a useful lesson, and make you feel the change more strongly than if they had never risen."

So saying, Phillip Arlines, after casting a withering glance of hatred at Arnold and Jessie, shut the door to with a great crash, and slowly descended the stairs, and in an another moment stood in the street.

It was some moments ere either Jessie or her father, spoke ; they were both much annoyed at the conduct of Arlines. Jessie could scarce comprehend what he said, especially as her father had braved his worst, and Arlines had at length quitted him with vague and distant threats.

Arnold, on the other hand, was as much astonished at his own firmness as at his success in defying and getting rid of Arlines as effectually as he had done. He turned towards Jessie, who stood watching her father's countenance a few paces from him.

"Well, thank Heaven ! he is gone," remarked Arnold ; " he is a strange man."

"And a very bad man, father," said Jessie, throwing herself into his arms, " a very bad man. I never felt so thankful at anything as I do at his departure ; but yet his dark and vindictive threats terrify me very much."

"Never heed them, Jessie, never heed them ; I do not ; he may try much, but he can do nothing."

"I am happy, very happy, to hear you say so much," said Jessie ; " it gives me new life and spirits ; but, father, there is another thing I should like to hear you say, as well as I did what you have done already, and that is not a little."

"What do you mean, my child ?" inquired Captain Arnold, with some uneasiness.

"I mean that I hope you will promise me that you will never enter one of those houses into which Arlines alone dragged you to lose your money."

"My dear Jessie," said Arnold, "surely this is unnecessary on your part ; but since you have thought it worth while to ask it, I will promise you that I will never enter one again under any pretence."

"Then we shall, indeed, spend a happy time of it, and nothing shall ever happen to vex you, I am sure."

"My dear Jessie," said Arnold, affectionately kissing her forehead, "you are a good girl ; make your mind easy about everything ; attend but to yourself and the children, and happiness, at least as much of it as I can feel, deprived as I have been of your poor mother, will be our reward."

As Captain Arnold uttered these words, a shade of sadness stole across his features, and he took his cane and hat, saying, he intended to walk a little way, and see some friends, with whom he intended to converse about his future plans.

With that he quittted the apartment, and sought the streets.

He walked some little distance, apparently without any object ; and at last he found himself in St James's-street.

He paused a moment or so, and considered within himself if it were prudent for him even to trust himself, unnecessarily, within the vicinity of such perilous temptation as that which now beset him.

CHAPTER XL.

THE TEMPTATION.—THE GAMING HOUSE. —ARNOLD'S SUCCESS.

CAPTAIN ARNOLD almost smiled at the fear that his own resolution might fail him at a moment like the present, and that, too, after he had so recently evinced his determination ; no, he was proof to this temptation, as well as he was to that that was of a far more actual value, and when opposition had something fearful to encounter.

"No, no ; I have nothing to fear now," he murmured to himself ; " the worst is now over. I will not fear temptation, when I have passed through the fire. The inducement to enter these places is no longer in being ; and I am free from its trammels. It would indeed be absurd in me, if I abstained from going into one particular street, because there is a house in it which I have no desire or need of entering—pho, pho!"

With this, Captain Arnold made his way up St. James's-street, and, as he did so, he was overtaken by a sudden shower of rain. Arnold hastened his pace, with the intention of reaching Piccadilly, and taking coach or seeking shelter in the Burlington Arcade; but the rain increasing to a heavy drenching shower, he was compelled to run up the steps of a large house, and stand under the portico until it abated.

But there were no signs of its abatement; the streets were all cleared in a few moments of the passengers, and cabs and coaches were rattling about in all directions. Several persons came up to the house-door of the house he had sought shelter in, and Captain Arnold recognised them as men who he had seen when in the company of Arlines at the various gaming-houses.

This for a moment or two rather astonished him, and he looked more narrowly at the place in which he had taken shelter; and, to his amazement, found he was standing within the very doorway of the house he most dreaded, the fatal gaming-house in which he had lost his whole fortune and estate.

For a moment or two, a chill crept through his frame, and he gazed into the street and saw it rained harder and more fiercely than before; he could not quit his position, and he resolved to stay.

"Why should I," he thought, "turn away from a shelter, because it is afforded by a house I do not intend to enter—by a house, indeed, that carries on within it that which, if I did enter, I should never join, or again be induced to share in the amusements that are offered to those who enter?

"'Tis mere childishness. I will stay, and that, too, as long as I have need. 'Tis the least they could do to afford me shelter from the storm: I have paid pretty dearly for it; but then, hard as it is, it is buying experience; and that is valuable at least, especially so as it leaves me with hope, resolution, and means. It would be difficult, I think, to fall into any new misfortune with the past before my eyes; it would be strange indeed!"

Captain Arnold, strong in his own resolution and the feeling that he was above temptation, turned his back to the green door at which he had looked with feelings of a mixed nature, and continued to gaze upon the streets and the effects of the shower.

The position of Captain Arnold was very unpleasant; the rain came pelting in the direction of where he stood; he looked out for a coach; but nothing of the kind was to be found for love or money; and it was raining by far too hard to attempt to quit the place he occupied.

The rain, indeed, beat against the face of the house, and the wind carried the spray quite into the passage, so that Captain Arnold began to think he must retreat from the post he occupied, under such disagreeable circumstances.

"Why should I not go inside? There is no more need to play than there is here; there is only a greater facility afforded. But what of that? my resolution is formed as immutable as fate."

Then came a long pause, during which the captain shifted his position more than once, and then he resumed—

"I cannot see the philosophy of getting drenched, when shelter is to be had for the trouble of walking into it. I might as well eschew the streets because evil men walk in them; 'tis a rank absurdity, and, were my motives known, I should be laughed at; indeed, they would be construed into the idea that my poverty was such that I dare not enter the place, if I would."

Stung with these thoughts, he quickly turned round and opened the green door. The bare thought that other people might think he was poor, was a reproach that he could not bear, or would not—perhaps the latter; for he eagerly seized the notion as an excuse to enter, which he did after some hesitation.

Once again in the gaming-house, Captain Arnold felt himself suddenly interested in all that was passing around him. His fears that held him in subjection, while he was on the outside, now deserted him, and he walked about with the assurance of a man who has the means of doing just as he pleases, but had so much self-denial, and could only do just what reason dictated, and no more.

Play was carried on, for some time, with varying success, and many bets were made upon the players, and yet Captain Arnold felt not disturbed; he kept a grave and stolid countenance, but at the same time he was resolved not to play or bet on any game.

He entered into conversation with several, who knew him by sight, and who, like himself, had sought shelter from the storm, and with no intention of playing at the tables.

One gentleman in particular attracted his attention. He appeared to be young, well educated, but not very conversant with the world, and, from the tone of his conversation, he gathered that he had not long been a frequenter at such places.

"I should like to play a game," replied the stranger, "but the table is so fully occupied, that there is no room."

"A private one is easily obtained," said Arnold, "if you desire it."

"I do not," replied the stranger, "unless I saw a friend here who would join me; otherwise I will wait till there's an opening at the table, and, if I can find any one who will lose half an hour with me, will have a game or two."

Captain Arnold said nothing. There were some strange fancies, that were floating about his mind; he could not have described them, had he been required to do so; they were a mixed and jumbled mass of fears and hopes, neither one nor the other, but compounded of both.

This mental disturbance caused the captain to have recourse to several glasses of wine, to quiet the disturbance and steady his nerves, which he thought suddenly became weaker, and weaker, though why he could not tell, until at length he found himself seated at a table with the stranger to whom he had been talking.

The stranger, seeing him unengaged, had put the question to him, and said, pointing to a table,

"That table is disengaged, sir; have you any disinclination to occupy it with me for half an hour's play?"

"None in the least," replied Arnold, before he was aware of what he had said, for he replied almost by instinct, and not from reflection.

Before, however, he could recall his words, the stranger had seated himself, and pointed to the vacant seat, which Arnold occupied. He could not retract, though he felt willing to do so; but after the first few admonitory thoughts that crossed his mind, and created some mental confusion, he was as cool, and cooler than ever he had been at such a place in his life.

They played for some time, with varying success; but towards the close of the game, Arnold was a gainer. They had played for some time, many games had been played, and many lost by the stranger, and some by Arnold, who finally rose the winner of the amount of one thousand pounds.

"You are successful, sir, to-day," said the stranger, rising. "I shall have my revenge on some other occasion."

"Certainly," replied Arnold, mentally thinking he would never enter the place again.

The stranger quitted the place, and Arnold stayed for a short time behind; then he went out alone, not ill pleased with his success, though he almost feared to think of it. It was so unexpected, and so contrary to his promise to Jessie.

<hr>

CHAPTER XL.

ARNOLD'S REFLECTIONS.—INTERVIEW WITH
ARLINES.—JESSIE'S REPULSE.

WHEN Arnold reached the street he felt a relief come over him difficult to describe. He had escaped from the scene of temptation not only without any loss, but with a positive gain of one thousand pounds. "What will Jessie think?" but he could not tell her of his success; he had promised her he would never enter a gaming-house again, and he had done so. But he was a winner.

There was a charm in the sound of that word; it appeared like music to his ears, and he gloried in the means by which he became possessed of large sums; and silenced the whisperings of conscience, which would often be more intrusive than welcome.

"Ah! well! well! I must not tell her anything about it," he muttered; "she is over gentle and ignorant of the necessities and usages of the world. Time—time will do much; but she is sensitive, and I will endeavour to learn her to look upon passing events like the clouds of a summer's day. 'Tis true they obscure the landscape; but they pass away and are forgotten. Necessity, indeed, knows no law; but was there any necessity for what I did? Had I not money, and, therefore, was there any stern and rigorous fate that drove me on?

"No, none; but stop—I am no casuist; else I might have known that inclination is as great a tyrant as ever one could be. Ay, I have it now. I see: who could fight against the onward and irresistible progress of his fate? Not I, certainly. He who can, is more than human.

"As I promised Jessie, however, I will say nothing about it to her. She shall remain in happy ignorance, though the knowledge might render others happy."

While these thoughts passed through his mind, he walked onwards towards his own home, and paused on the door step ere he lifted the knocker. His mind misgave him, and he could scarce blind himself with them, and he felt that the pure, simple-minded Jessie would reject the specious reasoning at once as untenable, and then he would appear as the only one likely to be deceived by his own arguments.

He turned to the door to lift the knocker, when he heard a step behind him; he instantly turned round, and perceived, to his astonishment, Phillip Arlines standing by him, with his hand extended towards him.

For a moment Arnold was too staggered to speak; but he did not attempted to take the proffered hand, but shrunk back, for there was a singular expression of cunning and audacity in Arlines' manner that perfectly astounded him. Arlines, however, took no notice of his confusion, but persisted in holding out his hand towards him.

"What is that for?" said Arnold, pointing to his extended hand.

Arlines took no further notice of the question, save by a provoking smile.

"What is that for? I again ask you," inquired Captain Arnold.

"My share," replied Arlines, coolly.

"Your share!"

"Yes; my share."

"Of what? I have nothing for you," said the bewildered captain.

"My share of your winnings," said Arlines. "I am entitled to my share."

"Your share!"

"Yes; I repeat, my share, Captain Arnold; you have not long won a thousand pounds in St. James's-street; you know that well enough; therefore, give me my share of it."

"And how do you know that I have won so much?" said Arnold.

"Oh, that can be of no consequence to you; and, besides, I never satisfy the unpardonable curiosity of a man, who merely wishes to inquire into my affairs."

"And I have no connection with you, remember that, and cease to trouble me about applications of this sort. I have no money for you."

"But you have; you have my share; surely you would not rob me of my own?"

"It is not your due. Recollect, I have had no aid, assistance, or confederation in this transaction; therefore, cease, I say, to trouble me."

"Captain Arnold, this will not do between us; I must have two-thirds, say, six hundred pounds; hand it over to me, and I will leave you."

"Six hundred pounds!" exclaimed the enraged Captain Arnold.

"Precisely."

"I shall give you nothing," said Arnold; "what I have, I have obtained without you; cease, therefore, to trouble me."

"I shall take measures, Arnold, to place you in a worse state than you have yet been in. All will be lost; and even what you have got will be rendered unavailable, for you will, before to-morrow, be the inhabitant of a gaol; and your character blown by this affair, you will be prevented from going into the same society again. Come, come, Arnold; that silly girl is not here now; you know my power, and your own resources; you know, also, how far the law can touch you, and how far it can touch me. Choose between us. I do not threaten you; far from it; I merely explain the case, as it stands, and what can be done. Don't you think it will be better to give me the money?"

Arnold hesitated; he knew not what to do; he did not like to part with so large a sum to Arlines, but he knew not how to avoid it. He put his hand in his pocket, and drew, instinctively, the money forth, and he gave it to Arlines, who seized it, and, having counted it out, quitted the spot, with a smile of triumph and contempt on his lips.

Captain Arnold now entered the house, and was soon in his own apartment, where he sat down somewhat agitated, while a feeling of disappointment slowly came over him.

Jessie came into the apartment immediately after. Her features betokened sadness and sorrow. She wore not the semblance of the hope her face betokened in the morning.

"Well, Jessie," said Arnold, as he saw she could not speak, "what has happened? Cheer up, and be patient."

"Patient, father! was I ever otherwise?" said Jessie, in a low tone.

"No, no, my child—my Jessie, never; but you are sad, and sadness ought not to trouble such as you."

"And yet such as I, father, suffer more than others who have, perhaps, less to be thankful for than I have."

"What do you mean, Jessie? Speak, and tell me the meaning of all this."

"I will, since you desire it, father. I had resolved that my heart should burst ere I said anything about it: but I have not the strength."

"Speak, Jessie, speak."

"Did you not, father, promise me that you would have nothing more to do with Arlines?"

"Yes."

"And have you not been in conversation with him for some minutes, father? I hope no future renewal of that man's acquaintance will rob us of our only hope of happiness and peace."

Arnold could not speak; he felt he was placed in a difficult position, and feared to trust himself with a reply; and Jessie, seeing he spoke not, continued:

"Father, father, there is yet more to tell you than that. You may not have been able to avoid Arlines; but you could avoid that house where you have lost your whole fortune. Oh, father! what will become of us all, of you, of these——"

"Say no more, Jessie; this is a subject that I cannot hear you speak of with patience; it is your place to be mute, and not to upbraid your father, when he has been unfortunate or even in fault."

"I do not, father, I do not upbraid you; I implore you, I beg of you, not for my sake, but for your own, for my brother's and sister's sake, nay, for my poor mother's sake, that this may not happen again. Never go near that place."

Arnold arose, and, in a half angry tone, he said, "Jessie, I did not think I had ever given you such liberty as to talk thus to me. I shall leave you for a time, till you come to a sense of the impropriety of your conduct."

So saying, Captain Arnold quitted the room. Jessie flew after him, and besought him with tears, and by every endearing word, to return and stay, though it were but to upbraid her.

Her tears and her supplications were in vain: he rudely pushed her on one side, and shut the door after himself. Jessie sunk into a chair, full of grief and tears.

CHAPTER XLI.

THE RECONCILIATION.—ARNOLD AND AR-
LINES.—THE GAMING-TABLE AGAIN.

WHEN Arnold had quitted Jessie, he paused for a moment or two on the stair-head, and bethought himself for a moment. He heard the deep sighs of Jessie; her sobs were quite audible; and he almost determined to return to her, and give her the assurance she desired; but then, again, he disliked the thought of explaining what had happened, and, more, he thought he should scarce be free if he permitted her to conquer. In the end, his worse feelings prevailed; and he turned from the door, and descending the stairs, he was soon out of the house.

Once out of the house, he knew not which way to turn, but went onwards at random; and, crossing the road, he suddenly came upon Arlines, who regarded him with a friendly look.

"Are you for a walk, Arnold?" he said, offering his arm, as he came up.

Arnold was somewhat staggered at first, and hesitated, but, seeming ashamed to do so, he took the proffered arm, and they both walked away together.

"Which way are you going?" inquired Arlines, with a malicious smile.

"Any way. I am going nowhere in particular," replied Arnold.

"I am westward bound," said Arlines; "that is as pleasant as anywhere else: we will go that way."

Saying this they proceeded through the principal thoroughfares for a walk.

Towards the end of the day London appears to be in a greater bustle than in the earlier hours; indeed, it would almost countenance the supposition, that its inhabitants had been idle and neglectful during the first hours, and had, as the decline of the sun warned them of the approach of evening, suddenly become alive to the importance of their affairs, and were hurrying to and fro, endeavouring to make up for the lost time by present speed and exertion.

This, however, is not the case, for, as the day recedes, there is so much to be done ere night closes upon them, and there are so many returning to their homes at early hours, that it gives a momentary impetus and bustle to the town.

The bright sun's rays glance over the house-tops, and are reflected strongly from the house windows, on the side of the way where they fall. The shops are all busy, and look their proudest and brightest at such a time; for their owners well know the effect arrangement has upon the passers-by who are usually attracted by a well-arranged assortment of goods.

On a fine day, in some of the principal thoroughfares, crowds of well-dressed people are seen promenading about, and adding a splendour to the gay scene, of which they form a part, and no unimportant part either.

The crowded streets have a busy, noisy sound, peculiar to the city, in which so many cries and noises are mingled together, and become one confused din, in which you can distinguish nothing.

Bustle and confusion are at their height, and a stranger would believe that all he saw had got into such an inextricable maze, that nothing short of a miracle could possibly save all from destruction; and yet how beautifully does this mass of people and carriages separate, one from the other, and each take its own devious course.

To strangers, who are unaccustomed to the habits of a large city, the mass of population and vehicles must, for some time, appear singular. Strangers are utterly unable to comprehend how it is, that so few fatal accidents have taken place; but a Londoner would, indeed, be surprised if any, barely any, took place at all.

The moment for fashionable people to dine has arrived, and the carriages of the nobility are seen hurrying to and fro, and driving furiously through the streets, to reach their destination at the appointed time.

The scene of bustle gradually subsides, until the moment when the theatres are about to open; and then amusement causes as much confusion and hurrying to and fro as ever the necessity for dinner had done.

The sun has by this time sunk in the west, and the subdued light that yet remained behind served but to show that preparations were being completed for a long evening, such as London alone can boast of; for evening here merges into night; and it is difficult, at times, to tell, from appearances, when one ends and the other begins.

"I do not know whether you feel any fatigue, Arnold; but I am very tired; for I have walked much to-day."

"I certainly feel fatigued," said Arnold; "I think a little wine would refresh us; after which, I will return home."

"As you please," said Arlines; "but I am out now, and intend to amuse myself fo the evening. I have not what you call a home to go to."

"I see," said Arnold; "but that evil might, you know, be easily amended, if you had the mind."

"Had I other things of that kind to distract my mind, I should not be fit to enjoy life, and keep pace with other men; and, besides, I have a great dislike to being fettered by any connection of the kind. 'Tis but a fight between two caged animals, you know, Arnold, and the

JESSIE DASHES THE POISONED DRINK FROM HER FATHER'S LIPS.

one who is the most insensible and obdurate gets the day."

"I cannot admit the truth of what you say," said Arnold.

"Perhaps not: your case was different; but had you lived in town—but here we are; will you come in, and have the wine you were speaking of?"

The house Arlines led Arnold to was the gaming-house in which he had so often been before. Here Arlines and Arnold sat down, and calling for wine they began to converse freely over many affairs that had passed, and

Arnold began to think he had acted unnecessarily harsh towards Arlines.

"The wine is uncommonly good, Arlines: I don't know that I ever tasted better in my life."

"It is," said Arlines, helping out the las glass; "we may as well have another bottl of the same sort."

This was agreed to, and the wine being brought, they resumed their conversation.

"I have been lucky here since you and used to come," said Arlines.

"Have you?" asked Arnold, drily.

"Yes, uncommonly lucky; and I think you have changed your luck, for you have been a winner."

"I was once, but you seem to know all about it," said Arnold.

"Yes," replied Arlines—"I am not on the town for no purpose; but the fact is, I know a great many things that people would not dream of."

"Indeed!" said Arnold; "what do you mean?"

"That as regards play, for instance—can either always win, or ensure myself against the fear of loss."

"Can you so?"

"I can."

"That would, indeed, be a secret, that would, like the wand of the enchanter, turn all things to gold."

"Two could work the scheme more effectually than one," replied Arlines.

"Would it do so, indeed?"

"Yes, it would; and, if you would promise to assist me, I would make you acquainted with my talisman."

Arnold was silent; he hesitated to have any further connection with Arlines: a host of fears rushed to his mind, and he said—

"I have but little to say, Arlines, about such a proposition; you know how far you are to be relied on in matters of this kind. I have lost much, and what I get is not mine."

"That is all past and done with," replied Arlines; "and you knew, when men feel dissatisfied with each other, they generally fall out about some trifle or other."

"Well, well, what is it?"

"Then tell me—will you aid me?"

"I will, if I find it may be done without too much——"

"There shall not be too much of anything; follow my advice, and all shall be well."

"But what is it you have to do?" inquired the captain.

"I will tell you, or rather show you. You must play a game with some one here, and I will ensure you against loss, under any circumstances."

"You will?"

"I will; before I leave the house, I'll pay the money down. Play, and play freely," said Arlines, "and I'll warrant you'll not lose, and then I'll tell you the secret; 'tis better understood thus than by mere word of mouth."

"Very well," replied Arnold, "I will try a game."

With that they both strolled about the place; and it was not long ere they found some one to play with Arnold.

They played with varied success for some time, and Arnold was expecting something to be done or said by Arlines, who was looking on cool and unconcerned to a degree. Arnold's mind more than once misgave him; but there was no way in which he could retrace his steps—he was obliged to play on.

"Play freely," said Phillip Arlines to Captain Arnold; "you can't hurt. I will undertake that you are no loser."

Arnold did play on, and lost hundred after hundred, till he became anxious and uneasy. He looked for Arlines, and saw him at another table, watching the progress of a game with apparent interest.

A curse was on Arnold's lips, and he would have paid his loss and played no more, but he had not the sum about him, and he was compelled to play to give Arlines time to quit the table, and come to him.

The voice of his antagonist recalled his thoughts.

"Do you play any more, sir? Your luck is against you to-night."

"Yes—yes," said Arnold; "another throw or two before we part, and then we will settle, if you please."

"As you please," replied the stranger.

They resumed their game, and yet Arnold felt that he was losing. Turning round, he saw Arlines walking towards him, and he came to the table just as he had lost another game, and Arnold paused a moment, and, turning to Arlines, he said in a low, bitter tone—

"What is to be done now? I have lost again."

"What is the amount?" inquired Arlines, with indifference.

"A thousand pounds!" said Arnold.

"Very well," replied the other; "pay it, then, and play no more on this occasion."

Arnold, for the moment, was struck dumb, for the thought rushed across his brain that Arlines had baited a trap for him, and intended to leave him to his own resources, and thus draw ruin upon him.

However, he was mistaken, for Arlines drew his pocket-book out of his pocket and took from it a roll of notes, which he gave to Arnold, who immediately counted them out, and handed them over to his antagonist, who received them with an air of satisfaction; and they quitted the table at which they had been seated.

"We will now go home, Arnold," said Arlines; and they quitted the apartments, Arnold too much bewildered at what had occurred to understand or ask any questions; and as they passed through the long dark passage that led to the room, Arlines said, in a low tone,—

"Arnold, you saw those notes?"

"Yes, I did," replied Arnold.

"Well, then, they are forged."

CHAPTER XLII.

THE FORGED NOTES.—THE APPOINTMENT.— THE DREAM.

THE words of Arlines acted like an electric shock upon the body and mind of Arnold, and he reeled for several yards, until the wall prevented his going further backward, and he would have fallen but for the same cause.

"Forged!" he gasped; "forged!"

"Yes; I make them," said Arlines; "I make them."

"Good Heaven!—what have I done? what have I not subjected myself to? Fool! fool! that I was."

"Pho! pho! don't alarm yourself—you have only uttered a few forged notes, that's all; and as for the danger or the punishment, why if it should ever take place, it will be either transportation or hanging; most likely the latter."

Arnold was for some time speechless; his faculties appeared to have flown, and he moved but from some instinct. Arlines looked at him, as they emerged from the gaming-house into St. James's-street, with the air of a fiend; triumph, malice, and pleasure were blended in one, and he inwardly chuckled at the internal commotion he had produced in the mind of Captain Arnold.

So exquisite was this emotion to him that he would not utter a word that would destroy the sensations that were giving Arnold so much pain and misery.

They passed on some distance before either spoke, and then Phillip Arlines said in a changed tone—

"Come—come, Arnold, recollect you are in as deeply as I am; therefore, be more of the man than to give way thus; you may as well, you know, be hung for a sheep as a lamb."

"What matters it to me," replied Arnold, "what it is for, so long as it is?"

"There is something like sense about that," said Arlines; "as it is not likely that so good an imitation will readily be discovered, and as you are now implicated with me, the best thing is to enjoy the pleasure it brings."

"The pleasure it brings?" echoed Arnold. "I can see but little, either in death or transportation."

"No—no; that is certainly unpleasant— most unpleasant," said Arlines, banteringly; "but I mean you may as well assist me to manufacture and pass these things, and share the proceeds between us. This can be easily done, and none the wiser."

Arnold gave an involuntary start, as Arlines said this, and would have refused it at once, but Arlines interposed by saying—

"Think over the matter, Arnold. I have some business on hand, and must quit you.

Think over it; there will be time enough between this and to-morrow. I will dine with you, and then we can talk over the matter together. It requires consideration: the advantages are so great that they only need an explanation to become perfectly apparent to you. However, in the meantime, keep your counsel, and adieu."

So saying, Arlines shook Arnold by the hand, and quitted him.

It was growing now very late, and Arnold turned his steps towards his own home, which he reached in a very short time, and having a latch key, he let himself in, thinking that he would not see Jessie, and so escape from any scene with her.

He entered the house, and had scarcely closed the door behind him, when the page, emerging from some unknown region, approached the captain with great deliberation, and, putting his hands into his pockets, he said, with imperturbable gravity—

"So, you are come home, are you? Well, and ain't you a nice young man to take care of yourself? We thought you had fallen through the flap of a cellar, and been converted into pies, by this time."

"Where is Miss Arnold, young impudence?" said the captain, not knowing whether to be angry or not.

"She's a bed, she is, like a good girl, where you ought to have been, too, had you been so minded; but here you are, injuring your precious health, and quite destroying my constitution."

"Come, sir, I will have none of this impertinence. I'll use my cane on your shoulders immediately."

"I should like to see you do it," remarked the page, taking a light and keeping at a respectful distance; "if you do, I'll drop the candle, and leave you in the dark, and then catch me."

"I'll have you discharged, you young scamp," said Arnold, getting warm, and really glad of something to attract his attention, and occupy his thoughts.

"Only think! what a violent man! I tells you what it is, sir, you've a notion of cut-tailing the liberty o' the subject and it's not to be borne in a country like this. There's Miss Jessie as ill as she can be, all owing to you, no doubt, and your late hours; come, go up stairs, and don't stand there admiring o' me, though I dessay you can't help it."

Arnold was soon convinced it was of no use to talk to the original that was before him, and he, therefore, gave up the task, and walked up stairs, simply telling him to follow him and give him a light.

"Oh! suttenly; that's civil now; but if you would keep better hours it would be more becoming; I have no mind to sit up myself, 'cept when I have an order for the theyatre—that's quite another sort o' thing."

By this time they had got into the room, and the light placed as the captain desired the page, when the latter remarked, that he hoped he wouldn't suffer from headache and want of appetite in the morning.

This was an unlucky speech, for the captain being within reach, brought his cane across his shoulders with such good intent, that he rushed from the room with a roar that disturbed several persons in the house and annoyed Arnold, who regretted he had either not struck him, or had done it much more effectually than he had.

Arnold now entered his own room, and, alone, he had every opportunity for his great enemy to happiness, thought, to attack him and cause him a sleepless night.

Thought was Arnold's great enemy, for it never served him effectually. His weakness of mind and want of decision and determination rendered all his reflections useless.

He well knew, and to himself acknowledged the dishonour and criminality of his present course; he saw now, with a vividness not to be mistaken, the first step he had taken in his present career; he saw all the difficulties, dangers, and disgrace that awaited, ay, surely awaited his pursuit of such a course, and yet he could not withdraw himself from the dominion of Phillip Arlines.

Each step, he knew, made him more and more securely the creature of the fiend who had woven around him such a net of entanglements that he could not release himself, and the more he plunged the more securely he was held.

He revolved matters over in his own mind repeatedly, and turn which way he would, he was met by difficulties on every side, and as that which was the most pressing and most immediate always turned the scale in favour of that mode of action, and as that always happened to be Phillip Arlines—and as he was the greatest difficulty that stood in the way of his quitting the proposed course of life—and the most dangerous enemy when he made him so that he had, his resolution gave way, and he was compelled to admit that he must be the obedient slave of that man's base designs.

Having come to this conclusion, he prepared to seek his couch and drive the uneasy thoughts that crowded his mind from him; and with many a bitter sigh he lay down to rest.

To sleep was, however, quite another thing —he could not—dark and sombre shadows of the future crowded on his brain, and he felt as though he had been transported to some deep shade where the souls of the departed wandered about, as if a warning to those who were permitted to behold them.

Thus he continued between sleeping and ......, until he fell into an uneasy slumber, and then he slept; but what a sleep! He rolled from side to side—he moaned and talked, but not distinctly—the words could scarce pass his clenched teeth—suddenly he started up, and uttered a cry of horror.

CHAPTER XLIII.

THE DREAM.—THE ADMISSION.—ARNOLD'S FEARS.

THE cry that Captain Arnold uttered when he started from his sleep, reached the ears of Jessie, who, for a moment, lay paralyzed with fear; but in another moment, as the conviction that it came from her father's room crossed her mind, she rushed to the bed-side of her only parent.

Arnold was sitting partially up, supported by one arm, and glaring around the room with a vacant stare, and he trembled excessively. Jessie approached him and took his hand, saying,—

"Father, dear father, what is the matter? Has anything happened?—what was the cause of that dreadful cry?"

"Is that you, Jessie?" said the captain, in an agitated manner. "Is that you, my dear child?"

"Yes, father—it is I. What—what is the matter with you? You tremble and appear to be suffering from some cause or other."

"Oh! 'twas but a dream, Jessie—'twas but a dream," said Arnold, nervously clutching her hand.

"It must have been a very dreadful one, at least," said Jessie; "but think no more of it, dear father—think no more of it, and be more composed."

"I shall be; but oh! it was very dreadful to look down such a dreadful gulf, the dark sides of which were too terrible to think of; and yet I cannot banish it from my mind."

"At all events," said Jessie, "you know it is not real, and reason will soon release you from the thraldom of nervous phantasies."

Captain Arnold gazed upon his lovely daughter, and reflected that but for his recent conduct and misfortunes he could have thought and argued the same; but now, alas! his mind was no longer strong and vigorous, and capable of resisting superstitious and dark thoughts.

"I will tell you what I thought," he said, slowly; "but sit down there, and you shall hear how dreadful a dream I had."

Jessie did as she was desired, and Captain Arnold proceeded to relate his dream to Jessie.

"I thought," said Arnold, "that your mother was alive, Jessie, and that we had strolled out together to enjoy the evening walk, and approached near the precipitous rocks that you have more than once seen,"

"Yes, father, yes," replied Jessie, when she

saw her father was looking at her as if he expected her to speak.

"You remember it well! we were watching the sun set, and approached the verge of the precipice, and looked down the long deep chasm that yawned beneath our feet.

"The sea beat below, and we could hear the waves plash against the bottom of the rocks. It was a dead, sullen sound, and caused terror to the ear. Beyond it was the ocean with its changing hues.

"The scene appeared beautiful—the glowing tints of the sky—the glitter of the sun's rays upon the ocean—all looked bright, and beautiful; but beneath our feet was fear and terror, and an undefined dread of death and danger to us.

"Your mother incautiously approached the edge of the precipice—I call to her not to do so, but she either did not hear me or heeded me not, for she ventured onto the very edge of the rock.

"I was silent, and clasped my hands in an agony of expectation. I saw her leaning over the dreadful depth below; she looked down steadily enough, and I saw her then remove, She is coming back—it is all over, I thought. and began to breathe again.

"But, alas! I was doomed to a deeper degree of agony than I had yet felt. Your mother wavered next. Great God! she had a kind of oscillating motion, as if she bent backwards and forwards, and was endeavouring to overcome a tendency to fall over the precipice.

"I could not move nor speak. I was spellbound, and presently saw her, with a loud scream, fall over the edge of the precipice.

"Heaven! I was paralyzed, and could not move a muscle. I heard the body of your unfortunate mother fall against the jutting rocks, as she descended the sides of the place, and, at length, I heard the dull, heavy plash into the water. Oh, God! then I was suddenly loosened from my trance, and rushed to the edge of the cliff, but she was gone.

"I crept to the edge and laid down, and looked over; but I could see nothing. The waves plashed and dashed against the base of the cliff, and threw the white foam high over the receding billows.

"I was dizzy and distracted; and, frantically at the moment, I called her, and held out my arms. I knew not how it was; but I fell from the summit of the rocks, and felt myself falling in the air; then it was that I called out in my agony.

"It was thus I awoke you, I suppose, Jessie," remarked the captain, when he had finished his narration.

"It was a terrible dream," said Jessie, "and I am not at all surprised at your being alarmed at anything so horrible. It must have been a fearful feeling."

"It was, Jessie—it was," said Arnold,

with a shudder. "I hope I may never have such another."

"I hope not, indeed," said Jessie; "but had you not better try to sleep again, father? You will be better by to-morrow morning."

"Ay—to-morrow morning," repeated Arnold, mechanically.

"What of to-morrow morning, my dear father?" said Jessie.

Arnold was silent; he endeavoured to think, but could not, his faculties were too confused.

"What is there in to-morrow that should render you so sad, father?" inquired Jessie, tenderly.

"Arlines!" ejaculated Arnold.

"Phillip Arlines—that bad man, who is the object of my abhorrence?"

"Yes, Phillip Arlines."

"What of him, father?—what should he have to do with you to-morrow, more than any one else?" inquired Jessie.

"Nothing, Jessie—nothing; but—but——"

"But what, father? Tell me. I dread to hear something has happened that will be a misfortune to us all."

"Oh, no—no! he is coming here to dinner with me; that is all, Jessie—that is all," said Arnold, hastily.

"Phillip Arlines coming here to dinner?" said Jessie, with an air of astonishment she could not disguise.

"Yes, Jessie; and why not—why not? I want company. I am quite lost without it, my child."

"Lost, indeed, father, with such men as this Phillip Arlines; but do you not forget you turned him out of the house?"

"No, no; I recollect it all, Jessie. I recollect it all," said Arnold; "but he will be here to-morrow to dinner — he told me so himself."

"He told you so, father?—then if he did, I declare I will myself complain to the nearest police magistrate, and denounce him——"

"Do not act rashly, Jessie; do not do anything of the kind."

"But, father, his conduct has been so bad, so wicked, and so insulting, that I cannot sit in the room with him, and it would be almost compelling me to think that you gave him permission to annoy me."

"Jessie, Jessie! you cannot mean to speak to your father thus;—you cannot do it," said Arnold, reproachfully.

"Father," said Jessie, "if that man comes here, I will denounce him, and he shall go to prison. If he stays, I will not—cannot stay."

"If you denounce him, Jessie, you denounce me also; for, believe me, he has the power and the means of placing me in a gaol. Cease, therefore, these reproaches. I am in his power,"

"Say not so, dear father; say not so!"

"I am, Jessie. Since you force the truth from me, I am, and cannot help myself. Go to your own room now, and leave me."

Jessie rose obedient to her father's commands, and slowly quitted the room, in a very desponding and dejected state of mind, while Arnold slunk between the clothes as if he feared some apparition.

CHAPTER XLIV.

THE DINNER.—ARLINES AND JESSIE.—THE PROPOSAL.

THE next day was one of some pain and anxiety to Captain Arnold; it was late before he rose, and took his breakfast by himself, and then quitted the house early, to escape any further interview, or any renewed solicitation from his daughter Jessie.

Jessie herself was but very poorly that morning, but yet she dragged herself down to the breakfast-table, in the hope of seeing her father, but was disappointed as he came not out.

Still she thought she should see him before he quitted the house; but there she was in error.

"Well," thought Jessie, "he has given no orders to any one about his dinner; I must do so, I suppose, else he will think I would not do it for his sake; but I will have it all ready."

Pursuant to this resolution, Jessie gave the necessary directions, though but very unwell in consequence of the fright that her father had occasioned her in consequence of the communication he had made to her relative to this Phillip Arlines; and the dream he related brought back to her mind her mother so strongly, that her spirits sunk, and she could scarce keep up.

Arnold walked about, and sought at one place and another amusement, to pass the time away until dinner-time should arrive.

In this he very well succeeded, though the day did not pass away without an occasional pang; he felt more than one alarm. As the time drew on, he more than once regretted the promise of Arlines that he would come to dine with him.

The time approached, and Arnold quitted the house he was in, and walked towards his own home, and quickened his pace, as the thought crossed his mind that Arlines might be there before him, and he dreaded the effect an interview might produce upon either of them.

Fortunately, however, he arrived at his door just as Phillip Arlines had arrived, and they both entered the house together.

"You see I am punctual, and have religiously kept my word," said Arlines as they entered the door.

"Yes, I thought you would," replied Arnold, devoutly wishing he had not done so much.

"Why, it is no more than we ought to do, besides keeping dinner waiting; and a cold dinner is an abomination."

"We shall not, however, have to call upon you to endure such to-day," said Captain Arnold, as he entered the drawing-room in which Jessie was seated.

"Ah!" said Arlines, "here is your lovely daughter. How do you feel to-day, Jessie? I am sure you appear quite charming, at least."

Jessie made no reply to this, but merely inclined her head towards Arlines, and appeared to wait until her father spoke.

"Jessie," he said, looking round him with a gaze that betrayed anything but confidence upon the table, "are we much too early to dinner?"

"It will be on table within a few minutes," she replied; and at the same time she rang the bell, and the page made his appearance very suddenly.

"Let dinner be brought up," said Jessie to the boy.

"Yes, miss. Any for that ere one yonder —the ill-looking one?"

It was lucky the door was immediately closed, else he had received the weight of Captain Arnold's walking-cane upon his person, but he escaped.

The little conversation that passed, chiefly emanated from Phillip Arlines, who talked of many indifferent topics, and directed much of it to Jessie; but she replied to very little of it, and then but very shortly.

The dinner, however, put an end to all this, and it was soon after that brought up. Captain Arnold felt gratified to find that Jessie had not neglected to put on as good a one as he could have desired to meet with; for, since Arlines was to come, he was desirous that there should be as good a one as could be obtained. It was a matter of pride with him to have a good table when he could at all obtain it.

"Your dinner does you credit, Arnold," said Arlines.

"It is due to Jessie; for I did not order any, but left it all to her discretion and management."

"Then Jessie will be a valuable acquisition to any one," replied Arlines, banteringly. "Suppose I were so blest, then dinners would become an object, were it but for affording the means of displaying taste."

"Your compliments are absurd and unnecessary, Mr. Arlines," said Jessie, coldly.

"Not undeserved, dear Jessie," he said, "but unappreciated by her for whom they are designed."

"I will not be insulted in this manner," replied Jessie.

"Arlines," said Arnold, "I must beg you will discontinue this conversation, or——"

"Or what, Arnold?" inquired Arlines, angrily. "You do not mean to say that I shall not address Jessie? because I will, and you know my power."

"I will of myself put an end to this," said Jessie, rising, and quitting the room on the instant.

When Jessie quitted the room, both Arlines and Arnold were silent for a few moments, when the former said,

"Arnold, do not imagine that I will be prevented from speaking to your daughter because she chooses to be in her airs, and persuade you to attempt the same, because I will do so."

"I can't help her quitting the room, Arlines," said Arnold, "if she do not like your conversation."

"My mode of conversation is as well adapted to her ears as it is to anybody that I may meet with, and I will not put up with this kind of treatment."

"What would you have?" inquired Arnold, much annoyed and bewildered. "I cannot control the temper of a child, at least I cannot cause her to endure your conversation, which, to say the least of it, was ill-adapted to the occasion."

"Indeed!" sneered Arlines; "ill-adapted to the occasion! Well, that may be a matter of opinion."

"It is."

"Exactly, but it is not my opinion, and that is of most consequence, as you are aware of," said Arlines.

"Be that as it may," said Arnold; "you promised to speak to me about some affair you had in hand at the moment."

"Ah! I recollect. Yes, it was respecting the forged notes."

Arnold started.

"Yes, some of these in which you paid your loss at St. James's-street."

"Yes," replied Arnold; "you spoke of my assisting you, though I cannot see that I am able to do so, for I cannot conceive how it is done."

"The manufacture of these things is not so difficult as you may imagine, but one man cannot do all; there's the pinch—whom can you trust?"

"Exactly," said Arnold. "Who indeed?"

"I, therefore, wish for your assistance in this branch, for to do them we must go through all the process of engraving, printing, and otherwise preparing them for use; and then there's the passing of them to be considered."

"Exactly," said Arnold, with a shudder, that evinced his fear of meddling with them.

"Now I want your assistance in all these perations."

"I cannot help you that I can see," said Arnold.

"Tut, man; did I not see, I would not ask you; but I know how serviceable you may be, you would scarce credit it; but secrecy and dependance are the greatest wants we have, and also one of the greatest qualifications of an assistant."

"But I dare not meddle with them, Arlines," said Arnold; "I dare not, indeed."

"Why, how nervous you are, Arnold," said Arlines, filling his glass; "one would almost imagine that this was the last dinner you would ever eat, and that you knew that that was the fact."

"I am not nervous," replied Arnold, a little excited; "but I am exceedingly afraid of meddling with anything that has to do with the forging of notes."

"You think they smell strong of strangulation, and produce a choking sensation, eh?" said Arlines, laughing.

Arnold made no reply, but gulped down the gibe and his wine together, and Arlines resumed.

"There can be no danger—none, at least, in which I do not share; and you may be sure that I make that as innoxious as possible. I have had no assistance as yet, because I would not expose myself to yet greater danger than I run. With you, however, the face of the affair is changed, for your interest is mine, and mine yours; besides, there is a yet greater degree of security for me, and that is you dare not betray me."

"And what should I have to guarantee me against such a contingency from you?" remarked Arnold.

Arlines laughed, and replied,—

"This, Arnold, and only this—that you may be a most useful instrument to me; therefore, it is, I would perserve you against all risk and unecessary danger; for, if you fell, I should be deprived of one who could always double my chances of success, and the amount of my profit; and, moreover, if I were caged, you could aid me with means, as I would you."

"And yet," said Arnold, "I cannot, I dare not meddle with them; the danger is so great, and the punishment, death, so fearfully heavy, that I shrink from doing that which would leave my children fatherless."

"I would be a protector to them," replied Arlines, "if such be needed, but I am persuaded it will not."

Arnold shuddered at the idea of Arlines becoming the protector of Jessie—she would die of want first.

"At all events," said Arlines, "you can begin with assisting me to pass them; you'll find that all fear will vanish as you become acquainted with their use—time and acquaintance will do much in that respect."

" And how do you propose to pass them ?" inquired Arnold.

" Upon every available opportunity," replied Arlines ; " but especially in paying losses at gambling."

" At the club ?"

" Yes ; a better plan could not be, for constantly paying debts promptly will beget the habit of playing with the highest players, and they must lose occasionally, and we shall be great gainers. The notes will pass unsuspected by them ; and when found out, will be entirely lost sight of."

" That," said Arnold, faintly, " may not be so dangerous or unlikely a place."

" I think so, too ; here are a thousand," he said, tossing them over to Arnold, " and now I vote we move towards St. James's-street and try what can be done."

He arose, and Arnold mechanically did the same, and both quitted the house.

CHAPTER XLV.

JESSIE'S SAD REFLECTIONS.—THE UNXPECTED MEETING.—A FEW HAPPY MOMENTS

JESSIE quitted the apartment in which her father and Arlines were seated at their dinner, and retired to her own room to mourn in secret on the unfortunate state in which she and her father should be placed.

She could not avoid thinking that Arlines would render her life more miserable and wretched than it really was; and yet that was needless—for, independent of all fear for herself, she had the strongest and most distressing apprehensions on her father's account.

It was not his future relapse into poverty that she so much dreaded, though she felt convinced that that must eventually come about, feeling assured that his present and temporary prosperity was founded on some accident, to name which she dreaded. She believed it to be connected with some gambling transactions, or worse, but, nevertheless, it must be subject to all the vicissitudes of a gambler's life ; but it was his own personal safety that she so much dreaded.

Surely the offended laws would one day have its victim. She felt assured that justice could not be constantly defied with impunity ; far from it : he would be hurried onwards by that vile being, Arlines, who, no doubt, exerted all his acquired power over him; first, for his own vile purposes, and then to urge him onwards to ruin and destruction.

How long that man would be allowed to triumph over the offended laws she knew not, nor how long he could exert his influence over her father ; but she dreaded to think it might continue until his ruin had been completed ;

then, indeed, Arlines might lose his influence. But would such a man as this stop even there ? No! he would pursue the child when the parent was no more. She would be the object of his mixed feelings, desire and revenge. Who, then, would stand between her and the direst persecution that could be endured by a helpless female ? Not her father; if he were a victim of Arlines, he would be no protector to her, and Arlines would even be deprived of the only motive that now appeared to prevent him from exerting his power and insulting her yet more cruelly; that motive was the belief that he could make the father useful to him—but that motive gone, she would have not even the shadow of protection.

Yes, there was one who would do his utmost for her, but yet she dared not name him. He was ever present to her mind, though his name never escaped her lips—and that was Alfred Pearson.

Strange to say, she had not seen him since the last time we recorded. Daily her anxiety grew greater, and yet she had no means of allaying it. Her fears for his safety were increasing, and yet hope found a place within her breast.

The thought that Pearson yet lived, was in itself a means of soothing her excited mind.

" Should he yet live, he will not desert me; but alas ! he knows not where I live, and I fear to attempt to seek him. I fear that I may bear more than I would wish."

At this moment she heard the door open gently. She looked up, and gave a faint scream, and then tremblingly rose.

It was Alfred Pearson, the object of her thoughts, and also of her fears and anxieties. He entered the room, and closing the door after him, advanced to Jessie, saying—

" Dear Jessie, pardon my intrusion ; but I saw no one in the way, and I sought you myself."

Jessie could not reply; he had clasped her round the waist, and she could not withdraw herself from his embrace, but sunk her head upon his breast.

" Dearest Jessie," he continued, " did you not think that I had quite deserted you ?"

" No, Alfred, I could not think that. I never thought of it even. I feared that something had happened too dreadful to name," she replied, with a shudder.

" That I was dead ? Why, Jessie, I have not escaped any great way from it. I have, indeed, been very ill—very ill, indeed, and that was the reason I could not attempt to find you out before."

" How did you do that ?" inquired Jessie. " I feared it would have been impossible for you to do so."

" It was purely accidental," replied Alfred. " I was passing, and saw your father and

THE COWARDLY ATTACK UPON PEARSON IN THE PARK.

Phillip Arlines go out of this house, and leave the door open, as if the servants had neglected them."

"Indeed!" said Jessie.

"Yes," replied Alfred; "I saw them go, and believing that you would be alone, I stole up to you. I need hardly say the pleasure I feel in once again seeing you."

"Nor I, Alfred," said Jessie; "but you have been very ill, indeed."

"I have, and appear somewhat different to what I was when I last saw you."

He smiled, but so sickly, that Jessie's heart heaved while she gazed upon him.

His appearance denoted great weakness; he was exceedingly thin, and very pale. His whole person appeared to have shrunk, while his features altogether appeared sharp and emaciated. It was to her a heart-rending sight to see the change that had been caused in one so young and vigorous as Alfred Pearson.

Jessie could not hide her tears; she could not look upon him without weeping; he drew her to him, and pressed her to his bosom, and said——

"Why do you weep, Jessie? Do not do so, it gives me great pain to see you thus."

" 'Tis to see the great change that has taken place in you, and that, no doubt, through your kindness to us, and detestation of our oppressor."

" Name it not, dear Jessie, for, while I have your tender sympathy and love, depend upon it it shall be the means of causing me to set a proper value on life. Love, Jessie, is the great balm for all wounds. Have I yours?"

Jessie's heart was too full; but she gave her hand into Alfred's, and sunk upon his breast, while he pressed her lips to his own.

Many kind words passed between them, and then the full tale of love. Vows were exchanged, and they swore to be true to each other while life remained.

Some time was passed thus, and much of past misfortune was forgotten in the calm happiness of the moment.

" Have you found out who it was that made that abominable attempt to assassinate you?"

" I have every reason to believe that it was Phillip Arlines ; and I should have been killed outright, but for assistance coming so opportunely."

" Indeed! And why did you not punish him? He richly deserved it."

" Yes, Jessie ; but, to tell you the truth, I feared to do so," replied Pearson.

" Feared to do so?"

" Yes, I feared that it would come out on his trial your father's name would be found to be connected with it, and hence my reason for letting the matter drop."

" And do you really think my father would consent to such an act of wickedness?" said Jessie.

" I do not think that he would do so willingly; but there is no knowing how far he may be involved in that man's schemes and crimes, and how far he might make it appear that your father might be mixed up in this affair. He, of course, would make it appear so for his own sake, and shield himself by the idea that I would not hurt your father."

" And you have dropped all thoughts of doing anything about it?"

" Yes," replied Alfred ; " I have given it up, and shall merely watch him until I find he has laid himself open to punishment for some past act."

" Do watch him, Alfred, and endeavour to prevent him from entangling my father; but I fear that he has already succeeded in doing so."

" I will, for your sake, Jessie," replied Alfred, " do all that I can to prevent his being too intimately connected with Arlines; but you know, Jessie, if the one has power over the other, he will exert it, and my persuasions will have no avail ; but if it should be in my power to thwart that man's schemes, or cross his purposes, I will."

Much more was said, and Jessie felt happier in the presence of her lover; but the time flew rapidly, and the moment for parting arrived, and Alfred Pearson bade her farewell for the time, telling her he would soon see her again, and then quitted the house.

CHAPTER XLVI.

THE GAMING-HOUSE.—ITS VISITORS.—ARNOLD'S SUCCESS.

ARNOLD and Arlines, when they quitted the house, walked to St. James's-street, where they proposed to spend the evening, or, at least, some hours.

" The notes you have, Arnold," said Arlines, " are excellently made, and will bear almost any test that may be made ; but they will be unsuspected, and you will gain all that you win."

" And receive a fair share of the winnings?" interrogated Arnold.

" Exactly," said Arlines, " that is not a bad thought though, and if we succeed, we shall amass a fortune in a short time ; but you must recollect never to pay your debts——"

" Not pay my debts— debts of honour you mean?"

" Yes."

" But how long should I be allowed to contract any?" said Arnold in some amazement.

" You misunderstand me," said Arlines, " or rather you spoke too soon, and did not leave me time to finish my sentence. I meant, you must not pay your debts of honour in the same coin you receive, else you may be either detected, or, if not, you have only your own useless notes still in your pocket, and notwithstanding all you may have won, you are still empty-handed."

" I see," said Arnold ; " it would not have occurred to me at first thought."

" I guessed as much, and hence I name it to you; but I think that you will find that if you were to assist me in the home department, you would do much better—act with more confidence and success."

" No," said Arnold, " I am sure I should fail; something would happen that would cause an entire failure of the whole affair."

" Absurd," said Arlines, " what on earth could? nothing, save your own sinking spirits, I am sure."

" And they would do more, Arlines, much more ; I should be completely disqualified from making the attempt, for I should not possess the necessary assurance and calmness of mind to carry me through it with anything like certainty."

" Well—well," said Arlines, " all in good time ; we will begin at the beginning: it will not do for us both to play, for, if we were to play together, we should not gain anything by it."

"Exactly," said Arnold, "and now that we are just arrived, what amount do you think will be the best to play for?"

"Any sum that is offered—take any bet, and cover the sum; be careful, but do not appear so, and fear nothing—should anything happen, I shall be at hand to back you."

So saying, Captain Arnold and Phillip Arlines entered the door of the gaming-house, after having given the usual signals to the porters, who, however, scarcely heeded them, so used were they to their forms and features.

The evening was yet early, and but few persons were present. Conversation and wine appeared to be the only kind of amusement that was yet resorted to by the denizens of this den of iniquity.

It was brilliantly lighted up, though it was scarcely dark; but such places are lit up all day, and artificial defies natural light.

The beauty and splendour of the furniture and appointments were such, that they threw over the whole an air of elegance and comfort scarce met with in the highest circles.

There were several individuals who were seated together and drinking wine, and Captain Arnold and Arlines sat down at a short distance, and immediately ordered wine for themselves, which being brought them, they proceeded to converse about different topics, until several others entered the gaming-room.

"Do you see that young man?" said Arlines, "with the peculiar sapient look of one who cannot imagine anything more manly or beautiful than himself?"

"Yes; with white teeth and an eyeglass, and with the air of an emperor?"

"Yes, he is the son of a lord, and he has much money. He is a great fool, but his folly is almost an impenetrable shield against all the attempts made to entrap him."

"How can that be, Arlines?" inquired Arnold; "because, as far as I can see, it must usually be people's folly that brings them to ruin."

"In general, I admit it; but the case is sometimes the reverse, as, for instance, the individual before you."

"And who is he?" inquired Arnold.

"The Honourable Mr. William Scapel, the son of Lord Scapel, a very rich young man, for he has much money left him by an aunt, over which the father has no control."

"Has he, indeed?"

"Yes; now, that young man is so capricious, captious and conceited, that you do not know what to do with him; unlike any one else, you cannot make sure of which is his tender point; he has many, but he shifts so often, and is so self-willed and so ignorant, and, of course, obstinate, that you cannot depend upon him for many minutes together."

"He is a singular young man, and as dis-agreeable a companion as could well be imagined."

"And for all that he is endured because he has money; but I think he can be had for all that. You will hear him offer some extravagant bet; accept it, and then let him win it: it matters little, win or lose, for it will be a good sum. If you win it, why, it is so much money made, if not, you have another chance, for you may claim your revenge."

"I see he is a most consummate fool to look at, certainly, and, in consequence of that, a disagreeable companion by anticipation," said Arnold.

"Exactly; but that can be of but little consequence," said Arlines, "provided we have the circulating medium from him."

"Who is that big man with the enormous quantity of black whiskers and ornaments about his person?"

"I don't know," replied Arlines; "but I will go and see: he was here the other night, and won some money. I expect, however, he is but one of ourselves, upon the look-out; but if he be so, we shall be one too many for him."

With this Arlines rose, and went and spoke to some of the persons engaged in the house, and after some short conversation, he returned to Arnold, saying—

"I was mistaken: he is a Russian count, who has the reputation of a rich man, though, from his vulgar appearance, I should have thought him some low-bred imitation of a gentleman."

"He would probably be the man to detect these——"

"Hush! do not utter a word. 'Let it not be spoken in Gath.' You know not who may be listening—be cautious. I always am. You need be under no apprehension at all—follow my advice implicitly, and all will be well. It will not be long ere you will have an opportunity of trying the scheme, for there are several who are impatient to begin, though none like to begin first—there, as I live, the fool is the first to open the dance with his folly."

As Arlines spoke, he pointed to the Honourable Mr. Schapel, who walked to the table and called a game.

Play now commenced in various parts of the room, and the various lights suddenly threw a glare all over the place, and the play beginning caused the scene to change so entirely, that it looked like the effect of magic.

A new spirit came over Arnold, who himself felt the full force of the enchantment, and rose from his seat, and in company with Arlines walked round the room.

After a time Arnold himself began to play, with various success for some time, and Arlines watching the game at a distance. At large he began to win, and continued to do so for some time, until at length he lost.

Arlines perceived this, and, hastening up to him, said—

"Arnold, leave off when you can, and come out with me."

This injunction Arnold obeyed, and after one more game he rose from the table, saying, that he hoped to see his adversary there on another occasion.

He then quitted the house and joined Arnold in the street.

"You have won about five hundred pounds, Arnold?" said Arlines, coolly.

"Yes, about that sum I believe," said Arnold; "but you must have kept a good account of debtor and creditor while I was at play, however."

"I did so. I am used to it, you see, and therefore am usually correct; but come, I want my share."

"How much do you call your share?" said Arnold, sharply.

"Three hundred out of five, at least, considering, especially, I gave you the means."

"You are moderate in your estimation of your own merits; but here is the money," said Arnold, handing it over.

"It is useless to quarrel about the amount of my share; it is but just. However, I must now go elsewhere, and shall bid you good evening."

CHAPTER XLVII.

ARNOLD'S RETURN HOME.—THE INTER-
VIEW WITH PEARSON.—A FRACAS.

CAPTAIN ARNOLD did not go home direct that evening; he had been too lucky, and thought he would stay out until he was sure he should not encounter the pale face and tearful eye of Jessie, which to him was one of the severest reproaches that could be directed against him.

He thought to dissipate his time, and scarce knew how to do so, until he thought of the threatre, and he at once entered the nearest one he came to.

Here he spent some hours watching the scenic representation until wearied, and then he sought the saloon. It was late that night ere he escaped from that scene of fascination and enchantment, and when he did, he was scarce in the condition he should be, for wine had made some havoc with his senses.

Homeward he went, and not being in a state fit for pedestrian exercise, he was some time in making his way to his room door. He went immediately to the drawing-room, with the intention of first helping himself to some more wine, for his recent exertions had rendered him

dry; and he became conscious that he required some rest before he sought his bed, lest he might in the confusion make a mistake and enter the wrong room.

When he opened the drawing-room door, however, which he did with some trouble, a sight met his view that at first somewhat astonished and bewildered him.

There were the lights burning on the table, and the young gentleman who had condescended to act the page was seated in the arm-chair, with his legs hanging over the sides, and resting upon the table. A book had fallen from his hand, and he was fast asleep.

Anger at the first moment seized upon Arnold's mind, and he grasped his cane, with the intention of inflicting personal chastisement on the unconscious sleeper, for this and other grave offences.

Fortunately, however, for Master Bob, or, when he would be propitiated, Master Robert, Captain Arnold's condition prevented him from taking a very steady aim, else he would have been most unceremoniously awakened.

As it was, he received a hearty blow across the shoulder, intended for his head. It was with a start of surprise that the youthful Bob jumped up and scrambled out of the chair; and when he had placed the table between him and the captain, he said—

"Oh, that's the way you does it, is it? Very well—very well. I shall know you for the future."

"You young scoundrel," muttered the captain, between his teeth, "I'll break every bone in your skin."

"Will you, though? I'll take precious good care I has yer dited at the pleiss hoffice, if yer tries that game."

Arnold sunk into the arm-chair, and held his cane threateningly at the page, who looked at it with an eye that betrayed mischievous intentions.

"Well, I am blowed if this ain't a pretty return for my kindness. Gratitude, eh? Yes, I thinks I sees it. Gratitude in human beans, eh? Yes, with a hook to it, or a stick,—cuss the stick."

"What do you mean by talking in this strain, you confounded abortion?" said the captain, stooping down to pick up the book that had fallen from Bob's hands, with the intention of throwing it at his head.

"Oh, this is what I calls gratitude! Here have I been sitting up on purpose to let you in, and destroying my own health—here's a pretty return. Why, what do you think of yourself, you old buffer,—eh?"

While young Robert was thus apostrophizing his master, Arnold looked at the title of the book, and, after some attempts, he contrived to read it. It was an old copy of the New-gate Calendar, and contained an account of the trial and execution of a forger and utterer of forged notes.

The book fell from his hands, and, rising, he seized a candle, and staggered into his own apartment.

"Well, well," said Bob, looking after him, "there's something in all this. What made him go away in that sort of fashion, I should like to know? The book—oh, it must have been the book! Well, he may have a tender conscience, arter all, and not like to hear of people being translated by means of a halter. I wonder what he would have done, had he read the whole? I'm sure I don't know. Well, well, I won't be too hard upon his indiscretions, only I hope he won't turn wicious."

Saying this, he took the book in his hand, put out the candles, and crawled to the door, and then retired to his dormitory.

* * * *

The next morning early, Arnold awoke, and thinking the cool morning air would refresh his fevered body, he determined to arise and seek the open air.

Dressing himself, therefore, he soon quitted the house, and did not return to it till towards the evening.

In the meantime Jessie, much distressed at her father's growing absence from his home, scarcely knew how it was; but he quitted the house early or late. It was a matter of constant regret and apprehension to her. She, however, could not help it; on the contrary, she endeavoured to prevent it.

The day was nearly past when a low and gentle tap was heard outside of the door. Opening it to see who it could be, she started back with a look of surprise and pleasure to see Alfred Pearson enter the room.

"Jessie, dear Jessie," said Pearson, clasping her in his arms, " I could not resist the temptation of coming in to see you."

"Ah! Alfred," she replied, "you have at least given me some cause for joy, while all else would make me melancholy and sad."

"Never fear the world, dear Jessie," said Pearson—" at least, that part of it that would make you unhappy; for believe me, it must be bad to do so, for who would endeavour to make the good and innocent miserable ?"

"But I am more unhappy on my poor father's account than on my own," said Jessie, sadly.

"Your father, Jessie?" said Alfred; " has anything new occurred since I was here ?"

"Nothing, save he was out late last night, and quitted his home early this morning. I cannot tell what to think of it; he seldom now stays at home, but seeks to pass his time at taverns and at gaming-tables, I am convinced of it."

"That will probably end in utter ruin, sooner or later; for no man ever yet had a continued run of luck at the gaming-table with fair play."

"Alas!" said Jessie, " I would not mind ruin so much as I would the loss of honour. I fear, Alfred, the worst from the connexion with that bad man, Arlines."

" His object is to draw your father into some scheme which he will make answer two ways; first profitably, and then use it as a means of forcing your father to do other things that may yet involve him more and more in ruin and destruction."

" What mean you, Alfred ?" said Jessie, in some alarm.

" That he will induce your father to commit some act for which he could make him amenable to some disgraceful punishment, and by holding out a threat of doing so cause him yet to sink deeper into iniquity."

A slight noise behind him attracted the attention of Alfred Pearson, and turning round, he beheld the angry and flushed countenance of Captain Arnold within a few feet of him.

Behind him, but unnoticed at first, stood the dark form of Phillip Arlines, with the habitual and satanic sneer upon his features, that gave them such a forbidding expression, a little altered, perhaps, by the feeling of hatred which he felt in all its intensity, and which was evident.

Alfred Pearson's surprise was for a moment so great that he spoke not, but stood rivetted to the spot. Jessie did not see her father or Arlines, neither did she hear the noise that attracted his attention, but surprised by his silence and attitude, she looked up into his face, and seeing him gaze so intently upon something, she also turned her head to see what it was, but what a sight met her eyes.

She started and screamed, and would have flown to her father, but she staggered across the room, and would have fallen but for the aid of Pearson, who immediately stepped forward and caught her in his arms.

"Do not be alarmed, Jessie," he said to her as he held her; " there can be no harm that will happen to you or anyone else, except any ill treatment or insult is offered you."

By this time the trance that appeared to have thrown a spell over the whole party broke, and Phillip Arlines, advancing a few paces, said, turning to Captain Arnold,—

"So, Arnold, you have an old friend: I was not aware you had any visitors when I walked out with you."

"I have none, Arlines—I have none," said the captain, in an excited tone.

"Then how can you account for that individual being in possession of your apartment and your daughter ?"

" He is unasked and unwelcome; this shall

be ended very speedily," said Arnold, who immediately stepped forward and took Jessie out of the arms of her lover.

Alfred Pearson stood calmly gazing on Captain Arnold and his daughter, while Phillip Arlines stood a mere spectator of what was going on.

CHAPTER XLVIII.

THE ALTERCATION.—OPEN DECLARATION OF ALFRED PEARSON.—THE AVOWAL.

"I ASK you, sir," said Captain Arnold, turning fiercely to Alfred Pearson, "by whose invitation you intrude yourself into my presence?"

"Captain Arnold," replied Alfred Pearson, calmly, "I have that to say which I wish to say to you in private."

"In private?" repeated Arlines, with a sneer; "has he not had privacy enough? he may have been here no one can tell how long or how often."

"You are beneath my contempt," said Alfred Pearson, in the same calm voice, "and a villain of the deepest dye."

"Cease to be insolent, else my cane and your shoulders may become acquainted, and I should not desire to have recourse to such a measure in your present state; but be assured I will, and that that consideration shall not save you, if you cease to be discreet."

"If I had not been in this state of weakness, you had not dared to say as much, as you know, from former experience, what kind of treatment you would have had at my hands."

Arlines' brows contracted, and it was with a flush of anger he turned to complain to Arnold, saying—

"I did not expect to be insulted under your roof, Arnold, and that, too, by an half resuscitated man only."

"Nor shall you be," replied Arnold. "Mr. Pearson, I insist upon your quitting my apartments, and never entering them again."

"Captain Arnold," again said Pearson, "I wish to speak with you in private."

"I decline having any communication with you in private or otherwise—you now know my mind."

"Then I must say what I have to say to you now, and before that bad man,"

"You will not stay, sir, to say anything, for I will have you removed instantly; and I will hear nothing that is at all disrespectful of any friend of mine; cease, therefore, to annoy and irritate me."

"You must know your own danger in trusting to Phillip Arlines; you must know the hollow-hearted villany of such a man, and how far you can trust to him without endangering you own safety. I say, Captain Arnold, you know the villany of that man; beware of him, beware of him."

"I will not hear any more of this," said Arnold, placing Jessie on a chair, and walking towards Alfred Pearson. "You must quit the room, sir; I shall be sorry to lay hands upon you, but you must quit the place."

"Father, father," said Jessie, starting up, and going between them, "do not harm him! his errand was one of good to you, and I could but wish you had listened to him instead of to that inhuman and treacherous man who will lead you to destruction."

"I will have no more of this; you are no friend of mine, sir, and had no invitation to come or to stop—indeed, most unwelcome."

"His advice, Arnold, would be more welcome to your daughter when you are not present," said Arlines, with a sneer.

"You can mean no good; honour was never yet intended to be the effect of such kind of proceedings," said Arnold.

"Can you say anything about that, Captain Arnold? Let your own heart speak, before you condemn another man; but my motives are honourable—most honourable."

"Ay, ay, whose are not?" said Arlines; "you do not cry stale fish, young gentleman."

"And I am willing to prove that they are so on the spot," said Pearson.

"Come, come," replied Arnold, angrily; "if I distrust your motives, I am not compelled to hear your justification or your explanation of them. Quit the room, sir."

"One moment before I go. Let me say this, Captain Arnold—I love your daughter—yes, honestly and fairly, I love her, and would make her my wife."

"I dare say you would," sneered Arlines; "and, as to keeping her, why that's quite another question."

"I can do that Arlines, and do it honestly; and that is what you never yet did in any relation of life."

"Liar!" said Arlines, hastily.

"It is easier to use hard words than to prove what you know to be untrue; but enough with you, it is Captain Arnold I have to do with. Do you hear and understand my offer, sir? I mean what I say, and have ample means of providing for her in ease and comfort."

"I hear no offer, and accept of no offer; quit the place this instant."

"If I had been Captain Arnold," said Phillip Arlines, with some asperity, "I would scarce have heard so much from a man who chose to attempt to beard me in my own house, much less should deem myself obliged to put up with his presence after I had repeatedly ordered him out."

"You, sir, have no right to dictate to my father what he should or should not permit;

your interference can only be accounted for on the same ground that other impertinences of the same character have been allowed to pass."

Arlines lifted his hat, and bowed with a smile, and said—

"It would be useless to argue with so good a casuist as Miss Arnold, but she will allow for the difference between an old friend and an unwelcome intruder."

"Such as you are, sir," retorted Jessie.

"Let this cease," said Arnold; "I decline any interference from Mr. Pearson, and I can readily guess the mode he has made use of to obtain my daughter's temporary good opinion, if, indeed, he has that; but he must not expect more. Sir, there is the door, let that suffice."

"No—no," said Jessie, suddenly, and with energy; "stay, father, hear me at once declare that Mr. Pearson has my love—the fullest and most entire confidence that woman can bestow on man have I in him, and no other man shall ever obtain love or esteem from me."

Phillip Arlines started at this full and unequivocal declaration. Captain Arnold himself was staggered: he had never seen so much energy and determination expressed by Jessie before, and he was for the moment perfectly bewildered, until Arlines said—

"Well, baffled by child, and defied by lover —all this would make a tableau for the stage. Weakness and indecision ought now to come and finish the scene."

"You shameless girl," said Arnold, seeking refuge in a passion, as he could not well argue the matter coolly, for it was all against him, the proposition being too reasonable and too generous an offer to be so refused—"can you do no less than avow such a declaration to my very face, before others, as if the knowledge of your disgrace would not be known to enough if only known to me?"

"It is no disgrace to avow an honest devotion to those we love, and to one who would and could shield and protect me from premeditated and deliberate insult."

"It is disgraceful," repeated Arnold, "and shameless to a degree; I wonder you could not occupy your thoughts with something less degrading."

"It would not have been surprising if I had occupied my thoughts, father, with something worse, left as I am day and night, at all hours, when you are haunting the gaming-tables of the metropolis."·

"Ha—ha!" said Arlines; "'tis well to chide a father, and step between him and his amusements."

"His ruin, say, rather," said Pearson; "for you, villain, know it well, and that you make him a dupe to your own schemes and objects; but I will keep such a watch upon you that it will give you much trouble to evade the punishment such a man as you merit."

"Ha—ha—ha! you can handle an old woman's tale admirably; but let me advise you, gentle Master Pearson, to look at home, for you may not be so invulnerable as you imagine."

"If you mean that my assassination shall be again attempted, I can understand your candour, and tell you that I shall be prepared for you, or any one you may employ to act the ruffian."

"I know not what you mean, but I tell you to beware."

"Father," said Jessie, "is that man ever to triumph over your better nature, and always to induce you to abandon me to his mercies? for, if you listen to him, you do indeed do so."

"Cease, Jessie," said Arnold, angrily; "I will not listen to any proposal of this kind; so now Mr. Pearson has my answer, and has no longer any excuse for remaining where he is not welcome."

"Go, Alfred, go," said Jessie; "you can do no good now by staying, but remember that I will never cease to love and esteem you."

"Farewell, then, Jessie; I go; but beware of that arch scoundrel, Phillip Arlines; I will watch over your safety, and thwart his schemes."

"You had better watch over your own safety," said Arlines.

"That I will do, and doubt not but the next act of violence will bring its perpetrator to condign punishment. Farewell, Captain Arnold; it was not thus when I first met you; but no matter, you will live yet to regret your present conduct and companionship."

"Quit the house, or by heaven, I will thrust you out," said Captain Arnold, in a loud, angry tone.

Alfred Pearson made no reply, but quitted the house, and they heard the door shut after him.

Jessie waited motionless till she heard the door bang, and then with a look of reproach at her father, she quitted the apartment, and sought the privacy of her own little bed-room, where she relieved herself by a flood of tears.

CHAPTER XLIX.

ALFRED PEARSON'S DETERMINATION.— THE FRIENDS.—THE LETTER TO JESSIE.

ALFRED PEARSON quitted the abode of Arnold with mingled feelings of anger, pain, and pleasure. He had heard Jessie's avowal with her own lips, and that, too, before her own father and Phillip Arlines; this, indeed, was a matter of gratulation with him, but the occasion was one that caused him to grieve.

It was evident that Arnold was either in the power of Arlines, or else he was yet deceived by his speciousness. He believed the former, for Arnold must by this time have seen enough of Phillip Arlines to be perfectly aware of his character, of which there could not be any doubt.

Arnold had refused his offer with contempt and in anger; he would not repeat it. It had been refused, he believed, because Arlines had opposed it, and he, of course, had a selfish motive to serve in doing so. Then Jessie would, he thought, now be subject to that man's insults and solicitations.

The thought was madness — his Jessie, to sit and hear the fulsome flattery and offers of such a villain, who was leading her father on to destruction. Could he not prevent any of their plots from bringing ruin upon even a wilful man? He feared not. Watch them how he would, there was no help for it. Captain Arnold he looked upon as a doomed man.

" But," thought Alfred Pearson, " if I cannot save the father, I may save the child. I may remove her from the vicinity of such baneful society. And if Arnold must needs sink I think he would, and could not be sorry, to see his daughter saved from such destruction that he himself must fall beneath."

This thought gave a brighter complexion to the affair, and promised eventually to be not quite so melancholy as he had first believed it must be.

But how to obtain Jessie's consent? how could he communicate to her? how could he for a moment induce her to quit the home of her father? That was a question which he could not well answer.

He would first try, and then he would be better able to tell what kind of success he might have. To leave her father, he thought himself would be a very prudent and advisable step. She was surrounded by comforts, it was true; but how long would they last?

As long as the gaming-house luck would stick by him, and then she must relapse into poverty and misery. No, she should never do that at least, until he had made an attempt to lift her out of the influence of such scenes of wretchedness and woe. He would make the attempt to do so, if he failed.

At that moment the thought struck him that he could not do better than have some friend whom he could employ to assist him to carry out his scheme. Some one in whom he could place confidence, and from whom he could expect reasonable and cool advice, without their discouraging him in his purpose; for to make the attempt to induce Jessie to elope he would.

"And none can be better suited for such a purpose," he mentally exclaimed, " than that rattling, but generous hearted fellow, Edward Nairs; he lives close by, and I will go there at once, and tell him candidly how I am placed in this matter, and hear what he says to it."

Pearson, who was yet weak and debilitated, was not sorry at the thought that he should at least obtain a rest before he went further, for the excitement of the scene he had gone through was almost more than he could then bear.

He fortunately found Edward Nairs at home, and was soon shown up into a handsomely furnished apartment, where his friend was seated, enjoying his wine and the newspaper.

"Pearson," said Nairs, rising. " I am glad to see you. I thought you had been dead, as I have not seen you for so long a time."

"I have been nearly dead, Nairs, I assure you; but I sent for you, and found you were out of town."

"Ay, so I was, that's true enough; but what has been the matter with you? You appear as if you had been buried some time, and but recently resuscitated. How is this?"

"I have been very ill. I was nearly killed in the Park by a fellow who assaulted me, and escaped. I was left for dead."

"Do you know him?"

"Yes."

"And have caused him to smart for it, I suppose?"

" No," replied Pearson; " I could not swear to him, and have no proof; but yet I am sure, in my own mind, of the villain who did it. But that is not what I came about. I am about to require your assistance."

" You shall have it in anything from running away with an heiress to the shooting of a parson," replied Nairs, gaily. " I am quite indifferent which, and yet I think the latter the best."

" If I were to do that," replied Pearson, " I should destroy my chance with the former."

" Not a bit—not a bit; birds of feather—you know. Plenty to be had; but I would sooner you had nothing to do with the latter. You don't know what havoc these fellows cause in a young man's prospects in life."

" But consider, when a man's in love, Nairs."

" Consider the devil!" replied Nairs, hastily. " Did you ever hear of a man in love who ever did consider anything? He goes head over heels, and leaves no time or room for consideration. A man in love, my dear fellow, has no more to do with consideration than old Falstaff had with honour."

" You give me a lively notion as to what advice and assistance I am to receive at your hands, at all events; but I dare swear you have been jilted, and are now smarting in consequence."

" Pho! pho! you don't know anything about it. Why, you were but little better than myself some time ago; but no matter, let me advise you to return to your native simplicity, and don't dabble in the sophistications of love. I'd as soon be a donkey and chew thistles,"

"I am not to be alarmed by such a description," said Alfred, laughing, in spite of himself, at his friend's vivacity,

"In that case I shall not attempt to dissuade you, for a wilful man must have his own way, and as to advising any of the human family against their own inclinations, I might as well attempt to persuade pigs from eating potatoes."

"Having come to that frame of mind," said Pearson, "we shall get on well, for I wish for your advice and assistance in furthering my wishes, and I ask this the more confidently as you are well qualified to advise or direct either way."

"If that ain't a compliment it is an insult, and I don't know which; but, speak out, and let me know the nature of this affair."

Pearson then entered into a full detail of all that had transpired since the first time he saw Jessie, until the interview he had just had, describing the conduct of her father, and the nature of his connection with Phillip Arlines.

"Well," said Nairs, "after all you have said, I should advise you to run away with the girl."

"It is for your assistance and countenance that I am now here," replied Pearson; "I have made the proposal to myself, and scarce know how to set about it."

"Write her a letter, and state all you wish, and endeavour to persuade her to elope, or see her."

"I can't see her, for I have been forbidden the house by her father."

"You ought to deliver the letter yourself, and make sure it does not miscarry," said Nairs, "else you may find more difficulties than you expect."

"If I could deliver the letter to her I could speak to her."

"Time and opportunity are not always propitious; but is there no one about the lodgings whom you could trust, no servant who would do it for love or money?"

"There is a kind of page."

"That will do; if you give him a crown he'll be as dumb as a drum with a hole in it. Now set about your letter, and go early in the morning with it, and watch for an opportunity of seeing the page before Arnold or any one else are about; give him the letter and the crown, and tell him the hope he may have of doing more business that way."

"I think your advice good, Nairs, and I will take it."

"And the letter, too?"

"Yes, in the morning, as then I shall have less chance of stumbling over some of those whom I don't want to see."

Anxious to put his plan into execution, he bade Nairs good day and sought his lodgings, where he sat down and concocted a long and persuasive letter to Jessie, urging her to quit her father and elope with him; assuring her that it would be better for all parties, probably disentangling her father from the company of Arlines, or, at least, setting his mind at rest on her account.

This letter he carefully sealed and placed in his pocket, and anxiously waited till morning came, that he might have the opportunity of delivering it.

He merely threw himself on the bed, dressed as he was, and fell into a short, undisturbed slumber, so that when he awoke it was scarce day. He could not sleep, but rose up, and throwing a cloak around him, he sought the streets, early as it was.

The dead silence of the streets, and the chill of the night air, were at first oppressive to his senses, and his spirits sunk; he, however, determined to proceed, and wait in the vicinity of the house.

The quiet stillness of night soon gave place to the busy tramp of foot passengers, as the sun's first bright rays were reflected back from the countless thousands of windows in the streets of London. The earliest dawn presents to the eye of the stranger a singular and curious sight.

Many noiseless figures were hurrying to and fro, as if something of the utmost consequence directed their steps, and some great event awaited their presence to become completed. Most of them are half cold, hungry wretches, whose employments call them from their homes at the earliest hour, long before the luxurious are up, and sometimes before they have even retired to bed.

The eastern sky becomes a mass of many coloured clouds; the bright and glorious tints that illumine the heavens can only be seen from some high place, or the summit of some tall house, which gives a greater extent of horizon, and then you may see the flamy clouds tinted with a furnace-like glow, and many a bright golden edge becomes lighter and lighter, till the sun's perpendicular rays, as they increase in strength, lose their glowing tints.

The streets, in the meantime, become more and more animated; the working population are now fairly afoot, and they may be met with in every street, and at every quarter of the town; not a moment elapses before you hear the hurried tread of some artisan or shopman going to his place of employment.

The early hours are the most pleasant, for then you escape the smoke from the many thousands of fires that are lit for some miles round this one spot, and often there are ten or twelve in one house.

The air of London must be greatly vitiated by this enormous congregation of fires, and hence the early hours in London are, no doubt, the most wholesome.

The busy throng in the streets is much increased by those who attend the markets, and carts and waggons are passing from one end of London to another; some are laden with what is going to market, and others with what they had bought at, and brought from, the markets.

The day clears up, and the busy scene is now increased by a mass of human beings that appeared not before. People engaged in trade and commerce, and their dependants, now begin to fill the streets of London, and moving streams of people, apparently without beginning or without end; no stop or break exists anywhere, and the most secluded spot is not without its own peculiar population, and those who wait upon their wants in endless ramifications.

The scenes and sights incidental to a London sunrise are new, even to many of its inhabitants, and are even peculiar to the metropolis, furnishing ample food for thought. In time, however, these things which we are apt to notice when they stand singly, are no longer seen by themselves, but are merged and lost in the continual wiles of people and things, and become merely parts of a whole.

These things all fled from the mind of Alfred

Pearson, whose impatience was great in proportion to the length of time he had been waiting.

At length, the opportunity that he had been looking for arrived, and the young gentleman who did the page came to the door, apparently to inhale the fresh air, for the benefit of his health.

Pearson immediately stepped up to him, and said,—

"Does Miss Jessie Arnold live here ?"

"Yes, sir, she does," said the youth, laying great emphasis on the last word.

"Will you deliver this letter into her own hands, and when she is alone ?"

"Oh, a *billet-deux*, eh ?" said Master Bob, with a knowing wink. "I knows what's what, I does."

"And you know the shape of a half-crown when you see it ?"

"Yes, I does ; but thinks it a pity it should ever be cut : 'tis unnatural, and oughtn't to be allowed, 'cept when you pays tradespeople ; if, indeed, 'tis worth while paying them at all."

"Well, there's the whole, instead of a half. Will you do my errand, as I require ?"

"Trust me alone for that, sir. I'm up to summut, especially in the morning. I'm wide awake. She's a precious nice girl, at all ewents, and I enwies your luck I'm blest if I don't. All right ; we needn't stop here—you'll be seen. I'll take care of the answer."

Pearson quitted the place, and returned to his lodgings, leaving Master Bob in possession of the letter.

CHAPTER L.

THE REFLECTIONS OF MASTER ROBERT.—
JESSIE'S INDECISION.—HER RESOLUTION.

PEARSON passed some hours at his lodgings in anxious thought respecting the effect his letter might have with Jessie, and the probability there was of her consenting to his wishes. At times he thought she would, and then he pictured to himself the many hours of happiness he would yet experience in her company, and the increased probability of his succeeding in rescuing her father, Captain Arnold, from his unfortunate connexion with Phillip Arlines.

Hopes now were flashed upon him in all their radiant colours, but they were often, like the arch in the heavens, swept away by some sudden change in the course of thought, and then he would be reduced to the lowest depths of despair and dissappointment.

Alternations of this character were as rapid as they were frequent, and they produced as various effects upon his appearance, for his appearance at one moment exhibited the beaming smile of joy, and at another the deep shade of dejection, occasioned by some adverse thoughts that might for a moment cross his imagination.

Thus influenced by the circumstances that affect a vivid imagination, we must leave him while we return· the bearer of the letter, and the fortunate possessor of five shillings, whole and entire, to wit, Master Robert.

Master Robert was as cunning a youth as you would meet with between here and any spot the reader may think fit to mention ; indeed, I think it would be very unlikely he would ever find his like.

He quietly put the letter in his pocket, saying to himself as he did so,—

"I tells yer what it is, Bobby—you're father's favourite—and 'll win the Derby this year, and if yer minds yer p's and q's you'll marry a duchess. I don't know," he added, after a pause, "whether I won't spoil this affair, and keep the young female for myself. Of course she'd be willing, especially if I were to make up a honourable 'tachment to her."

Bob paused again, and then gave a loud whistle, shook his head, and laughed outright, and then slapping his leg, he exclaimed,—

"No, no, demmit—that won't do at no price. A young fellow ought not to be scotched in the early part of his career—no, no, it will never do to be tied at such a price ; besides that, a man about town never thinks of getting married until he has seen something of life ; no, I can't consent to be tabooed in this manner. Plays, gals, and wine ; I must enjoy all, and when I've had enough, why then I will, perhaps, permit myself to be married to somebody as has got plenty of tin, and then there can be no objection. Then I'll let these unfortunate people get into a scrape as they can't get out of. I'll deliver this billy dux, and let her know I am awake, and knows what's what."

In pursuance of this determination, Bobby shut the door and walked up stairs, and became fidgety, as he became aware that the captain would take his breakfast alone, and Miss Jessie was too unwell to leave her own room.

"This is a blessed fix," he muttered to himself ; "here am I—I wants to deliver this 'ere blessed 'pistle, and can't go into the bedroom on no account, 'cause I ain't upon intimate terms with the young un ; hows'ever, I can't do more than wait, only I hope I sha'n't wear it out, as the breeches o' mine are something tight, and the pockets fit close."

The captain, after spending some time in apparently no very pleasing reflections, rose up and quitted the house.

"Now," thought Bobby, "here's the time for me to deliver the billy dux ; well, I'm blest, here she comes ! Talk of What's-his-name, and sure enough here he is ; why, I am as good as a prophet, for here she comes. I'll let her eat some breakfast, though, else she won't be able to read the interesting communication I have got in my pocket."

Indeed, Jessie needed something, for her appearance betokened anything but happiness or health; her face was pale, and sorrow sat there. Sad and sorrowful was the expression of her features, while every movement betrayed a subdued but settled melancholy.

When Jessie had taken such a breakfast as was scarce sufficient to support nature, the page said to her—

"Does you expect to hear from any of your country friends, miss ?"

"What do you mean, Robert ? You are a very singular child."

"Child ! Well if anybody else had said so, I would have told 'em my mind ; but you, Miss Jessie, are quite privileged. What I means is —ain't you got no private correspondence, as the newspaper calls 'em, eh ?"

"None that I am aware of," said Jessie quietly.

"Then I am afraid, miss, this 'ere letter, or dilly dux, ain't for you, 'cause you ain't got anybody to send one."

"Let me see the address,' said Jesie ; " and if it be for me, I suppose you have no objection to part with it ?"

"Certainly not, miss," said Bob, producing the note in a most positive state of crumple ! "this 'ere's the crittur."

Jessie took the note, and at once perceived, by the handwriting, whence it came, and said, angrily—

"Why have you dared to keep this letter back ; why did you not give it before ?"

"You wern't up, miss, when it come," said Bobby.

"But you have had it all breakfast time, you tiresome boy."

"I didn't wish to spile your appetite," said Bobby, with a malicious grin.

Jessie arose and quitted the room, seeking the solitude of her own apartment, in which she could read the letter of one she loved so well.

It was with a beating heart and flushed countenance that she opened the letter and read its contents, and her varying emotions were visible enough in her beautiful countenance.

Alternations of cloud, sunshine, and rain, were never more rapid than the alternations of sorrow, pleasure, and tears, were in Jessie during these few moments that sufficed to enable her to peruse the letter of Alfred Pearson.

She read and re-read it, till she had almost every sentence by heart ; she knew not what emotion was strongest ; each for the moment held full sway over her heart, and she would have been induced to comply with any sug-

gestion that Alfred himself had made in person.

Full of gratitude for this expression of his entire and disinterested attachment, she could scarcely bring herself to give a refusal, for she never for one moment doubted his honour, far from it ; she would have relied upon his integrity as she would upon a solid rock—but then there was her father.

Could she, at such a moment, leave his side —at a time when she believed he had renewed his connection with that dangerous man, Philip Arlines ?—no.

But what said Alfred Pearson ? He said— "that her quitting her father, and becoming his bride, would in all probability tend to withdraw him from that man's society, and give him greater freedom of action, as he would not be fettered by the reflection that his daughter's comforts were necessary to be obtained. He would know, too, she was happy, and had a protector who was both able and willing to support and care for her."

She thought over this, but her active mind led her to a different conclusion.

Her father, she thought, would not be induced to give up Arline's society ; on the contrary, he would find another restraint removed ; a motive for the care of his own safety would be lost, because whatever became of himself, his daughter would not suffer ; and more, might not the same power be exerted to cause him to endeavour to entangle Alfred Pearson in the same net that had been so effectually thrown around him ?

No, no, she could not consent ; her heart, indeed, prompted her to the deed ; but reason forbade her. It was with a deep sigh she determined on rejecting the proposal so generously made her by Alfred Pearson ; and she sat down with a saddened heart to write a reply to that effect, which ran as follows :—

"DEAR ALFRED,—Forgive me, if I refuse your generous offer—for generous it is, to one in my state ; but I do so because I am convinced that totally opposite results will be the consequence of the act, to those that you predict. My mind is in a wavering state ; I would do anything that I believed would ensure your happiness and my father's, but I dare not sacrifice the one for the other, especially as I hope that a different state of things will, ere long, enable you to obtain my father's consent. Adieu.—Ever yours,

"JESSIE ARNOLD."

This letter was no sooner written than she despatched the page to the nearest post-office with it, in preference to Pearson's residence.

Having done this, she felt herself more at ease, not perhaps from the course she had adopted, but because she had come to some determination which she resolved acting upon.

It is usual for people to feel uneasy while they are arguing a matter with themselves, but they are less anxious after having once made up their minds, and this was Jessie's case.

CHAPTER LI.

PEARSON'S DISAPPOINTMENT. — INTERVIEW WITH NAIRS.—HIS ADVICE.

THE letter that Jessie had posted to Alfred Pearson found him in a state of anxiety and fever difficult to describe. A lover's doubts and fears are usually of that mixed, eccentric character, that might, for want of a better term, be called nondescript.

The moment the letter came, he seized it with a trembling hand, and hastily tore it open, and greedily perused its contents, and then the letter fell from his hand to the floor.

"Refused by G—d!" he exclaimed, and he sank upon a sofa, overwhelmed with disappointment.

Some moments elapsed ere he moved, and them he again picked up the letter, and perused it again carefully through, and more carefully, for at the first he merely read it with a view of arriving at the one thing he most wished to learn, and that was, her determination. This was averse to his wishes, and his disappointment was so great, that he forgot all else for the moment.

"It is kind—very kind," he muttered; "her devotion is great, and her expressions of confidence strong, stronger than I could have expected. No one doubt appears to be on her mind—save in connection with her father.

"He is not deserving of such a daughter—'tis almost more gratifying than a doubting consent, and yet a consent I would it had been, for I could have converted doubt into confidence."

He paused again, as if communing with himself as to what course he ought to pursue.

"Ought I or not to see her?" he muttered. "I know not what to say or what to think. Perhaps a personal interview would effect what a letter has failed to do; but should I go, I may again encounter Captain Arnold, who has more than once ordered me out of his house. I cannot submit to such treatment; but should I do so, I may render Jessie's position more unhappy—that I would not do for a trifle. I will go and see Nairs; he is a young man tolerably well versed in the ways of the world, and therefore, perhaps, the best able to give me available advice."

Having determined upon this, he was soon ready for the street, en route for Nair's residence. He did not lose time until he reached there, and was fortunate to find him at home, for confirmed bachelors are seldom found at home.

"Well," said Nairs, "I perceive you have come for a consultation; there's all the determination of a weather-cock nailed to one point in your countenance, despite of whatever wind that blows; yet you are determined to stick to one."

"That is true, Ned," said Pearson; "I am for effecting one object, be the impediments what they may. I have, however, come to consult with you as to the propriety of making the attempt."

"Indeed!"

"Ay, indeed; and then we will talk over the propriety of the measures to be adopted in case we agree to the first."

"Suppose we blink the first, and come to the second; it is a lover's course, and why not honestly adopt it?"

"Because my mind is divided, and I know not which way to act; but read this letter; 'tis an answer to the one I sent her, or rather left her."

"My dear fellow, your mind is as likely to be biassed to do anything by my advice not to do it, as if I were to persuade you it ought to be done."

Nairs read the letter, and then returned it, saying—

"It is, certainly, a very gratifying letter, and shows the indecision of the writer's mind. She has the most perfect confidence in you. Well, if that does not extend to trusting herself in your power during an elopement, I mean to say you have no tack nor talent for intrigue."

"Granting all that," replied Pearson, "your knowing my object and wishes, what would you advise me to do under these very peculiar circumstances?"

"If it were my own case," replied Nairs, "my way would be clear enough. I would see her, and use every endeavour to induce her to comply, because you have no object in view that can be accomplished by delay; on the contrary, everything to lose."

"Exactly so," said Pearson.

"If I were you, I would go and obtain her consent, and then it would be time enough to make the necessary arrangements."

"But," said Pearson, "if I make arrangements with her, how am I to be able to tell if they be practicable or not?"

"Leave that to chance," replied Nairs, "and it will be odd to me if, in London, you cannot do impossibilities with money. I'll undertake to do almost anything, and accomplish it, too."

Pearson paused for a few moments, and Nairs said to him—

"Do not let me urge you on with my advice; it was given only in consequence of my entering into your feelings : my own, you know, induce me to eschew matrimony, for you know the old song—

'But wine neither nurses nor babies can bring
And a big bellied bottle's a mighty good thing.'"

"A truce to your bachelor predilection; I know you are not a marrying man."

"I'faith, you may make sure of that; thank Heaven the veil has been lifted off my eyes, and I can look coldly on human nature, and especially the tender portion of the community, yclept woman."

"Hold your brag; you will marry your cook before you die, I'll wager my head—nay, my hopes of success in this affair."

"'Tis a bold offer; but if I win, I don't see the gain in such a wager, and I fear it will not be won or lost till I find myself blowing my last breath; but what do you intend to do?"

"Endeavour to obtain an interview with Jessie Arnold as soon as I can, and endeavour to obtain her consent, and arrange all for her, leaving you to make it all practicable."

"That I will do."

"Then for the present, adieu," said Pearson, as he quitted his friend Nairs, to seek, if possible, an interview with Jessie Arnold.

He quitted the abode of his friend, and made his way, regardless of time or distance, at once towards the lodgings of Captain Arnold, where he arrived without any precise intention or plan of how he was to obtain an interview; but a lucky thought struck him, and the intervention of fortune's favourite, in the person of Master Bob, was the grand talisman that opened the portals of the house, and Alfred Pearson found himself suddenly in the presence of Jessie before he was well aware of it, and before he had arranged, in his own mind, the nature and order of the arguments he intended to use to induce her to quit her father's protection and submit to his.

"Jessie, dear Jessie," he said, advancing, and taking both her hands, "pardon my intrusion; but I was so unhappy that I could not refrain from coming to see you and talk over with you the proposition I made you by letter."

"This is scaacely kind of you, Alfred, to attempt to disturb my resolution in this matter," said Jessie.

"Do not say so," replied Pearson; "let me rather hope you have not made up your mind; or if you have even done so partially, that you have done so but from a partial consideration of the consequences of it. I am convinced that, not only will it conduce to our own happiness, but it will be the means of securing your father's safety, as far as that can be effected by human agency now."

"What do you mean, dear Alfred, by now?

Has anything fresh occurred that places him in greater danger?"

"I know of nothing, save that there has been much money paid away between them, and some gained: farther than that, and the knowledge that the mere association with such a man as Phillip Arlines must be dishonourable and dangerous, I know nothing; but do not let me alarm you on that account, it is from cool reflection I wish you to consent to become my wife, for you may depend upon it, that as soon as your father is aware that you are no longer dependant upon him, that whatever may become of him you are safe, his own sense of honour will return to him and induce him to sever a connection, that, perhaps, the fears he entertains for your welfare may alone induce him to continue."

"Do you think he would do so from such a cause? He knows I have besought him to sever it long since."

"Possibly; but as you have not removed the cause you have not succeeded in destroying the effect."

"If I thought so," said Jessie, and then she paused.

"If you thought so," said Pearson, "would you be persuaded to take the step that I so earnestly advise as conducive to the welfare and happiness of us all? Say that you consent, and as I hope for mercy hereafter, you shall not have cause to repent of having trusted to me so far."

Jessie was silent, and Alfred pressed her tenderly to his heart, and extracted a whispered consent.

Alfred Pearson's raptures and Jessie's fears occupied some time in expressing and subduing, but it was eventually agreed that she should elope with Alfred Pearson the next night a little before midnight, as by that time Captain Arnold would then be at home, and retired for the night, or else occupied at the gaming-house, where he would in all probability be kept for some hours, and when he returned he would not expect to see Jessie that night.

It was with a greater degree of happiness and rapture than he had yet ever experienced, that Alfred Pearson, after promising that he would be punctual, quitted Jessie and hastened off to his friend, Edward Nairs, to consult with him regarding the details, and the best mode for completing his happiness by an instant marriage.

CHAPTER LII.

"WELL," said Nairs, "back again; you are much like the pendulum of a clock, ever going there and back again. Have you succeeded yet?"

"I have," replied Pearson, "and have

now come to claim your promise of assisting me to complete this affair. I am to meet her to-morrow at midnight, or before that hour. Now what I want is, either to make off for Scotland, or else to have a special licence, and be married the next day."

"Either can be done; but I should recommend a trip to Gretna, as that will probably prevent any pursuit, or at least baffle it, and there can be no objection to the validity of the marriage, and there might a dozen accidents happen if the ceremony were performed in London."

"Well—well, I will leave it all to you, if you say all shall be ready before midnight to-morrow."

"You may depend upon it I will have such footers for you as shall carry you down the road at a whirlwind-like rate, just suitable to young lovers, and anxious-to-be-married people."

*   *   *   *

The next day was one of great anxiety to Alfred Pearson, and he more than once visited Nairs to ascertain the state of his preparations; and when satisfied on that point, wandered about early in the evening in the vicinity of Captain Arnold's lodging. The weather was threatening and unpropitious, and he was left to contemplate London scenery by lamp light.

As darkness approaches, the shops of London exhibit a peculiar brilliancy, that gives the stranger at once a vivid idea of the vast extent and resources of the metropolis. The lighting of London must form a curious speculation to the thoughtful; few cities in the world present such a speculation.

The cold bleak wind that swept through the streets was laden with moisture, that came floating in the air, and, gradually getting heavier and heavier, at length settled into a drizzle, that promised a continuance of the same miserable weather as the night set in.

The increase of the rain was accompanied by an increase of the wind, which rendered it doubly troublesome and disagreeable.

There were, it is true, moments when a few rays of the moon struggled through the mass of swift riding clouds that crossed the sky, and discharged their humid contents upon the earth. At such moments, a slender prospect presented itself of a cessation; but no, the moon was soon hidden, and the heavy, steady showers again commenced.

The streets were now cleared of all such pedestrians as are usually found promenading the metropolis on pleasure; and there are a great number whose only time is at this hour, and many more who care but little to stir abroad until the bustle of the evening has begun.

But on a wet night, the streets of the metropolis are bare of such persons, and yet there are vast quantities of individuals who are abroad in the main thoroughfares. The shops exhibit the same goods, the same tasteful display, and the same enormous expense is incurred in lighting them, as when there is every prospect of their being well remunerated by purchasers who flock about on fine nights.

The shops shut earlier, however, on such occasions, and yet but very little earlier, for they have all the lingering hope that still clings to the mind, though repeated disappointment has taught them the futility of the hope that animates them.

Thus the evening wears on, and the heavy rains have washed the very streets of the accumulated filth of perhaps many days' standing. The population out of doors grows thinner, and the footfall of the passengers become fewer and more distinct; the noises grow less frequent and more subdued, and the hour of general repose approaches.

It was with much anxiety and impatience that Alfred Pearson walked about the streets waiting the signal that was to assure him that all was in readiness; and she, the beloved girl of his heart, was prepared to trust him, and seek the means of uniting herself to him for life.

It was a cold, miserable night, and one that Alfred would not have ventured out in if he had had a less inducement; much less would he have waited in all the inclemency of the weather, weak as he yet was, had it been for a less cause than the one he had hopes now to effect.

At length he determined to go to the door, and ascertain if it had been left open to admit him. He crossed over, and pushed open the street-door, which was not entirely closed, and made his way up stairs.

Pearson had to pass Jessie's room. The door was partly open, and he saw Jessie lighting the lamp that was to be the signal for his coming. She did not see him, and he entered the room.

"Jessie, dear Jessie," said Pearson, as he advanced towards her.

She turned, and gave a half-stifled scream, as she perceived who it was.

"I feared," he continued, "that some accident had happened to prevent your getting clear of the premises."

"I can't go, Alfred—indeed, I can't. I have been thinking about it ever since, and I haven't heart to leave my father—I can't do it."

"Not for his sake as well as mine, and for yours also?" said Pearson reproachfully.

"I deserve your anger, Alfred, I knew I do, for having thus deceived and disappointed you; but if you knew the struggle I have had between love and duty, you would, I am sure, pity and forgive me."

"Do not speak thus, dear Jessie," said Pearson, with much tenderness; "do not speak thus, nor think that I have wished to hurry you into a measure from selfish motives only, which you think you ought not to do, and will repent hereafter. I would not, for the world, be the cause of your neglecting any duty that it was a pleasure to you to perform; no, Jessie, no; but I do urge it from my heart, because I believe it will tend to help you in the discharge of such duties as you wish, as well as from the love I feel for you. For these reasons, dear Jessie, think—think, again, before you entirely refuse me."

"I have thought, Alfred, until my head is nigh to burst, and cannot do it. My father has not yet returned."

"He will not expect to see you, love, to-night, and will scarce find it out until to-morrow."

"Ah," sighed Jessie, "I could not go without seeing him, even if I could consent to go at all. Do not press me, dear Alfred; you do not know the unhappy hours I have spent since I last saw you, for I know how I must have caused you pain and disappointment."

"Speak not of pain and disappointment, though they will be great enough; think only of the probable results—our mutual happiness and your father's welfare, which I am well assured, whatever might be his present opinions—and they are, I know, founded on misapprehension—will be best consulted by this marriage. But, ceasing to urge it as a matter of selfishness on both sides, consider your peculiar situations—you without friends, exposed to the insults of that scoundrel, Phillip Arlines; and I, exposed to the chance of all the accidents and ills of life that may deprive me of the only being who can render my life happy. Your own love, too, Jessie, I should hope, would teach you different, and help you to come to another determination from the one which you have named."

"I can't help it, Alfred; you are better skilled in argument than I; but it matters not, I cannot quit the house."

"But, Jessie, I have a post-chaise and four ready to start the moment you step into the vehicle."

"I regret the more that you should have done all this, and that for my sake: but, dear Alfred, do not urge me to this step, at least now. I should render you unhappy by the sorrow and sadness that would be my portion, if I did consent to leave my father's roof. He may need such care and consolation as only a daughter can afford to a father."

"You will not be the less his daughter, and your power will be increased of aiding him," replied Alfred Pearson; "but, believe me,

Jessie, not to press you merely because of your having given a promise, I do not see that any one, or all of the reasons you have alleged, is or are of sufficient importance to cause you to decline this proposal."

"It appears much different to me, Alfred; therefore, urge me no more."

As Jessie spoke, the door of the room opened, and Captain Arnold entered the apartment.

CHAPTER LIII.

ALTERCATION BETWEEN CAPTAIN ARNOLD AND ALFRED PEARSON.—THE FAREWELL. —SOOTHING A FRIEND.

THE confusion of Jessie and Alfred Pearson was great at this sudden and unexpected appearance of Captain Arnold at such an inopportune moment, and for some minutes not a word was spoken by any of the persons present.

Jessie stood irresolute whether to fly to her father, and beg his forgiveness, or seek instant protection in the arms of Pearson, and defy his anger, which she believed was very great.

Alfred Pearson stood calm and quiet, determining in his own mind to avow everything, and justify himself should there be need or opportunity, and, if Jessie were willing, to take her away from him. He did not expect this; but he was prepared for any emergency that could arise, and he could almost anticipate much from Captain Arnold's appearance. Indeed, his flushed face, and excited appearance, gave him such an air of wildness as to give Jessie great alarm.

"'Tis well, sir," exclaimed Arnold, in a hoarse voice, "'tis well of you to endeavour to seduce the affections of the daughter from the father, and 'tis better indeed to do that under the most specious pretexts you could well procure to suit your vile purposes."

"My purposes are not vile, Captain Arnold, but pure and honourable, and my motives for doing so will bear both scrutiny and comment."

"'Tis false, base man! you know it is false! Could you once get Jessie to trust you, and then she would indeed want a protector. I have forbidden you the house, I have done all that could be done to deter your coming hither, but meanness and assurance go hand-in-hand, and I must adopt measures that will place you in an unequivocal situation."

"Dear father," said Jessie, interfering, "hear me? you have entirely mistaken Mr. Pearson's principles and intentions."

"There can be no mistake. Jessie, hold your tongue. Do you, sir, leave the house, or I'll——"

"Father, father," exclaimed Jessie, as she

PEARSON WARNS ARNOLD OF THE VILLANY OF ARLINES.

interfered to prevent what was apparently about to happen—violence; "you are, indeed, about to do what you will live, I hope, to repent of."

"It is an ill wish, Jessie, an ill wish; but thus it has been with you ever since that man has thrust himself where he is not welcome, and whence he has received no invitation, and no welcome."

"Did he not save my sister's life, father? Think of that. I am sure he is—must be welcome."

"'Tis a heavy price to pay for the safety of one daughter at the expense of the welfare and happiness of another. To save one and bring worse than destruction upon the other, deserves not thanks, but scorn and hatred."

"Captain Arnold, I have allowed you to go on thus without interruption; you have now made a definite charge against me; I can repel that as being false."

"Words are but words, and no man ever yet admitted the baseness of his designs, or intended dishonourable conduct."

"You, Captain Arnold, should not judge too severely; but I am willing to place my conduct beyond dispute. I have ample means to support a wife in ease and comfort; I now offer my hand and fortune to Jessie, and am ready to make her my wife. Do you consent, Captain Arnold?"

"No, sir, I do not. The audacious manner in which such a proposal has been made to me is sufficient to ensure its rejection. Leave the house instantly, and never enter it more."

"At least acquit me, Captain Arnold, of all dishonourable intentions, for I call upon you, as a man of honour, to declare in my own presence that I have at least conducted myself without stain or reproach. Either allow me to prove my words, or cease to reproach me with aught that can be called dishonourable."

"Mr. Pearson, there is the door; am I to use violence towards you, and put you out?"

"Go, dear Alfred," exclaimed Jessie, "go—we shall meet in better times. Farewell; but go; leave the place, for my sake."

"For your sake I do, Jessie," replied Alfred, sorrowfully. "I would it were otherwise; be assured, however, of my faith and my honour."

"I am—I am."

"Farewell."

As Alfred uttered the last words, he slowly descended the stairs, leaving Arnold frantically gesticulating at him, but restrained by Jessie, who sought to calm her father's anger.

Alfred Pearson, when he reached the street, scarce knew which way to turn. Chagrin and disappointment almost drove him to madness. To be so broken in upon as he had been was vexatious in the extreme, and to be baulked in a scheme so nearly affecting his own happiness was, of all things, least to be patiently borne. It was useless to do otherwise, and yet his philosophy shrunk under it, and he nearly broke out into a fit of violent execrations upon Captain Arnold and the whole world.

"Why, what on earth's the matter?" exclaimed Nairs, who had come up unperceived.

"Eh—what, are you here?"

"Yes; where did you expect me?"

"With the post-chaise."

"I have it all right; I thought you were gone some time, and thinking you were too modest to press the question, or carry her off, I came to help you."

"There was no need of help this time, Nairs," replied Pearson.

"Why, what's the matter? Has any bitter disappointment occurred?—you look truly chopfallen."

"Disappointments enough to madden any one, I believe," said Pearson; "and interruptions worse than all."

"Very well," said Nairs. "I'm no way disappointed; there's always plenty of vexation where there are women. I never met with one yet who was not always more ready to cross than please, and who took more pleasure in the first than a grand Turk would in his seraglio;

but come along, 'twill do you good to come and see the post-chaise I have got ready waiting, with four good horses, and men who would drive you to the devil, if you paid them according."

"Oh, I can take your word for all that," replied Pearson; "you are too good by half; I don't want to see them."

"Oh, but you must," replied Nairs, taking hold of his arm; "it will soothe your spirits to tell the men you don't want them, and order them back; it will help, too, I should think, to cure you of your sweet passion."

Pearson and Nairs quitted the neighbourhood, after given the necessary counter-orders to the postilions; and as neither of them could well reach their lodgings, at that hour, without disturbing the whole house, they determined to ramble about, and witness daybreak in London—a novelty even to them, Londoners as they were.

The beauties of the summer are gone, and nothing but strict winter is apparent, and the extreme cold and humidity of the atmosphere cause unpleasant sensations to be felt by those who walk the streets of London at the earliest hour at this season of the year.

Long before the faintest glimmering of daybreak may be heard the hasty footsteps of ill-clad artisans who are compelled to rise early, despite of the inclemency of the season, to seek their various places of employment and labour, for the support of themselves and their families.

Many, besides, have to seek the factory and workshop to prepare them for the reception of those who work at their various trades, and whose time is accounted too valuable to be wasted in attendance even upon themselves.

Then the daylight is retarded in its progress, and is not so sensibly felt by the inhabitants in consequence of the heavy atmosphere and humidity that hangs over the city, like a cloud mixed with many particles of foreign matter, from the many thousand fires that are lit.

The day, however, does break despite these impediments, and the inhabitants become visible to each other, and the shops are observed to be gradually unclosing, and the streets present the appearance of having been glazed on either side.

The whole town appears to be emerging into life, and struggling to do so against difficulties and adverse circumstances, such as we have enumerated.

The streets are now gradually filling; at first with the more humble of the working population, who throng the streets as they leave their homes to seek the spot their employment calls them to.

Then might be heard the heavy and sonorous bell, and cry of "dust ho!" through the back streets—coaches and carts of all descriptions, and the bustle of a winter morning in London has commenced.

But, winter or summer, there is one unvaried round pursued. The town may be what is termed empty or full, and yet you see no diminution of vehicles or persons.

Chill and gloomy, and with a dead-coloured sky above, the day-break of London, at this season of the year, presents as few points of attraction as could well be imagined; and few as these are, they are sufficient to make the appearance of winter welcome to some were it but for the sake of change, and no other.

After breakfasting together, the two friends separated, to seek that repose which they had been deprived of during the night.

CHAPTER LIV.

SCENE IN A GAMING-HOUSE.—THE ARREST.— THE ESCAPE FROM THE OFFICER.

THE anger of Captain Arnold was great when Pearson left, but he did not continue, at least, the expression of it, for he confined himself to upbraiding Jessie; and he would hear no reply, for had he done so—and he was conscious of it—he would have been discomfited; but he soon ceased, and abruptly retired to his own room.

* * * *

The following day was one of some moment in our history. Captain Arnold was late, as was his custom latterly, and then he left the house, and lived at different hotels until towards the afternoon, when he met with Phillip Arlines, who appeared in very good spirits, and said,—

"Arnold, I have a fresh supply of notes, and there will be a very good opportunity of using them."

"Indeed!"

"Yes, there will be some fresh persons there, who have plenty of money to spare, and are admirably adapted to our purpose."

"Yes, indeed," said Arnold, "if they be willing, and do not discover anything unpleasant."

"There is no danger. But come, it is getting towards eventide, and we may as well walk towards the place to which we are bound."

"Very good," replied Arnold; and they both rose and quitted the place.

"It is a fine evening," remarked Arnold.

"It is," said Arlines, "and a walk will help to arrange your ideas and strengthen your nerves."

"They require something of the sort, I believe."

Sunset in London, and during the winter, is a short-lived and somewhat cheerless affair. If the weather be ever so fine, it cannot render it more than pleasant. There are none of the gradually increasing masses of vapour, that become illuminated and appear in gorgeous tints, and then gently fade into the indistinctness of twilight. There is none of this; on the contrary, the few warm tinges that may occasionally be seen, are there but a few moments, and then the temperature sensibly diminishes; warm clothing and sharp walking are in requisition.

Here and there may be seen a row of windows sparkling with, and throwing back the cold rays of the winter sun, and that but for a very short time; for the rapidly sinking sun causes these evidences of his presence to disappear almost suddenly.

At this time the streets are full of bustle and animation. The stream of human beings that have been going one way principally, now turn, and it would appear as though the city were emptying itself of its inhabitants, who come pouring out in the main thoroughfares towards the outskirts of the town, where a great portion of them live, for the benefit of having their wives and families at a distance from their places of business, and in a more healthy place of abode.

As the sun's rays disappear, the operation of lighting this vast metropolis commences, and here men may be seen hurrying to and fro with long ladders, and little curiously constructed lanterns; running up the former with charateristic speed, and, having lit the lamp, running down again, and then on to the next lamp, until his district is completed; and thus the whole of London is lighted up in the course of an incredibly short space of time.

These lights are much increased by the many thousands of lights of every shape and variety that are found in every street. The brilliancy of the illumination is very great, and forms a very great attraction; and many evening loungers exist, whose chief amusement consists of strolling along the streets of this metropolis, and viewing the appearance of both shops and goods at such a moment.

And the sight of a well lighted and elegantly fitted-up shop, with costly articles disposed with care and taste, will repay the idler for any care and thought he may have bestowed upon it. Many hundreds of such, ay, whole streets are to be found in the City of London.

It is difficult for those who are used to look upon such sights every day to imagine what must be the sensation produced in the mind of any one for the first time witnessing so imposing a sight as scores of well lighted streets, with shops, and filled with goods such as we have described.

They now arrived at the gambling-house, and once more entered it, Arlines preceding Arnold.

CHAPTER LV.

THE PURSUIT.—THE SPY.—THE PROJECTED
DEATH.

THERE was such a scene of splendour and
excitement presented to their gaze that few
were able to resist its enchanting and magic
influence; but it made little impression upon
Arnold, connected, as he was, with these scenes,
and their various means of passing time, and
affording one of the most dangerous and seducing
amusements that has ever been invented by the
genius of man.

Here were several strangers of great promise
to Arnold and Arlines, and the latter whispered
to the former,

"This promises to be a lucky evening.
Take these notes and play freely, but not incautiously, as that may breed suspicion; play, and
pay as a man who has the means and will to act
rightly, but who would rather win than lose."

Thus, then, they quitted each other's society
and mixed in the gay throng, and were soon
busy at the tables, were large sums of money
quickly exchanged hands, and Arnold, though
he had lost much, had, upon the whole, been a
considerable gainer.

At length some one entered the saloon and
fixed his eyes upon Arnold, and watched him
very closely. The same occurred to Arlines;
but they did not trouble themselves about it for
some time, as they had seen them and played
with them on several previous occasions.

But, at length, Arnold's suspicions produced
fears, and he seized the first opportunity of
quitting the table and seeking Phillip Arlines,
to whom he communicated the fact.

"I have observed it," replied Arlines, "and
cannot think what it means; nevertheless, do not
be alarmed—take no notice of it—I will think
of some mode of action. Perhaps it would be
as well to pick a quarrel with them, and, as we
are known, it is probable they will be ejected
from the place."

"That would be dangerous," remarked
Arnold, "and, perhaps, be unnecessary."

"It may, but I think not; however, we will
leave this place, and you must hold yourself in
readiness to quit unobserved when I give you
the word—by the way, as there are no eyes on
us now, we may as well steal the opportunity
and leave."

They immediately left the saloon by a side
door unobserved, and thence into the passage.
The porter was there.

"All is right," whispered Arlines, as they
passed through the outer door and were once
more in St. James's-street.

They had scarce gone a dozen yards ere they
heard the sound of a hasty footstep behind them.

They turned and saw a big bulky man close to
them, who said—

"I am sorry to interrupt your conversation,
gentlemen, but I have business with you both."

"What do you mean by this insolence?" said
Arlines sharply.

"Exactly what I say."

"Explain what you mean."

"Then you are both my prisoners. I am a
Bow-street officer. Take it quiet, gentlemen,
and nobody won't suspect anything; but you
must allow me to walk between you."

"Your prisoners?" said Arlines. "I do not
know what you mean; are you drunk, or are you
mad?"

"Neither, gentlemen; but I have a warrant
for the apprehension of Captain Arnold and
Phillip Arlines, for forging and uttering forged
notes."

"Let me see it," demanded Arlines, coolly;
"I cannot believe in such an absurdity."

"Oh, I am reasonable, and will convince
you," said the officer, producing the warrant;
and the instant he did so, Arlines seized the
warrant, and a desperate struggle ensued between him and the officer.

"Arnold! Arnold!" exclaimed Arlines;
"help! help! or we are locked up."

"I'm d———d if you ain't, too," said the
officer, as he bent Arlines to the ground with a
powerful grasp.

He had scarcely uttered these words, however,
before he was felled by a powerful blow across
the head from Arnold's cane. This released
Arlines, who again struck the officer, as he was
endeavouring to rise, a dreadful blow that laid
him senseless. They both immediately fled
across Piccadilly, and thence through a number
of streets towards Oxford-street; when they
had got a considerable distance, Arnold, who
was trembling with apprehension, and could
scarce speak, inquired, in a low tone, what was
to be done now they were marked.

"I have not brought you into this danger,
Arnold," replied Arlines, "without having it
in my power to succour and secret you where
no police-officer could ever find us, were the
whole of them put upon the scent—follow me,
and do not speak."

Arnold obeyed in silence, and Arlines began
to make for the suburbs of the metropolis,
closely followed by his now terrified companion
in guilt, whose fears were all in the ascendant,
and who now looked upon himself as entirely
lost, without a hope of future succour.

"Arlines," he said, "the end of all the vice
and iniquity in which you have plunged me has
come at last; we may escape one officer,
charged with the task of apprehending us, but
we cannot escape the whole machinery of the
law, which will be set in operation against us."

"A plague on the law and its machinery

likewise; we not only can escape, but we will."

"By death."

"Not at all. I have not the remotest intention of dying yet. I can assure you we have ready money, and what is to hinder us, with ordinary tact, from getting out of the country, if such an extreme measure should become of very pressing necessity?"

"What! in spite of the vigilance of the police?"

"The vigilance of nonsense. The police are but men as we are, and with the disadvantage, too, in most cases, of being men of slow comprehension and defective education. For one success that crowns the efforts of the police, they make a hundred failures, which are never heard of. I am convinced, Arnold, that it needs but common tact and prudence to escape from the police, and we possess uncommon tact and prudence—therefore our escape shall be certain."

"But how are we to live?"

"We have money."

"Which will not last long."

"Pshaw, Arnold, you are full of fears. Come on quicker, and we will talk over our affairs more at leisure. Here we are, you see, near the suburbs of the city. Camden Town lies but a little way now in advance of us, and while all the hells of St. James's will be hunted for us, no one will suspect that we are enjoying the cool breeze that blows from the Hampstead Hills. Come on, expedition will soon bring us to the end of our journey."

"And where is that?"

"Why, you have heard the old proverb that 'truth lies at the bottom of a well.'"

"I have, but what has that to do with us?"

"Simply, that we shall be compelled, if pushed very hard, to imitate the goddess's example."

"Explain yourself."

"My meaning must be evident. We must find safety at the bottom of a well, where I have already, with a forethought that would, were I a general commanding an army, have insured me immortality, made such preparations as will make us as comfortable as such a place will admit of."

"You surprise me."

"Of course I do."

"But what is to become of my daughter, Jessie? I cannot wholly desert her, Arlines. Although of late our intercourse together has not been marked with much affection on my side, I grieve to say, yet when a question concerning her arises in my mind, I find that she is still dear to me, and I cannot desert her entirely."

"She has not shown any remarkable wish lately to consult your feelings."

"True; but—"

"Peace, peace! We will talk of that another time. I will myself undertake to pro-vide for her safety if you write an authority for me to act. But at present we have something of far greater importance to look to; our personal safety is a first and foremost consideration."

They had now reached the extensive and important district of London, which lies between Hampstead and the New-road, a district which, with each revolving year, is increasing, and there cannot be a doubt but that, in a very short time, the London rambler must go beyond the once villages of Hampstead and Highgate to get a sight of a green field. Arlines frequently paused, and stood for some minutes in a listening attitude in order to be certain that they were not followed, and long before he had, with his jaded and miserable companion, reached the road, on each side of which gardens and villas began to appear, instead of regular rows of brick houses, he was convinced that no one was on their track; but they had made good an escape from a danger which had threatened at one time to be of the most formidable character, for whatever difficulty the London police officers may occasionally have in finding those gentleman who may, in their own phraseology, be "wanted," when once they do find them, no one has ever doubted their courage in effecting the capture.

To shake off, therefore, as Arnold and Arlines had done, one of the most effective and experienced of the Bow Street runners, was no mean adventure, and could only have resulted from the accidental circumstance of no one being near at the time of the encounter.

"Are we near our place of destination?" asked Arnold.

"Yes," was the reply; "but you must not expect a great amount of comfort where we are going."

"Comfort? Do not mention it. If we can procure safety I shall be abundantly satisfied."

"That, then, I can assure you of, I think; and what is more, there is no reason on earth why we should not continue to enrich ourselves by the same means we have already adopted."

"God Heavens! you do not mean to say that you would again venture to any of the old haunts?"

"Yes, I do. You must know, that during my rather chequered career of life, I went through a variety of adventures, and one of them consisted in, for a whole year, being one of a batch of strolling players, where I made it a particular study to find out all the known modes of disguise and personal alteration. I became an adept at such matters, and have no hesitation in saying that I would disguise you in such a manner that your most intimate friend would fail to have the least suspicion of your identity."

"You surprise me."

"You would be still more surprised were you

to see what I can do in that way; but we will talk more at leisure over future operations when we shall be safe in the place of concealment I am about to conduct you to."

"Have you had that place long?"

"I have; but there was no use in troubling you about it until some occasion like the present made it absolutely necessary that we should retire to it, and I hope you consider it as a great proof of my confidence and friendship that I now take you to a place of concealment which I have for months laboured at to make comfortable as well as secure."

"You awaken my curiosity," said Arnold, "as well as allay my fears. Have we got far to go?"

"No, we are near to our destination. Hush! be cautious. Do you see that man?"

"Where, where?"

"With the paper in his hand, and which he looks at so earnestly for a moment, and then at us. By heavens! I should not be a bit surprised if that paper contained our description, which, no doubt, has been forwarded to the different police authorities; we must be careful. Come on and quicken your pace gradually; do not look behind you whatever you do."

"More danger, more danger," groaned Captain Arnold. "Oh, what a dreadfully perilous career have we commenced upon! Where will it end—where will it end?"

"Pshaw! at the bottom of a well, to be sure; come on and don't be making a fool of yourself by groaning, and muttering miserable speeches—come on, I say. D—n the fellow, he is coming after us."

"Are you sure, Arlines?"

"Quite; do not look—I can see with less appearance of looking, probably, than you. He is coming!"

"Is he? only one?"

"That is all; but if he stop us here he will get plenty of assistance. My object is to get him out among the fields if I can."

"And—and then?"

"Murder him, if you like; you have a taste for calling all your own actions by the ugliest possible names I know."

"Good God!"

"Oh, very likely; you can say your prayers if you like, but you will excuse me for saying, that I think them not a little out of place. Come on, will you? By God, Arnold, if you hang back so, I will leave you to your fate."

"Get rid of him in some other way, Arlines. Do not murder him—do not take life if it can, by any possibility, be avoided."

"Dead men tell no tales. He's most likely a remarkably clever fellow, and won't be satisfied with anything short of a knock on the head that will settle him at once. We are gaining time every moment, for see, there are the open fields before us, every inch of which I know

well, and if he is but goose enough to follow, he is a dead man as sure as my name is Arlines."

Captain Arnold could now plainly hear the footsteps of the man who was following them, and each one seemed to strike upon his very heart, as, in obedience to the injunction of Arlines, he hurried onwards, heedless whither he was being led, so long as there was any chance of safety from the horrible consequences of the crimes he had committed at the instigation of his villanous companion.

"Listen to me," said Arlines, in a low tone; "I cannot think how the fellow who is following us can be such a fool as to do so, except that he is not quite sure we are the persons he is in search of, and is determined upon dogging us to where we may be going, in preference to risking our arrest. There are a hedge and a stile immediately in advance of us now, at the end of this footpath. You see it is very dark, and I will pause on this side and hide myself in a ditch, while you cross the stile, and immediately that you have done so, turn and face our pursuer, and ask him what he wants with us. If necessary, then I will hit him down from behind, and we shall be free of him."

"But—but you will not leave me?"

"How suspicious you are; if you have any such doubts, do you hide in the ditch and I will do the other part of the business. Only remember, you must strike surely, or by heaven and earth I will leave you to your fate."

"No, no; I am satisfied. Let it be as you first proposed; I place myself entirely under your protection."

"Very good; move on faster then. Do not speak again, but when I leave your side, make not the least pause, but cross the stile, and then turn sharp round, so as to prevent him from crossing it while you question him. You shall not be much troubled, for, I assure you, I have no sort of intention to waste time."

Arnold trembled, but he said no more, silently making up his mind to obey the directions of Arlines, and congratulating himself that if a murder were committed, he should have no actual hand in it, inasmuch as he would not have to strike the blow.

The hedge and the stile, as Arlines had stated, were but a very short distance in advance of them; but, owing to the extreme darkness of the night, it was not seen until they were quite close upon it.

Giving, then, Arnold a slightly propelling push forward, Arnold sunk down by the side of the hedge, and was lost to sight in a moment among the thick underwood that grew there in abundance. In another instant Arnold crossed the stile, and turned round at the exact moment that the man who had been following them came up, which he did at great speed, as if he had made up his mind to bring affairs to a crisis at that particular spot.

They confronted each other for nearly half-a-minute, without speaking, and then Arnold summoned courage to say—

"Well, my friend, what do you want?"

"Friend or not," said the man, in a hoarse, brutal voice, "as the case may be, who are you?"

"Am I bound to answer the questions of any fellow who may come to me on a public pathway?"

"You must answer mine. I am an officer."

"In the army or navy?"

"Come, come, none of that nonsense; it won't go down with me. You know what I mean well enough; I'm a police-officer. Where's your pal?"

"I really don't understand you."

"Indeed! I pity your ignorance. You are very green, no doubt—uncommon; but, to make a long story short, I rather think your name is Arnold."

"You are mistaken."

"Then I must take the consequences of my mistake in an action for false imprisonment, I suppose. You are my prisoner, and if you attempt to run for it, I'll shoot you as sure as you are a living man; so now you know all about it, and you'd better submit quietly. I'm not the sort of fellow to be trifled with, when I am sure of my man."

He made a movement as he spoke to cross the stile, and as he did so, Captain Arnold, who retreated a step or two, could see the dim outline of the figure of Arlines, as he rose from the long grass and heaps of decayed leaves in the dry ditch, where he had been concealed during the very brief dialogue we have just recorded.

Arnold felt a deadly sickness come across his heart, as he knew what was about to happen. Each fleeting moment was an hour of agony. He trembled like one at the point of death, and it required all his efforts to keep himself form falling to the ground in a swoon, so powerfully excited and terrified was he at what was now certain to occur.

CHAPTER LVI.

THE MURDER OF THE OFFICER.—THE PURSUIT.—THE FLIGHT.—THE MURDER.—THE CONCLUSION.

THE officer had one leg over the stile, and would quickly have succeeded, no doubt, in capturing Arnold, when, like a flash of lightning, a dreadful death-dealing blow came down upon his devoted head.

The crash of bone as the powerful implement of destruction descended upon him was awful to hear—a sickening sensation came over Arnold, and it was with the greatest difficulty that he succeeded in saving himself from fainting on the spot.

For a moment the officer stood in the same position he was in when he received the blow that had brought death with it. Then, as if impelled by some power of great energy, he fell to the ground so dead and dull a mass, and with such a strange heaviness, that had the body fallen from a great height it could scarcely have reached the earth with greater force.

There was one long groan—it was the escape of air from the lungs in consequence of the sudden change of position, and then all was still. The man was quite dead—a portion of his skull had been beaten in upon the brain, and death must have been instantaneous.

"Now, Arnold," cried Arlines, "we are free from that danger—this meddling fellow is effectually out of the way. Come over here again."

Arnold shrunk back, and holding his hands before his face, he said,—

"No, no—I dare not cross at this point. I—I will find some gap in the hedge lower down, and come over, but not here—not here."

"Curses on your cowardice," muttered Arlines; "when I am done with you, it would serve you right to make you share a similar fate."

These words, although not uttered with an intention of their producing such an effect, came upon Arnold's ears with the force of a thorough conviction of their truth, and in his heart he now felt certain of what had been a dim and indistinct idea several times in his mind; namely, that Arlines would some day murder him.

"Yes—yes," he muttered to himself, as he walked along the side of the hedge to find an opening through which he could pass. "Yes, he will murder me, or I must murder him—there is no resource for either of us. In self-defence I now make the determination to take his life at the first opportunity that shall offer itself of doing so with absolute safety. Then I may know some peace, but not till then."

With these thoughts he burst through a part of the frail hedge which offered less resistance than any other, and gained his infamous companion.

"Now," said Arlines, "this neighbourhood will be the one searched principally for us. We shall be traced here no doubt, and the murder of the officer will be attributed to us; therefore, it is an unsafe one."

"But you talked of your only place of refuge being hereabouts?"

"Do you think I come the nearest and most direct way to any place which I consider one of great importance on account of its secrecy? No, Arnold I am not the poor trembling fool that you are. Ask no explanation, but follow me silently and closely."

"We shall be awfully hunted for this murder," groaned Arnold; "it was imprudent."

"Imprudent, was it? Curses on you and your prudence. It will bring you to the gallows, if——"

"If what?"

"No matter ; silence—silence!"

Arnold in his own mind could add the remainder of the sentence to that "if" of Arlines, and he did so. "It means," he muttered in a low tone, which could not reach his companion's ear; "it means if he does not murder me himself ; but I will be beforehand with him—I am now on my defence. He has made me the desperate man I am, and he shall feel the consequences of it."

Where he was now being led Arnold had not the least idea, for he was ignorant of the neighbourhood, and timidly followed his conductor, who after a time paused at a wooden gate, which appeared to lead into a large piece of waste-looking ground, where there were a number of hovels, or outhouses, of a squalid, miserable appearance.

The moment they passed through the gate they were saluted by the loud barking of a dog, and Arnold drew back in some alarm, which was noticed by his companion, who said—

"Come on : he is chained up, and I will lead you clear of him. Take hold of my arm."

Arnold did as he was desired, and after going on for about a hundred yards or so Arlines stopped, and taking from his pocket a small whistle he blew it once loudly, when scarcely had the sound subsided ere a door opened in the side of one of the miserable-looking hovels, and a man appeared with a light, which he was shading with his hand, unconsciously by that means throwing a strong glare of light upon as villanous a looking countenance as ever mortal possessed.

"Hilloa !" he cried, "who are you?"

"The old customer," said Arlines. "Don't you know me?"

"Oh, it's you, governor, is it? What's the row?"

"Nothing particular. Is the horse and cart in?"

"Yes—yes."

"Then I want it. You will have it back in the morning."

"Very good, governor. Will you walk in or wait where you are while I get it out?"

"I will wait where I am. Be quick, for time has become a matter of some importance."

"Oh, has it? Humph! I understand—I understand."

So saying, the man disappeared, and Arnold remarked, in a low tone of voice—

"What do you want with a horse and cart, Arlines? Are we not near your much-vaunted hiding-place?"

"Not so near as you might imagine ; but hold your tongue; we shall have loads of time for talking."

In an incredibly short space of time, considering that the horse had to be put to, a common small chaise-cart, of very light construction, was brought out by the villanous-looking man, who held the horse with one hand, while he carried a light in the other.

"Here you are, governor," he said ; and then, upon seeing Arnold, he cried—"Hilloa ! is this the cove you——"

"Hush, d——n you !" cried Arlines. "Who told you to wag your tongue at such a wonderful rate, I should like to know?"

"Oh, I'm mum, if mum's the word, governor."

"Is the horse fresh?"

"As a daisy the first thing in the mornin'."

"Get in," whispered Arlines to Arnold, and they both, in another moment, were in the cart. The man handed the reins to Arlines, and then he walked on and opened the gate, which was soon passed. It was very dark, but Arlines seemed to know the road exactly, and walked the horse quietly till they reached a good hard road, and then he said—

"Now, Arnold, you will see what this horse can do, if put to it a little."

Upon the word, he gave the horse a slight touch with the whip, and slackening the reins at the same time, the creature stepped out in tremendous style, passing every vehicle with prodigious speed.

"Where are you going," said Arnold, " at this really terrific pace ?"

"You will soon know. It ain't above forty minutes' drive, at the rate we are now going."

On—on they sped, without a pause, and so confused was Arnold by the rapidity of recent events, that, although he gazed about him all the way, he had not the least idea as to where he was, even when Arlines drew up at a country-looking public-house, and said aloud—

"Hilloa—hilloa ! Ostler !"

"Here you are," said a man, who spoke as if he were half asleep.

"Take care of the nag till the morning, will you ?"

"I should think so."

"Come on this side," whispered Arlines to Arnold, and, in another moment, they both left the chaise-cart on the furthest side from the public-house, and Arlines, leading him by the arm, led him on at a rapid pace.

"Do tell me where we are now," said Arnold. "What can be the use of keeping the place a secret from me?"

JESSIE AND HER LOVER SURPRISED BY CAPTAIN ARNOLD.

"Do you mean to tell me that you really know not where you are?"

"Indeed I do not; we are in some country lane, and there appears to be a ruined house here to the right, but where we are I know not."

"Then we are in the village of Mortlake, not far from Richmond, and the ruined house you see there is Merton Vil'a."

"Mortlake?"

"Ay, you ought to know it; we have been here together before, although not down this lane. Come on—come on."

"What, to the ruin?"

"Yes; for in the grounds of that ruin, to tell the honest truth, is the well that I have spoken to you of, and which I have thought it prudent to reach in the round-about manner I have, rather than come to it direct."

Arnold followed him in wondering silence, and the two were soon within the precincts of the ruined villa, a full description of which we gave in the second chapter of this work.

* * * *

We have already recorded how two men one night sought Merton Villa, and were overheard, as well as seen, by a young girl, named Mary Sedgemore. In these two men our readers now recognise Arnold and Arlines; we have recorded how they sought the old well, how Arlines descended it, and how thoughts of murder came more thickly and strongly over the mind of Arnold, and he felt that he might never have such another opportunity of taking the life of the man who had led him to destruction, and of whom he now had become fearfully afraid.

We have related Arlines' descent into the well, and how he drew himself slowly up until he could speak to Arnold, who he wished to assure of the safety of the place of concealment, and then "he looked up as he spoke, for his head was very near the level of the well's brink, and in a moment a sense of his danger flashed across his mind. He seemed for the instant paralysed, and with a ferocious cry the other made a swinging blow at his head with a hammer. Instinctively he threw his head back, and the blow came upon his face, smashing one of his eyes from its socket, and falling with such a sickening smash as was horrible to hear. In an instant the blow was repeated—and then a shriek so wild and agonising, and so awfully loud, that it was heard far and near, burst from the frightfully injured man. The lantern dropped from his grasp.

"'Down—d——n!—down!' cried the murderer.

"He gave another swinging blow with the hammer. A cry of horror burst from his own lips. He had overreached himself, and missing his blow, fell heavily upon his victim. The rope flew over the pulley like lightning, and both went to the bottom of the well, locked in a dreadful embrace."

And thus to a terrible death came those two men, both of whom, it is no exaggeration to say, possessed talents and opportunities which might have placed them in most enviable and honourable positions in society; but, alas, we always find that the greatest amount of evil in this world is produced by perverted ability of some kind or another, and when we see a great criminal, or one who has defied morality and social law, we generally have to mourn the fact, that there were talents that, if properly directed, would have achieved good of as widely celebrated a nature as the evil that has perhaps convulsed society, and plunged the individual in destruction.

Oh, who shall picture the death-struggle which ensued when Captain Arnold did reach the bottom of the well, along with his still

breathing, desperate, maddened companion, who, feeling that he had his death-wound upon him, was only anxious to drag with him to perdition the man who had been his dupe, and had now become his executioner—a fitting retaliation.

Let us fancy how they clung to each other's throats—how they dashed each other against the sides of the well—what oaths, what screams, what dreadful imprecations came from their lips, as each feared he should die before the other.

But Arlines had received the greater injury. He had but few minutes to live, but those minutes, short and fleeting as they were, surely we can imagine what desperate ones they had become, and how he laboured to make them tell against the life of his false companion.

He never released his hold of Arnold's neck—a hold he had got in the first few moments of the desperate struggle. The position of the dead bodies afterwards showed that; and thus it was that Arnold, if he had not died from the numerous injuries he had received in consequence of the dreadful concussions against the brick wall at the bottom of the well, must have been suffocated by the determined grasp which Arlines would not release—no, not even after death was upon his brow, and he no longer was aught but a senseless mass of inanimate matter.

With broken limbs and dislocated joints they lay at length calm and still—those two men of fierce passions, of unholy desires, and of deep wickedness.

From the frightful wound which Arnold had given to Arlines, the hot blood flowed freely, and Arnold, too, had received so many injuries now, that many a vein was torn and broken, from which the sanguinary fluid bubbled forth in a hot stream, mingling with the blood of him who had been the first to stir up, by his pernicious counsels, all the latent evil which was in his disposition.

It was, indeed, a dreadful sight. They lay half immersed in a pool of their own blood—those mangled bodies, for they were both so heated, so fevered by the frightful conflict they had had, that their blood was in its most liquid state, and flowed freely from its overcharged veins.

Oh, could Jessie, the young, the gentle, the beautiful, and the compassionate, have seen the dreadful sight which presented itself at the bottom of that old dried-up well—the spring which once fed it had not for many years produced so much liquid as now, in the colour of blood, lay upon its ancient foundation—what horror, what agonising, what maddening horror would have been hers.—How vividly would have come back to her recollection the dream she had once had, which had faintly pictured to her imagination a dim outline of the dreadful fate that was now her father's in reality.

But she was spared the sight. Indeed, by the care of one who loved her fondly, she was spared even the description of the scene, each word of which would have been a pang to her heart greater than as if an assassin's poniard had searched its utmost recesses.—Yes, she was spared it.—A holy, Heavenly influence was around her and about her. He who loved her —Alfred Pearson—stood between her and her once sad reflections. He shielded her with his dear love from a knowledge of all the past; and when busy thoughts would sometimes picture to her some terror connected with her father's death yet greater than she had heard repeated by any one, and a question rose to her lips upon the subject, he would say,—

"My Jessie, ask nothing of the past—it is with Heaven. You cannot add to, or alley a pang that he who has gone has suffered. Think of the happy future, with those who love you, and at the same time you may well believe that imagination, such as yours, is apt to picture scenes of far greater horror than ever yet actually occurred."

And, after all, who shall regret the death of Captain Arnold, steeped as he was up to the very lips in crime? It would indeed have been well had he had time for repentance—time to say more than the few brief words that did burst from his agonised heart as he found himself descending with such frightful rapidity down the well; but so far as his own sufferings were concerned, he had, perhaps, met with an easier death than, as the violator of the laws of his country, he had any right to look forward to.

"God have mercy upon me!" were the words that came last from his lips. Let us hope that they reached Heaven, and that some pitying angel recorded them as some evidence of contrition that, had there been time for such feelings, might, and would, have ripened into sincere sorrow and repentance for the past.

He did think of Heaven—he did feel himself unworthy—he did even in that moment of mortal agony solicit the mercy which is infinite. May he have found it! But for Arlines—the wicked—detestable hypocrite— for him we may well tremble, and fancy that if there be a place of punishment where the wicked pass many ages, secluded from the glories of Heaven, there will his vexed spirit be.

Surely, surely, when once men embark in such desperate schemes of villany and crime as Arlines all his life seemed to have luxuriated in, they must think themselves immortal, and real life is far from being the fleeting, feverish dream it is. They must think they have a thousand years before them, and that it is worth while to be wicked and detestable for fifty of them, in order to have a hope of enjoying nine hundred and fifty more with the proceeds of their iniquity. Truly, it is strange that man should hoard, cheat, scheme, rob, and murder, and yet know himself to be the creature of a moment.

And where was poor Jessie while these dreadful events were occurring?—events which made her an orphan, her father a murderer, and cast a stigma upon that name which was once and should ever have been an honourable one, and one which could have been mentioned by her with pride as belonging to one in whose praises his country had reason to be eloquent, because he had been one of its bravest defenders.

She sat alone; a feeling of disquietude came over her, for there had been a strangeness about her father's manner when last she had seen him that had seemed to her as if he contemplated each moment saying something to her, and yet never could summon courage sufficient to utter the necessary words.

Some people may laugh as they will at what they call presentiments, but there are too many well accredited instances of such strange, shadowy forewarnings of events to be completely disregarded; and if ever there was in a human mind a strong and overwhelming presentiment of some dreadful coming blow of fate, it was in the mind of Jessie Arnold after she had last parted with her father.

A shuddering feeling of alarm crept over her, and after some time spent in striving to dissipate her nervous apprehensions, and restore the tone of her mind, she was compelled to give way to them completely, and in a voice of agony she exclaimed,—

"I shall never see him again—I shall never see him again. My father has gone from me for ever. Something dreadful is surely about to happen, and by the goodness of Heaven the shock of it is being decreased to me by this dim shadowing of it to my soul beforehand."

So deeply impressed was she with this idea, that for some minutes she contemplated making an effort to find her father, if he was yet living; but a very little reflection convinced her how utterly futile her search would necessarily be, being as she was without the least data as to where she was likely to meet with him.

When this conviction thoroughly possessed her, she sat down again, looking as pale as some finely chiselled marble statue made to adorn some monument, to show the world how deeply regretted was the still form that slept beneath that sleep which knows no waking but in a world beyond the stars.

This species of torpor which now came over her did not last long; it was the striking of a clock which dispelled it, and then she started to her feet as if the sound had been a signal for the perpetration of some dreadful tragedy in which she was to act some harrowing part.

She listened until the last echoing intonation of sound had died away in the far distance, and then, as she trembled excessively, she knelt down by the chair on which she had been sitting, and joined her hands in prayer.

CHAPTER LVII.

THE CONCLUSION.

THE young girl, Mary Sedgemore, who, up to this moment, had remained in the ruins of the old villa, rushed out, and hastening to the village, gave such an alarm as brought the whole village to the well. They found it uncovered, and the rope hung over the temporary pulley, while the spade and the other implements, used by Arlines, lay about the brink. All was still as the grave, and although loud calls were made down the well, no answer was returned. Her lover, who was amongst the number, would have himself descended to ascertain the fate of those below, but Mary, with such frantic earnestness, implored him not to do so, that he desisted from the attempt, and a young fellow, a farm-labourer, who said he feared nothing alive, and, therefore, was not likely to fear anything dead, volunteered to go down, which he did with a light in his hand.

All was breathless expectation till he shouted—

"Pull me up—pull me up," and in a few moments he was at the brink again. He looked as pale as death, and in answer to the numerous inquiries made of him, he said—

"I saw two dead men. They were holding each other by the throat, and one of their brains was dashed out."

*   *   *   *

Our tale is nearly over—virtually it is wholly concluded.

We see how Captain Arnold, the once respected, gallant officer, with a competent fortune, and loving, gentle beings about him, to whom he was bound by the tenderest of ties, became in consequence of gaming — the liar, the hypocrite, the thief, and, finally, the murderer. Peace be to his ashes, for the mercy of Heaven is infinite, and rather considers man's strength and man's temptations than his acts, so that even Arnold may hope for forgiveness.

*   *   *   *

In the morning the police took possession of Merton Villa, and workmen were procured who very soon brought the bodies of Arnold and Arlines to light, when they were recognized as those of the two forgers, against whom warrants had been issued, and who must soon have fallen into the hands of the police.

The publicity thus given to the whole transaction, of course, very soon enabled Jessie to know all that had occurred, and she identified both the bodies. Her grief was for a time excessive, but there was one who whispered consolation to her in such tones of love and true feeling, that, although she had lost her father, and all the natural ties of life were nearly severed, she could not feel herself lonely, or that there was no one yet worth living for.

We need not say that it was Alfred Pearson, who thus spoke to her, and who, with such tenderness, assuaged her grief, and assisted her to dry those natural tears she could not help shedding for her father's death, despite all the misery he had inflicted upon her by his dreadful conduct.

"My darling Jessie," he said, "after all those things that we at first sight view as great calamities, are sometimes really great mercies. 'Tis true, you have lost your father, and you have had to sustain the shock of losing him very suddenly; but bear in mind, while you weep for his death, what a dreadful catalogue of evils he has avoided by that death, and how much more bitter must have been your grief to have known that he had to expiate the crimes he was led into by the villain Arlines, in a manner I dread myself to think of."

"You are right, Alfred, you are right," said Jessie, as she threw herself upon his breast. "God bless you, for you are the only friend I have."

"Jessie," he added, "I will not be your friend. You must call me by a dearer title."

"Dearer, Alfred?"

"Yes, my Jessie; you must call me husband. Be wise at once, and give me the right to protect you, as well as the will to do so."

Our readers will easily anticipate Jessie's answer; within one week she was Mrs. Pearson, and being kindly and affectionately received by her husband's friends, she looked forward, not in vain, to a long career of happiness with the chosen object of her heart.

Children blessed their union, and as years rolled on, their happiness increased rather than diminished, and they at length learned to look back to the sorrowful scenes which had occurred during the early part of their acquaintanceship with a chastened feeling, to consider that all was perhaps for the best, and now and then to talk of the past with composure, and not to shrink so sensitively when any casual mention was made of "The Murder at the Old Well."

www.ingramcontent.com/pod-product-compliance
Lightning Source LLC
Chambersburg PA
CBHW082010170626

46817CB00009B/3054

9 781535 806152